LOVE AT FIRST FIGHT

MARY JAYNE BAKER

HEAD
of ZEUS

An Aria Book

ALSO BY MARY JAYNE BAKER

First published in the UK in 2021 by Head of Zeus Ltd
This paperback edition first published in 2021 by Head of Zeus Ltd
An Aria book

9 7 5 3 2 4 6 8

A CIP catalogue record for this book is available from the British Library.

ISBN (PB): 97811800246164
ISBN (E): 9781800241640

Head of Zeus
5–8 Hardwick Street
London EC1R 4RG
www.ariafiction.com

Print editions of this book are printed and bound by CPI Group (UK) Ltd,
Croydon, CR0 4YY, on FSC paper

MIX
Paper from
responsible sources
FSC® C171272

Some Cupid kills with arrows, some with traps...

Much Ado About Nothing (act 3, scene 1)

ONE

Bridie peered through the peephole of her house from the wrong side, trying to see if Hattie was up yet.

If her housemate was already in the living room, Bridie had no chance of sneaking in unnoticed through the front door. She'd have to walk round to the corner shop and buy a magazine or something so she could pretend that was why she was up and about at this time in the morning. Pretty hard to pull off when she was still in the same little black dress she'd worn out to the restaurant the night before. But if Hat was still in her bedroom then there was a chance Bridie could creep into the house, get back to her own room and throw on her pyjamas before her housemate realised she hadn't come home last night.

No, it was no good. The peephole was a dead loss. God only knew what they did to the glass in those things to make them work, but she couldn't see a thing from this side.

Dare she try the letterbox? The hinge was a bit creaky, but if she was really, really careful… Very quietly, very slowly, Bridie bent down and pushed it open.

Nope, that was no help either. She could see the standard lamp, the telly, the back of the sofa, and that was it.

'I can see your knickers when you bend over like that, you know.'

'Shit!'

Bridie jerked straight up, pulling her tiny dress down to cover her bethonged bum. Hattie's boyfriend Cal had appeared behind her, smirking.

'As, in fact, can the rest of the street,' he said, waving one hand around the sleepy cul-de-sac bursting with May blossom. 'You were giving the old chap across the road quite a show there, Bride.'

'What the hell are you doing spying on our front door?' she demanded, giving her dress another yank as she tried to cover a bit more flesh.

'Well I wasn't hanging around waiting to get a view of your pulling undies, if that's what you're thinking.' He nodded to a cardboard carrier he was holding containing three takeaway coffees. 'I'm bringing Hattie coffee in bed before she gets up for work, aren't I? Like the almost indecently perfect boyfriend I am. Why the hell are you breaking into your own house?'

'I'm not.' She snatched up her handbag from the step. 'I was just trying to see if Hat was up yet.'

'I get it.' He brushed past her to unlock the front door with Hattie's key. 'Home in the early morning, desperately trying not to be spotted, wearing the same clothes as when you went out on your date last night. So it's the classic walk of shame then, is it?'

'No. Shut your face.'

He shook his head solemnly as she followed him inside. 'Bridie Morgan, you shameless harlot. And you a teacher, responsible for all those impressionable young minds. I'm

2

shocked, really. Shocked and appalled. Shocked and appalled and disgusted. Shocked and appalled and disgusted and—'

'God, I hate you.' She glanced longingly at the third coffee on his tray. 'Is that for me?'

'That was the idea, yes. I had assumed when I went out for it that you were tucked up all snuggly in your own bed, alone. I'm innocent like that.'

'God, I love you.' She snatched at the coffee, sat down in the armchair and swallowed some down, hardly caring about the way it scorched her throat in her desperation for a caffeine hit. 'Ahhh. That's the stuff.'

'Hattie!' Cal called down the hallway. 'Come on, you're missing all the fun. Bridie's been staying out past her bedtime with unsuitable boys and she just flashed her tiny knickers at me.'

Bridie was sure she heard that running-in-the-air sound effect from the Scooby-Doo cartoons before, within literally a fraction of a fraction of a second, her housemate appeared in the doorway.

'Oh my God!' Hattie said, hurtling into Cal in her rush to get into the room. He caught her deftly and pushed a cup of coffee into her hand before pulling her down onto his knee on the sofa, none of which even broke her concentration. 'Tell tell tell! What happened, Bride? Did you get a humpable one at last?'

'Not exactly.' Bridie fortified herself with another mouthful of coffee. 'Do we have to do this now, Hat? I'm badly in need of a very long, very cold shower to wake me up a bit before work. I'm knackered.'

Cal grinned. 'I bet you are. Scarlet woman.'

'I notice you stayed over again last night, you enormous hypocrite,' Bridie said, glaring at him.

'Hey, me and Hattie have been together a year. You can't

3

compare our loved-up long-term-relationship shagging to your one-night bounceathons with randoms off Tinder.'

'Come on, Bride, you have to tell,' Hattie said. 'It's not fair to roll in at this time and not share the gossip. Did you meet someone good at long last or not?'

Bridie sighed. 'Well, I thought I might have. This guy Jake really seemed like he might tick a few boxes, at least as far as being worth a quick roll-around to break my long run of celibacy. I mean he was good-looking, well-groomed, plus he didn't manage to bore me into a coma within the first hour of the meal, which is about as much as I expect of blokes these days. But…'

'But?' Cal said.

Bridie frowned at him. 'Do we have to have you here for this? This is girl talk, Cal Kemp.'

He shrugged. 'I can do girl talk. Men, am I right? What a bunch of bastards. With their leaving the toilet seat up and their inadequate foreplay and their… socks.'

'Is that the best you can do?'

'Ah go on, Bride, let me join in. Your disastrous dating stories are always worth sticking around for.'

'Yeah, let him stay,' Hattie said, snuggling comfortably back against him while he buried his face in her neck. 'You know I'll tell him later anyway.'

Bridie shook her head. 'Traitor. What about sisters before misters and all that jazz?'

'Hey. Cal and me have no secrets from each other.'

'Speak for yourself,' Cal murmured into the ear he'd started nuzzling.

'You think, do you? I've seen your browser history.'

'Oh,' he said. 'All right, in that case we have no secrets from each other.'

'Besides, it's only Cal,' Hattie said to Bridie, tilting her head to give him better access to her ear. 'Who's he going to tell?'

'Fine,' Bridie said, folding her arms. 'I'll tell you both. But only if you cut out the heavy petting – it's making me queasy.'

'Don't see why we should,' Cal mumbled from Hattie's neck. 'Even you got some action last night, probably for the first time since school. Me and Hat can't be lagging behind just because we're in a long-term relationship, can we? Otherwise we'll be doomed to Mateus-Rosé-fuelled dinner parties and Sunday afternoon garden centre trips for all eternity.'

'It would've been the first time in nearly a year, if you must know. Not that I actually got any action in the end.' Bridie finished her coffee and put the empty styrofoam cup down on the table. 'Although I did go back to his place with that in mind, yes.'

'Tsk tsk tsk. And on a school night too.'

'I've been celibate for ten solid months, Cal. School nights be damned, I say.'

Hattie pushed Cal away from her neck so she could lean forward, the better to absorb all the juicy details. 'Well, what happened? Did he ask you to dress up in his dead wife's lingerie or something?'

'Worse.'

'Oooh, I love this!' Hattie said, clapping her hands. '"Guess the Pervert" is my favourite post-Bridie-date game. Did he want to draw you like one of his French girls?'

'Or wear one of those Furry suits?' Cal suggested.

'Ball gag?'

'Sex swing?'

'Gimp mask?'

'Strap-ons?'

'All right, you maniacs, stop.' Bridie groaned. 'Again, I'm going to have to say, worse. God, I don't even know if I can tell you. It's just too humiliating.'

'You have to tell us after a teaser like that,' Cal said.

'Only if you promise not to breathe a word to a soul, both of you.' She frowned at him. 'Especially you, Cal. I'd never hear the end of it if your brother found out. I bet he'd pay the roaming rate from South America just to ring me up for a gloat.'

'I swear he won't hear it from me.' Cal licked the end of one finger and crossed himself solemnly. 'There. Spectacles, testicles, wallet and watch, as we used to say at Sunday school. Now go on, spit it out.'

'Yeah, what was wrong with Jake?' Hattie asked. 'He looked normal enough in his Tinder photo.'

Bridie sighed. 'He still lives at home. With his parents.'

'How old is he?' Cal asked.

'Same age as me.'

'All right, I'll admit his parents being at home is a pretty big mood-killer,' Hattie said. 'Still, it's a bit unfair to judge him just on that, Bride. Lots of people in their late twenties are forced into that situation these days, aren't they?'

'That wasn't the only problem.' She scrunched her eyes closed and moaned faintly. 'You know, he really had me fooled with the sharp suit and the normal job and everything. I should've known Tinder could never match me with just an ordinary, well-adjusted human male.'

Cal shuffled Hattie off his knee to get a better view of his old schoolfriend's abject misery.

'Go on,' he said with a grin. 'I bet this is going to be good.'

'He shared a bedroom with his brother,' Bridie muttered.

Hattie's eyebrows shot up. 'Oh my God!'

'There's more.' Bridie buried her face in her hands and lowered her voice to a pained whisper. 'It was… bunk beds.'

Cal let out a snort of laughter, then covered his mouth.

'Oh God. Sorry, Bride, that just slipped out,' he said. 'This Jake surely didn't think you were going to do it with him while his brother was in the bottom bunk, did he?'

'Don't be ridiculous.' The absurdity of the situation finally ate through her epic humiliation and Bridie's lips twitched into a smile. 'His brother was in the top bunk.'

'Shit! You didn't actually do it, did you?' Hattie said, her eyes widening.

'Course we didn't. There isn't enough wine in the world, Hat.'

'Then where've you been all night? Topping and tailing with the brother?'

'No. I didn't have the fare for a taxi on me so I kipped on their sofa until the buses started running. His mum woke me up half an hour ago with a fried egg sandwich.'

Hattie shook her head. 'This twenty dates in twenty days challenge you set yourself is not working out, Bride. I really think you ought to jack it in.'

Bridie watched as Cal half unconsciously trailed his fingers over his girlfriend's thigh. 'What, so I can sit here every night watching you two touching each other up like love's young and excessively randy dream? No thanks, it's too depressing.'

'Why don't you just date normally, like normal single people? Wait for the good matches to pop up before you swipe right? There's no need to cram a year's worth of dates into a few weeks. I always said it was a daft idea.'

'Cramming them in is the whole point.' Bridie pushed herself to her feet and went into the kitchen to hunt for something carbohydrate-based for breakfast. 'I'm trying to prove something to myself here, guys,' she called back through the open door to the living room. 'After this little experiment is over, I'll either have found The One – or at least someone who doesn't make me want to swallow my own eyeballs every time he opens his mouth, which when you've been single as long as me amounts to the same thing – or I'll have seen enough of men to finally accept that true love is a fiction created to sell boxes of Milk Tray and embrace my inevitable singledom with resigned contentment. I think if I can just do this, it'll teach my brain that there's no need to have any regrets about giving myself up to spinsterhood.'

After hunting through all the kitchen cupboards, she discovered a half-pack of jaffa cakes that were two weeks out of date and took them back into the living room.

'How many of the twenty dates are left?' Cal asked.

'Two, then that's it,' Bridie told him. 'I haven't had a single decent match so far, and I can't imagine the last two are going to be any better. Come this time on Sunday, I'll be resigned to my fate and looking into cat adoption.'

'The male of the species aren't all lost causes, you know,' Cal said. 'I'm all right.'

Bridie snorted. 'That's a matter of opinion.'

'Hey. I brought you coffee, didn't I?' He folded his arms with an air of self-satisfaction. '*And* I don't even want to get into your pants. Just did it out of the kindness of my heart. That's pretty noble, right?'

Hattie patted his knee. 'You're a prince among men, darling.'

'You see, that's the whole problem. He actually is,' Bridie said to Hattie, nibbling around the edges of a stale jaffa cake.

'That's more like it,' Cal said, nodding. 'Cheers, Bridie. Nice to be appreciated.'

'Hadn't finished, had I?' She glanced back to Hattie. 'You

know why? Because the rest of them are setting such a stupidly low bar. These days, any bloke who brings his girl-friend a takeaway coffee and manages to keep his knob in his knickers for five minutes thinks he's treating her like a bloody princess. The problem with heterosexual men en masse is that for every Cal there's also far too many…'

'Too many Bens?'

'Yeah,' Bridie said with a thin smile. 'The sort of arro-gant, swaggering twats who shag their way around every woman within a ten-mile radius and are convinced they're God's gift to the female sex. The thing that really pisses me off is that so many women actually seem to fall for Ben's brand of laboured charm. It reflects badly on the rest of us.' She finished off her jaffa cake and helped herself to a second.

'You two do know that I'm sitting right here while you're slagging off me and my brother, right?' Cal said. The girls ignored him.

'I'm reliably informed that you liked Ben well enough once, Bridie,' Hattie said with a knowing smile.

'Yes, well. I was a kid then; too naive to know any better. He soon showed his true colours.'

'So that's why you're so down on the rest of us?' Cal asked. 'Because my brother stood you up the night of your sixth-form leavers' ball ten years ago? I mean, I hate to go all #NotAllMen about it, but… well, that's just Ben, isn't it?'

'Oh yeah, I bet he'd love to believe he put me off men for life, the raving egomaniac,' Bridie said, curling her lip. 'It's not just Ben, thank you very much, Cal. It's Ben plus every lad I've been out with since.'

'Kind of harsh on our kind, isn't it?'

'It's not just you lot that are the problem.' She pushed the jaffa cake packet away and propped her chin on the heels of her hands. 'It's me. I'm a tosspot magnet, you guys. The only decent lads I seem to meet are either spoken for or they just don't fancy me.'

'Or they share a set of bunk beds with their brother,' Hattie said.

'Yeah, and you know what? I'd still take that guy over Ben bloody Kemp and his ilk.' Bridie hesitated, then reached for the jaffa cakes again. 'Still, we're at least free of the magnificent Ben's company while he's riding llamas up Machu Picchu or whatever it is,' she mumbled through a mouthful of sponge and citrus. 'It's been a lovely, peaceful year without him around.'

Hattie laughed. 'I'm sure there must've been a collective sigh of disappointment from the female population of Messington on the day he announced he was leaving us.'

'Huh. I'm pretty sure that was a sigh of relief.'

'Well, ladies, sigh no more,' Cal said, smiling. 'Because you'll never guess who's just come home.'

TWO

'And I want at least two sides of A4 on the death of hope in *The Great Gatsby* by next Tuesday, no excuses,' Bridie called to her Year 12s as they filed out of the classroom for lunch.

Josh Abercrombie pulled a face as he went by her.

'Why does English have to be so depressing, miss?'

Bridie shrugged as she swept her books and papers into the cavernous bag she used for lugging them around in. 'That's just the way it is, I'm afraid. Writers are a morbid bunch. Just count yourself lucky the exam board didn't foist any Hemingway on you.'

He squinted at her. 'You all right, Ms Morgan? You look knackered.'

'Mmm. I was up late... planning lessons. You know, teacher stuff. Go on, go get your dinner.'

When the kids had disappeared off to the canteen, Bridie slung her bag over her shoulder and headed to the staffroom. There'd been a summons from Mr Duxbury, the head, asking all members of staff to congregate there before breaking for lunch. When she arrived, Hattie was already there with Meg and Ursula, the two other teachers they were friendly with.

'Love, you look shattered,' Ursula said as Bridie threw herself into a chair beside them.

'Don't you start,' Bridie muttered. 'I've had enough piss-taking off the kids.'

'What's up?' Meg asked. 'Late night?'

'More like an early morning,' Hattie said, grinning. 'Our Ms Morgan's a dirty, filthy stop-out, ladies. She crawled in on her hands and knees this morning after a fraternal threesome in a bunk bed.'

'All right, keep your voice down,' Bridie hissed. She cast a glance towards the door, where the remaining teachers and assistants of Messington Secondary School were filing in. 'There was no threesome and no bunk bed sex, all right? Just a date that went bad.'

Ursula raised an eyebrow. 'Another one?'

'Yes, Urs, another one. It's me, isn't it?'

'Poor old Bride.' Hattie stood up and rested a hand on her shoulder. 'Those guys don't know what they're missing out on. Here, let me get you a coffee before you slip into a sleep-deprivation coma.'

'Thanks, Hat,' Bridie said, patting the hand on her shoulder. 'The more caffeine I can get inside myself today, the better. Honestly, I've never been so tempted to pull a sickie as I was this morning.'

'You really need to ditch this twenty dates thing, Bridie,' Meg said when Hattie had gone to the kitchen area to make her a drink. 'It's been an unmitigated disaster from start to finish.'

'I know it has, that's the whole point. I'm trying to prove something to myself, aren't I?'

'What, exactly?'

'That retiring from the world of men and dating will be no bad thing. The twenty dates challenge is supposed to be kill or cure for my love life.' Bridie shrugged. 'I'd say it's working a treat.'

'But they've all been awful.'

'Exactly,' she said. 'Girls, I can honestly say that right now, I never want to go on another bloody date again. And if I'm ever even slightly tempted in future then all I need to do is remember the tedium of Alistair the tropical fish breeder, or think about the bloke who'd lied about his age and turned out to be at least sixty, or that sweaty pervert who kept trying to play footsie with my crotch, and I'll be cured instantly. Best idea I ever had. I've saved myself a world of pain in the future.' She yawned. 'Although I could wish I didn't have another one tonight. I'll be in serious danger of falling asleep on him, especially if he's as boring as they usually are.'

'You must want to meet someone though, don't you?' Ursula asked. 'Everyone does.'

'No they don't. Some lucky bastards just live happily single, doing exactly what they want every day, watching whatever they like on telly and never having to fight for the covers. And after my last date tomorrow, I'm looking forward to joining their ranks.'

'You seriously don't want to fall in love?'

Bridie snorted. 'Are you kidding me? What is love anyway but a combination of endorphins and self-delusion? The rose-tinted haze soon wears off, and it's then you realise what sort of slobby, farting, football-obsessed, lager-guzzling meat-head you've gone and lumbered yourself with.'

'If that's how you feel about it, why not just give up now?'

'Oh, I don't know,' Bridie said, sighing. 'Perhaps I've been clinging on to a last sliver of hope that there might be someone out there for me. Not hearts and flowers; just a mate I can sit in my PJs with while we split a Domino's and watch *Cobra Kai*. Someone I fancy enough to cuddle up to at night, with only minimal periods of feeling semi-homicidal towards each other. Let's face it though: if I haven't met him by now, he obviously doesn't exist.' She summoned a smile. 'Anyway, it doesn't matter. I'm fine on my own, and I'd rather be single than settle for some wanker just for the sake of a bit of company.'

'You're taking Number Twenty to Hattie's fancy-dress party tomorrow, right?' Meg said. 'Maybe he'll be the one if tonight's doesn't make the grade. Saving the best for last.'

Bridie smiled to herself. 'I very much doubt that. He looks as dull as death.'

Meg laughed. 'You seem very happy about it.'

'I told you, I'm looking forward to being free of the whole business. Men only mean stress. I've not met a single one who was worth the bother of it all, in bed or out of it.' Bridie glanced fondly at Hattie as she made her a coffee in the kitchenette. 'Still, I'm glad Hat got a good one. I sometimes think Cal Kemp might be the only decent bloke in town – Nature's way of compensating for his brother, I guess.'

'I heard Ben was back from his year out.'

Bridie pulled a face. 'Yeah, more's the pity. He'll be there tomorrow night too, I suppose, letching over all the female guests.'

'Suits me,' Meg said, a dreamy look coming into her eyes. 'Ben Kemp's welcome to letch over me any time.'

Bridie rolled her eyes. 'Do you have to encourage him? He's insufferable enough as it is.'

'He's also utterly gorgeous. Sorry, Bride, but that does kind of cancel out the ego.'

'Ugh. Traitors to womankind, the lot of you. Wouldn't

you rather have a great personality than someone who thinks he's it just because he's got himself a decent set of cheekbones and some abs?'

'Depends what you're looking for, doesn't it?' Meg said, shrugging. 'A decent set of cheekbones and some abs are fine for what I've got in mind.'

'So are Hattie and Cal still as loved up as ever?' Ursula said, diplomatically changing the subject.

'Yeah, it's pretty nauseating,' Bridie said. 'I can't go anywhere in the house without hearing their loud squelchy snogging – or worse. I wish the walls weren't so thin.'

'Sounds like I ought to start shopping for hats.'

'Well, it's not quite reached that stage yet, thank God. If Cal takes my Hattie away from me, I might have to revise my good opinion of him.'

'Of who?' Hattie asked as she joined them again. She handed over a mug of coffee and Bridie cuddled it to her gratefully.

'Your boyfriend,' she said, blowing on her drink. 'Ursula was wondering if wedding bells might soon be ringing out.'

Hattie flushed as she reassumed her seat. 'Don't be daft.' She smiled. 'He is wonderful though. Honestly, every time I wake up next to him I can't believe my luck.'

'See?' Bridie said to the other two. 'This is what I have to live with now. I can't decide if it's sickening, adorable or a bit of both.'

The head, Mr Duxbury, entered the staffroom and cleared his throat for silence.

'What's this meeting about anyway? Do you know?' Bridie whispered to Ursula.

'Two months until we break up for summer, right? I guess it's the usual recruitment drive.'

'Oh Christ, no.'

'OK, you're all here. Good,' the head teacher said. 'Now as you know, this is traditionally the time of year when I ask – stop!' He spun to face Adrian Verges, the deputy head, who'd been trying to sidle to the door. 'Nice try, Mr Verges. Sit yourself back down.'

Adrian fell reluctantly into a nearby seat. Duxbury marched to the door and stood with his back against it, in case there were any more escape attempts.

'Right,' he said. 'As I was saying, this is traditionally the time of year when I appeal for volunteers to supervise the Duke of Edinburgh Gold training expedition during the six-week holidays.'

There was a collective groan from the staff.

'Now I don't know why you always react like that,' Duxbury said, frowning at them. 'I've been going on the trips for years, they're always a basket of laughs.'

'Traipsing dozens of miles across soggy countryside then spending all night trying to stop hormonal spotty-faced kids from sneaking into each other's tents for a fumble?' Hattie muttered to her friends. 'Yeah, sounds like it.'

Duxbury spun to fix a Grinch-like smile on her. 'What was that, Miss Leonard? Did I just hear a ringing "yes please" from you?'

Her eyes widened. 'What? No!'

'Mmm, you know, I'm sure I did. Very generous of you to offer your time, thank you.'

Hattie turned a horrified look on her friends while he scribbled her name down on a clipboard. Meg tried unsuccessfully to smother a laugh.

'Ah! And Miss Collins too,' Duxbury said, turning on Meg with the same dangerous grin. 'I see you're in full agreement with your friend Miss Leonard. What a lot of fun you're going to have together. I'm sure my delightful cousin

Ursula will want to join you both as well, what with you all being as thick as thieves in the night.'

'No way!' Ursula said.

'Of course you do. You were a Girl Guide, weren't you?'

Ursula folded her arms. 'You can't use inside information like that against me, Eddie, it's unethical. Plus I'll tell Nana on you.'

'Go ahead, she'll be on my side. She always did think you ought to get outside more.' Duxbury scanned the rest of the assembled staff, every one of whom seemed to be trying to make themselves as small and as silent as possible. 'Well well well, this is going to be easier than I thought. Anyone else here with a comment to make?'

'Help me,' Hattie mouthed to Bridie while the head wrote down Meg and Ursula's names.

Bridie grimaced before raising her hand to ask a question.

'Um, Mr Duxbury?'

'Yes, Ms Morgan?'

'How does it work, please? I mean, where are you going to be taking the D of E kids?'

'We'll be doing a twenty-five-mile yomp over the North York Moors, carrying all our own equipment, tents and food. The children will have to plot the route and navigate by OS map – none of this mobile phone GPS nonsense. This is a practice walk to prepare them for their final expedition, which they'll do with minimal supervision and guidance at a later date.' He puffed himself up. 'This is the way they build resilience and self-sufficiency. Skills I think a few of you could benefit from learning too.'

'Yes, but we don't actually have any skills, do we? Hattie doesn't know how to read maps or put tents up or anything like that.' Bridie shot Hattie an apologetic look. 'Trust me as someone who's frequently had to help her navigate: she could get lost in her own backyard.'

Hattie looked put out at this summary of her navigation skills. She opened her mouth to object, then caught Duxbury's eye and closed it again.

'Not a problem,' Duxbury said airily. 'Teachers are only expected to supervise the students. There will be a professional instructor present to take responsibility for the expeditionary side of things; I've arranged it with a local company that organises treks and other outdoor activities. Really, it'll be like a free holiday for you. I can't understand why you aren't all fighting for places.'

'But what if we lose our way on the moors?'

'Well, we can burn that bridge when we come to it.' His pencil hovered ominously over his clipboard. 'So, Ms Morgan? Can I write you down? I'm sure you want to keep your three friends company, don't you?'

'I can't believe I agreed to go on this bloody expedition,' Bridie grumbled as she got ready for her date back at the house that evening.

She pulled a top out from the cupboard and chucked it to Hattie, who was sitting on the edge of her bed.

'Hmm,' Hattie said as she held it against herself. 'Bit revealing, Bride. You'll have him drooling into your cleavage all night.'

'Good point. I'm far too tired for cleavage-drooling.' She glanced at the life-size cardboard cut-out of George Clooney that inhabited one corner of her room. 'What do you reckon, Georgie?'

Bridie could sense from George's expression of quirked-eyebrow amusement that he agreed with Hattie's assessment. Her housemate threw the top back to her and Bridie put it away in the cupboard again.

'Anyway, the D of E thing wasn't my fault,' Hattie said. 'You saw what happened. That arse Duxbury bullied me into it.'

'Only because you had to go and open your big mouth about how shit it was going to be. And now you've dragged me, Meg and Ursula down with you. Cheers, mate.'

'You never know, it might be fun. If we all fill our rucksacks with boxes of wine we'll get through it.'

'As you so perceptively pointed out in the meeting, it'll be wet, miserable and full of randy kids trying to get off with each other whenever we turn our backs,' Bridie said. 'I remember it well from when I was a horny seventeen-year-old making life hell for the poor suckers who'd been roped into supervising our D of E training.'

'Oh, right. So you have got some outdoor skills then.'

'Well yeah, some, but I was hardly going to tell Duxbury that, was I? The main thing is, I know from personal experience that it's bound to be awful.'

Hattie propped her chin on her fist. 'Yeah, I know. I was trying to find a bright side.'

'There isn't one. Sorry, Hat.'

'Thanks for offering to keep me company anyway. I promise I'll make it up to you somehow.' She sighed. 'The worst part is having to spend a weekend away from Cal. Not sure how I'll cope for two whole days without a cuddle.'

'Well it's no good looking at me, sweetheart.' Bridie shook her head. 'You've really got it bad for that boy, haven't you?'

Hattie hugged herself, smiling dreamily. 'I know. I never knew it could be like this. Love, I mean.'

'I'm half sorry I ever introduced the pair of you.'

'You don't mean that.'

'No, I suppose not,' Bridie said, smiling too. 'As much as I want to play up to my reputation as a hardened cynic about all things romance-related, you two are obviously made for each other. And Cal's a good guy, despite his evil big brother's influence. Nauseating as you are together, I'm glad you're both happy.'

Hattie stood up to give her a squeeze.

'You don't have to go on this date, Bride,' she said. 'You know it's only going to make you miserable. Why don't you text the lad to say you've got a cold or something, then we'll get into our PJs and watch a film? You need time to recover from last night's dating disaster before my party tomorrow.'

'That does sound nice.' Bridie hesitated a moment, then sighed and carried on rifling through her cupboard. 'But I have to go. I made a promise to myself that I'd see this thing through to the bitter end. Besides, I'm presuming you've got Cal coming over.'

'Yeah. So?'

'So, if it's a choice between watching you two being sickeningly loved up on the living room sofa or going out for my daily dose of man-cure, I think I'll choose the latter.' She glanced over her shoulder. 'I take it Ben'll be there tomorrow night?'

'Well, yes. He's my boyfriend's brother, Bridie, I had to invite him.'

'Huh. He's a man-cure all by himself.' She groaned. 'Oh God. I hope this guy Craig I've got lined up for tomorrow isn't too horrendous. Ben'll take the piss something chronic if I turn up with a total dud.'

Hattie smiled. 'Come on, admit it. For all your slating of Ben, you get off on winding him up.'

'I won't deny that scoring off Ben Kemp is one of my

life's few pleasures. Still, I wish he'd stayed in South America until I was done with the twenty dates thing. That's just the sort of ammo he'll delight in using against me forever.' Bridie finally selected a yellow strappy top and chucked it onto the bed. 'This'll do. Now help me hide the bags under my eyes before I have to go.'

THREE

Ben glanced around the familiar surroundings of the Crossed Garter from his seat at the bar, smiling slightly.

It was weird. He hadn't been looking forward to coming home again – back to boring old Messington, the sort of dull Yorkshire seaside town where nothing much had happened since the invasion of the Spanish Armada, filled with the same old faces he'd been seeing since the day he was born. When Ben had pictured the muddy ocean and colourless beach of his hometown while he'd been away, the contrast with the lush mountainous beauty of Peru couldn't have been stronger. God, the freezing drizzle that had met him when he'd stepped off the plane last week had almost sent him scurrying to book an immediate return flight.

But now he was here, back in the same pub he'd been drinking at since he was… well, eighteen if you believed that fake ID he'd bought online, or sixteen if you didn't. Anyway, he was forced to confess it did feel sort of good to be home. Back with his friends; his family. His memories.

'Bloody hell, I don't believe it! So young Ben Kemp's back in town, is he?'

Ben spun his stool to face the bar, where the landlord was beaming broadly at him from behind a row of beer pumps.

'Hiya, Pete,' he said, holding out a hand to him. 'You miss me?'

'What, my best customer? I nearly went bust when you sodded off.' Pete pumped his hand enthusiastically. 'Good to have you home again, lad. It wasn't the same without you. How long have you been back?'

'A week. Hey, was it always this cold around here?'

Pete laughed. 'You'll soon readjust. So is it the usual then?'

Ben smiled to himself. It was nice to be back among people who knew what your usual drink order was without needing to be told.

'Yeah, cheers,' he said. 'Pour one for our Cal as well, will you? He's meeting me here in a bit.'

'Tell you what, you can have these two on the house. Homecoming present.'

Ben clapped him on the shoulder. 'Ta, mate.'

Pete started pulling his pint as Ben scanned the pub for familiar faces.

There were a few people he recognised, a handful he didn't – tourists, probably. You always got some in a seaside town, although the Garter was really more of a locals' pub.

A pretty girl he didn't know, one of a pair sharing a bottle of wine at a nearby table, smiled as his gaze fell on her. Ben smiled back, and she blushed slightly at the attention. He let his gaze linger for a moment, holding eye contact, before drawing it away. That could definitely be worth further investigation later on.

And... oho! Who was this he spied tucked into a corner,

looking bored as hell while she shared a basket of chips with some lad? Bridie Morgan, no less! Surely she hadn't actually settled down while he'd been gone? Cal hadn't mentioned anything. Anyway, if Bridie was in a relationship now then she looked bloody miserable about it. She had her chin propped on one fist as she nibbled with little enthusiasm on a chip, literally seconds away from dozing off by the look of her.

Bridie looked a bit different than she had when he went away. She'd filled out a little in the curves, and changed her hair to a shorter style. It was bobbed now, with added caramel highlights blending with her natural copper tones. They suited her: both the hair and the curves.

She was a lovely-looking girl, there was no denying that. Not that the lad she was with seemed to have noticed as he chattered on, oblivious to the fact his date clearly wasn't interested. Ben noticed though, seeing her with fresh eyes after his year away, and his wasn't the only male gaze drifting appreciatively in her direction either. If she didn't have such a sharp gob on her – and such stupidly high standards – she could easily take her pick of the lads round here. As it was, Bridie was like a hedgehog: cute, but far too prickly to get cuddly with.

She did look good tonight. Ben might tell her so later – tongue in cheek, naturally. It was always fun seeing her go that lovely shade of mauve when he teased her, and hearing her comebacks. She never held back from giving as good as she got, and she never backed down. Ben hadn't realised just how much he'd missed sparring with Bridie while he'd been away.

Not wanting his old schoolfriend-slash-nemesis to catch sight of him yet, he took his and Cal's drinks to a table out of sight of Bridie and her boyfriend. He'd just swallowed his first sip of beer when his brother arrived.

'All right, tiny?' Ben stood up to give Cal a hug, towering over him at six foot two to his brother's six foot one and a half. 'Got you a pint of that Blonde you like. I'm hoping your drink order hasn't changed while I've been gone.'

'Cheers, big brother.' Cal sat down and drew his beer to him.

'Now this I missed – us two setting the world to rights over a pint,' Ben said. 'Come on then, fill me in on everything that's happened round here while I've been away.'

'You first. How was the job interview?'

'Really good. They offered it to me on the spot actually. Senior Instructor Kemp, if you don't mind.'

Cal blinked. 'Seriously? That's brilliant, Ben. Did you like the look of the company then?'

'Yeah, Grand Adventures has got a great reputation in the outdoors industry. I know you and Mum thought the Peru trip was a mad idea, but the manager there was dead impressed. He said trekking Machu Picchu was just the sort of experience they were looking for. I told you a year's travel could be a good career move for me.' Ben took a sip of beer. 'There's only so far you can wow prospective employers with the Three Peaks Challenge, right?'

'I'm glad to hear you'll soon be rejoining the ranks of the employed.' Cal leaned over the table to slap his brother's arm. 'Well done, mate.'

'Cheers.' Ben lowered his voice. 'Guess who's here.'

'Who?'

'Bridie Morgan. In the far corner, eating chips with this hipster lad. She's never managed to coax some poor bastard into a relationship while I've been gone, has she?'

Cal smiled. 'Not quite. She's on a date. She goes on a lot of them these days.'

'What, Bridie?' Ben said, quirking an eyebrow. 'Last time I saw her, that knobhead Chris had just ended it with her and she was declaring she was renouncing men for life.'

'She's doing some sort of last-ditch experiment to see if any of us might be salvageable: twenty dates in twenty days. Yesterday's went so well, she flashed her thonged-up bum cheeks at me in excitement.'

'Miss Sensible Knickers wears thongs now?' Ben shook his head. 'Things really have changed around here. What did she flash you for?'

'It was an accident. I caught her trying to do the tiptoe of shame back into the house without Hattie seeing. Still, if I wasn't spoken for I might have to admit it wasn't a bad view.' Cal looked up from his pint. 'But I forgot. I'm talking to a man who's seen it for himself, aren't I?'

'Well, I'm not sure I ever saw it in the naked light of day. It was all under-the-duvet stuff when we were that age.'

'Why did you two break up?' Cal asked. 'All I remember is you asking her to the sixth-form leavers' ball and then suddenly deciding you weren't going to go.'

Ben tapped the side of his nose. 'A gentleman never tells, young Calvin.'

'Right. And what about you?'

He picked up a beer mat and chucked it at his brother. 'Look, we didn't break up, OK? We didn't break up because we were never going out.'

'Yeah? I might've been a year below you guys, but I was old enough to know what those noises coming from your room were whenever she came round to ours.'

Ben shrugged. 'That was only a casual thing. A bit of

friendly fumbling, the way kids do. We were never officially boyfriend and girlfriend.'

'Then why did you ask her to the ball?'

'She didn't have a date and I thought she'd look a bit sad turning up on her own, so like a good mate I asked if she wanted to go with me. Which was pretty noble of me really, given I'd had a few tempting offers in other areas.'

'Well then, why stand her up? There's not much noble about that.'

Ben glanced at the table where the attractive woman who'd smiled at him earlier was drinking wine with her equally attractive friend. 'Hey, fancy chatting up those two in a minute? It'll be just like old times, the Kemp brothers out on the pull.'

'Come on, you know I'm with Hattie now. Anyway, don't change the subject.'

'I got cold feet, all right?' Ben said, feeling his cheeks heat. 'It felt like Bridie was starting to see us as more than just friends with benefits; we were both about to go off to uni in different parts of the country, so I freaked out and hid at home. I'm not proud of it, but I was a kid, wasn't I? Come on, let's go talk to the girls. The blonde one keeps looking at me.'

'How many times, Ben?' Cal said, looking irritated. 'I've got a girlfriend. Unlike you, that does actually mean something to me.'

Ben shook his head. 'Harsh. After what Dad did to Mum, you really think that doesn't mean anything to me?'

'Everyone knows you don't do commitment.'

'Which is exactly why I don't do infidelity. No girlfriend means no obligations, which means no one gets hurt. And I'm not about to start encouraging you to misbehave either.'

'I never realised you felt so strongly about it,' Cal said in a softer voice.

'Well, now you know,' Ben said. 'I wasn't suggesting you get off with her. I just need a wingman to keep her talking while I try my luck with the friend, that's all.'

'No, bruv, I can't. Innocent or not, I'd have some serious explaining to do if it got back to Hat that I'd been chatting up another woman down the pub.'

'Ugh. Fine.' Ben took a gloomy sip of his pint. 'When did this place get so boring?'

'It's not boring. We just grew up, that's all.'

'Same difference.'

'You should give the relationship thing a go yourself,' Cal said. 'You might discover you like it.'

Ben scoffed. 'No chance. When that day comes, just stuff me, mount me and stick a plaque under me saying "RIP Benjamin Kemp: taken from us far too soon".'

'Ben, you're twenty-eight years old. Most of our mates are either married or engaged now, if they aren't already sprogging out. Don't you ever think about settling down?'

'What, so I can get myself a mortgage, a couple of kids who think I'm old and pathetic and a wife who's long since bored of shagging me, then resign myself to the highlight of my day being cracking one off in the shower every morning before work? Trade the Audi in for some hideous family estate? I might as well just chop my knackers off now and have done with it.' He patted his brother's hand. 'Not that I'm not happy for you, kid. But that stuff's not for me.'

'Gee, thanks,' Cal said drily. 'You can't seriously be planning to bounce around women the rest of your life, can you?'

'Why not? Sounds pretty good to me.'

'Life with someone you love doesn't have to be all Volvos and shower wanking, Ben. I know we weren't set the best example as kids, but I promise you some people have these things called happy, fulfilling marriages. Have you really never met anyone you thought might be worth getting to know a bit better?'

Ben shrugged. 'Maybe I have, but when I made the effort I discovered they rarely were worth it once you scratched the surface. I certainly can't imagine falling for any of them. I'm not sure I believe there is such a thing as love, to be honest – I mean, maybe for someone like you, but not for me.'

Cal shook his head. 'God, you're a cynical bastard.'

'I'm a realist. Until I meet a woman who combines sex appeal with wit, humour, intelligence, good conversation and great taste in films – all the qualities I'd want in an ideal mate, in other words – then there's no chance I'd throw away my precious freedom for anything less.'

'Well, do what you like. But I've found my ideal mate and I'm buggered if I'm letting her get away,' Cal said. 'Hattie's perfect.'

'Oh Christ.' Ben groaned deeply. 'Is this what you're like now? Do I need to start bringing sick bags with me every time we go out for a drink? You'll be writing her bloody sonnets next.'

'Love isn't a dirty word, Ben.'

'That very much depends on how and when you say it.'

Cal cast a glance behind him and lowered his voice. 'Look, there's something I need to talk to you about. That's why I asked you out for a drink.'

'What is it?'

'It's about the fancy-dress party tomorrow night. I need you to do me a big favour.'

Ben frowned. 'OK. What?'

'At ten o'clock I'm going to bring out the cake I'm

making for Hat, all right? And I want you to help me serve it.'

'Me? Why?'

'Because there's going to be something very special in the third slice from the top, going clockwise. I'm going to cut it up and I want you to hand out the pieces. But you have to make completely sure no one gets hold of that piece except Hattie. Understand?'

Ben stared at him. 'Oh, no. No! Cal, please say you're not doing this.'

Cal smiled dreamily. 'I am.'

'Seriously, bruv, how can you do this to me?' Ben shook his head despairingly. 'I thought we were brothers. Mates. The two musketeers. Now you're abandoning me for some lass?'

'She's not just "some lass". I love her, don't I?'

'I can't believe you're turning husband on me. What happened to our plan to stay single for life and buy a cabin in the Swiss Alps with a heated pool and an Xbox?'

'We made that plan when I was seven and still thought girls were icky,' Cal said. 'Sorry to have to break it to you, Benjy, but my priorities have shifted a bit since puberty set in.'

'This is all Bridie's fault. Introducing you to those schoolmistressy sirens she works with, in their tweed twinsets and pearl-studded G-strings. We never should've stayed friends with her.'

Cal smiled. 'Look, don't think of it as losing a brother so much as gaining a Hattie.'

'God, if I'd known I'd have a bloody family wedding to come home to I'd have stayed in Peru,' Ben said, groaning.

'You get to be best man though. You'll enjoy that, right? You can write a speech about what a twat I am.'

'Hmm. Suppose. Can I organise the stag as well?'

'Course.'

'There's that, I guess.' Ben managed a smile and clapped his brother on the shoulder. 'Well, congratulations, little brother. Underneath this cynical exterior I am happy for you, I promise. I mean, I think you're mad to want to do it, but since you do then all the best to you both. Hattie's a lovely girl.'

Cal laughed. 'Cheers, but let's not get ahead of ourselves, eh? I need her to say yes yet.'

'You reckon she will?'

'Let's say I'm quietly confident.'

'I suppose I should be grateful it's her and not Joanna,' Ben muttered as he finished his pint.

'Oh, Jo wasn't nearly as bad as you always make out.'

'She bloody was, mate.'

'Well, let's not fall out over it. She's gone now.' Cal drained his remaining beer and stood up. 'I'll get us a couple more in.'

FOUR

As dates went, Bridie had been on worse – but not often. In terms of awfulness, this was definitely a candidate for top three.

She probably should've run when she'd noticed Joel's man bun, but, reminding herself why she was putting herself through this, she'd resolved to stick it out. The highlight of the evening had been right at the start, when they'd arrived at the pub and Joel had offered to buy them a basket of chips to share. From there, it had quickly gone downhill.

'Of course, people from outside the fandom just don't understand how all-consuming it can be,' he was saying now as she nibbled on a chip. 'That's why I was so excited to see from your profile that you were into them too. It's rare to find someone who really appreciates good music.'

Bridie hadn't thought much about it when she'd added to her Tinder profile that she liked the Spice Girls. It was actually supposed to be semi-ironic: something a bit retro and cheesy that she hoped might attract someone with a decent sense of humour. But Joel, it seemed, was almost holy in his adoration for Ginger, Baby, Scary, Sporty and Posh. He'd been to every gig he could, both with the actual band and their numerous tribute acts. He also belonged to a ridiculous number of online fan groups, collected obscure memorabilia and had very probably sent Emma Bunton pairs of his underpants through the post.

His entire conversation during their date had revolved around the music of the Spice Girls, the inferiority of modern girl bands when compared with the Spice Girls, the overlooked yet career-defining merits of Mel B's performance in *Spice World: The Movie*, and fan theories on the true meaning of the phrase 'zig-a-zig-ah'. If Bridie was tempted to go back to Joel's place later – which she absolutely was not going to be doing no matter how much alcohol she swallowed down to cushion this horrendous experience – she imagined she'd be expected to shag him in some sort of Spice shrine while wearing a replica of Geri Halliwell's Union Jack dress.

'So what's your favourite of their albums then, Bridie?' he asked her.

She roused herself. After last night's kip on Jake's mum's sofa, she was only barely managing to stay awake for this evening's disastrous date.

'Oh, er... the last one, definitely,' she said, nodding sagely.

He frowned. '*Forever*, really? Wow. Not sure how you can defend a choice like that.'

'Well, you know. I'm a rebel.' She glanced around at the sound of approaching footsteps and groaned. 'Oh God.'

He followed her gaze to Ben, who was making a beeline for their table with a big grin on his face. 'You know that guy?'

'Yes, he's an old schoolfriend. Well, I say friend...'

'All right, Sweet Pea?' Ben said when he reached them. He leaned over the table to help himself to a chip. 'Still alive then, are you?'

She flashed him a wide smile. 'Well I almost pined away when you went off on your geriatric gap year, but then I don't know, after about ten minutes I somehow seemed to make this miraculous recovery. How's your substitute penis?'

'The Audi? Just like the real thing, love: sleek, sexy and ready to ride.'

'Mmm. Or over-hyped, over-polished and comes too quickly.'

Ben looked Joel up and down as if he were some sort of specimen impaled ready for dissection, taking in his man bun and selection of Spice-themed tattoos. 'What number's this one then, Bride?'

'Bloody Cal, I'll kill him,' she muttered. She summoned a smile for her date, who was watching their gleeful bickering with a puzzled expression on his face. 'Um, I'm out of wine here, Joel. Do you think you could pop to the bar and get us another couple of drinks?'

'Have you got any money?'

She lifted an eyebrow. 'Seriously?'

'Hey, I bought us the chips, didn't I?'

'Of course, you're right. And I only bought the last two rounds, how selfish of me.' She pushed her empty glass towards him. 'Just tell Pete to stick it on a tab. I'll settle up when I leave.'

'Well, what number date is it then?' Ben asked when Joel had gone to the bar.

She glared at him. 'Nineteen, if you must know. And please tell your brother from me that he might want to start wearing a cricket box when he comes over to ours.'

'So how are you finding Joel?'

'He's great. Really, really nice guy. Some sort of big-shot music producer, apparently.'

'Liar.'

She grimaced. 'All right, so he's not a music producer. But he's still pretty cool.'

Ben leaned over her to take the last chip. 'What're you two planning to do after this? Will it be the standard post-date shag, do you think, or will you be spending the night picking through Mel C's bins together?'

She scowled at him. 'Have you been eavesdropping on us?'

He shrugged. 'Couldn't help hearing a bit on my way over. Look, how about you ditch this loser and come have a drink with me and Cal? You must've got tired of only seeing me in your more erotic dreams this past year.'

'No thanks. Joel might be boring, obsessive and tight as fuck, but I'll still take his Spice Girls fixation over your tales of sleeping with the entire female population of Brazil.'

'Peru.'

'Whatever.' She cast a glance over his deeply tanned arms and curled her lip. 'You look like you've been Ronsealed. What do they call that shade, Werther's Original?'

He grinned. 'Missed you, Bride.'

'Not mutual.'

'You're looking pretty sexy yourself,' he said, looking over her outfit of yellow strappy top and skinny jeans. 'I'm told you're into wearing thongs these days.'

'Tell Cal to make sure that's a steel-lined cricket box, will you? Because just for him I'm about to get into wearing hobnailed boots as well.'

'It was only a matter of time.'

She nodded to his jeans. 'You do know your flies have been undone the whole time we've been talking, right?'

'Shit, have they?'

Bridie smirked as he cast a worried glance in the direction of his crotch. 'Made you look.'

'Funny.' He nudged her. 'So do you think you'll be going back to Joel's place later, or is it a cosy night in with the alternative entertainment you've got hidden in your knicker drawer?'

She looked up to smile dangerously at him. 'Bend over and I'll show you.'

'Hey, don't threaten me with a good time.'

'Look, just sod off, Kemp, can you? Go back to Darkest Peru, see if you can get a job making marmalade sandwiches for Paddington Bear or something.'

'Come on, Bride,' he said, putting an arm around her shoulders. 'Ditch Joel and come have a drink with us. You can have lots of fun insulting me and I promise I won't tell a single story about my many sexual conquests on the South American continent. Although you're right, there were loads.'

'Nope. Fine where I am, thanks. And look, here's my date back again.' She shrugged off his arm and fixed her face into a smile as Joel arrived with their drinks and a couple of bags of crisps. 'Cheers, honey.'

'Oooh. Nice touch,' Ben mouthed.

'Hope you don't mind, I stuck a couple of bags of Kettle Chips on your tab as well,' Joel said as he sat back down. 'I spent all afternoon in the gym working on my deltoids so I'm craving carbs tonight.' He cast an underwhelmed glance at Ben. 'Oh. Your friend's still here.'

'I know, he's failing to take the most obvious of hints,' Bridie said. 'He thrives on attention though. Just ignore him and he'll soon go away.'

'I was going anyway.' Ben clapped Joel hard on the shoulder. 'Look after this one, mate, she's a real treasure.' He winked at Bridie before strolling back to his own table.

Bridie scowled after him. God, she hated that guy.

———

Hattie smiled fondly at Cal as he lay sleeping beside her, his arms wrapped tightly around her naked body as if afraid she might disappear in the night. She ran her fingertips lightly over the bare skin of his back, and he grunted appreciatively in his sleep at her touch.

Even after more than a year together, the novelty of this part – of waking up in his embrace – had never quite worn off for her.

Hattie had had a couple of longish relationships in the past; even lived with someone for a while – Scott, her last serious boyfriend. It was after they broke up three years ago that she'd landed here in Bridie's spare bedroom, and, after the two friends had discovered that living together suited them, she'd ended up staying put.

Hattie had really thought she'd been in love when she'd moved in with Scott; had even idly dreamed about marriage, and the kids they'd have together one day. She thought she'd been in love once before that too, with Tyler, her university boyfriend. But she'd never dreamed she could have anything like what she had with Cal Kemp; lovely Cal, who made her laugh, supported her, believed in her and loved her in a way no one else ever had. This time, Hattie knew for certain she'd met the one person she was destined to grow old with.

She leaned over him – his breathing soft and regular as he slept – and planted a gentle kiss on his cheek.

The peace was shattered by a loud voice from outside the bedroom door.

'Wakey wakey!' it yelled, followed by the elephant honk of a vuvuzela.

'Jesus Christ!' Cal's eyelids popped open like a doll pushed suddenly upright. 'What is it? Are we at war?'

Hattie smiled. 'No, love, we're just getting Bridied. I've been expecting her for the last twenty minutes. She does this every year on my birthday.'

'All right, you two, I'm coming in!' Bridie called from behind the door. 'Please cover all bums, boobs, willies, fannies and anything else you don't want me to see.' A second later the door flew open and she marched in, still in her pyjamas, honking the vuvuzela like the boogie-woogie bugle boy of Company B.

'Ugh. Talk about a rude awakening,' Cal muttered, pushing himself into a sitting position. 'What kind of a birthday tradition do you call this, Bride?'

'One that worked perfectly well before you started practically living here rent-free. Hattie likes me to wake her up early on her birthday, don't you, Hat?'

'I don't, in fact,' Hattie said. 'When my birthday's on a weekend, I like nice, long lie-ins snuggling with my boyfriend.'

Bridie smiled fondly at her. 'I know. Why do you think I do it?'

Cal laughed. 'I have to pop into the garage this morning, as it happens, so I'll clear out and leave you to your girly birthday shenanigans.' He leaned over to plant a lingering kiss on Hattie's lips. 'Happy birthday, gorgeous. I'll see you at the party tonight.'

Hattie smiled, blushing slightly. 'OK. Can't wait.'

'I'll miss you.'

'I'll miss you more.'

'Love you lots.'

'I know you do, Cal. Me too.'

Bridie made a gagging noise. 'Christ, do we have to have this every time he leaves the house? He's going to work, not the Russian Front.'

Cal turned to frown at her. 'Nobody invited you to come in and watch, you know. How about buggering off for a minute so I can kiss my girlfriend goodbye properly and get dressed without flashing you?'

'Oh no, not a chance. If I leave you alone it'll be hours until I can get Hattie to myself, waiting for you two to finish snogging. Not to mention what tends to come after that.' She turned to face the wall. 'There, I'm not peeping. Get your clothes on and sod off, Cal Kemp.'

'Ever the charming hostess,' Cal said. 'All right, but no looking. Eyes away from that mirror.'

'Cal, I promise, you've got nothing under that duvet I want to see.'

'Ouch. That hurts, Bride.'

Hattie gave his arm a consoling pat. 'Never mind her. She doesn't know what she's missing.'

'Well, you have to say that. But thanks.' He gave Hattie a last kiss and hopped out of bed to put his clothes on.

When Cal had left to go to work, Bridie bounced on to Hattie's bed, beaming broadly.

'It's your birthday, Hat!' she said, giving the vuvuzela another ear-splitting honk. 'Get your clothes on and let's go have fun. There's presents to be opened downstairs.'

Hattie groaned. 'It's too early for this. Stop honking my eardrums off, can you?'

'It's quarter of an hour later than last year. Serves you right for staying up all night shagging.'

'Hey. Pre-birthday treat. I'm entitled.'

'Come on, you're awake now,' Bridie said, nudging her. 'You might as well get up and come to play.'

'Why are you so bouncy?' Hattie demanded. 'You normally spend the morning after a date muttering to yourself about all blokes being a dead loss and the possibility of entering a convent. Nice and quietly, in your very own room.'

'Not today. Today it's my best friend's birthday. Here, I brought you a coffee to help you wake up.'

Bridie jumped up to grab the two mugs she'd left on top of the bookshelf outside Hattie's room and put one down on her friend's bedside table.

'Thanks.' Hattie reached for a bobble to push her morning bed-head hair into a rough bun before drinking her coffee. 'What are you in such a good mood for then?'

'Aren't I allowed to just be happy?'

'No.' Hattie narrowed one eye. 'You didn't get lucky last night, did you?'

'Nope, another total write-off. He had the lyrics to "Two Become One" tattooed on his lower back.'

'God, you're kidding.'

'I'm not. He flashed me with it and everything. And he was wearing those slouchy trousers so he included a generous amount of bum crack as a bonus.' Bridie shrugged. 'Suppose I'm just relieved I'm coming to the end of this twenty dates thing. After tonight I'll be done with the whole business and I can finally relax.'

'You're not really going to swear off men forever, are you?'

'Yep. I think the fact I'm looking forward to it so much is proof that twenty dates in twenty days was a great idea. I'm now completely sanguine about the fact I'll never have to spend another tedious evening with another tedious man as long as I live.'

'What time did you get home from the pub?'

'Nineish. I must admit, I feel better for a full night's sleep.'

'That's early,' Hattie observed. 'How did you manage to escape the clutches of "Two Become One" bum crack guy then?'

Bridie gave a wry smile. 'Someone phoned Pete behind the bar and told him I needed to go home straight away because my adorable Schnauzer puppy had been injured by a falling piano.'

'Eh?'

'In other words, Ben Kemp bailed me out. At least, I assume it must've been him.'

'Oh yeah, Cal said they ran into you last night,' Hattie said. 'So Ben phoned Pete, did he?'

'Must've done. I saw him leaving with some unfortunate girl he'd been chatting up, right before I got the message. I guess he must've rung somewhere on the way back to her place.'

'That was nice of him.'

'No it wasn't. He just loves the idea of rubbing the fact he rescued me in my face, that's all. I never asked him to stick his nose in.'

Hattie shook her head. 'You're really too hard on him. I know Ben can be kind of up himself, but he's a good laugh, isn't he? I like him.'

'You haven't known him as long as I have,' Bridie muttered. 'Plus you've got Cal prejudicing you in his brother's favour. Believe me, Ben Kemp is a royal pain in the arse and he always has been.'

Hattie examined her for a moment.

'What did happen between you two at school, Bride?' she asked. 'The whole story.'

'You know what happened. He stood me up for a date after A levels.'

'What, and you're still sore about it ten years later?'

Bridie glared into her coffee cup as if she could see Ben's stupid cheekboney face in there, smirking up at her.

'No,' she said. 'I'm sore about the fact that he struts around this town like a randy alpha gorilla with a permanent hard-on, thinking every lass he meets is sizzling with lust for him.'

'Hmm.' Hattie took a sip of her coffee, still with her eyes fixed on Bridie. 'Why should that bother you? It's no skin off your nose who Ben gets a hard-on for, is it?'

'It's the way he loves to flaunt it, that's all,' Bridie muttered. 'Smug git.'

'Did you have feelings for him then? Cal seems to think you might've been pretty serious about each other at one point.'

'So do you want to open your presents now?' Bridie asked, turning away. 'Then I thought I'd take you out for breakfast at Chicolini's. My treat, obviously.'

'You're not getting out of it that easily.' Hattie made her eyes wide and leaned round to flutter her eyelashes at her friend. 'It's my birthday, Bride. You have to tell me secrets on my birthday, especially after you chased Cal away during cuddle time.'

Bridie smirked. 'Yeah. You know, I've started to realise what it is you see in that boy.'

'Oh my God, you peeped!' Hattie gave her arm a playful slap. 'Bridie Morgan, you randy little pervert!'

She shrugged. 'Hey, don't judge me. I haven't had sex in ten months, remember? Besides, Cal got a flash of my bum yesterday so I'd say it's a fair trade-off.'

'OK, if you've been getting your sex-starved rocks off

spying on my boyfriend in the buff then you definitely owe me secrets. Did you have feelings for Ben or not?'

Bridie sighed. 'Honestly? I don't know. I was a kid, Hat; I'm not sure I'd have recognised them if I had. I guess... I felt like I did. You know, at the time.'

'What happened the night he stood you up?'

'You really want to know?'

'Yeah, go on.'

'We weren't seeing each other,' Bridie said, flushing. 'Not officially anyway. He was essentially the same Ben then as he is now: flirting with every girl in our year, teasing me constantly. I didn't mind his cockiness so much then. I actually thought it was kind of sexy, although I'd appreciate it if you didn't tell him that. It's easy to be impressed by that level of confidence when you're eighteen and shy as fuck.'

'So how come you had a date if you weren't seeing each other?'

'We weren't a couple but we did have a thing going on; sort of casual. I'd go round to his on Sundays and we'd have a bit of a grope while we watched TV together. Nothing heavier than third base – just to pass the time really. And then...' She hesitated. 'I mean, Ben had been with plenty of girls, even in those days. I thought if I was going to do it, I might as well do it with a mate. Someone with experience who'd know what he was doing.'

'You mean...'

'I asked if he'd go all the way with me. My first time. I really wanted to lose my virginity with someone I knew and trusted – someone I saw as a friend.'

'What happened? Was it awful?'

'I never got to find out,' Bridie muttered. 'We'd made a plan to do it after we'd been to the leavers' ball together. I spent all the money I'd got saved from my Saturday job on some sexy pants from Ann Summers and a packet of condoms from the toilets at the Garter. And…' She blinked. 'And he never turned up. I guess he got a better offer.'

'Aww. Poor little Bridie. That must've hurt.' Hattie rubbed her hand. 'Didn't he ever tell you why?'

'No. He never mentioned it again, and I was far too humiliated to ask him what the hell happened. Not long after that we both went off to uni, and since then we've been… well, like we are now.' She smiled grimly. 'It's probably for the best I didn't shag him. The last thing I want is to be just another lass round here who's been to bed with Ben Kemp.'

'It was a long time ago though.'

'Yeah, and he hasn't changed a bit, has he? He's only been home a week and already it's back to business as usual, picking up girls down the pub.' Bridie shook her head, scowling. 'God, that guy pisses me off. I just don't understand why the women in this town let him get away with it.'

'It's always going to be easy for someone who looks like him.'

'Huh. A few good, solid knock-backs could be the making of him, I reckon. It's a shame everyone's blinded by his stupid pretty face.'

'Well, never mind Ben,' Hattie said, squeezing her hand. 'Maybe you'll finally meet Mr Right at my party tonight, eh? I bet Fate's been saving him for the last of the twenty dates. You know, for dramatic impact.'

'With my luck, I doubt that very much.' Bridie forced a smile. 'Come on, time to get up. Birthday breakfast of Danish pastries and croissants at the caf, on me. Calories don't exist on your birthday, it's a well-known fact.'

FIVE

Hattie's twenty-eighth birthday party was being held that evening at her parents' home, one of the big Victorian townhouses on top of the cliff that overlooked the sea. Mr and Mrs Leonard were the sort of people who liked to make a fuss of their only child's birthday.

Bridie wasn't really looking forward to it. According to his Tinder profile her final date, Craig, was a chartered accountant with a keen interest in angling, so she wasn't anticipating much in the way of stimulating conversation. Still, at least after tonight it'd all be over. Already she was picturing the nice, quiet Sunday she'd be having tomorrow, with no need to change out of her pyjamas, put on make-up or spend an hour getting ready for yet another tedious date. No need to move, in fact, from her lovely, snuggly bed.

Hattie's birthday bash was a fancy-dress party with a difference: sort of the modern equivalent of a masked ball. Guests could go as anything they wanted so long as their faces were covered, then there'd be a big reveal at 11pm. Bridie was sure there'd be very few surprises when it came time to unmask though. These were small-town folk who for the most part had known each other nearly all their lives; masks or no masks, it was going to be pretty obvious who was who.

'Hi,' a man said to her when she arrived outside the house, stepping out of the shadows. 'Bridie, right?'

'That's me.' She turned to look at him. 'And you appear to be… an ogre. Wow. You know, I've seen some misleading Tinder photos in my time but…'

He laughed and pulled off his rubber Shrek mask. 'Craig. Nice to meet you.'

'You too.'

She scrunched her eyes closed as he leaned forward to kiss her. Surely a handshake was more appropriate to a first date, wasn't it? Why did some of them go for the full-on lip lunge right away? Still, at least Craig had kept it confined to her cheek. To be honest, this one seemed like he was probably more awkward than grabby.

'So, um, which Catwoman are you then?' Craig asked, glancing down at her figure-hugging black leotard.

'One of the Sixties ones, I think. I didn't have the nerve to go for the full Michelle Pfeiffer PVC.'

He smiled. 'Pity, it'd suit you. I mean, not that you don't look great as you are. I'm not about to start complaining when my date turns up in skintight Lycra.'

Bridie squinted at him in the light of the little lamps that lined Hattie's parents' drive. He actually wasn't bad-looking, especially when he smiled – a big improvement on his Tinder photo, in which he'd been proudly showing off some unfortunate fish he'd caught. Full, thick hair, green eyes, and his flirting game so far was pretty on point: just the right amount of sexy, without crossing the line into creepy. She couldn't have actually stumbled on a good one, could she? Maybe the girls had been right. Maybe Fate, with her keen sense of dramatic irony, had been saving the best for last.

Bridie felt a twinge of irritation at the idea. If Craig was halfway decent, that meant she'd have to make the effort to see him again. Just when she'd been looking forward to a nice, quiet life of duvet days and Netflix boxsets with only her George Clooney cut-out for company.

Shit, that wasn't normal, was it? Craig wasn't awful – at least, not so far. She was supposed to be pleased about that, not annoyed. Forcing herself to return his smile, Bridie fixed on her Catwoman mask and nodded to the door.

'Well, shall we go in?' she said. 'We'll grab a drink, then you can tell me all about yourself.'

———

When she and Craig had helped themselves to a cold beer each from an ice bucket in the kitchen, they found a quietish corner where they could talk.

Bridie glanced around the room, looking for familiar figures under their disguises. She'd been right: it wasn't hard to tell who was who. She knew Hattie at once, of course, since they'd hired their costumes together. As the birthday girl she had a licence to be the best-dressed person in the room so she was in a huge Regency ballgown with a Marie Antoinette wig, her face covered by an elaborate Venetian-style mask decorated with sequins and feathers. She was chatting with Elastigirl from *The Incredibles* – Ursula, obviously – and Pete Prince, the landlord of the Garter, who'd gone to no effort at all as Clark Kent. He was in his normal clothes, with an unbuttoned shirt showing a Superman-logo T-shirt underneath, plus a pair of fake glasses that hardly counted as a mask. Meg was here too, in a black tulle skirt and steampunk-style basque with a studded leather mask covering the top of her face. She was standing near the buffet table, getting chatted up by a well-built lad dressed as Spider-Man.

'Some people seem to have gone to a lot of effort,' Craig observed, rolling up the bottom of his Shrek mask so he could sip his beer. 'Is there a prize for best costume?'

'I don't think so. Just the kudos and admiring glances.' Bridie turned back to face him. 'So why Shrek then?'

He shrugged. 'I had it left over from a mate's stag do last year. We did a masked bar crawl.'

She grimaced. 'Ugh, poor you. Stag and hen dos, is there anything worse?'

'I know what you mean. Still, at least your lot aren't usually expected to go to strip clubs. Being surrounded by hordes of naked strangers is the kind of thing that sounds great on paper, but it's torture for us shy boys.'

'Yeah, but you don't have to wear hats with inflatable willies on them and play hoopla. We women have our crosses to bear too.' A tall man in school uniform was passing them clutching a couple of drinks, and Bridie reached out to grab his arm. 'Oi. You.'

'Hiya, Bride. I mean, hiya, mysterious masked stranger.' Cal nodded to Craig. 'And hi, Bridie's date.'

'Craig,' he said, standing up to shake Cal's hand. 'Good to meet you.'

'And you. Glad you both made it.'

'I want a word with you,' Bridie said, glaring at Cal as Craig sat back down. 'I'd have brought it up this morning but it seemed only fair to wait until you had some clothes on.'

'Me? What did I do?'

'Did you or did you not...' She trailed off as her gaze fell on his short trousers, blazer and school tie, topped off with a

Zorro-esque black eye mask. 'Speaking of clothes, Cal, who exactly are you supposed to be tonight?'

'Right now I'm Number Five from *The Umbrella Academy*. After the unmasking, I think I'll be either Angus from AC/DC, Wee Jimmy Krankie or one of the Bash Street Kids.'

'All right, Wee Jimmy, then answer me this: did you or did you not tell your brother last night that you'd seen my arse?'

Cal grimaced. 'Ben dragged it out of me. Kicking and screaming, I was.'

'You are in so much trouble, Cal Kemp.'

'I don't know why you're so coy about it, Bride. He's seen it, hasn't he?'

'He's seen… some of it. I see no reason why that should make it a topic of general conversation down the pub. Where is he anyway?'

Cal gestured in the direction of Meg and her Spider-Man suitor, who was whispering in her ear while she laughed. 'Over there.'

'Seriously, he's at it again?'

'Well, you know what he's like.' He nodded to Craig. 'I'll leave you both to it. Enjoy your date, guys.'

'Sorry, what was all that about your arse?' Craig asked when Cal had gone to join his girlfriend.

'Oh, nothing.'

'Did you used to go out with his brother then?'

'Not exactly go out. We had a bit of a fling when we were kids, till Ben buggered it up.' She cast a dark look at Ben in his Spider-Man suit, practically nibbling Meg's ear through the spandex while he whispered to her. 'We've all got that one ex, right?'

Craig laughed. 'Tell me about it. My ex-wife's a real piece of work.'

'Go on, how bad?'

'Well, when we split she logged in to my Facebook account and posted a screencap of my recent internet search history.'

'Oof.' Bridie paused. 'You know, that's actually sort of impressive. I mean, as revenge gambits go.'

'My mum didn't think so. Jenny tagged her in the post.' He nodded to her beer bottle. 'So, you want another?'

'Yeah.' She smiled. 'Yeah, that'd be nice. Thanks, Craig.'

———

'Hi, you,' Hattie said, beaming at Cal as he came back to join her in his giant schoolboy outfit.

'Hi, miss.' He bent down to give her a kiss before pressing a drink into her hand.

'Oh God, please don't call me that,' she said, laughing. 'I'd feel like a right perve if you weren't so enormous.'

'And how's my beautiful birthday girl? Having fun?'

She returned his kiss. 'I am now you're here.'

Pete mimed retching at Ursula, who nodded her whole-hearted agreement.

'I notice you didn't get me and Pete a drink, Cal,' Ursula said.

He shrugged as he detached himself from Hattie's lips. 'I'll get you guys one when you start sleeping with me.'

'Not worth it,' Pete observed to Ursula.

She cocked an eyebrow. 'You'd know, would you?'

'I've got second sight, love. All pub landlords have, it goes with the job.' He nodded in Bridie's direction. 'Who's young Miss Morgan out with tonight then?'

'He's called Craig,' Cal said. 'He seems relatively normal actually, for one of Bridie's dates.'

'God, I hope so,' Hattie said fervently. 'She really sounded like she meant it this morning when she said she was giving up on dating. I'm relying on Craig to convince her there's still some decent single lads left in the world.'

'Is your brother here?' Pete asked Cal.

Cal smiled drily. 'If there's women, there's my brother. He's the Batman by the buffet, schmoozing Hattie's mum.'

Pete glanced over to the buffet table behind Meg and Spider-Man. A Tim Burton-era Batman was talking to Sandra Leonard, Hattie's mother, who was dressed up as a Pierrot.

'Oh,' Ursula said, blinking. 'I sort of assumed he was the Spider-Man. Who's Meg getting drooled on by then, if it's not Ben?'

'Some bloke called Adrian from your school, I think.'

'Seriously, deputy head Adrian? Mr Verges?' Ursula nudged Hattie. 'Hey, you know he's coming on the D of E trip with us? That could be interesting. I thought it was only the kids we'd have to stop from misbehaving.'

Hattie frowned at them. 'Can you lot stop giving away who everyone is? The whole idea of this party is that it's supposed to be a surprise when we all unmask.'

'Sorry.' Cal slipped an arm around her waist. 'Not another word, we promise. Although to be fair, it is mostly obvious.'

'Hey,' Pete said, pushing his Clark Kent glasses up his nose. 'Master of disguise here, ta.' He looked from Ben in his Batman costume to where Bridie was chatting with Craig. 'Are those two ever going to stop kidding themselves, do you reckon?'

'What, Bridie and Ben?' Ursula said. 'How do you mean?'

'Well, you don't need the psychic ability of a bartender to

see what's behind the constant bickering. You could cut the sexual tension between that pair with a lemon slicer.'

'You really think so?'

'Absolutely. It's like when you ping the bra strap of the lass you like at school to show her you fancy her. At least, that's the way we did it back in my day.' He shook his head. 'God, ten years' worth as well. That'll be one hell of an explosive shag when they finally give in to it.'

'Nah, surely not. She hates him, she's always on about it.' Ursula glanced at Hattie. 'She does, doesn't she?'

'Hmm. To be honest, I'm tempted to side with Pete – when it comes to Bridie anyway,' Hattie said. 'She'll swear herself blue that men are a waste of time, and not one of them worse than Ben Kemp, but she'll still talk your ear off about him any opportunity she gets. A bit of the lady protesting too much, it seems to me.' She took a sip of her beer. 'Plus you should've seen what a good mood she was in this morning after she bumped into Ben at the pub last night. I reckon she missed him a lot more while he was away than she's letting on.'

'Didn't he dump her when they were at school or something?'

'He stood her up for a date at their leavers' ball,' Cal said, glancing over at Bridie. 'Not sure why. Ben's always liked girls a bit more than was good for him but he's not usually a cad about it.'

'I heard there was more to it than just him not showing up.' Hattie lowered her voice. 'This is top secret, you guys, so don't spread it around, but I'm told Bridie had a deal with Ben to lose her virginity to him the night of their sixth-form ball. She bought special pants and everything. I know it was a long time ago, but that's the sort of humiliation that stays with you.'

'I never knew that.' Cal looked at his brother, who was helping himself to a plate of food from the buffet. 'In that case, it was even more out of character. Our Ben ducking out when he knew he was on a promise.'

'Maybe he got another offer.'

'He didn't. Our dad was due to drive him over, Ben was all dressed up in his hired dinner suit, then at the last minute he refused to go and shut himself up in his room all night playing computer games. Mum was really worried about him, I remember her stressing.'

'Why do you think he did it?'

'He told me he got cold feet when he thought Bridie might be getting serious about him,' Cal said absently, his gaze still fixed on Ben. 'You know, I've always thought he liked her a lot more than he ever admitted at the time. Too worried about trying to uphold his reputation as the school stud, I think.'

'Yeah, and he still does,' Pete said. 'Come on, am I right or am I right?'

Hattie looked up at Cal. 'What do you think? I'm convinced Bridie still fancies him, whatever she says.'

'Well, I'll answer for my guy if you'll answer for yours. It's occurred to me before that the reason my brother's never done relationships is that he's in denial about his long-standing monster crush on Bridie Morgan.'

'Oh my God, that's so sad,' Ursula said in a sober tone. 'Poor Bridie. Still nursing a broken heart after all these years, and never knowing Ben feels the same way about her.'

Cal laughed. 'Don't let the pair of them hear you talking like that. They'll scoff you into the middle of next week.'

'Honestly though, it's tragic, isn't it? Bridie's about to commit to a life on her own and Ben's going to spend his days having empty sex with strangers, all because they're too proud to admit how they feel about each other. I could just cry about it.'

'I never had you down for a sentimental drunk, Urs,' Hattie said.

She shrugged. 'It's sad, that's all. I don't mind admitting I'm a sucker for a happily-ever-after.'

'All right, then let's do something about it,' Pete said.

Cal frowned. 'About Bridie and Ben? Such as what?'

'There must be something we can do. I've been serving you lot since I was still pretending to let you kid me with those crap fake IDs, and I've known for a good decade that those two are their own worst enemies. I'm not averse to dishing out some happily-ever-afters if I can.'

'Well, all right, me neither. I'd love to see my brother happily settled, and if it isn't with Bridie then I can't see it being with anyone else. How would we do it though?'

'I've got an idea,' Hattie said in a low voice.

They huddled closer. 'Go on,' Cal said.

'OK. So Bridie resents Ben because he humiliated her when they were kids and then never acknowledged it, right?'

'Right. And?'

'And then he spent the next decade sleeping his way around most of the women we know, basically rubbing salt in the wound. She's convinced he's got no romantic interest in her and so she's afraid to make herself vulnerable by admitting she has in him. She just puts up this shell of cynicism and sark.'

'I know she does. I just don't see what we can do about that.'

'Bridie needs to know how he really feels about her, don't you see?' Hattie's eyes sparkled as she glanced from one of them to the other. 'See his softer side – all those feelings he's been hiding from her all this time.'

'She'll never believe us though, and Ben's hardly going to tell her,' Pete said. 'He's as bad as she is.'

'Yeah, because he thinks she hates him and so he's afraid to let his guard down with her. They're trapped in this stupid emotional catch-22.'

Cal rubbed his face with his palms. 'God, I feel like I've accidentally wandered into a psychology lecture. Where are you headed with this, Hat? We're going round in circles here.'

'Exactly, and so are Bridie and Ben. She's afraid to show her feelings to him; he's afraid to show his to her. Each of them is convinced the other feels nothing so they lock their own feelings away to avoid being hurt, retreating into denial mode. But if one of them believed the other did have those feelings – I mean, if we could make them believe it – they'd know it was OK to drop their defences. That's how we break the circle.'

'But it's like you just said. Neither of them are going to admit their feelings for as long as they think the other one doesn't have any.'

'Which is why we need to convince them the other *does* have them, using all the deviousness at our disposal. Because that's what good friends do, right?' Hattie lowered her voice. 'OK, listen up, you guys. I've got a plan.'

SIX

'...and this was us in the Maldives on our honeymoon,' Craig said, showing Bridie the next photo in the album on his phone. 'That was Jenny's choice. I wanted to go to the Galapagos Islands. Typically she pulled the spoiled brat act and got her own way.'

'Mmm. That's classic Jenny,' Bridie muttered.

Craig swiped to the next image. 'Oh, and this is at her thirtieth birthday party. I caught her flirting with this old giffer from my angling club in our kitchen. Can you believe the audacity of that bitch?' He smiled fondly at the photo. 'God, she was beautiful.'

And to think Bridie had believed this date might actually turn out to be tolerable...

She roused herself from her semi-catatonia. 'Craig, look. You've talked about nothing but Jenny all night. I agree, she sounds like a nightmare and you're well out of it. Now can we please talk about something else?'

He blinked. 'All right. What do you want to talk about then?'

'Well… OK, what sort of films do you like?'

'Films?'

'Yeah, you know, films. Moving pictures. They've been around for a while now. People sometimes like to talk about them on dates.'

He looked blank for a moment. 'I like *The Godfather* trilogy.'

Bridie exhaled with relief. 'Right, great. Me too. Although I always thought Part III was—'

'You know that when me and Jenny got together, she'd never even seen them? I mean, how do you get to twenty-seven without seeing *The Godfather*? Unbelievable.' Craig laughed. 'Then when I finally got her to watch the first one with me, she fell asleep halfway through. All she ever wanted to watch were stupid soppy romcoms and reality shows. That should've rung alarm bells, I guess, but I was blind then. Thank God my eyes have been opened, right?'

'Right.' Bridie drained her remaining beer in one go, even though there was still half a bottle left. 'Oh look, I finished my drink. Would you mind?'

'Sure,' Craig said, blinking at her empty bottle. 'Wow, that was fast work. You're not a drunk, are you?'

'Not as a rule, but I'm always happy to explore new experiences.'

'You know, when Jenny had had one too many she always used to—'

'Craig, please. I'm gasping here.'

Craig looked bemused. 'OK. I'll be back in five then.'

As soon as he'd disappeared into the kitchen, Bridie grabbed her bag and made a beeline for the French doors that led out onto the veranda. She closed the blinds to shield herself from view before heading outside.

'Oh. Hi.' A man dressed as Batman was leaning on the

balustrade, looking out over the sea. 'Sorry. I didn't realise there was anyone else out here.'

'I don't mind a bit of company.' The man seemed to be wearing some sort of voice changer. It made his voice sound all deep and gravelly – just like the real Batman, if the real Batman had had a North Yorkshire accent. 'Who're you hiding from?'

'My date. He's got some very complex feelings towards his ex-wife that he wants to work through and I'm buggered if he's going to do it with me. How about you?'

'I just fancied a timeout.' He turned back to look at the reflection of the Milky Way being mangled by the waves. 'It's not a bad view, is it?'

'Nothing like it in the world.' Bridie went to stand by him and inhaled a lungful of salt sea air. 'That's better. I was starting to feel seriously claustrophobic in there.'

'Well, you're safe now.' He glanced at her empty hands. 'But you haven't got a drink. You want me to fetch you one? I won't tell your date where you're hiding, I promise.'

She smiled. 'Cross your heart?'

'Batman's honour,' he said, solemnly holding up three gloved fingers.

Bridie tried to place the real voice behind the robotic echo of the changer, but she couldn't match it to anyone she knew. The man was disguising his tones naturally too, she was sure: making them deeper and throatier before they even reached the electronic device built into his mask. Evidently this was someone taking the masquerade theme far too seriously.

'Yeah, all right,' she said. 'Cheers.'

He disappeared inside. Bridie let out a deep sigh as she gazed out over the ocean, feeling the tension that had crept into her body while she was with Craig slowly dissipate. Five minutes later the Batman guy was back, clutching a couple of bottles of beer.

'OK, you can feel free to go back in whenever you get chilly,' he said, handing her one. 'Your date isn't there to bother you any more.'

She frowned. 'What?'

'You were here with the Shrek lad, right?'

'Yeah, why?'

'I told him you'd had a sudden attack of hereditary scrofula and had to go home. He didn't seem too bothered, to be honest. He's leaving now.'

'Huh. Probably off to key his ex-wife's car and leave a dozen roses on the back seat.' She clinked her beer bottle against his. 'Thanks, mate.'

'Hey, that's what us heroes do: rescue damsels in distress.'

'Not the hero Messington needs but the hero Messington deserves. Yep, I can see that being you.' She squinted up at him, trying to identify the jawline. 'I know you, don't I?'

'You tell me.'

'What's your name?'

'I can't reveal that information, I'm afraid. First rule of Superhero Club: no giving away your secret identity.'

'Ah, go on.'

'Just call me Bruce.' He glanced at her Catwoman outfit. 'Looks like we were destined to meet tonight, eh, Selina?'

'Well, it's just Bridie for short.' She shook his glove. 'Nice to know you, Bruce.'

'So who do you know here then?' Bruce asked her.

She peered through a slit in the blinds at the now swinging party. Cal and Hattie seemed to have morphed into a single entity while they enjoyed a slow dance. Ben had lifted the bottom part of his Spider-Man mask and was sucking face with Meg, whose dream of being the next notch on his bedpost was obviously about to come true.

'He could at least have done it hanging upside down, for the sake of authenticity,' Bridie muttered to herself.

'Sorry?'

'Hm? Oh.' She turned back to Bruce. 'I know the birthday girl and her boyfriend pretty well.'

'You know Cal, do you?'

'Yeah, we were at school together. His girlfriend's my housemate. I was the one who introduced them actually.' She glanced up at him. 'How do you know him?'

'We've got a few friends in common.'

She nodded to Ben and Meg snogging. 'What about his brother, do you know him?'

'Not really. Are they alike?'

Bridie snorted. 'Luckily for Hattie, thankfully not.'

'Oh? Why do you say that?'

Bruce actually sounded more like Lego Batman than Batman Batman, Bridie decided. Extra gravelly. It was pretty sexy.

'God, Ben's just such an arse,' she told him. 'I don't know how he manages it given his severe personality defects, but he only needs to look at a woman and her knickers seem to fall off. And there's no sign he might start giving it a rest as he creeps towards thirty. He's going to end up being one of those sad middle-aged men with Peter Stringfellow haircuts who prop up the bar in seedy pubs, thinking they have a shot with girls half their age.'

'The woman he's with seems to like him,' Bruce said, glancing over his shoulder at Meg acquainting herself with Ben's tonsils.

Bridie shrugged. 'Meg knows he's a good bet for a one-night stand. All the girls round here know that if you want an evening of no-strings-attached fun, Ben Kemp's your man. Messington women might get their kicks with him, but you'd never find one mad enough to actually date him.'

He turned back to look at her. 'You don't think so?'

'Nah. Ben's a cut-rate gigolo, that's all: decent body but not much going on in the personality department other than a good line in brag and swagger. More importantly, he never says no. He's a human vibrator, basically – that's how the local girls see him. I swear, a nice dose of the clap would do his vanity no end of good.'

'Bloody hell,' Bruce muttered. 'I wouldn't want to get on your bad side, love.'

She shrugged. 'Hey, don't shoot the messenger.'

Bruce was silent for a moment, watching Ben nuzzle into Meg's neck through the glass door.

'I take it you're not one of this Ben's many conquests then,' he said at last.

'Are you kidding?' Bridie sent a black look in Ben's direction. 'We did have a bit of a thing going on, back in school when I was too young to know any better. That was before I knew what he was really like. Honestly, I'd shag anyone before that guy.'

'What sort of a thing?'

'Oh, we…' She looked up at him, frowning. 'Why am I telling you all this? I never even met you before tonight.'

'Well, I'm the Dark Knight, aren't I? Protector of the innocent, champion of the weak. I'm inherently trustworthy.'

She squinted at him. 'Turn that voice changer thingy off. Let me hear your real voice.'

'Can't do that. Told you, I've got a secret identity to protect. I'd be drummed out of the Justice League.'

'All right, have it your way, Man of Mystery. I'll find it out at the unmasking anyway.' She turned back to look at the softly plashing ocean. 'Perhaps Ben did mean something to me once. I thought he did at eighteen, at least. We used to mess about a bit, just as friends, but then he asked me to our big leaving ball after exams had finished and I thought... I suppose I thought that'd be our first proper date. I was all set to lose my virginity to him that night. Then when I got to the ball... no sign of him.' She blinked hard. 'Can you believe that? The man who never says no didn't want me. That seemed to set a template for my relationships ever after. My entire love life has been an unmitigated disaster from that day forward.'

'I'm sorry,' Bruce said, and his voice sounded softer under the gravelly Batman tones. 'Still, if this bloke's as much of a tool as you say, it sounds like you had a lucky escape.'

'I know. It hurt like hell at the time though. That first broken heart.'

'Seriously, he broke your heart?'

'That's how it felt when I was a kid.' She shrugged. 'I should probably be grateful. Ben taught me to be wary. I know better now.'

'Did he ever tell you why he stood you up?'

'He never mentioned it again, not once in ten years. I suppose he ditched me for a better offer.'

'I don't believe that.'

'Well, I can't think of any other reason he'd turn down sex. That was always his favourite hobby.'

'Maybe he was nervous.'

She laughed. 'Ben? You really don't know him, do you?'

'No.' He put his hands on her shoulders and turned her to face him. 'But I do know that if I was an eighteen-year-old boy about to go to bed with a girl who looked like you, I'd be scared to death.'

'Why?'

He glanced down her body. 'Why do you think? Because you're bloody gorgeous. That's kind of intimidating when you're that age.'

Gorgeous… did he really think that?

She shook her head. 'Not for Ben.'

'Well, I can't speak for Ben.' He drew a gloved finger down her cheek. 'I can only speak for me. And what I think is that you're the best-looking girl at this party.'

That jawline… it did look familiar. Had she met Bruce before tonight? She felt fuzzy-headed from the beer she'd drunk and lulled by his soft words and the gentle sound of the waves, but she was sure that behind the voice changer there was something… a tone, a trick of speech. Where did she know it from? She felt like she was in a dream, and something she knew, or ought to know, was hovering just out of her reach.

'Are you sure we haven't met before?' she whispered as Bruce brought his face closer to hers, his fingers resting on her cheek.

'You tell me.' He pressed a soft kiss to her lips, and Bridie, in a pleasant haze of alcohol and ocean and Batman, let her eyes close as she returned it.

'Well?' Bruce said quietly when he drew back. 'Have we met before, Bridie?'

'I… I'm not sure.'

She looked up into the eyes that glittered from behind his cowl. They were a deep, compelling brown, sort of laughing and sad both at the same time. She did know them. She knew them from somewhere in… in the past? Knew them well, so well…

God, she really shouldn't have had that last drink. She held on tightly to Bruce's thick arms around her, feeling suddenly dizzy.

'Who are you?' she whispered.

'You genuinely don't know?'

'No. Tell me.'

The sound of people singing 'Happy Birthday' echoed out to them from inside the house, and Bruce jerked straight.

'Shit! Bridie, what time is it?'

'Um, just after ten, I think. Why?'

'Oh shit! Shit shit shit! Sorry, love, I have to go.'

'Er, hey,' Bridie said, blinking dazedly. 'Can I… do you want to maybe swap numbers or something?'

'Not right now. Later. I have to be somewhere.' Without another word, he darted back into the house.

SEVEN

When Ben got back inside, Cal had already begun slicing Hattie's birthday cake and was looking panicked.

'There you are,' he hissed when his brother joined him. 'Where the hell have you been?'

'Sorry, I got distracted.'

'Ben, seriously, could you stop chasing muff for five bloody minutes and do your only brother the one favour he's asked you for in his life?'

'Sure. Sure. Look, I'm here now, aren't I?'

'Will you turn that voice thing off please? You sound like you've got a thirty-a-day fag habit.'

'All right, fine.' Ben reached up to switch off the voice changer built into his mask.

Only half a cake now remained unsliced. Ben glanced at the identical pieces arranged on paper plates. 'Which one of these is third-from-top-clockwise then?'

'This one,' Cal muttered, jerking his head towards it.

'This one?' Ben asked, pointing.

'No, not that one. The one next to it.' He elbowed Ben as

he reached for the neighbouring slice. 'Not that side, the other side.'

'This one?' Ben picked up the slice and squinted at it for any sign of an engagement ring nestling in the sponge.

'Yeah, that's it. I think.'

'You think?'

'I'm… ninety-six per cent sure it's that one.' Cal groaned. 'Oh God. It's jinxed, isn't it? The whole thing's bloody jinxed.'

'It's not jinxed. Although a slightly less elaborate proposal after the beer's been flowing all night might've been advisable.'

'Look, I'm trying to be romantic here. I'm only doing this once in my life and I want to make it an occasion to remember. Where've you been anyway?'

'I went outside for some air.' Ben turned to face him, still holding the slice of cake. 'Cal, do you reckon the birds round here think I'm just some shallow cut-price gigolo who's only good for one-night stands?'

'Well yeah, probably. Not sure why that revelation should shock you. Who've you been talking to?'

'Bridie.'

Cal raised his eyebrows. 'She said that to you? That's a bit harsh, even by her standards.'

'She didn't know she was talking to me. Well, she might've. I can't work out if she did and was just trying to wind me up by playing dumb while she slagged me off or if she genuinely had no idea.' He frowned. 'But then if she did know, why would she have told me… and why would she have let me…' He stared thoughtfully at the cake for a second. 'She said some stuff, Cal – stuff I wish I'd known before. About me and her at school.'

'Look, do we have to do this now?' Cal whispered. 'I'm

about to propose here, I've got my own worries. Just hand out the cake while I give my speech, can you? We'll talk about your problems later.'

'Right.' Ben picked up another slice of cake and went to hand it to someone in the assembled crowd, keeping the special Hattie piece carefully in his left hand.

'Here you go.' He approached the bloke dressed as Spider-Man and handed him a paper plate. 'No, hang on. Not that one. You have this one.'

Spider-Man blinked as Ben swapped the cake he was holding for the one in his right hand. 'But they're all the same, aren't they?'

'I'm keeping the thinner slice back for myself. Er, watching my figure,' Ben said, patting the rubber abs of his Batman suit. 'You know how it is, right? Not much left to the imagination by the uniforms in our line of work.'

The guy stared blankly at him, seemingly having forgotten that he was currently dressed entirely in spandex. Ben shot him a weak grin and went to grab more cake.

Cal banged a fork against the side of his beer bottle for attention and the room fell silent, everyone turning towards him.

'Er, hi folks,' he said, smiling bashfully. 'I just wanted to say thank you all for coming to Hattie's party, which Dafydd and Sandra have been kind enough to host, and, um, I hope you enjoy this birthday cake that I baked with my own fair hands.' He glanced at his girlfriend. 'Especially you, Hat. Because I think if you look carefully, you'll find a very special ingredient in your slice.'

She blinked. 'OK. It's not one of those hash cakes, is it?'

Cal nodded to the slice of cake Ben had darted forward to hand her. 'Take a look for yourself.'

Frowning, she broke her slice in half, then in half again, until her plate was just a pile of crumbs and jam.

'All I'm seeing is an increasingly inedible piece of Victoria sponge, Cal.'

'You're not looking hard enough. It's in there, I swear.'

There was a sudden choking noise from Sandra Leonard, who'd just taken a bite of her own slice of cake. Cal's eyes widened.

'Shit! Ben, you've given her the wrong bit!'

'Er, right. Bollocks. Bollocks!' Ben glanced around the guests. 'Does anyone here know the Heimlich manoeuvre?'

'Oh God, Mum!' Hattie darted over to her mother, who'd gone a bit purple, and started slapping her heavily on the back of her Pierrot costume.

'Er, surprise,' Cal said, grimacing as Mrs Leonard finally coughed the engagement ring up into her cupped hands. 'Are you all right there, Sandra?'

'I'm… fine,' she said hoarsely. She wiped the ring with her handkerchief and handed it to Hattie. 'Here you go, love. You can take it with my blessing if he promises not to try to murder me every anniversary.'

Hattie stared at it, then up at Cal. 'What is this?'

'Well, it's me trying to be romantic, isn't it?' Cal said with a sheepish smile. 'I wanted to make it a proposal for you to remember. Something we can tell the grandkids about.'

'What, the day you nearly killed their great-nana?' Hattie shook her head, smiling. 'You big idiot.'

'So will you?'

She shrugged. 'All right, go on then.'

He laughed and came forward to embrace her. 'Thanks, Hat. Sorry I messed it up.'

'No, it was sweet. And very you.' She looked up to smile at him. 'Only Cal Kemp could manage to propose by half-choking his future mother-in-law while dressed as Just William.'

He took the ring from her to slide it on and gave her a lingering kiss, to the ringing applause and cheers of the other party guests.

'God, this is the best day,' he whispered. 'I love you so much, Harriet Leonard. So much.'

'I love you too, Cal. Forever.'

'Forever? You promise?'

'I promise.' She gave him another kiss before freeing herself from his embrace. 'I'll be back in a minute, darling. I want to go find Bridie so I can tell her the news. I don't know where she's hiding but she's typically managed to miss the whole thing.'

When Hattie had gone, Cal turned to frown at Ben.

'Well you cocked that right up, didn't you?'

'Me? It was you who told me the wrong slice!'

'That is completely untrue.'

'Yeah?'

'And even if it is true, it's still your fault for not being here at ten to back me up like I asked you,' Cal went on, ignoring the interruption. 'Seriously, the one occasion I'm going to propose in my life and you can't even manage to get here on time.'

'I said I was sorry. Anyway, it all worked out in the end, didn't it? Sandra survived the assassination attempt and Hattie said yes.'

'Hmm. Suppose.'

'Well, congratulations, tiny.' Ben pulled him into a hug and slapped him on the back. 'My baby brother about to become a married man, eh? Never thought I'd see the day.'

Cal smiled as he hugged him back. 'You should come on in, Benjy. The water's lovely.'

'Oh, no. Not this Kemp.' Ben glanced towards the French doors, which Hattie was opening to go search for Bridie outside. 'Look, you stay and have fun. I'm going to get off home.'

Cal frowned. 'You all right?'

'Yeah, just… I'd rather not stay for the unmasking bit.'

Cal squinted at him. 'What did happen with Bridie tonight, Ben?'

'Never mind that now.' He gave his brother's hand a hearty shake. 'You and Hattie enjoy the rest of your night. Be happy, little brother.'

———

Bridie stared into the distance with unfocused eyes as Hattie hooked an arm through hers.

'Engaged?'

'Yep.'

'Engaged to Cal?'

'That's what I said.'

She shook her head, trying to free herself of the floaty state she'd been in since her kiss with Bruce.

Where was Bruce anyway? She was back inside the party now, being guided by Hattie towards Cal and a tableful of cake, but there was no sign of the man she wanted to find.

'Hello? Anyone in there?' Hattie said, waving a hand in front of her friend's face. 'Come on, Bride, wake up. I need someone to be excited with. I know you think marriage is stupid and pointless and a massive stressful faff for no reward, but I was hoping you'd be able to fake it for my sake.'

'Sorry.' Bridie managed a smile and gave her friend a hug. 'I am excited for you – genuinely, not faking it. I'm just in shock, that's all. All the happiness in the world, Hat.'

'Where were you while Cal was proposing?'

'Oh, just… dreaming, out on the veranda.'

Hattie quirked an eyebrow as she let her friend go. 'With Craig? Cal said he seemed a good prospect when he talked to you earlier.'

'Well, he wasn't. Ex-wife issues. No, I was with…' Bridie scanned the crowd again. 'Never mind.'

'So, can I count on you for maid of honour duties then?'

'Ugh. Will I have to wear a dress?'

'Yes, Bridie, you'll have to wear a dress. You're going to look like a princess on my wedding day if I have to bundle you into the thing kicking and screaming.'

'Oh God. All right, but just this once.' Bridie frowned at Cal as they joined him by his cake table. 'So what's all this about you stealing my housemate, Cal Kemp?'

He smiled. 'I'd prefer to think of it as sharing custody. You can have her every third weekend and select bank holidays.'

Bridie wrapped him in a hug. 'Well, congratulations, you lucky sod. If it had to be anyone, I'm glad it was you.' She glanced at Ben in his Spider-Man costume, feeding Meg forkfuls of cake from his plate. 'Although I don't envy Hat one in-law.'

'What happened to your date, Bride?'

'He turned out to be another dud, unsurprisingly. A real-life superhero scared him away for me.' She let him go. 'Cal… do you know a guy called Bruce?'

He frowned. 'Bruce? No. What was he, Australian?'

'No, he was local, I think. He said he knew you.' She looked around the room again. 'I was talking to him on the veranda, but I can't see him anywhere now.'

Cal exchanged a look with Hattie. 'What was he wearing, this Bruce?'

'Like a Michael Keaton-era Batman costume. He had this voice changer thing on that made him sound all gravelly.'

Hattie lifted an eyebrow. 'Seriously? You met a guy dressed as Batman who told you his name was Bruce and you thought his name was actually Bruce?'

Bridie blinked. 'Oh. Right. So who was he then?'

'Don't you know?'

'Well, his eyes looked familiar but I couldn't place them.'

Cal opened his mouth to respond, but Hattie subtly shook her head.

'Doesn't sound like anyone I know,' she said. 'How about you, Cal?'

'Um… sorry, Bride, I don't think I saw him,' Cal said, registering his fiancée's waggling eyebrows. 'If I do, I'll let him know you're looking for him.'

'Why are you looking for him?' Hattie asked Bridie.

'Oh, he… seemed kind of interesting, that's all.' She stared absently for a moment before rousing herself to smile at them. 'Well, I'll stop making a gooseberry of myself when you two obviously have some important engaged-people snogging to do. I'm going to get off home.'

'You're not leaving before the unmasking, are you?'

'Yeah, I'm all partied out, to be honest. Plus the only person I didn't know seems to have buggered off, so there'll be no surprises for me.' She cast another dirty look at Spider-Man and Meg necking. 'Getting horny at a party while dressed entirely in spandex is something I'd really have expected your brother to think through, Cal. Still, I don't suppose he'll care if everyone can see his willy, given most people around here already have. See you later, guys.'

———

'She thinks Adrian's your brother,' Hattie said to Cal in a low voice when Bridie had gone.

'Yes, I'd worked that out. And she obviously has no idea that her pal Bruce Wayne was actually Ben.'

'What do you suppose happened between them?'

'Dunno, but Ben was being pretty strange before. He thought she might know who he was really and just be messing with him. Sounds like she served up a few home truths while they were out there.' Cal pulled his fiancée into his arms to make it easier for them to talk in whispers, and also just because he liked having her there. Mainly the second thing. 'As soon as he saw you going out to fetch her, he was out of the door like a whippet,' he murmured close to her ear. 'Said he wanted to go home before the unmasking.'

'Did he now?' Hattie narrowed one eye. 'Interesting. Very interesting.'

'How come you stopped me spilling the beans? Is it part of your big plan?'

'I think it could be a useful bit of information to sit on until we can work out the best way to use it to our advantage, yes.'

'I never knew my future wife was so sneaky and devious.' He kissed her ear. 'It's kind of turning me on.'

'In that case, you're going to love what I'm going to suggest next.' Hattie leaned back to look into his face. 'Cal, we're a modern, progressive sort of couple, right?'

'I like to think so.'

'And if we can find some convenient way to bring my maid of honour and your best man together in the run-up to the wedding, we obviously want to jump on that, right?'

'Well, yeah.'

'Great, because I just had the best idea.'

EIGHT

'What?'

'A Sten party,' Hattie said as she stretched her legs lazily out onto the coffee table the next morning. 'Joint stag and hen, for boys and girls. They're all the rage among young couples like me and Cal.'

'But what about our old plan for a weekend in Cambridge?' Bridie demanded. 'We were going to go punting and have a picnic, just me, you and the girls. A small, classy ladies' weekend with not a penis in sight, inflatable or otherwise. You told me that if you ever found yourself engaged, that's what you wanted to do.'

'Well that was before I met Cal, wasn't it? I want to spend my hen night with him, like I want to spend the rest of my life with him. He's my best friend and I want him to be there.'

'Oh, right. Thanks a lot.'

Hattie smiled. 'All right, my joint best friend then. It'll still be fun with the boys there, won't it?'

'No it won't. Boys ruin everything. We'll end up on a

boozy weekend in Magaluf watching Pete Prince being sick on a lap dancer.'

'We won't because I'm the bride and I have power of veto.'

'But it's supposed to be all girls, that's the whole point of the tradition,' Bridie protested. 'One last night of freedom with your sisters before you settle down. A chance to make tits of ourselves with no men there to judge us.'

'I thought you hated all that tradition stuff.'

'Not as much as I hate lairy, testosterone-fuelled lads' nights out with a side order of toxic masculinity.'

'Oh come on, stop living in the past,' Hattie said, flicking a hand dismissively. 'Stag and hen dos are anachronisms in this day and age. I want a pre-wedding night out with all my friends, not just the female ones.'

'How do we find something everyone's going to enjoy though? Cal's mates from the garage are all blokey-type blokes. I can't see a bunch of macho car mechanics punting down a river swigging sparkling rosé, can you?'

'Stop making problems. There's loads of fun things we can do together.' Hattie examined her nails, casually buffing them with her thumb-tip. 'I'm sure you and Ben can come up with something we'll all enjoy.'

'Me and...' Bridie laughed grimly. 'Oh, no. Not a chance.'

'He's Cal's best man, Bride. We have to let him have an equal say in the planning. Besides, marriage is about compromise, right?'

'Yeah, which is one of the many reasons I never, ever want to do it. You and Cal are supposed to do the compromising, not me and Ben.'

'Well once you've practised it, you can show us how it's done.'

'I am not planning a Hag do—'

'Sten. The men come first.'

'Huh, so what else is new?' Bridie muttered. 'I am not planning a Sten do with that arrogant bellend Ben Kemp. No way. Ask Ursula or Meg to be maid of honour if that's how it has to be.'

'But I want it to be you, Bridie,' Hattie said, fluttering her eyelashes. 'You're my best friend.'

Bridie folded her arms. 'I thought Cal was your best friend now. Why don't you get him to be maid of honour?'

'Aww, come on, you're not allowed to sulk when I'm all excited. You want to make me happy, don't you?'

'No.'

'Please, Bride. I'm only doing this once, then you'll never have to be my maid of honour again.'

Bridie sighed. 'You'll really be miserable if I don't organise this bloody thing with Ben?'

'Inconsolable.'

'And will you take over washing-up duty from now until you move in with Cal?'

Hattie blinked. 'Wow. Hard bargain.'

'Well, will you?'

'Yes, yes, all right.'

'Fine. I'll do it,' Bridie said. 'But I want it minuted that I was against the idea from the start, and if the lads ruin your night by showing up in matching pink mankinis or flopping their tackle out in the pub then it's not my fault.'

'OK, your objections have been noted.'

'When are we having this Sten do anyway?'

'We're looking at late October for the wedding, so I guess earlier that month.'

Bridie frowned. 'That's only five months' away. I'm no expert, but is that really long enough to organise a wedding?'

'It'll be tight, but an autumn ceremony would be so perfect, don't you think? All the gorgeous colours,' Hattie said with a blissful sigh. 'Besides, my mum's got contacts she can exploit. That gives us a head start.' Sandra Leonard was a professional wedding planner, highly sought-after by newly engaged Messington couples.

'Where will you have it?' Bridie asked.

'Mum thinks she can get us booked in at Lindley House.'

Bridie gave a low whistle. 'Bloody hell, that place? That's a bit posh for oiks like us.'

'I know, it'll be a dream come true if she can wangle it. They've got the most amazing little wedding chapel in their orangery. It'll be stunning, with the lake outside and all the trees blazing red and gold through the glass.'

Bridie smiled at her friend's sparkling eyes. 'I bet your dress'll look beautiful against a backdrop like that. And you in it, obviously.'

Hattie patted her hand. 'Thanks for being excited for me, Bride. I know this isn't your scene, weddings and dresses and all that stuff.'

'Well. It's hard to stay grumpy when your little face is all glowing and happy.'

'Since you're being good and cooperating, I'll make the tea. Even though it's technically your round.' Hattie swung her feet off the table and got up to put the kettle on.

'Did you find this so-called Bruce you were looking for before you went home last night then?' she called through to the living room.

'No. He'd definitely left.' Bridie sighed. 'So that's another man I managed to scare away within the first half-hour of meeting them.'

A few minutes later, Hattie came back in with the tea.

She handed Bridie a mug and sat down on the sofa with one of her own.

'You're sure it was the first half-hour?' she asked. 'I thought you said you recognised him.'

'His eyes looked sort of familiar, but I've been through everyone I can think of and I still can't place them,' Bridie said. 'Maybe I was just imagining it. I was pretty tipsy by that point.'

'No kidding. What happened with you and him then?'

'He…' Bridie coloured. 'He rescued me from Craig and we had a beer together. I drunkenly offloaded on him a bit about my love life woes, which would normally be enough to send any half-decent man running, but he was a good listener and he seemed sympathetic. Then we… kissed.'

Hattie lifted her eyebrows. 'You kissed him? Bloody hell.'

'He kissed me, but I kissed him back, yeah. I was a little bit pissed but also a little bit… sort of dreamy. It felt kind of unreal, with the costume and the sea behind us and the stars and… everything.'

'How was the kiss?'

'Only brief, but nice, really nice. Soft; not pushy at all. Then he just dashed off like Cinderella on the stroke of midnight, saying he had somewhere to be. That was the last I saw of him.'

'Maybe it's a sign you shouldn't give up looking just yet. This guy obviously got your pulse racing and your knickers in a twist. That shows there are still men out there capable of exciting you, despite the twenty dates disaster.'

'Or it's a sign I'm destined to scare off any decent man I do manage to meet.' Bridie sighed and sipped her tea. 'I don't know, it did feel like we might have chemistry. I guess the main chemical at work was alcohol after all.'

'Maybe he really did have somewhere he urgently needed

to be. Maybe Fate saved your Mr Right till last, just like I said.'

'I wouldn't go booking us a double wedding just yet,' Bridie observed wryly. 'If I've got a Mr Right – and I'm pretty sure I haven't – one of his qualities is definitely not disappearing for no reason and then never acknowledging it. I've been there before.'

'You're not on about Ben again?' Hattie said, shaking her head. 'Seriously, Bride, you're obsessed.'

She snorted. 'Yeah, in his dreams.'

'Honestly, I wish I had some sort of app that could calculate just how much of your conversation is dedicated to what a twat you think Ben Kemp is. Even when he was away, you were forever talking about him.'

'Because you'd started seeing his brother. I might've managed to put him out of my mind if Cal wasn't suddenly here all the time, reminding me of the constant irritation of Ben's existence.'

Hattie shot her a sly look. 'If I didn't know better, I'd think you were trying to cover up a secret crush.'

'Now you're entering the realms of fantasy,' Bridie said, laughing. 'No, I can say with all honesty that I wish Meg joy of the man – not that he's ever likely to call her now he's got what he wants from her. I promise you, he's the last eligible bachelor on this single girl's list.'

———

Ben kicked at a pebble he'd taken a dislike to and watched it bounce a couple of times before settling in a pool of sandy saltwater.

He'd woken this morning still thinking about the party. He hadn't slept much, but when he had, his dreams had been full of it too: Bridie's hard words – hard but fair, as his brother had ruthlessly observed – and the kiss that had taken him as much by surprise as it had her. Unable to shift the whirl of thoughts, he'd walked down to the beach in the hope of clearing his head, but the sea air wasn't really helping. If anything it was making things worse, with the soft splashing of the waves and the scent of spring blossom wafting down from the trees that lined the promenade bringing back last night's veranda kiss all too clearly.

What had made him do it? He was so used to seeing Bridie bristle and spit like an angry cat in his presence that it had been pleasant, just for once, to find her warm and relaxed, enjoying his company. She'd been sad – sad because of something he'd done – and he'd wanted to comfort her. That was just instinct. But then she'd looked so… God. Ben knew she had a great figure, but seeing her in Lycra had been a revelation. There was a lot more to her than there had been when he'd last had an intimate view of her body, and just as he'd suspected, she'd filled out in all the right places.

That must surely have been it: the reason he'd let himself get carried away. He'd always been physically attracted to Bridie – he'd never denied that, not even to her, although she probably thought it was a piss-take – but she was usually wrapped in a thick cocoon of sarcasm and hostility. She wasn't like the other girls round here when it came to succumbing to his dubious charms. Finding Ballbreaker Bridie all soft and marshmallowy for once in her life, and in that figure-hugging Catwoman costume too, had been more than any hot-blooded man could be expected to resist.

She hadn't known it was him; Ben was certain of that now. He'd believed she had, at first. Smiled to himself as he'd heard her lay into him while pretending she had no idea who he was. But when they kissed, and the things she'd told him about that night at school... she couldn't have known. He was the last man she'd ever knowingly let kiss her.

He felt a twinge of something he couldn't identify at that thought. It had been nice to kiss Bridie, but it would've been even nicer if she'd wanted him to – as Ben Kemp, that is, not Bruce Wayne. He could just imagine her responding in kind, opening his lips with her tongue, caressing his body with her fingertips just like she used to during their hesitant, fumbling teenage make-out sessions, only now with all the confidence of a grown woman... fuck, yes. That would've been so much better.

No, the Bridie who'd kissed him with that degree of gentleness, who'd confided her innermost secrets to him, who'd confessed he'd broken her heart, couldn't possibly have known he was her old sparring partner. Which meant that everything she'd said, all those charges she'd levelled at him... she hadn't just been trying to get a rise out of him, it was actually what she felt. That was what she thought of him. What everyone thought of him.

He glared at a seagull that had alighted in front of him to peck at a discarded chip wrapper. It took one look at his grim expression and flapped off again.

The biggest shock, when Ben had mulled it over last night in bed, was discovering that he and Bridie weren't the friends he'd believed them to be. He'd always thought they were mates, more or less. Yes, they spent most of the time they were together trying to push each other's buttons, but that was just play, wasn't it? He enjoyed trading quips with Bridie – that teasing back-and-forth, trying to coax a reluctant smile out of her – and he'd always believed she relished trying to outmatch him just as much. But when he'd heard the way Bridie spoke about him when she thought she was talking to someone else... Had that really been her true opinion of him, all this time? That he was a gigolo – a shallow pretty boy with nothing to recommend him but a good game in the bedroom? Ben knew Bridie loved to hate him, but he'd never realised she didn't respect him.

And not just her either. 'The women round here', she'd said. Did Messington girls gossip about him? Compare notes on his technique? Give reviews to their randy girlfriends so they could look him up, like some dodgy call girl ad in an old phone box? Was every woman he'd ever been to bed with laughing at him behind his back?

Strange that the idea should bother him so much. He'd internalised the old double standard, he supposed, when he was young; seen himself as some sort of James Bond figure while he'd easily charmed the town's female population into his bed. Now that he found himself on the receiving end of the same sorts of sneers as the girls who were seen as 'easy' back when he was a teen, he realised that perhaps in these days of greater sexual equality, sleeping around just made him seem a bit of a loser. Christ, he'd be twenty-nine in two months' time. He was past the age where the jack-the-lad act was sexy rather than pathetic.

It also meant that since school – since the night of the leavers' ball – he'd been shagging around without even thinking about how it might make Bridie feel to be the one woman he'd rejected. She'd never mentioned that night to him since it happened: not once. He'd honestly thought she must've forgotten all about it, although he often found himself thinking of it when he bumped into her.

What did she call him? The man who never said no? That wasn't fair. He'd had a lot of sex in his time, yes, but he doubted it was nearly as much as Bridie believed he'd been having – his own fault, perhaps, for playing up to his reputation. Still, that must hurt, thinking she was one of the few girls in town he'd spurned. Hurting her had been the last thing he meant to do. He was fond of her, underneath it all. It upset him to realise she hadn't known even that much.

He could hardly explain what had really happened on leavers' ball night now though, could he? Quite aside from the humiliation of admitting it – and to Bridie of all people – ten years after the event was a bit late for an apology. Plus then he'd be forced to confess that he was the man she'd confided in last night – and that he'd taken advantage of the situation to get a snog. She already thought the majority of the male species were only out to get laid; him more than most. He didn't want to give her yet another reason to despise him.

He just needed to keep acting normally, and try to be a bit more sensitive to this lingering resentment Bridie still felt about the way things had ended all those years ago. That shouldn't be too hard. They only saw each other every once in a while anyway, through their mutual friends or when they ran into each other in town or at the pub. Perhaps they were likely to find themselves in each other's company a bit more often in the run-up to Cal and Hattie's wedding in October, but not, he hoped, too regularly.

Ben jumped as his mobile buzzed in his pocket. He took it out and scanned the screen.

Bridie, shit! What was she ringing him for? Did she know? Someone at the party could've enlightened her as to who was under the Batman suit – Hattie, Cal or any number of others. Besides, she'd have found out at the unmasking that he wasn't really the randy Spider-Man she'd mistaken for him.

He screwed his eyes closed as he answered, preparing himself for the tongue-whipping of his life.

'Bridie, look, about last night—' he began before she could start berating him.

'God, Ben, please spare me the gory details,' she said with a groan. 'I'm not interested in what you and Meg got up to after the party, all right? At least keep it to yourself if you're incapable of keeping it in your Spidey-pants.'

Oh. So she didn't know then. Obviously she hadn't stuck around for the unmasking, and none of their friends seemed to have filled her in – yet.

'Right,' he said, blinking. 'So, er… why are you calling? Did I do something else to piss you off last night?'

'Probably, but I haven't got time to go through a list. I'm ringing about the Sten.' She paused to listen to the background noise. 'Where are you anyway?'

'Down by the sea. I went out for a walk. What's a Sten when it's at home?'

'Didn't Cal tell you? Him and Hat have decided to hold a joint stag and hen do. Girls and boys together.'

Ben groaned. 'Oh, what? The promise I could arrange Cal's stag was the whole reason I agreed to this bloody best man business. That's the only thing about weddings that doesn't suck.'

'Yes, well, I'm not happy about it either, but for Hattie's sake I said I'd grin and bear it. Or bear it anyway. So when do you want to meet?'

'Meet?'

'Yes, Ben, meet,' she said, sounding irritated. 'I'm the maid of honour, you're the best man. It's our job to organise the bloody thing and I want to get it thrashed out sooner rather than later. Ideally in no more than half an hour, the quicker to be free of your company.'

'So… I'm planning this thing with you, am I?'

'What do you think I've been saying?' she said impatiently. 'Has last night's sex made your brain go gooey or something? You know, you should get that checked out. There's a good chance it's syphilis.'

'Um, right,' he said, feeling a bit dazed. 'OK, I guess we can meet. I'll make a list of suggestions, you do the same, then we can talk it through in the pub this weekend.'

'Look, are you OK?' she said, her voice sounding ever so slightly softer, unless he was imagining it. 'You sound really spaced out. And you haven't tried to wind me up the whole time we've been talking, which has to be a first.'

He managed to rouse himself enough to sound at least a bit like his usual self.

'Disappointed?' he asked, smiling.

'I'd be lying if I said no.'

'I'm just a bit tired, that's all. I promise I'll be back on form when we go on our date.'

'Do not call it that, Ben: I mean it. And don't sit too close to me either. The last thing I want getting around is that I was seen out on a date with Ben "The Cock" Kemp.'

Did people call him that? He hoped it was in reference to his reputation with women and not just... well, because they thought he was a bit of a cock.

'I'll be as chaste and respectful as a monk,' he told her solemnly. 'But a sexy one with a full head of hair.'

'You'd better. I'll see you at the Garter, seven o'clock Saturday. Don't be late.'

NINE

Hattie glanced at her classroom door to make sure none of the students were peeping in at her illicitly using her phone during school hours, then flicked to the wedding make-up tutorial she'd saved to watch in her morning break.

The presenter, Jojo Fitzroy, was one of the top beauty influencers in the world. Her 'Beauty With Jojo' YouTube channel subscribers were in the millions. Hattie had never tuned in before, but there was a first time for everything.

'Now, brides, this is where we really make the most of those cheekbones,' Jojo said in her trademark husky purr. 'I'm going to get hate mail from the pros for this, but I'm about to show you some contouring hacks that will have you ready not only for the altar but for the red carpet. So, my queens, grab those beauty blenders and together let's find our power.'

Currently Jojo looked a bit like 'she was doing skeleton make-up for Halloween, with highlighting cream around her mouth and cheekbones and dark powder either side of her nose, but Hattie knew that in a moment she'd work her magic and end up looking like a Hollywood star at the Oscars. She was beautiful even without the make-up, as well as exuding an easy, sophisticated glamour that Hattie couldn't help envying. With her 'face' on, as she liked to say, Jojo looked like a supermodel.

Hattie paused the video as a knock sounded at the door. Ursula and Meg were waving to her through the glass and Hattie beckoned for them to come in and join her.

'Naughty naughty, Miss Leonard,' Ursula said as she pulled up a chair beside her. 'You'd better not let Eddie catch you with your phone out. What're you watching?'

'Just a Jojo Fitzroy make-up tutorial. She did a new series for brides-to-be in the run-up to her big wedding last month.'

'You're thinking make-up already? There's months to go yet.'

'I thought I might as well get some practice in.' Hattie looked glumly at the paused video before turning it face down on the table. 'Honestly, though, there's so much to it. I always thought I was going it a bit, just sloshing some foundation and lippy on, but there're people who won't leave the house until they're contoured and highlighted and tweezed and false-eyelashed to within an inch of their life. I don't know how they have the energy for it every single day.'

'I'm sure Cal'll think you look gorgeous whatever you do,' Meg said. 'It's you he fancies, not the face paint.'

'Yeah.' Hattie gazed thoughtfully at the phone. 'I guess so.'

'No Bridie?' Ursula asked. It was a tradition that the four of them would congregate for coffee and a gossip in Hattie's classroom every morning break.

'She'll be on her way.' Hattie lowered her voice. 'Actually, I'm glad I caught you both before she got here.'

'Have you been thinking about the plan?' Ursula whispered.

'Yes. I was trying to work out where she could overhear us talking without it looking like a total set-up, and I thought, where better than on the D of E trek? We can easily wangle it so we're having a conversation outside her tent while pretending we don't know she's in there. The boys are going to arrange to set Ben up at some point too.'

'That's not for a while though. Is it not better to do it sooner?'

'Well yes, probably, but I can't think of another setting where we'd be able to get away with it so easily. Anyway, I've set the wheels of romance in motion in the meantime.'

'Oh?'

'Yep,' Hattie said, feeling pleased with herself. 'Me and Cal have decided to hold a joint hen and stag thing. And guess who has to organise that?'

Ursula laughed. 'Oooh, very devious. I like it, Hat.'

'Aww,' Meg said, looking put out. 'I actually really fancied that girls' punting weekend.'

'Well, tough,' Hattie said. 'This is in the cause of true love, Meg.'

Ursula nudged her. 'Plus now Adrian will get an invitation too. I don't suppose you'll object to that, will you?'

Meg smiled. 'I have got a good feeling about him. We're going out on a proper date this weekend. You'd better keep schtum though, girls: you know how Duxbury is about staff dating.'

'That's another thing,' Hattie said. 'Meggy, I know this is a big ask, but… I'm not sure how I can explain this, but I kind of need you to pretend you were getting off with Ben on Saturday.'

Meg frowned. 'You want me to lie? Why?'

'Well, you don't need to lie as such – just don't correct Bride if she asks you about it. Be vague or change the subject or something. She had the idea it was Ben and not Adrian in the Spider-Man costume, and… well, I haven't quite worked out how all the pieces are going to fit together yet, but my own Spidey-sense is telling me I ought to keep it quiet a bit longer.'

'How come?'

'Because at the party, her and Ben—'

'Her and Ben what?' a voice at the door asked.

All three of them jumped as Bridie entered the classroom, closing the door behind her.

'Er, just party gossip,' Hattie said, smiling feebly. 'Meg was telling us what a good night she had.'

She shot Meg a pointed look.

'Oh. Yeah, right,' Meg said. 'Well, it's been a while since I had any of that sort of fun. It was nothing serious really.'

'When is it ever with that guy?' Bridie said, joining them at the table. 'So how was he?'

Meg's face took on a dreamy expression. 'He may quite possibly be the best I've ever had. And I don't say that lightly.'

'Oh God. Don't tell him that, whatever you do. He's bad enough already.'

'How was your night, Bride?' Ursula asked, tactfully changing the subject to save Meg the necessity of telling too blatant a whopper. 'Good date?'

'Nope, awful.' Bridie shrugged. 'Man-cursed as ever, right? Tell you what, if I've got a fairy godmother then she's one sadistic bitch.'

'So that's it then, the last of the twenty dates,' Meg said. 'How does eternal singledom feel? I can't imagine knowing I'd never have another date as long as I lived.'

'Well, not quite,' Hattie said, smirking. 'Bridie's got a date this weekend actually.'

Bridie shot her a sharp look. 'I have not got a date, and I'd thank you not to start spreading it around that I have. I've got a planning meeting – one I agreed to greatly against my better judgement after my so-called best friend guilt-tripped me into it.'

Ursula laughed. 'With Ben, right? Hat was just telling us about the stag/hen thing.'

'Sadly, yes. I hope it won't be too painful.' Bridie sipped her coffee thoughtfully. 'I don't suppose either of you know who was at the party dressed as Batman, do you?'

Hattie tried to say with her eyebrows everything she was unable to say with her mouth.

'Batman?' Meg caught Hattie's look. 'Er, no. I didn't notice any Batman.'

'Nor me,' Ursula said.

Bridie shook her head. 'That's what everyone's said. I'm starting to think I dreamed him up.'

'Why, did you fancy him?'

'Yep,' Hattie said. 'He kissed her on the veranda.'

'Did he? That was forward of him.'

'Well, the kiss was mainly fuelled by beer,' Bridie said. 'Still, I wish I knew who he was.' She turned to examine Hattie. 'Are you all right, love? You look preoccupied by something.'

Hattie smiled vacantly. 'I'm all right.'

'Are you sure? I thought you'd still be walking on air, soon-to-be-Mrs Cal Kemp.'

'Well, I am, but…' She sighed and turned her phone over so Bridie could see the screen.

Bridie frowned. 'You're watching the "Beauty With Jojo" channel? What for?'

'She's done a new series on bridal make-up. To celebrate her wedding to that hunky actor from the Regency thing.'

'Conrad Benson,' Ursula said with a faraway look in her eyes. 'Lucky cow. I'd kill to wake up with that guy every morning.'

Bridie was still looking at Hattie, who squirmed under her shrewd gaze.

'There are other beauty vloggers you could watch,' she said. 'Why this one, Hat?'

'Well, she's supposed to be the best, isn't she?' Hattie sighed. 'And… I guess I couldn't help myself.'

'Sorry, are we missing something?' Meg said, looking from Bridie's keen stare to Hattie's flushed cheeks. 'What's wrong with watching Jojo? Every man and his tarted-up dog gets their make-up tips from her these days.'

'Go on, tell them,' Bridie said to Hattie.

'She's Cal's big ex,' Hattie murmured.

Ursula's mouth dropped open. 'You're not serious!'

'I wish I wasn't.'

'Cal really went out with Jojo Fitzroy? I mean, your Cal, Cal Kemp?'

'Yeah. Long time ago, well before me and him met.'

'But she's worth a bomb,' Meg said. 'No offence to Cal, Hattie, but he's a car mechanic from the arse end of nowhere. Where would Jojo even meet someone like him? Did he fit her a new spark plug or something?'

'She wasn't worth a bomb when they met,' Bridie said. 'She was just someone he got chatting to on a night out in Leeds with a group of mates: I was there. He was only twenty-one.'

'How long were they together?'

'Nine months. He was kind of besotted with her.' Bridie grimaced. 'Sorry, Hat.'

'That's all right,' Hattie said, trying to quash the uncomfortable twisting in her belly that arose whenever she thought about Cal with Jojo – or just plain Joanna, as she'd been before she rebranded. She looked at the frozen image on the phone. 'She's very beautiful, isn't she?'

'Nah, she's nothing but lip fillers and falsies,' Bridie said staunchly. 'You don't need that stuff to make you gorgeous; Nature already did it for you.'

Hattie smiled. 'I appreciate the loyalty, Bride, but we both know she looks great. She's got Kate Moss's bone structure and she talks like bloody Marilyn Monroe. Not to mention the fact she's probably a multi-trillionaire by now. Every time I think about her with Cal, I feel like I gain a stone, shrink about four inches and develop a moustache.'

'Why? Him and her are well in the past. Plus she's married now, off living her best life for the benefit of the *Hello* photographers. There's no need for you to compare yourself to her.' Bridie raised her eyebrows at the other two. 'Is there, girls?'

'I can't believe you never told us Jojo was Cal's ex,' Ursula murmured, a starstruck expression in her eyes. Bridie shot her a look, and she coughed. 'I mean, Bridie's right, Hat. Cal loves you now. Right, Meg?'

'Absolutely,' Meg said, nodding. 'In fact, I wouldn't even stoop to asking Cal to ask Jojo to get you some signed photos of Conrad for us. Unless you wanted to, that is. Totally up to you.'

Bridie shook her head. 'You two are useless.' She turned back to Hattie. 'It's true though: Cal and her have been over for years. I bet he never even thinks about Joanna these days. He's too busy being head over heels in love with you.'

'You think?' Hattie opened her Facebook app to show them an old photo of Cal and Joanna at a nightclub somewhere. The young Cal had one arm around his girlfriend's waist and was beaming like a lad who couldn't believe his luck, while Joanna, in the tightest and shortest of little black dresses, looked askance at the camera with her familiar pout. She'd posted it to her timeline with the words: *Thinking of you, babes,* and a kiss.

'She posted it this morning,' Hattie said. 'Cal was tagged in, so it showed up in my feed – they're still Facebook friends.'

'It's just a memory from this day seven years ago,' Bridie said dismissively. 'It popped up; she shared it. That doesn't mean anything, I do it all the time.'

'Cal's responded with a hug react though, look.'

'Oh, he's just being polite.'

'A like react is polite. A hug is… well, a hug,' Hattie murmured. 'And what's all this "thinking of you, babes" business?'

Meg shrugged. 'That's just Jojo. She gushes, it's part of her persona. Everyone's "babes" or "sweetie" or "queen" in her vids.'

'I never took to her,' Bridie said. 'She was friendly enough, but something about her always felt false to me. Whatever she might have going for her looks-wise, in personality she's no Hattie Leonard.'

'And we all know men value personality over everything, don't we?' Hattie muttered.

'Hey. I thought I was the gang's official man-cynic.'

'You must be rubbing off on me.' Hattie sighed. 'I mean, I know Cal's not like that. It hurts, that's all, thinking he was once with someone like that and now… now he's only with someone like me.'

'Exactly, and thinks he's the luckiest man in the world.'

'You're reading too much into this hug react, love,'

Ursula said soothingly to Hattie. 'It's an emoji, not another woman's knickers in the glove compartment. If it bothers you, discuss it with Cal.'

'No.' Hattie forced a smile. 'No, I know I'm being daft. I don't want Cal to think paranoia over minor Facebook interactions is a taste of what our married life's going to be like. The photo got me reflecting on the fact that his ex is this wealthy, glamorous celebrity and I'm just some dowdy little chemistry teacher who doesn't know how to contour – that's all.'

'You're the one he wants to spend his life with,' Bridie said. 'He asked you to marry him, didn't he?'

'I know.' She put her phone away. 'I'm being ridiculous, aren't I? Early wedding jitters, probably. It just felt like a bit of a kick in the gut, seeing them together.'

'You're only going to make yourself feel worse watching her videos,' Meg said. 'Do yourself a favour and find another channel, eh?'

'Yeah, you're right. Thanks, girls. I'm OK now.'

There was a knock at the door, and they all turned to see who it was. Mr Duxbury had appeared, with Adrian Verges, the deputy head, lurking at his elbow. Adrian caught Meg's eye and smiled.

'Ah, good. Just the young ladies I wanted to see,' Duxbury said, barging in. 'We need to have a quick meeting about the plans for the Duke of Edinburgh expedition. Mr Verges, you'll take notes, please.'

'Oh, what?' Ursula said, groaning. 'I'm not sure the management here understands the meaning of the word "break". I ought to report you to the union, Eddie.'

As Duxbury's younger cousin, Ursula was able to get away with speaking to the head in a way none of the others could.

He glared at her. 'This is important. I've got your kit lists from the trekking company.'

'Oh God, there's kit lists,' Ursula muttered as Duxbury and Adrian helped themselves to seats and Adrian took out a pad to make notes. 'We don't have to bring our own potties, do we?'

Duxbury looked down one of the lists. 'That's not on here. Loo roll is though. I think if you get caught short between campsites, you're just expected to make like the pope and do it in the woods.'

'What? But we're ladies!' Meg protested. 'We can't be as disgusting as you lot, it's not in our nature.'

Duxbury shrugged. 'Then you shouldn't have volunteered, should you?'

'You volunteered us, you rotten sod,' Ursula said.

'Well, you shouldn't have been cheeky and answered back to the boss. See, you've learned a valuable lesson already.'

He handed out a kit list each, plus a photocopied map that made absolutely no sense to Hattie no matter which way round she turned it. Hopefully Bridie, with her Duke of Edinburgh experience, could make more sense of it.

She scanned down the kit list. Tent, one between two. Sleeping bag. Mess tin. Nope, she didn't have any of this stuff: not even a torch. Cal and Ben were outdoorsy sorts though, so hopefully they'd have things they could lend. She only hoped the tent would come with instructions.

'This is a map of the region we'll be traversing, with overnight camping spots marked,' Duxbury said, pointing them out.

'And we're supposed to be able to follow this, are we?' Meg asked, squinting at her copy of the map.

'It isn't exactly rocket surgery, Miss Collins. Map-reading is intuitive.'

Ursula snorted. 'Intuitive, are you kidding? It's just a load of squiggly lines and random triangles.'

'There's a symbol key on the bottom,' Duxbury said. 'Besides, the trek leader will be there to help you out if you get stuck.'

'We'll be meeting the kids at the campsites though, right?' Bridie said brightly. 'I mean, they're supposed to be learning independence. We only need to supervise them camping; we don't need to trudge over the moors with them.'

'On the real expedition, yes, supervision will be minimal,' Duxbury said. 'For this training expedition, I want everyone walking together. It'll help give them confidence for the final thing.'

'Well, it was a good try,' Meg whispered to her.

'We've got twenty kids going. They'll be in two-man tents, strictly segregated by gender, and I want you lot all keeping a careful eye on them.' Duxbury shot a sharp look at Adrian, whose pencil had frozen in mid-air as he gazed dreamily across the table at Meg. 'And it shouldn't need to be said that the same rule applies to staff, by the way. Perhaps you might like to write that down, Mr Verges.'

'Hmm?' Adrian snapped out of his daydream. 'Oh. Right you are, boss.' He licked the end of his pencil and made a note of rule one. 'No... shagging...'

'Hem. Yes. Now the company who will be leading us are called...' Duxbury consulted a piece of paper. 'Grand Adventures. They will provide expeditionary equipment: OS maps, compasses and so on. I'm assured we've been assigned a very experienced trek leader after I told them my lot were going to be bugger all use.'

Hattie sat up a bit straighter, casting a sly sideways glance at Bridie. Her friend's face showed no glimmer of recognition, but Hattie had known the name immediately. Grand

Adventures: that's where Ben's new job was. Could he be the experienced trek leader? God, how perfect would that be – the two of them in the great outdoors, bonding while they toasted marshmallows over the campfire and sang 'Ging Gang Goolie' or whatever happened on these things? The only difficulty would be keeping it quiet until they were actually out there and it was too late for Bridie to back out, which she almost certainly would if she knew Ben was going too.

'OK, rule number two,' said Duxbury, who seemed to swell a little with each self-important pronouncement. 'No mind-altering substances. Everyone coming along will be searched before we set off. I think we all learned a lesson from the magic mushrooms some young scallywag put in the campfire stew a few years ago.'

Adrian stifled a snort.

'That'll have been the year when you hoisted Mrs Camberwell onto your back and bounced halfway up Pen-Y-Ghent with her, will it?' he said soberly.

'Yes, thank you, Mr Verges. Mrs Camberwell has been very understanding about that incident, knowing as she does that I believed at the time I was a species of rare wallaby rescuing her from a bushfire.'

'Do you want me to minute that?'

'No.' Duxbury frowned. 'Actually, yes. The minutes must be a true and accurate record of what's been discussed. Everything we say must be written down.'

Adrian shrugged and scribbled down 'no drugs – may lead to wallabies'.

'And as with the previous rule, this goes just as much for teachers as students,' Duxbury said, fixing them with a stern frown. 'No wacky baccy, no pills, no booze. I know what you lot are like.'

Bridie groaned. 'Oh, what, no booze? Come on, not even

a bottle of wine to share after the kids have gone to bed? Surely we've earned that much mind-altering.'

'I will not have Messington pupils going home to their parents and telling them the supervising staff were all three sheets to an ill wind. No.'

'Right. So you'll be leaving your fags at home, will you?' Ursula said.

'That… is not the same thing.'

'Nicotine's a drug, isn't it?'

'Surely a couple of bottles of wine between us is OK, boss?' Adrian said, catching Meg's eye as he obviously tried to ingratiate himself with her.

'It is not. No wine. That's my final decision.'

Ursula shook her head. 'You can be such an arse at times, Eddie.'

'I'm a… well!' For a second, Mr Duxbury looked like steam might be about to come out of his ears. 'Ursula, you will respect my position. In this building, I'm your boss first and your cousin second. Mr Verges, I'll thank you to write that down.'

Adrian blinked. 'What, that you're an arse?'

'Yes. Everything must be recorded.'

He shrugged. 'All right, you're in charge.'

Adrian went to make a note, but the lead in his pencil snapped.

'Damn it,' he muttered. 'Sorry, boss. I'll add it when I get back to my desk.'

'Just make sure you do. I wish it to be minuted, so it may stand as a permanent record.'

'Oh, that's all right, Eddie,' Ursula said, smiling brightly. 'I'm sure we can remember that you're an arse whether or not it's written down.'

'Right. The bell's about to go so that will be all,' Duxbury said, ignoring her. He stood up and waved a warning finger around all of them. 'And remember. No wine. I have spoken.'

'Don't worry about it, guys,' Bridie whispered when he'd gone. 'We'll smuggle some there in shampoo bottles. That's how we used to do it when we were kids.'

'Unless you know where we could find some magic mushrooms,' Adrian said. 'I'd bloody love to see his wallaby impression.'

TEN

When Bridie arrived at the Garter on Saturday night Ben was there waiting for her, all dressed up in dark jeans, fitted T-shirt and a smart blazer. He'd claimed a corner table, a candle flickering merrily in the centre. He stood up when she joined him, smirking in a way that instantly made her suspicious.

'Evening, Sweet Pea.'

'Please don't call me that, Benjamin.' She nodded to the candle. 'What the hell is that?'

'Just a little mood lighting. Here, let me get that for you.'

He darted to her side of the table before she could sit down and pulled her chair out for her.

She cast him a wary glance as she took a seat. 'All right, what are you playing at?'

'Hey, it's our first date. I just want to make sure it's perfect, that's all.'

'You know very well it's a planning meeting. I don't date any more, and I certainly don't date you. Did you order drinks?'

'Yep. Pete's bringing them over.'

She glared at Ben when Pete turned up with a bottle of fizz in a wine cooler and two champagne flutes. Each flute had half a strawberry in the bottom.

'For the lady,' Pete said, putting one down in front of her with a flourish. 'And for the… for want of a better word, gentleman. I hope you two have a lovely romantic evening.' He winked at them before heading back behind the bar.

'You think you're pretty damn funny, don't you?' Bridie asked while Ben poured them both a drink.

'That would be a fair assessment, yes.'

'I can't believe you bought us bubbly. You are such an insane amount of bellend, Ben Kemp.'

Ben smiled at an elderly couple who shot them a surprised look as they passed by. 'Don't mind her. It's our first date, she's a bit nervous. We're going to have a wonderful time.'

The couple hurriedly walked off, tossing worried glances over their shoulders. Bridie couldn't stop her lips from twitching. It was pretty funny, to be fair.

'All right, now you're scaring the tourists,' she whispered to Ben. 'Can we get on with this meeting now, or is Pete Prince about to come back over with a plate of spaghetti and meatballs and a violin?'

'You're the lady to my tramp, sweetheart. We'll do whatever you want to do, just as long as it ends up at my place.'

'It ends in hopefully no more than half an hour, when we've got a plan for this Sten thing and I can go back to avoiding you until the day of the wedding.'

'What, their wedding or ours?'

'Ours, are you kidding?' she said, laughing. 'Quite apart from the fact you disgust me, I will never, ever understand what people see in weddings.'

Ben shrugged. 'Nor me, but most folk seem to like them. I think it's to do with love or something. That's what they say anyway.'

'Surely you can be in love without mangling the business with a wedding. Once couples have been buried up to their necks in party favours and table plans and warring relatives and snotty flower girls and tantruming page boys, I'm surprised they can still bear to look at each other.' She paused to take a sip of her fizz, which actually tasted like the good stuff: champagne, not prosecco. Ben had obviously developed expensive tastes while he'd been away. 'All you get out of weddings is misery and debt, and then something like one in three marriages ends in divorce anyway. If it was me, I'd spend the cash on a once-in-a-lifetime holiday instead.' She shrugged. 'Might take the bloke, might not.'

'Yeah, I know what you mean. Weddings are so old-fashioned as well: all these stupid traditions about who speaks and in what order, who gives who away, when to lift the veil and whatever. It's daft.'

'Tell me about it, it's like going back to the bloody Middle Ages. Instead of exchanging rings, they might as well just get a branding iron with the groom's family name on it and tell the bride to drop her knickers and bend over.'

'I know, right?' He smiled. 'Heh. You notice what just happened?'

'What?'

'We agreed on something.'

Bridie couldn't help smiling too. 'I suppose we did. I wouldn't get used to it though.'

'Perhaps that's the secret. We can only get along when we're agreeing what a sucker everyone else is for sticking their necks in the noose.'

'And here's the ultimate irony: we've just been appointed

best man and maid of honour at our nearest and dearest's upcoming nuptials. Architects of our own misery, right?'

'Well, as long as it keeps them happy. Cal's promised me he's only doing this once.'

'Hattie said the same. Fingers crossed they're one of the two in three that make it, eh?'

'If anyone's going to, it's those two.'

'Yeah, I know. Sickening, aren't they?'

'Excruciatingly.' Ben sipped his champagne. 'Cal was always going to be the marrying type though; he used to arrange ceremonies for his Action Men. Hattie'll be good for him. Plus she isn't Joanna Fitzroy, which is a definite plus.'

'At the risk of inflating your already blimp-sized ego by agreeing with you twice in as many minutes, you're right there.' Bridie squinted at him. 'Why did you always dislike Joanna so much?'

He shrugged. 'I don't like phonies. I don't think I ever heard a sincere word come out of that woman's mouth. She was like the anti-Bridie or something.'

'Thanks. I think.'

'I mean, insofar as you never let a little thing like good manners get in the way of saying exactly what you're thinking.' He topped up their glasses. 'You didn't like her either. Did you?'

'No. I'm not sure why, she was pleasant enough. It just felt like she could never quite conceal the fact she was bored in your company.'

'No surprise she made a career out of showing people how to hide their true faces,' Ben said, his lip curling. 'She was always an expert at that.'

'See, this is what I don't get,' Bridie said. 'Yeah, I never took to her, but you *really* didn't like her. Why do you feel so strongly about it?'

'Because it was my brother, wasn't it? Cal's the best lad I know – I mean, obviously don't tell him I said that. He deserved better than someone like her.'

She smiled. 'You know, Ben, for all your many faults, you're a pretty good big brother.'

He lifted one eyebrow. 'I'm sorry, I'm not sure I heard that correctly. Was that… did you just pay me a compliment?'

'No. I was just… giving credit where it was due, that's all. On Cal's behalf, not mine.'

'Waiter!' he called, waving to Pete behind the bar. 'Can you send over a dozen oysters, some monkey glands and a dash of powdered rhino horn please? This date's definitely taken a turn.'

'It wasn't a compliment and this isn't a date,' Bridie hissed. She grabbed his arm and pushed it down again. 'Stop that. There might be people I know in here.'

'Can you say it again for me? I want to commit it to memory, so I can moon over it in private forever.' He sighed dreamily. 'The day Bridie Morgan paid me a compliment. I'm marking it down in my diary.'

'God, I hate you.'

He grinned. 'You love to hate me. Admit it.'

'No, I actually do just hate you. Sadly though, I also need you right now.'

He nodded. 'We all have needs. You want a bit of that powdered rhino horn to go before we head off to my place?'

'Stop, can you? I've got better things to do with my Saturday night than sit here listening to your crap fake flirting.'

'Really?' He sipped his drink. 'Then what did you turn up for?'

Bridie smothered a smile. 'Enough, Ben.' She leaned

down to get a notepad and biro from her bag. 'So come on, what ideas have you got?'

He opened the notes app on his phone. 'All right. Go-karting.'

'That's a no.'

'Paintballing.'

'Another no.'

'Zipwiring.'

'Absolutely not. Hattie's scared of heights.'

'Weekend in Magaluf?'

'I bloody knew it,' she muttered. 'No, again.'

'So this planning meeting-slash-date is actually just going to be you vetoing all my ideas, is it?' Ben asked.

'No, only the shit ones,' Bridie said, shrugging. 'It's not my fault they're all shit ones.'

'Well, what've you got then?'

'OK.' She flicked to another page in her notepad. 'Creating our own tea sets at that pottery-painting café in town.'

'Christ.'

'Punting weekend in Cambridge.'

'Ugh.'

'Spa holiday at a stately home?'

'I think I just spontaneously sprouted a pair of ovaries.'

'We could do a murder mystery weekend in fancy dress.'

'Yeah, OK. Or we could just scream "KILL ME NOW" in unison into the void of our own despair for forty-eight solid hours.'

'Jesus, this is hard work.' Bridie looked up from her notepad. 'There must be something we all like.'

He shrugged. 'Strippers?'

'We do not all like strippers, Ben. Or not the same-shaped ones anyway.'

'All right, how about clay pigeon shooting or something like that?'

She lifted an eyebrow. 'You really think the two of us ought to be in the same vicinity as a fuckload of guns?'

He reached over to pat her hand. 'I'd never shoot you, Bride. There's far too much entertainment value in you.'

'Mmm. You say the sweetest things.' She shook her head. 'No, I can't see Hat going for that. What else do we all enjoy?'

'We all like a good night out. Why don't we just do a bar crawl somewhere? We could go down to Blackpool for the weekend, hit a few bars, a club, maybe a casino. It's the Vegas of the North, you know.'

Bridie's pencil hovered thoughtfully over her notepad. 'I suppose that's not a terrible idea. Plenty to do in Blackpool, whatever your tastes.'

'It's a great idea. Lots of fun for boys and girls. Plus, if we're going in October that means the illuminations will be on.'

'Right, so they will. They'd make a pretty impressive backdrop for our bad behaviour.'

Ben grinned. 'Go on, admit it. I had the best idea.'

'It's not a competition, Ben.'

'Right. But I won though, didn't I?'

'I feel like I'm on a date with a twelve-year-old,' Bridie muttered.

'Aha!' Ben jabbed a finger at her across the table. 'You just called it a date.'

'That was… a slip of the tongue.'

He folded his arms with an air that told her there'd be no living with him now. 'Nope. You said we were on a date. You, Bridie Morgan, are on a date with me, Ben Kemp. That is a competition, and I definitely won it.'

'And now it's over.' She finished her drink, stood up and threw her handbag over her shoulder.

He looked up at her. 'Is that it? Are we done?'

'Yep. Apparently we're going to Blackpool. Because you won.'

'Well all right, but I was kind of hoping we might…' He nodded to the bottle of champagne. 'I mean, aren't you going to help me finish this?'

'I'm sure you can recruit some other female company to drink my share. You usually do.'

'Yes, but… what about the rest of the planning? We'll need to make a guest list, hire a coach, get T-shirts made, all that kind of thing. Not to mention booking the strippers.'

'We are not having strippers.'

'Hey, we'll be fair and equitable about it. One for the ladies, one for the gents. That's what you call feminism in action, right?'

'Yeah, if you get your definition of feminism from the articles in *Playboy*.'

'*Playboy* has articles?'

She rolled her eyes. 'Bye, Benjamin.'

'Come on, Bride, don't go. There's still a lot to sort out here.' He shot her what he probably thought was a winning smile. 'Sit down and have another drink with me. I'll behave, I promise.'

'We can talk through the details another time, when I've replenished my cringe faculty a bit. Right now, I'm going home to put my pyjamas on and watch *Strictly* on iPlayer.'

'You really won't stay?'

'Nope. I'll see you soon, Ben. Unfortunately,' she muttered to herself as she walked away.

ELEVEN

Cal was waiting for Ben outside Messington Climbing Barn some weeks later when his phone rang. His brother always took ages to get changed after their regular Thursday climbing session, with his mysterious and elaborate grooming rituals. Apparently it took a lot of time to look as fashionably scruffy as Ben.

'Hiya, Hat,' he said when he answered the call. 'What's up?'

'I just wanted to check you were ready for tonight,' Hattie said. 'Does Pete know what he's got to do?'

'Yes, we've synchronised watches.'

'All right, talk me through the plan. Just so I know you've got it down.'

'OK, so Ben and me arrive at the Garter at approximately 7pm,' Cal said. 'At 7.33 precisely, Pete's going to come over and ask if I can help him shift a barrel down in the cellar in exchange for a free pint. Ben's going to offer to do it in my place because he's so obsessively macho, I'm going to talk him out of it. I'll go with Pete, leaving my phone on the table. At 7.39, you're going to text and tell me I need to ring you urgently. Ben will see it and come find me to let me know. Pete will have locked the door from the bar to the cellar, forcing Ben to go round to the delivery doors outside. Let's estimate the whole thing from your text to delivery doors will take him about five minutes. So at around 7.44, that's when me and Pete start loudly discussing Bridie's secret feelings for him. We'll just have to trust to the fact he's too vain to walk away when he hears people talking about him.'

'I think when it comes to your brother, we can count on that,' Hattie said. 'OK, it sounds like you've planned it all out with military precision. Well done, sweetie. And don't worry, I won't forget my part.'

'When will you and the girls work the same trick on Bride?'

'We're going to do it on the D of E trip next month. There ought to be ample opportunities there. Did you find out if it is Ben they're sending from Grand Adventures?'

'Yeah, it's him,' Cal said. 'Lady Luck seems to be smiling on our devious plans. I don't think it's occurred to Ben that Bridie might be one of the supervising teachers, her not being an outdoorsy sort.'

'It hadn't occurred to her either until that bastard Duxbury press-ganged us all into it.' Hattie paused. 'She is a bit outdoorsy though, isn't she? She told me she was a D of E alumnus.'

'Only because she fancied Ben. She never had any interest in going outside until she heard he'd signed up for the scheme.'

Hattie laughed. 'Ah, I see. I was wondering how someone as incurably lazy as Bride ended up trekking over miles of countryside. Well, let's just hope we can reunite the child-hood sweethearts on their next expedition together.'

'The lengths we go to for love, eh?' Cal said, smiling. 'A right couple of Cupids we are.'

'It's only fair to pay it forward. God, Cal, wouldn't it be wonderful to see those two as happy as we are?'

Cal laughed. 'If they don't end up throttling each other first.'

'I feel sort of bad lying to them though, don't you?'

'It's a half-lie really. They do have feelings for each other; that's pretty plain. The only part we're making up is claiming we've heard them confess it.' He glanced towards the climbing barn. 'I'd better go, love – he'll be out any minute. I'll come over later and tell you how it went.'

As Cal ended the call, a message popped up in Facebook Messenger. He blinked at it.

Long time no see, babes!!! Fancy a catch-up? It's been far too long x

Joanna. OK, that was kind of unexpected. The date on the message before this one was over three years ago: her to him again, just a generic celebration GIF in honour of his twenty-fifth birthday. What was with the interest in catching up all of a sudden?

Relations between Cal and his ex had always been amicable enough. They often liked each other's Facebook posts, and occasionally commented on them. Not friends exactly, but cordial online acquaintances. Cal had wished Jo well on her recent wedding to the actor chap, Conrad, and she'd congratulated him on his engagement. It was all very grown up. But private messages were a rarity now they'd both moved on with their lives.

Cal had noticed Jo liking his posts more often after she'd shared that old photo of the two of them. Was that behind the sudden desire for a catch-up? His recent posts had mainly been about the big, and very adult, changes coming up in his life – the wedding in four months, and Hattie moving into his place in six weeks' time. Perhaps that and her own recent wedding had got Jo nostalgic for the days when they were just two young people with their whole lives ahead of them. Cal had been feeling a bit like that himself, if he was being brutally honest: excited about his future with Hattie, naturally, but wistful, in some ways, for his youth. Anyway, he was flattered that amidst the wealth, celebrity and glamour of her current lifestyle, Joanna still occasionally found the time to think of him.

Just off out, he replied. *Later though?*

I actually meant in person. Con and me will be over your way soon. I've got a speaking gig up in York. How about we grab a coffee: us two, you and Hattie? x

That sounded nice and civilised. He'd noticed Hattie always went a bit quiet whenever Joanna was mentioned, but Cal was sure they'd get on fine once the ice had been broken. He glanced at Ben, who was finally approaching from the climbing barn, and tapped a quick message back.

Sure, sounds good. Text when you're in the area.

He stuffed his phone into his pocket before Ben asked who he was messaging. Cal knew his brother wouldn't approve. He couldn't stand Joanna, for reasons Cal had never been able to work out. OK, Jo was an acquired taste in some ways, but Ben's dislike of her seemed stronger than her quirks really warranted.

'You took your time,' he said.

'Hey, it takes a lot of effort to look this beautiful,' Ben said, running a hand through his dark curls. 'Where are we going for a drink then? We could try that new craft ale place.'

'Let's go to the Garter. Then if we decide to stay for another pint or two, you can leave the Audi in the car park till tomorrow and walk back to yours.'

'Right, so we're making it a session, are we?'

'I need to make the most of these boys' nights while I'm still a single man, don't I?' Cal said, shrugging.

Ben smiled. 'Get it while you're young, eh? Come on then.'

At the pub, they ordered a couple of pints and claimed a table. Cal took out his phone and put it down in front of him.

'Expecting a call?' Ben said.

'Hmm?' Cal glanced up. 'Oh. No, just keeping an eye on the time.'

'What for?'

'Just… you know, so I know what time it is. So, how go the Sten plans?'

'Ugh, that sounds so wrong,' Ben said, grimacing. 'It's not even a real word. I can't believe you're not letting us have a proper stag.'

Cal grinned. 'We can always have one when you get married, eh?'

'Ha! What a comedian.'

'It won't be so bad having girls there, will it? You love girls.'

'Well yes, in specific contexts.' Ben took a glum sip of his pint. 'I won't even be able to enjoy the ones I do hit it off with, with Bridie glaring at me disapprovingly the whole time.'

'Been seeing a lot of our maid of dishonour, have you?'

'More than I can stomach. I wish she'd take that lemon-sucking look off her face whenever she's with me and lighten up. I know it's hard to believe, but Bridie can be a great laugh when once in a blue moon she actually lets herself go a bit.'

'I know she can. Where are we going for this Sten do anyway?'

'Can't tell you that. Me and Bride decided it ought to be

a surprise. You guys just have to pile into the coach and trust we're taking you somewhere good.'

'Ooh, is it a spa weekend?' Cal said, brightening. 'I've always wanted to try one of those hot rock massages.'

Ben shook his head. 'Mate, you've been spending too much time with Hattie. I mean, do you actually have a vagina of your own now or what?'

'You know you'd secretly enjoy it, hanging out in the hot tub drinking Grolsch,' Cal said. 'Aren't you glad Bridie's going? Hattie told me about your veranda smooching at her party.'

'That was entirely fuelled by alcohol and her arse in that Catwoman costume. I can take no responsibility for my actions.' Ben frowned. 'You didn't tell her that was me, did you?'

'Course not. I'm famed for minding my own business, especially where your sex life is concerned.' Cal took a sip of beer. 'You ought to tell her though.'

Ben snorted. 'Yeah, right. I'm actually quite attached to my testicles, thanks.'

'Well, what did you do it for if you don't want her to know it was you?'

'Because...' He hesitated. 'Dunno, she was just being all nice to me. I mean, that hasn't happened since before I started shaving. I got carried away by the novelty of it.' He stared thoughtfully into his pint. 'Did you know she was still upset about that night at school?'

'I guessed she was, yeah. Didn't you?'

'No. She's never mentioned it in ten years – not to me anyway.'

Cal shrugged. 'She feels humiliated, I should think. That's how I'd feel if someone had done that to me.'

'Suppose she does.' Ben was silent a moment. 'Do you think I should apologise or something?'

'Bit late now, bruv.'

'I know. I feel bad, that's all.'

Cal raised an eyebrow. 'What, you? When did you develop a conscience?'

'Well, she's a mate, isn't she? I mean, sort of, in that weird way where I feel she's only seconds away from kicking me in the nuts at any given moment. I never meant to hurt her.'

'Then what did you stand her up for? You knew that'd hurt her but you still did it.'

'All right, I suppose what I mean is that I never meant to keep hurting her,' Ben said. 'I was just a stupid kid then. It's the ten years afterwards I feel worse about.'

They glanced up as Pete approached them from the bar. Cal shot his phone a sly sideways glance to check the time: 7.33, right on schedule...

'Just the man I wanted to see,' Pete said, slapping Cal on the back. 'How'd you like to earn yourself a free pint, young Calvin?'

'Depends what I have to do for it.'

'I've got a couple of barrels down in the cellar I need to tap. Fancy giving me a hand to shift them? It's a two-man job and I can't take Noah off the bar.'

Cal shrugged. 'All right, that seems a fair deal.'

'That's OK, I'll do it,' Ben told Pete. 'Cal's only got little puny arms. He can stay here and mind our drinks.'

'Oh, no.' Cal stood up. 'He asked me first. You're not having my free pint, mate. Anyway, I need the macho points to compensate for that half-inch you've got on me.'

Pete raised his eyebrows. 'Oh?'

'In height, you elderly pervert.' Cal patted Ben's head. 'Although I've long been convinced it's mostly hair. Shave that off and I bet I'm at least four inches taller. Come on then, Peter.'

'If you're not back by the time I've finished my beer, I'm pinching yours!' Ben called after them.

Cal followed Pete behind the bar and through the door that led down into the cellar. At the top of the stone steps, the landlord flicked the light on and locked the door behind them.

'Right,' he said in a low voice. 'It's 7.37. Hattie's going to text in exactly two minutes. Let's get into position, shall we?'

———

Ben was absently watching Sky Sports on the Garter's big TV when he noticed Cal's phone buzz.

A message flashed up from Hattie.

Sweetie, can you call me straight away? Something urgent's come up. ASAP please, I need you right now!!!

Hmm. Urgent. Did she mean *urgent* urgent, or was that just the sort of thing girlfriends said to get you out of the pub early? Hattie probably wanted Cal to pick up a bottle of wine on his way over later or something. Anyway, Ben was sure whatever it was could wait ten minutes.

He was about to go back to watching the football when the phone buzzed again.

And I mean urgent urgent, not finish-your-pint-first urgent. I'm talking major disaster. NOW, Cal, or I swear I'm going on sex strike for a fortnight!

Ben sighed. So this was life in a relationship, was it? It really wasn't selling the idea to him. He pocketed Cal's phone and went to the bar.

'You mind if I pop down to the cellar for a sec, Noah?' he

asked the barman. 'My brother's helping Pete shift some barrels and I've got an urgent message from his missus.'

'Yeah, help yourself,' Noah said, nodding to the door behind him.

Ben went to try the handle, but the door wouldn't open.

'Seems to be locked,' he said.

'Oh, right. Pete must've locked it behind him. He's always paranoid someone might lean against it and fall down the steps,' Noah said. 'Tell you what, if you go outside you can bang on the delivery doors and they'll be able to let you in that way. They won't hear you knock from up here.'

'Right, cheers. Keep an eye on our drinks a sec, will you?'

'Yeah, no problem.'

Ben nodded his thanks and headed outside to the double doors that led into the beer cellar.

He could hear voices as he approached, his brother and Pete obviously deep in conversation. He frowned as a snatch of it reached his ears.

'Yeah, I know, poor cow. Still, I don't suppose your Ben cares, does he?'

Eh? They were talking about him? That was Pete who'd just said that. What poor cow was he on about?

Ben was about to knock on the door and ask when Cal chimed in.

'He doesn't know,' Cal said to Pete. 'Me and Hattie swore to her we'd keep the secret. It's probably for the best, knowing Ben like I do. I really hope she'll get over it, given time. That's the best solution.'

Secret? What secret? Too curious now to stop eavesdropping, Ben lowered his fist and moved nearer to the door.

'Will she though?' Pete said. 'If she hasn't got over it in the past decade then I can't see it happening now. Even him sodding off for a year didn't help.'

'Yeah, it's ironic really, isn't it? That it should be him, after all the time the two of them have spent doing battle. I don't think she even realised how deep she was in until he came back from Peru. She'd been in serious denial before that, with this twenty dates thing, but after Ben came home she found she just couldn't lie to herself about it any more.'

Bridie! They were talking about Bridie. Bridie and… him? What on earth did it mean?

Pete sighed. 'That poor lass. Tell you what, if I was ten years younger I'd be tempted to see if there was anything I could do to cure her.'

Cal snorted. 'Fifteen years younger, more like.'

'Yeah, all right. Still, she's a lovely girl, Bridie Morgan. Good laugh.'

'I know. She deserves someone who'll make her happy, and with her looks she could easily take her pick, whatever she says about being jinxed when it comes to men. I just can't see her ever making a go of a relationship while she's still hung up on my brother.'

'Did she know it was Ben she was playing tonsil hockey with at the party that night?' Pete asked.

'No – well, maybe on some level she did, in her subconscious or whatever. She'll never admit it though. I reckon she'd be devastated if she knew she'd let him see just how deeply in love with him she is.'

Ben smothered an exclamation. He couldn't believe he was hearing this! It wasn't true, was it? It couldn't be. Bridie Morgan, in love with him? No. She hated him – he'd heard her say so. She'd hated him ever since…

'I'm surprised she can even bear to look at him after he broke her heart when they were at school,' Pete said to Cal.

Broke her heart… yes, that bit was true, wasn't it? Bridie had told him as much when she'd believed he was Bruce – at least, she'd said that's how it had felt at the time. She'd genuinely had feelings for him once, when they were kids. But the idea that she could still have them now, today, after all the years they'd spent merrily at war with one another…

'He didn't break it enough to stop her loving him,' Cal said. 'What amazes me is that Ben can't seem to see it. The way she pretends to hate him because she's so afraid of him finding out her true feelings, yet she talks about him constantly. The failure of every relationship she's ever had while she's been lying to herself about it. Her jealousy over his track record with women. She fell for him at school and it's my belief she never stopped having those feelings.'

'Did she say that?'

'More or less. She was a bit drunk one night and it all came spilling out to me and Hattie. How she puts up this shell of sarcasm because she knows he'll never be able to love her back. How much it hurts, having to watch him with other girls all the time. How she feels she'll never be able to make a go of it with someone else because she can't stop herself loving Ben.'

'Why doesn't she just tell him all that?'

Cal laughed. 'You have met my brother, right? He doesn't do love: just sex. She'd only be setting herself up for another broken heart when she became another notch on the bedpost he's practically whittled away to nothing.'

'You're not planning to tell him then?'

'God, no. I love Ben, but Bridie's an old friend. I couldn't bear to see him hurt her again. Not that I think he'd do it on purpose; he's a womaniser but he's not a bastard. Still, I know that's what would happen. You'd never be able to convince someone as cynical about love as my brother that it's possible to have feelings as deep as Bridie's are for him.'

Pete sighed. 'That poor kid. I hope she gets over it.'

'Me too. But let's face it, it's not looking good,' Cal said soberly. 'Well, there's nothing to be done about it, I suppose. Just one of those things. Come on, let's finish shifting these barrels before Ben nicks my pint.'

Ben slid to the ground, his back against the doors.

He could hardly believe it. And yet Cal said Bridie had told him, in her own words, with her own mouth. She loved him – she'd loved him since school! And the way she was with him – the insults, the sparring – that was just her way of defending herself because she was so afraid of getting hurt by him again. Now he looked at it like that, it made perfect sense.

She loved him. Bridie Morgan loved him. No woman had ever loved him in his life before. No one had ever thought he was worth it – hell, even he didn't think he was worth it. Ben felt a strange sensation creeping into his belly: excitement, mingled with a sort of warm gratitude.

So Cal had been keeping this from him, had he? Trying to protect Bridie from his selfish, shagging wolf of a big brother. And all this time, all these years, every time he'd been with someone else it had been another kick in the gut for the poor lass. No wonder Bridie had sounded so angry at the party when she'd talked about his sexual history, calling him conceited; shallow; a gigolo. Those words had been haunting him ever since that night – it was a relief, in some ways, to realise she hadn't really meant them. Now he knew all that he knew, Ben was starting to wonder if she had known who he was after all…

What should he do? Should he talk to her about it, or… or what? His head spinning with unfamiliar, frightening thoughts and feelings, Ben stood up and wandered dazedly back into the pub, his errand entirely forgotten with the shock of this new discovery.

TWELVE

'So we were thinking melon boat starter, then lamb for the main with a pea risotto alternative for the veggies and vegans,' Cal said as he, Ben and Pete sat around a table in the sun-drenched beer garden of the Crossed Garter. 'Sound good to you guys? Hattie's devolved responsibility to us.'

Pete, who was sorting out the wedding catering, looked up from the iPad he was making notes on.

'You'll be paying through the nose for lamb in the autumn,' he said. 'What about chicken? That never goes out of season.'

'Dunno, seems a bit boring. Hattie liked the idea of minted lamb. Ben, what do you think?'

Ben, absently tearing strips off a beer mat in the seat next to him, didn't answer.

Cal poked him, and Ben started. 'Hm? What?'

'Come on, bruv, you're the deciding vote,' Cal said. 'Chicken or lamb, what do you reckon?'

'I've eaten, thanks.'

Pete shook his head. 'What's up with you today? You've not listened to a word we've said, have you?'

'Yes I have.' Ben racked his brains to remember any snatch of the conversation that had been drifting around him. 'Lamb... gets up your nose in the autumn. Or something.'

'You jumped about a foot when I prodded you then,' Cal said, turning to examine him. 'Something on your mind?'

'Course not.' Ben tore the beer mat into halves, then quarters. 'Bad night's sleep, that's all.'

Pete squinted at him. 'Here, have you changed colour?'

'Eh? Don't be stupid.'

'You have. You've gone beige.'

Cal looked down at Ben's bare arms and laughed. 'He's right, you have changed colour. You've had a spray tan, haven't you?'

Ben felt his cheeks heat and took a sip of beer to hide his face. 'No. There's a new sunbed at the gym and I thought I'd give it a go, that's all. What's so funny about that?'

'Since when do you do sunbeds? That's a whole other level of vanity, even for you.'

Ben shrugged. 'Missed my holiday tan, didn't I? I don't know why you're making such a fuss over it.'

'New haircut too, right?' Pete asked.

'Yeah. So?'

Pete grinned at Cal. 'Tell you what, if I didn't know your brother better then I'd think he was going to extra effort for some lass.'

'What, this guy? Surely not,' Cal said, smirking at his brother.

Ben scowled at the table. 'Give it a rest, can you? Let's just get this menu settled.'

'No one special you're trying to impress, is there, lad?' Pete asked, raising an eyebrow.

'Don't talk daft.'

'It's an interesting thought though,' Cal said to Pete. 'Ben with an actual, full-on crush on someone. I'd kind of like to see that.'

'What's up with you two today?' Ben demanded. 'Has all this wedding talk sent you soft? I don't have a crush on anyone and I've got no interest in impressing one particular woman out of the throng, all right? It's just a bloody tan.'

'All right, mate,' Cal said, patting his shoulder. 'No need to be so touchy. You know we're only winding you up.'

'That's being in love for you,' Pete said with a knowing nod to Cal. 'Rips your nerves to shreds. Trust me as someone who's done the marriage thing more than his fair share.'

'And the divorce thing more than his fair share.' Ben finished his pint and stood up. 'I've got to go, Bridie's coming over with some Sten stuff. Apparently this bloody wedding's destined to take over my entire life until it's done with. If you want my opinion on chicken over lamb, it's that I couldn't give a toss.'

'What're you in such a foul mood for?' Cal demanded.

'I told you, bad night's sleep. Got a toothache. I'll see you both later.'

'Mood swings are another sure sign,' Ben heard Pete whisper to Cal as he marched off in the direction of his flat.

Ben had never felt more on edge. This would be the first time he'd seen Bridie since he'd overheard Cal and Pete discussing her feelings for him just over a week ago and he'd been losing sleep for days thinking about it. Was he going to be able to act normally around her? Would she be able to tell? Oh God, what if she told him she loved him? She'd be so hurt if he didn't say it back.

Obviously he was fond of Bridie. He always had been, despite the games they loved to play: she was one of his oldest friends. He'd missed her a lot when he'd been away; missed matching wits with her, and making her smile all those times she just couldn't help showing her amusement at something he'd said. He'd thought about her on the long nights sleeping up in the mountains too. Wondered what she was doing, what she was thinking, who she might be with. But love – like, proper, romantic, Cal-and-Hattie-type love? Just the thought of it made him queasy.

Unless that was love. Could love make you feel sick? Ben had no idea, he'd never felt it before. That could be what the twisty feeling in his tummy was, but it could just as easily be horror, or the lentil dhal he'd had for lunch.

God, that in itself was pretty pathetic, wasn't it? He must be the only man this close to thirty who didn't know the difference between love and lentil dhal.

Ben shook his head to snap himself out of it as he unlocked the door of his flat. Of course he wasn't in love. Ridiculous notion. If he was capable of falling in love – and he was far from convinced that was even remotely possible – then why now? And Christ, why *her*? He'd known any number of sexy, funny, captivating women – known them in both the social and the Biblical sense – who would've been more than capable of exciting that emotion in any other heterosexual man, and yet Ben had never felt a flicker of anything other than sweet, uncomplicated lust. And these were women who actually enjoyed his company: who flattered him and made no secret of the fact they found him attractive. Bridie was beautiful, yes, but she was also a huge pain in the arse. It would be insane to be in love with Bridie. Laughable, even.

Ben let out a laugh as he entered his bedroom, as if to

prove his point, but it sounded kind of hollow. He guessed he just wasn't in a laughing mood.

He was right though. His feelings were definitely of the friendly variety and nothing more. He wasn't sure why it had taken him quite so long to come to that conclusion. Then again, that just proved it couldn't be love, didn't it? If people were in love, they must know it right away, like a thunderclap. It'd be pretty unmistakeable, surely. The fact Ben had spent so many sleepless nights puzzling over it just meant he'd been right in what he'd told Cal – he didn't do love. He couldn't.

Anyway, where did love lead if you let yourself get sucked into it? Nowhere good. Marriage, monogamy, mortgage, mundanity. A straitjacket, in other words. Love was a slippery slope that ended with the death of your way of life – of adventure, youth and fun. Ben was damned if he'd make that sacrifice. No, not even for Bridie.

He pulled off his T-shirt and took his favourite smart shirt from the cupboard. He was about to put it on when he stopped.

Christ, what was he doing? Getting dressed up for her? It wasn't a date, for fuck's sake. He wanted to help the poor cow get over it, not taunt her when he knew she had feelings he could never reciprocate. Maybe he couldn't love her, but he still liked her a hell of a lot and the last thing he wanted was to cause her more pain.

If he was going to cure her, he needed to make himself less appealing, not more. Ben put the shirt away again and went to rummage in his drawers.

It was early evening when Bridie knocked at the door of Ben's flat with a folder under her arm. She'd suggested meeting at his place rather than the pub, where there were no witnesses to misinterpret the situation if Ben started playing his usual games.

'All right, let's get this over with,' she said when Ben opened up. She frowned as she took in his outfit of baggy grey sweatpants and oversized hoodie. 'Bloody hell, what's up with you?'

Ben shrugged. 'Last time I checked, you weren't my girl-friend. I don't need to dress up to impress you, do I?'

She blinked. 'All right. Never said you did. Can I come in then?'

'Suppose you'd better. The sooner you come in, the sooner you can go again.'

Bridie followed him to the kitchen, feeling puzzled. Usually when she saw Ben, he had some sort of quip for her: a tease or a taunt, a bit of fake flirting. Not that she'd ever admit it, but she'd been looking forward to doing battle with him tonight. Why was he being so abrupt? He seemed genuinely pissed off with her.

In the kitchen he sat down at the dining table, not bothering to offer her a seat.

'All right, let's get on with it,' he said, his usual laughing tone missing entirely.

'Not going to offer me a cuppa?' Bridie asked.

'If you want one, you know where the kettle is.'

She frowned as she took a seat. 'Don't think I'll bother, thanks. What the hell's wrong with you today?'

He scowled down at the table. 'Nothing. Why would there be anything wrong? I'm fine.'

'Ben, you're dressed like you live in a bus shelter and you're snapping at me like I just ate your pet hamster for a between-meals snack.' She took a worried look at the purple semi-circles under his eyes. 'Seriously, are you all right? You look really tired.'

'I'm tired of this fucking wedding. Can we just get this done please?'

'OK.' She opened her folder and paused. 'Sure there's nothing else wrong? You're not acting like yourself.'

'Maybe I am. Maybe this is the real me.' He looked with little interest at her folder. 'Have you got quotes from the coach hire companies then?'

'Here.' She pushed some of the papers across the table to him. 'Did you book the hotel?'

'Yes. Ten twin rooms and a single.'

'We'd better keep boys and girls separate when we draw up the room-sharing list.' She quirked an eyebrow. 'I mean, if your libido can cope with an entire night of no sex?'

Normally that would elicit some sort of jibe in return, and Bridie waited hopefully for a response, but Ben just shrugged.

'I'll manage,' he said.

She summoned a smile. 'Seriously, mate, no comeback?'

'Not today. Not in the mood for it.'

'Ben, are you sure you're OK? This isn't like you.'

'It is though.' He rubbed his fingers through unkempt hair. 'Sorry, Bride, but when you get right down to it I'm just a grumpy, slobby bloke with questionable personal hygiene and a sex addiction, like every twat I've heard you whinging about after another crap date. You were right, I'm the last man any woman in her right mind would want to go out with. So... now you know.'

'When did I say no one wanted to go out with you?'

'Maybe you didn't. It's what you think though, right?'

There was silence for a moment as Bridie regarded him curiously.

'Ben, I think I'm going to go,' she said quietly. 'I don't know what's going on with you today, but it's clear you'd rather I wasn't here. The quotes are all there: just text me when you've had a look at them.'

She stood to leave. Ben had lowered his head, his eyes tight closed, but he opened them when he heard her chair scrape back.

'Bridie, wait,' he said in a softer voice. 'Look, I didn't mean to upset you. If I was rude, I'm sorry. It's… it's for your own good, that's all. I can't do it, all right? Maybe there's a part of me that… but I'm not that guy. I couldn't ever be him, not even if I wanted to.'

Bridie shook her head, feeling more bemused by the second. 'What are you burbling about, Ben? You're scaring me.'

'Sorry.' He closed his eyes again. 'Sorry. I was just trying to… actually, I think I might be coming down with something. You're right, you should go.'

'Right.' She turned to leave, then hesitated and turned back. 'Coming down with what?'

'Dunno. Just something.'

'Well, do you need me to get you anything?'

'I just need rest. Rest and to be left alone.'

'But if it's a fever, you shouldn't be on your own. Let me call your mum, or Cal. Or I could stay, I guess, if no one else can come sit with you.'

'Bridie, I'll be fine. Please, just… just go.'

'All right.' She hesitated again. 'Are you sure though? I'm worried about you.'

His mouth flickered. 'Are you?'

'Well, yeah. I mean, if you're ill.'

Ben sighed and stood up to rest his hands on her shoulders.

'You're a great girl, you know that?' he said quietly.

She turned to look at the hands on her shoulders. 'Wow.

You really are ill.'

He gave a hollow laugh. 'You have no idea.'

'What do you think it is? Flu? You must be delirious if you're paying me compliments. Do you want me to bring you over some Beechams?'

'No, not flu. This is… something else.' Ben gave another strange little laugh. 'Funny really. I always thought I was immune.'

'OK,' she said, blinking. 'Does it feel like a fever?'

'A bit like that.' He bowed his head. 'I mean, no. There's no temperature.'

'All the same, I think you ought to go to bed. Do you need me to help you to your room?'

'I'll be OK.' He smiled. 'You, offering to put me to bed. I'm supposed to make some sort of crack about that, right?'

Bridie smiled too, pleased to see a glimmer of his usual personality. 'Well, save it for me until you're better.'

'I will.' Ben planted a soft kiss on her cheek, then blinked, looking puzzled. 'Sorry. Not sure why I did that. Bye then, Bridie.'

'Right. Um, bye.' Feeling bewildered, Bridie headed for the door.

THIRTEEN

'God, this is like waiting for Sting to orgasm,' Bridie muttered as, with her fellow Duke of Edinburgh volunteers-slash-chumps, she stood next to her huge rucksack by the coach that was going to be taking them to the starting point of the training expedition. 'Where the hell's Duxbury? I'm getting soaked through here.'

It was a typical British summer day in July: grey, drizzly and cold.

'Yeah, where has your cousin got to?' Hattie asked Ursula. 'I thought we were supposed to be getting checked for contraband before the kids arrive.'

'He's talking to the trek leader in the staffroom, I think,' Ursula said. 'Probably telling him what a bunch of useless reprobates we all are.'

'Have you got your shampoo, Bride?' Meg asked.

'Yep. Five bottles. You?'

'Six. I, er, brought extra conditioner.'

'How long until the kids get here?' Adrian asked.

Bridie glanced at her watch. 'They ought to start turning

up in fifteen minutes. I wish Duxbury would get a bloody move on and do this inspection he insisted we get here early for.'

The head teacher soon appeared, looking even more pompous than usual. He was in an oversized purple walking jacket and woollen socks pulled up to the middle of his calves, with a pompom hat sticking straight up on his bald head.

'Right,' he said, clapping his hands. 'Get those rucksacks open, ladies and gent. I want to make sure we're all abiding by the rules before the kiddies arrive. Leading by example and all that.'

Bridie shot a look at Hattie before opening hers up for him to rummage through.

'It's nothing that isn't on the kit list,' she told Duxbury as he poked about. 'Lightweight trousers, thermal vest, three pairs of knickers, towel, walking socks and a torch, plus a mess tin, cutlery, first aid kit, wash stuff and all that. Hat's got our tent.'

Duxbury drew out a bottle of shampoo. Then another. And another. And another and…

'Bugger me,' he muttered. 'How often were you planning on washing your hair, Ms Morgan?'

'Oh no, you see, I need all those.' She picked up one bottle. 'See, this one's for dry hair – I use that on my ends. And this one, for greasy hair, I use on the roots. Then I have to use the colour treatment serum for my highlights, and of course the special argan oil conditioner—'

'All right, all right, I get the picture. Pack it up again then.'

He moved on to Meg, who'd already started arranging her shampoo bottles in a row for him.

'Do all women need this many different shampoos?' Duxbury asked her.

'Well, that depends. The bald ones probably only need two or three.'

'Right.' He blinked at them in puzzlement, then moved on to Ursula, who'd made a little pile of her clothes next to a single, industrial-sized two-litre bottle of shampoo.

'Only the one for you?' he said.

'Yes, but I need a lot of it. You see, I get terrible dandruff if I don't use big dollops of this medicated stuff—'

'All right, I don't need to know any more about feminine hair-cleansing rituals. Put it away again, please.'

He moved down the line to Adrian, who immediately started pulling out his own selection of shampoo bottles.

Duxbury shook his head. 'Surely not you too, Mr Verges.'

He shrugged. 'I'm a metrosexual modern man, boss. Is it a crime to want to be salon-smooth?'

'OK, well, pack it away. I hope the extra weight is going to be worth it when we're carrying all this over miles of rolling countryside.'

'Oh God, it'll be worth it,' Hattie muttered. She summoned a smile as Duxbury looked at her. 'Er, for the benefit of having glossy, fragrant hair, I mean.'

'Ah.' Duxbury nodded towards the man striding in their direction from the school. 'Here's Mr Kemp, the walk leader, to introduce himself before the children start arriving.'

'Oh, no.' Bridie stared at the broad figure heading their way, then spun to face Hattie. 'No! Not him.'

Hattie shrugged. 'Hey, I'm as surprised as you are, Bride. It's no good looking at me like it's my fault. I didn't book the thing, did I?'

'Friend of yours?' Duxbury asked.

Bridie folded her arms. 'Absolutely not.'

'He's my fiancé's brother,' Hattie informed him. 'He and Bridie have... history.'

Bridie put up her hand. 'Sir, may I please be excused? I'm not feeling well. I don't think I can go actually, now I come to think of it.'

Hattie grabbed her arm and pushed it down. 'Oh no you don't. All for one and one for all, remember? Besides, you're the only one with any... jojoba shampoo. Don't forget you promised to share it with all of us.'

Bridie glared at Ben as he reached them. 'Kemp. Want to explain what you're doing on my trip?'

'Bridie.' Ben looked taken aback. 'What are you doing here?'

'I work here, don't I? Don't pretend you didn't know I was coming.'

'Why would I? I mean, you're lazy as fuck and you hate the outside world. You're the last person I'd expect to see on a hiking expedition.'

'Oh yeah, a likely story. I take it you've recovered from your man flu then.'

'It wasn't man flu.' Ben reached up to rub his hair, looking awkward. 'So, um... how've you been then, love? All right?'

She frowned. 'What, do we do pleasantries now? Usually you just insult me.'

'Well, I... I never meant to be bad-mannered. I mean, I'd hate to ever upset you or hurt your feelings or... anything like that. I hope you know that, Bridie.' He met her gaze then immediately dropped eye contact, grimacing as he rubbed his hair again.

Bridie snorted. 'You'd hate to hurt my feelings? Since when?' She turned to Hattie. 'What's he being weird for? Is he still ill?'

'He's being nice, Bride.'

'For him, that is weird.'

Duxbury clapped his hands again. 'All right, I can see mums and dads pulling in. Get on the coach while I do inspection, everyone. I hope you know some good community songs – we're going to be on this thing for at least the next two hours.'

'Oh *God*,' Bridie groaned as they climbed aboard.

———

The kids they were taking on the expedition were all Year 12s, sixteen and seventeen years old, and certainly old enough to give them a few headaches when it came to policing the sleeping arrangements later. But while they were mature enough to be sexually active – or at least, aspiring to be – they weren't above acting like primary-schoolers on the coach. By the time the group arrived at their destination, the adults on the trip had broken up two snogging couples, one headlock and a snot-flicking fight, but had been entirely unable to quash the rousing chorus of 'Stop the Bus I Need a Wee-wee!' that broke out after the first half-hour – and continued for the next two.

'Well that was hell,' Ben muttered to Bridie as they got off the coach. 'Is this what kids are like then?'

'Yep.'

'Why do people have them?'

'Contraception malfunctions mostly, I think.'

He rested a hand on her arm. 'Bridie, look... can we talk? Later, I mean.'

She shook her head. 'I'm really not happy about you being here for this, Ben. The least you can do is try to stay out of my way for the duration.'

'Please. This is important. I've been thinking about it ever since… for ages.'

'Thinking about what?'

Before Ben could elaborate any further, they were interrupted by Duxbury.

'All right, Mr Kemp, the children are ready for you,' he said, gesturing to the kids waiting expectantly in front of the coach.

'Er, right.' Ben cast a last look at Bridie before going to address the group of students.

'OK, you lot,' he said, clapping his hands together briskly. 'I'll be your instructor for this expedition so feel free to ask me anything you want. I'm not a teacher so we don't need any of that "mister" or "sir" stuff. You can just call me Ben.'

He grinned broadly at them and Bridie noticed a couple of the girls flush, nudging each other and giggling. She rolled her eyes.

'First of all, can you get into pairs?' Ben said. 'You'll be sharing the OS maps and compasses one between two.'

After the kids were paired up, Ben handed out the equipment and gave them a talk about safety on the moors, care for the environment, techniques for walking long distances with minimal discomfort and other things they might need to know. He was good with them actually, striking just the right note between matey nonchalance and authoritative leadership. Already they were looking at him with liking and respect – and lust, in the case of some of the girls and at least one of the lads. Bridie felt annoyed that this was something else he was apparently good at with no effort at all.

After Ben's talk he guided kids and teachers through some stretches to loosen their muscles, then they shouldered their giant rucksacks and set off. Bridie was expecting Ben to take the lead, but he hung back, letting the kids go ahead.

'Aren't you supposed to be up front showing them the way?' she asked as he fell into step beside her.

'They're supposed to find their own way, that's the whole point. I'm just here in an advisory capacity, and to help them out if they get stuck.' He tapped Josh Abercrombie, who was walking beside them with his partner, on the shoulder. 'Strides shorter and faster, lad. You want to finish your day's walking at the same pace as when you set off. Better for your muscles.'

'Right. Cheers, Ben.' Josh regulated his pace accordingly and he and his partner soon caught up with the pair in front of them, leaving Bridie and Ben to bring up the rear.

'Look, Bride,' he said when they were alone. 'Sorry about last time I saw you. If I was weird.'

Ben Kemp, apologising to her for being weird. That was even weirder than the original weirdness. What was going on with him? Last time Bridie had seen him, it felt like he could hardly bear to look at her. Today, he couldn't seem to stop staring at her. She'd noticed the inscrutable glances he kept flinging in her direction all through the coach trip.

'Well, you were ill, I suppose,' she conceded graciously.

'Yeah. I was. And hey, thanks for checking up on me.'

Bridie flushed as she remembered the text she'd sent to make sure he was OK. 'Just wanted to make sure you hadn't passed out on the floor or anything.'

'More than I deserved after the way I snapped at you.' He nudged her. 'Remember when we were doing this?'

Bridie couldn't help a small smile. Yes, she well remembered the first weekend she'd spent walking the fells with Ben and the rest of their D of E group in sixth form. Ben was the whole reason she'd signed up. As he'd truthfully pointed out, she really wasn't the outdoors type, much preferring to stay warm and cosy indoors than face the elements out in open countryside. Only the mammoth crush she'd had on him at seventeen could've convinced her that all that time spent trudging through mud was worth it. And it had paid off too – it was on the weekend of their training expedition that their friendship had first become more, when they'd started their not-quite-relationship one night in his tent with a cheeky grope under their sleeping bags.

'I remember,' she said. 'You were a cocky, insufferable little git that weekend, swaggering about flirting with everyone. Not a girl on the trip was safe from you.'

'That's not how I remember it. I only remember one girl not being safe from me.' He glanced at the kids. 'I hope this lot are better behaved than we used to be.'

'Are you kidding? They're teenagers. Hormones on legs.' She turned to face him. 'Listen, why don't you go up ahead? I've got the back.'

'Trying to get rid of me?'

'Yes.' She nodded to Meg and Adrian. 'Go talk to Meg. I bet you haven't spoken to her since the night of the party, have you? It's only good manners to at least pass the time of day with your former one-night stands.'

'She looks happy enough with the company she's already got,' Ben said, glancing at Adrian as he said something to make Meg laugh. 'I'd rather stay with you, Sweet Pea.'

She frowned. 'Can you stop calling me that?'

'You used to like it when I called you that.'

'Yes, well, that was a long time ago. Look, you're supposed to be the instructor for this trip. Just be professional, can you?'

'I am professional.' He pointed to her compass. 'I can tell you you've got that the wrong way round, for a start.'

'Ugh.' She glowered at the compass in her hand. 'I bloody hate all this stuff.'

He smiled. 'You never could get the hang of it, could you? Here.' He took the compass, turned it until the needle was aligned with 'North' and handed it back. 'There you go.'

'How is that supposed to help me? All I know is which way is north. So, what, if I keep walking I'll eventually get to the Arctic Circle and be gobbled up by a polar bear?'

'It'll help you make sure you're following the route correctly,' Ben said, nodding to the map in a waterproof case around her neck. 'Well, never mind, I'll look after you. I got you through this before, I can do it again.'

'Why are you being so weirdly nice to me?' She leaned towards him and sniffed. 'And why do you smell like that? Are you wearing aftershave?'

He flushed. 'Yeah. Hugo Boss.'

'You weren't wearing it earlier.'

'I, um… I bought it when we stopped at the services.'

'Ben, why're you wearing Hugo Boss to a Duke of Edinburgh expedition?'

'Well, I saw it there behind the counter and I… remembered that you liked it. Back at school, I mean, when I used to wear it.'

She flashed him a puzzled frown. 'What've you gone all nostalgic for suddenly?'

He shrugged. 'I've just been doing some thinking lately. About the old days.'

'What for?'

'It's been on my mind, that's all.' He looked at her. 'Can we talk later, Bride? In private, I mean.'

'Talk about what?'

'There's something I need to tell you. Something I want to apologise for.' He rubbed his neck. 'It's not going to be easy, but I'll hate myself forever if I don't.'

She shook her head, bewildered at this sudden personality shift. 'What do you want to apologise for this time?'

'I'll tell you later, when there's no one else around.' Very briefly he squeezed her arm. 'I want to call pax, Bride. Make it better between us.'

'Ben, I don't understand.'

'Look, that night – there's something you don't—'

He broke off as Kelly, one of the sixth-formers, came to ask him a question about the symbols on her OS map. Afterwards he was commandeered by Mr Duxbury, and Bridie was left alone with her thoughts for the rest of their day's walking.

FOURTEEN

'Oh my *God*!' Bridie wailed as she sank onto one of the benches that surrounded the fire circle at their campsite.

Josh, who was helping his friends Kelly and Emma build a fire, looked up at her. 'What's up, miss?'

'I think I'm broken, guys. Have any of you seen my feet? I can't feel them so I assume they must've dropped off somewhere along the way.'

Emma shrugged. 'I feel all right.'

'You're young and newly minted. I'm old and falling to bits,' Bridie said. 'All right, hold your noses.'

'Why?' Kelly asked.

'Because I'm about to take my boots off.'

She eased one painful, blistered foot out of her walking boot and rolled her sock down to massage her tender ankle.

'I can't believe we've got another full day of this,' she said. 'My shoulders hurt, my feet hurt, even my nose seems to hurt. And I don't get a badge at the end of it like you lot do. It's totally unfair. I want a badge.'

'You've already got a badge,' Hattie said as she joined

them and took off her rucksack. 'You did your D of E Gold at school, didn't you?'

'Then I want another, shinier badge. In fact I want two, because I'm old and knackered now so it's even more of an achievement.'

She saw Kelly nudge Josh. 'Hey, that Ben guy's a bit hot, isn't he?'

'I know. He reminds me of a black-haired Chris Hemsworth.'

'Yeah, like if you took Chris's face and put it with Aidan Turner's hair then you'd get him,' Emma said. 'I wonder if he's hairy under his top.'

Bridie frowned at them. 'Oi. No letching at teachers, children.'

Kelly shrugged. 'He's not a teacher though, is he?'

'He's a sort of teacher. Anyway, it's not appropriate.'

Josh glanced at her filthy trousers and boots. 'How'd you get so muddy, Ms Morgan?'

'I stepped in a cowpat. And a puddle. And then another cowpat. I seem to have a knack for discovering filth, like those pigs that can sniff out truffles.'

'Come on, Ms Morgan, up you get,' Hattie said, patting her shoulder. 'I'm hoping you know how our tent goes up, since I've got no idea.'

'Oh, you'll work it out,' Bridie said, holding her hands up to the now crackling fire.

'No I won't. Get up and help me.'

'I'm still getting the feeling back in my legs. Ask Ben to do it. He needs to be earning his fee.'

'Ben's busy helping the kids with theirs,' Hattie said, nodding to him showing a couple of the students how to angle their guy ropes at a little distance from where the teachers were setting up camp. 'Come on, up.'

Bridie groaned as she got painfully to her feet. Hattie looked at her expectantly.

'What?' Bridie said.

'Well, where is it?'

'The tent? I thought you were carrying it.'

'No, I gave it to you when we stopped for that last break, remember?'

'Oh right, so you did. Well, then it must be…' Bridie turned to her rucksack and trailed off.

Hattie frowned. 'Bridie? Please tell me that look on your face doesn't mean what I think it does.'

'It's… gone,' Bridie whispered. 'Hat, the tent's gone. I had it strapped to the back of my rucksack.'

'It can't be gone. How the hell do you lose a two-man tent?'

'I don't know. Maybe it fell off while we were walking.'

'What, and you didn't notice?'

'Well no, obviously not.' Bridie rubbed the heels of her hands into her eyes. 'Oh God. I bet I didn't attach it properly and it's back at that last rest point five miles away. What the hell are we supposed to do now?'

———

Hattie summoned an emergency meeting of the teachers plus Ben while they tried to work out what they could do about their sudden tent deficit.

'Right, so there's seven adults and we've got two two-man tents and a one-man between us,' Adrian said. 'I suppose some of us will just have to squeeze someone extra in, that's all.'

Meg cast a doubtful glance at one of the tents that had already been put up. 'The two-man tents are a bit small for three, aren't they? They look a bit small for two, to be honest.'

'Yes, they're trekking tents,' Duxbury said. 'They're designed to be as minimal as possible, to keep them lightweight.'

'I don't think the one I brought is a trekking tent,' Ursula said. 'Anyway, it's a bit bigger than this one. I think we could get three in it at a push.'

'It'd only be for tonight,' Ben said. 'I can ask my brother to drive over to where we're camping tomorrow with a spare.'

'I don't mind squeezing in with Adrian and Mr Duxbury in the trekking tent, if that'll help,' Meg offered. 'Then you can take Bridie and Hattie, Urs.'

Duxbury shot her a sharp look. 'Oh no. No mixed-sex tents.'

'This is an emergency though.'

'What sort of example is that for the children? I'll have parents making complaints left, right and centre if they think you lot have been bonking on the job. Besides, ours is too small to fit another in unless they want to lie on top of us.'

'I'm game if you are,' Adrian whispered to Meg.

'We don't have to mix,' Hattie said. 'What if three of us girls share one two-man tent, then the lads can take the other and the spare girl goes in the one-man?'

Duxbury shook his head. 'Look, we can go round the houses on this until the cows freeze over. I told you: we're not going to get three of us into that trekking tent, no matter how we squeeze up.'

'Well what do you expect the extra person to do then, Eddie?' Ursula demanded. 'Sleep up a bloody tree? We have to find some solution.'

Suddenly, Bridie burst into tears. They all turned to stare at her.

'Oh God, I'm sorry,' she said, laughing as she wiped her eyes on her sleeve. 'It's just been such a long day, and I'm so tired, and I stink of cow shit and my feet hurt and...' She choked on another sob. 'Hat, I'm sorry I lost the tent. Look, you go in with Meg and Ursula. I'll sleep out.'

'Out in the open?' Ben said. 'Don't be daft, Bride. You'll freeze.'

'Serves me right. I should've been more careful.' She swallowed hard as another sob tried to force its way out. 'I... I have to go hide, before the kids see me crying. I'm really sorry, all of you.'

Blinded by tears, Bridie ran in the direction of the toilet block where she could cry her eyes out in peace.

————

When she finally emerged, Ben was leaning against a tree, waiting for her.

'Got it all out then?'

She sniffed. 'What do you want?'

'To tell you I'm not going to let you freeze your peachy little bottom off sleeping out in the open air.' He approached her and slipped an arm around her shoulders. 'It's all right, we've got it sorted. You're taking my one-man tent.'

'But then where will you sleep? Duxbury's adamant they can't fit another in his and Adrian's tent.'

'I packed a waterproof bivvy bag. I'll sleep out.'

She shook her head. 'No, Ben. I was the one who lost the tent. It should be me.'

'I told you I won't let you,' he said, a gentleness in his voice that she hadn't heard there for a long time. 'I'll be all right; I've done it a thousand times. This is what I'm trained for: survival skills. Besides, it's summer, even if it is a bit of a chilly one. Whereas with your record of bad luck, you'd probably get eaten by a wolf or something.'

She looked up at him. 'Are there wolves?'

'Technically they're extinct in Britain, but I wouldn't put it past you to attract a couple all the same.' He gave her a squeeze. 'Now cheer up, eh? You did well today, tent loss aside.'

'Are you kidding? I hurt everywhere.'

'So do I. So does everyone. That's all part of the fun.'

She managed a weak smile. 'Masochist.'

'That's what made me the rough, tough macho man I am today,' Ben said, smiling back. 'Come to the fire. The kids are making a big pot of curry for everyone. I wouldn't stake my life on it being edible, but it doesn't smell too bad. Then I'm told that after they go to bed, Meg's got some aloe-vera-infused vodka we can share.'

'All right.' She realised his arm was still around her shoulders, and it occurred to her that she ought to push it away. But it felt comforting, strong and supportive, and right now she needed that, even if the arm in question was attached to Ben Kemp. She still felt very wobbly.

'And you are taking my tent,' he said. 'No arguments.'

'Thanks, Ben,' she whispered. 'I appreciate it.'

'Bride…' He looked down at her. 'You know that I like you, right?'

She frowned. 'What?'

'I mean, you know that in spite of everything, I'm actually really bloody fond of you? I've always thought of you as a mate. I thought you felt that way too, until… well, I know we wind each other up, but you do know that, don't you?'

'I think… I'm not sure. Maybe.' She stared vacantly for a

moment, her gaze drawn by the glow of the campfire in the distance. 'Was that the thing you wanted to talk to me about?'

'No. That was… something else.'

'What?'

'Not now. Later.' He gave her a last squeeze and let her go. Bridie felt vaguely disappointed at the removal of the strong arm from around her shoulders. 'Come on, Sweet Pea, let's get some grub.'

———

Three hours later, the kids were all in bed. Mr Duxbury, after staying up long enough to ensure there was no tent-hopping taking place, had retired to his tent likewise, and Ben was with the remaining teachers passing a slightly soapy bottle of vodka disguised as L'Oreal Elvive between them.

'I know whose idea this was,' he said, glancing at Bridie. 'This is how we smuggled booze to our Duke of Edinburgh expedition back in the day.'

Bridie smiled too – and did she colour slightly, or was he just imagining it? Perhaps that was the glow from the fire, but he was sure she looked pinker than she had a second ago.

'Happy days,' she said, sighing. She took a swig from the shampoo bottle and passed it to Ben. 'You know, this part of the great outdoors really isn't bad at all.'

'What was Bridie like at school, Ben?' Ursula asked. 'I bet she was a little hellraiser, was she?'

Ben smiled. 'Nah, just a big old swot. Shy too. Hard to believe now that there was a time when she was all quiet, blushing maiden modesty, right?'

Bridie nudged him. 'Oi. Unfair.'

'I didn't say it was a bad thing,' he said, shrugging. 'I thought you were cute.'

She raised an eyebrow. 'Cute?'

'Sexy cute. But adorable cute as well.'

'And you were an arrogant, strutting knobhead who thought he could charm any lass in our year into bed just by winking at her,' she told him. But she was smiling.

Hattie yawned and stood up. 'Well, I think I'm going to get to bed. We've got a long day again tomorrow. Night night, everyone.'

Ben was sure he saw her flash a look at the other two women before she disappeared into their tent.

'You know, I'm pretty knackered myself,' Ursula said, glancing at Meg. 'How about you, Meggy?'

'Mmm. I could sleep.'

Adrian shrugged. 'I'm not tired.'

'I think you are,' Meg said.

'Eh? No I'm not.'

'Yes, Adrian, you are.' She lowered her voice. 'Or maybe you don't fancy a quick kiss and cuddle behind the toilet block before bed?'

'Oh. Right.' He faked a yawn. 'Wow, suddenly I can barely keep my eyes open. Night, chaps.'

FIFTEEN

'Just us then,' Ben said when they were alone. He passed Bridie the shampoo bottle. 'Nightcap?'

'Thanks. Better make it the last one though.' She swallowed down a mouthful and gave it back to him.

'Look, I'm glad I got you to myself.' He took a swallow too and put the bottle down on the ground.

'Yeah, what is this mysterious thing you've been wanting to talk to me about?'

Ben looked into her face. Perhaps it was the vodka or perhaps it was just the warm, fuzzy feeling that came after a day of releasing endorphins out on the moors, but she looked softer to him, somehow. Sort of faintly amused, like she always did around him, but without the familiar prickliness he was used to seeing alongside it. He shuffled a bit closer.

It was funny, how suddenly the realisation had hit. He'd tried so hard to lie to himself; to convince himself that love was a nonsense, and his feelings for Bridie strictly friendly with just a healthy amount of lust for an undeniably attractive woman mixed in. In the end, though, all it had taken was that evening in his kitchen, and the tender concern she couldn't conceal when she was worried he was ill. As soon as Ben had seen the look of genuine love in her eyes, his walls of self-delusion had shattered and he'd been forced to acknowledge the answering stirrings inside himself. Now he knew about the velvety cushion of soft, lovely Bridie-ness that she kept hidden under her scathing wit and acid tongue, he couldn't help wanting more of it.

He'd believed he was immune to love, his emotions remaining unaffected by any woman he'd been with. What Ben realised now was that he wasn't incapable of love at all; he'd just been lying to himself about the fact he'd fallen long ago.

But that didn't matter. He couldn't tell Bridie any of that – at least, not yet. There was something he needed to put right first.

'I wanted to talk to you about...' He took a deep breath. 'About the sixth-form leavers' ball.'

Her expression hardened instantly, the way he'd known it would, and the old hostility flared in her eyes. But Ben had been thinking about this for weeks and he was determined to see it through. Even if he got a slap in the face for his trouble, he was going to apologise for that night – ten years too late or not.

'What the hell makes you think I want to talk about that?' she demanded.

'Because you're still upset about it. Aren't you?'

'Christ, Ben, get over yourself. Do you seriously think I'm still dwelling on something that happened when we were teenagers? I mean, do you actually believe you were ever important enough to me to even give it a second thought?'

'That's all right. You can tell me off if you want – I know

I deserve it,' he said. 'Just promise me you won't flounce off until I've explained.'

'Explained what? I barely even remember it so you're wasting your breath. And I do not *flounce*.' She picked up the shampoo bottle again and took a defiant gulp of vodka.

'I think we both know you remember it perfectly well,' he said gently. 'Can I tell you what happened?'

'I know what happened, I was there. Which makes one of us.' She pressed her eyes closed. 'You knew it was going to be my first time. You knew what a big deal it was for me to have it with… with you. And then you weren't even there. You didn't turn up, you didn't call to tell me why, and you never, ever apologised. I mean, how the fuck can you explain something like that?'

'Is that it? Are you done?'

She went on as if she hadn't heard him, ten years' worth of resentment and hurt spilling out of her now the floodgates were open at last. 'Jesus, Ben, I'd even bought sexy pants. I had an Ann Summers red lace bra and thong set and a packet of Pete's best ribbed-for-her-pleasure johnnies from the ladies' loos in the Garter. It cost me all I had saved from my Saturday job and…' she swallowed hard '…and it was also the single most humiliating, devastating experience of my entire life.'

'You know, for someone who barely remembers it, that's a lot of detail.'

She turned to him, the film of tears over her eyes making them glow red in the firelight. 'Do you know who I actually lost my virginity to? Some chinless wonder at university whose name I can't remember and who never even bothered to call me afterwards. I was so drunk I didn't know what was going on. I wanted it to be special – I wanted it to be with you. And instead it was… a mess. Like every date and relationship I've had since. It was you, Ben. You were the one who jinxed me.'

'Bridie, I'm sorry. If I'd known that was how you'd been feeling, all this time…' He hesitated before stretching an arm around her. 'I feel awful about it. I really want to apologise, and to explain if you'll let me.'

'Huh. Explain. I'd love to know what you think you can say that's going to make it all OK again.' She pushed his arm away from her.

'I was a virgin too,' he said quietly. 'Just like you.'

She frowned. 'What? No you weren't.'

'I was, Bridie. I'd never been with a girl before. It was bullshit, all of it — teenage bragging, the sort lads that age excel at. I had a reputation I never earned and I worked hard to hang on to it, because when you're a kid that's the sort of thing that puts you right at the top of the food chain. I never told anyone, least of all you.'

She shook her head. 'No. That can't be true. Louise Marsh told me she'd shagged you after GCSEs.'

'Well, Louise had a reputation of her own to uphold. Everything back then was done through Chinese whispers. I didn't sleep with her, or with anyone until after I'd left school.'

'So… why?' She turned those big, wet eyes up to him again, and he fought against the urge to take her in his arms and kiss the tears away. 'You didn't want to lose it with me. Is that it? You wanted to hold out for someone special?'

'Now come on, does that sound like me?' He caught the look in her eye and dropped the teasing tone. 'You were special to me, Bridie. I pretended you weren't and it was just mates messing about, like I pretended I had a lot of experience. The truth was, I really liked you. A lot. That's why I never showed up that night.'

She frowned. 'You really liked me so you stood me up for a date and turned me down for sex? Wow, Ben.'

'I was terrified, that's why. Scared shitless I'd get it totally wrong with the fittest, sexiest, funniest girl I'd ever known. And being a teenage boy, instead of facing up to it like a man I ran away and hid from it, head firmly thrust into the sand. God's honest truth, that was what happened.'

'But… why not just tell me that? You think I'd have cared you had no experience?'

He sighed. 'I meant to. Not to confess – I was far too embarrassed for that – but at least to apologise for standing you up. I was trying to get my nerve up to talk to you about it when everything kicked off at home – I mean, with my dad. It wasn't long afterwards that Mum found out what he'd been up to and slung him out. And then… then we'd both gone off to uni and I'd missed my chance. I'm sorry, Bridie.'

Bridie was silent for a moment, frowning.

'Why not tell me after though?' she asked. 'You've had years to put it right.'

'I was ashamed. Worried you'd laugh at me,' Ben murmured. 'I genuinely thought you'd forgotten all about it. You never mentioned it.'

'Well, no. I told you, it was the single most humiliating experience of my life. I thought if you knew how much you'd hurt me, you'd just use it as ammo.'

He shook his head. 'That's not fair, Bridie. I know I tease you but I'm not cruel, am I?'

'No. Just annoying.' She gazed into the fire, watching the flames lick around the big log blazing in the centre. 'I wish you'd told me before.'

'I should have. I'm sorry.'

She looked up at him. 'Why now, Ben?'

'I just… it's been on my mind.' He met her eyes. 'So now you know everything, are we proper friends?'

'Well, I don't know. Maybe. I need time to think about it.'

'And… there isn't anything you want to tell me, is there?'

She frowned. 'Like what?'

'Well, sort of anything you might want me to know. About how you feel or… anything.'

'Not that I'm aware of, no.'

'Are you sure? Because I wouldn't… I opened up to you because I trust you, Bridie. You can do the same. It's OK, really.' He reached out to tilt her chin up so he was looking into her eyes. 'I think you might be surprised by my answer.'

'This is… strange,' she murmured. She gazed into his face, her brow knitting into a puzzled frown, as if there was something in his features she couldn't quite place. 'What does it remind me of?'

'I don't know, what does it remind you of?'

'I'm… not sure.'

He ran a finger over her cheek. 'Tell me what you're feeling, Bridie,' he whispered. 'I need to hear it from you.'

'Honestly, I don't know what you mean.' She stared into the crackling fire for a moment, then seemed to rouse herself. 'I'd better go to bed. We have to be up early. Thanks again for the tent, Ben.'

He looked up at her as she stood to go. 'And do you forgive me? I'm sorry, genuinely.'

She hesitated.

'I don't know,' she said at last. 'It hurt a lot, for a long time. Like I said, I need time to think about it.'

'I never meant to break your heart.'

She snorted. 'Oh right, I bet you'd love to believe that.' But she softened when she saw the earnest expression on his face. 'No, you're right. It did feel… devastating, at the time. I don't know if I can forgive you just like that, but... well, it means a lot that you apologised finally.'

'I'm sorry it wasn't sooner.'

'Me too.' She turned to go, paused, then turned back. 'Ben?'

'Yeah?'

'Happy birthday, eh?'

———

Bridie had been snuggled into her sleeping bag for an hour, but she couldn't fall asleep. Her brain was too preoccupied with thoughts of Ben and what he'd told her.

So there had been an answer to the mystery of The Great Sixth-Form Leavers' Ball Jilting after all. Ben Kemp, the biggest slapper in their year with a reputation almost as huge as his ego, had had no more experience with girls at eighteen than she'd had with boys. She could scarcely believe it.

And... he had liked her. Liked her as more than just a friend who happened to come with a convenient pair of boobs attached. God, if she'd only known all this before! For years she'd let that night colour her love life, her view of men; everything. Her view of men like Ben in particular – or what she'd thought were men like Ben.

But today, he'd seemed... different. Warmer, kinder, genuinely solicitous for her comfort and good opinion. There'd been no teasing that wasn't affectionate and good-natured, no sparring, no sarcasm, no barbs of wit at her expense; not even when she'd goaded him. He was the Ben of old again – the boy she'd fancied rotten back at school – and in spite of their history, she'd felt herself softening towards him.

She pulled the sleeping bag higher. It was chilly in the one-man tent with no other human bodies to keep her warm. Bridie was sure she was going to wake up with an icicle dangling from the end of her nose, like in the old Tom and Jerry cartoons or that bit at the end of *The Shining*. And if it was cold in here, Ben must be shivering like a jelly sleeping out by the fire – which was probably by now no more than a glowing ember.

The trekking tent was designed to be as compact as possible but it was just about big enough to accommodate another person, if they didn't mind sleeping on their side, sardine-style, and forgoing all sense of personal space.

Bridie closed her eyes and counted a few sheep, trying to ignore the voice of conscience in her head. But it was no good. Sighing, she shuffled out of her sleeping bag, put on her crocs and went to find Ben.

When she emerged, an ostentatious sunset was bathing the moors in lilac and yellow. Ben lay awake by what was left of the fire, taking in the spectacular sight through the slit in his bright orange bivvy bag. Bridie approached and poked him with her foot.

'All right, come on,' she whispered.

He blinked. 'Why, where am I going?'

'There's room for you in the tent if you don't mind squashing right up. No funny business, OK?'

'Are you sure?'

'No, but I can't have your frozen corpse on my conscience. It'll upset Hattie and Cal if you drop dead right before the wedding. Up you get.'

He shuffled out of his bag, slung it over his arm and followed her inside the tent.

'Don't touch me, all right?' she whispered as she watched

him extract his sleeping bag from the waterproof outer layer of his bivvy bag.

'I'll have to touch you a bit, Bride. There isn't space to keep my hands completely to myself.'

'Well, OK. But no touching any of the important bits.'

He smiled. 'That's not what you said on our Duke of Edinburgh.'

'That was then. This is now. And you'd better be out of here by the time the kids wake up too.'

'OK. And hey, thanks for rescuing me. It was bloody freezing out there.'

'Well. I couldn't let you catch hypothermia on your birthday, could I?' she said, with just the hint of a smile. 'Why didn't you tell anyone it was today?'

'There's just something about twenty-nine I can't help finding a bit depressing,' he said, sighing.

'I know what you mean.'

'How come you knew? I thought you'd have forgotten the date years ago.'

She shrugged. 'Saw it on Facebook.'

'You couldn't have. I took it off my profile a while back.'

'Well, then I guess… it just stuck in my head,' she said, feeling her cheeks pinken. 'It's no big deal. I've got an amazing memory for dates.'

Ben smiled. 'OK.'

When they were both cocooned in their bags, he spooned into her back and flung one arm over her.

'We don't have to cuddle, do we?' she whispered.

'We do in a one-man trekking tent. Anyway, it'll help if we share body heat.'

'Well, just watch the boobs, that's all.'

'Always.'

Bridie could feel his hot breath on the back of her neck.

Half unconsciously, she shuffled back a bit so her body was pressed more closely against his. For the warmth, naturally. Nothing more than that.

Already she could feel herself drifting towards sleep. The comfort of another body against hers seemed to have a lulling effect, convincing her inner primordial cave-lady that it was now safe to drop defences.

'Night then,' Ben whispered, his mouth close to her ear. 'Thanks again for this. As birthday presents go, I've had worse.'

'That's OK.' Her eyes felt heavy, and she snuggled more tightly against him. 'Ben?'

'Sorry, Bride. I promise, that's completely involuntary.'

'Oh, for God's sake.' She glanced over her shoulder to look at him. 'That night at the leavers' ball…'

'What about it?'

'Was that a date? Did you ask me to go with you because you wanted me to be your girlfriend, officially?'

'Course I did. I told you, I really liked you. More than liked you. I wish I'd had the guts to tell you that back then.'

'I liked you too.' She fell silent for a moment. 'Long time ago, eh?'

'Very long time ago.'

'Yeah. I guess so. Night, Ben.'

'Goodnight, Bridie.'

SIXTEEN

Cal was rummaging around in his loft looking for the spare two-man tent Ben had asked for when a message from Joanna popped up.

How are you feeling, babes? I bet the wedding nerves are kicking in now! x

He threw the tent he'd been looking for down through the hatch then picked up his phone to reply.

Bloody terrified! That's normal, right?

No good asking me ;-p BTW I'm round your way tonight. You still fancy meeting up? I'm dying to meet Hattie x

Hat's away this weekend, Cal messaged back. *She'll be back Sunday though.*

No good, I'm only here till tomorrow x

Well, I'm free this evening if you're happy to make do with me. Chicolini's in town good for you?

Mind if we make it your place? Sorry if that's a bit cheeky. I don't want to spend the whole time signing autographs, that's all x

Wow. Jo really did occupy another world now, didn't she? It was weird to think of his ex as this big celebrity who couldn't go anywhere without being mobbed by fans. Cal struggled to make sense of it. Maybe if she was a film star or something he could get his head around it, but online make-up tutorials? Still, that was the world now, he supposed. Anyway, he was glad she was doing well for herself.

OK, come on over, he said, and texted her his address.

Thanks, babes. Can't wait to see you xxx

You too. Oh, but I've got none of that special milk for Conrad's coffee. What kind does he have? I'll nip out for some. Cal knew from Joanna's Facebook posts that her new husband was vegan.

It's just me. Con couldn't make it. See you at your place in half an hour x

Half an hour, bloody hell! He hadn't realised she was that nearby.

Cal hesitated a moment, his gaze still fixed on the phone. This was OK, wasn't it? When the plan had been for all four of them to meet up somewhere in public it hadn't felt like there was anything wrong, but now... he had this nagging feeling Hattie might be a bit peeved if she knew Joanna was coming over, alone.

That was fair enough, he supposed. Having his sexy ex over to the house while his fiancée was away on a trip did look a bit... well, if it was the other way round Cal wasn't sure he'd be too keen on it. But it was all innocent, despite how it might look to a casual observer. Joanna's fame meant coffee shops and pubs were off limits, and Cal hadn't realised she wasn't bringing her husband when he'd invited her. Besides, they were just two old married people – or nearly married, in his case – catching up after a lot of years. That was fine. Hattie trusted him; he knew that.

Still. There was a look he'd seen on her face when anyone brought up the subject of Joanna that made him think Hat was... not jealous of his ex exactly, but at least uncomfortable about the idea of him with her. Cal didn't want anything upsetting Hattie in the run-up to the wedding, just when she ought to be enjoying her status as a bride-to-be. Innocent as it all was, it might be best if he didn't mention Joanna's visit. His ex would be gone tomorrow and that, Cal expected, would be the last he'd hear from her.

'Darling!' Joanna said when he opened the door to her half an hour later, her face glowing with pleasure and immaculately applied cosmetics. She threw herself at him for a hug. 'Oh my God, it's been so *long*!'

'Hiya, Jo.' Cal patted her back while she embraced him, casting a nervous glance at the surrounding houses. 'Um, come in, please. I've got the kettle on.'

He showed her into the living room and gestured for her to take a seat on the sofa.

'I'll make some coffees,' he said. 'Still milk, no sugar?'

'You haven't got anything stronger?' Joanna asked. 'It's a little late for caffeine.'

'I've got some of Hattie's chardonnay in the fridge.' Cal paused as it occurred to him that if Jo drank that, Hattie would notice it was missing – he never drank white himself. That meant he'd either have to lie about who'd visited or top it up, which felt like a level of subterfuge beyond just keeping quiet about his ex-girlfriend's visit. The idea made him uncomfortable.

'Er, actually, no, she's run out,' he said. 'Merlot?'

'Oh no, I can't drink red. I've just had my teeth whitened,' Joanna said, looking appalled at the idea. 'Never mind. I was saving this for later, but we may as well open it now.'

She reached into her handbag and handed him a bottle.

He stared at it. 'Veuve Clicquot. Bloody hell. I hope you didn't buy this specially.'

She shrugged. 'It was a gift from one of my sponsors. They're always sending the stuff. I've got a fridge full of it at home.'

'Um, right. I'll pour us a couple of glasses then. I haven't got any flutes, I'm afraid.'

He went into the kitchen and popped open the bottle, peeping back at Joanna skimming her phone on the sofa. She was wearing a knee-length skirt – probably by some big-name designer, not that he was any sort of expert – which she'd pushed higher so she could cross her long, silken legs. Joanna looked out of place in his little living room, among the pot plants and IKEA furniture: too colourful, too beautiful, too... unreal. Suddenly, Cal really wished Hattie was there.

'Here you go,' he said, presenting Joanna with a glass of champagne. He was about to sit down in the armchair when she patted the seat next to her on the sofa.

'No need for you to sit so far away, babes,' she said with a broad smile. 'We did share a bed for quite a long time, in case you'd forgotten.'

'Er, no. I hadn't.' He hesitated a moment before sitting beside her, trying to keep a bit of distance between them on the two-seater sofa. 'So, um... what was the gig then?'

'Sorry?'

'The speaking gig you came up for.'

'Oh, that. Just a trade conference I was asked to address. Huge bore, but the money was good.' She glanced at him. 'Are you still at that garage?'

'That's right. I run the place now.'

'Oh, well done you,' she said, patting his arm. 'I knew you were destined for big things one day.'

OK. Did she mean that to sound patronising, or was she genuinely trying to pay a compliment? It was hard to tell with Joanna. Everything she said was in that same soft purr, the tone giving nothing away.

'Thanks,' he said. 'I guess life's pretty different for you these days, right? You've certainly come a long way from the make-up counter at John Lewis.'

She smiled. 'I forgot that's where I was working when we met. Feels like a lifetime ago, doesn't it?'

'It was a lifetime ago.' Cal awkwardly sipped his champagne, hoping it wouldn't make him belch. 'Um, so, what happened to Conrad?'

'He got a better offer,' Joanna said, smiling a little sadly. 'The wrap party for this thing he's been filming. To be honest, I was glad I had an excuse not to go. I know they look down on me, all his friends from the TV world.'

'Really? Why?'

'They never say anything, but it's as if… as if acting's a legitimate talent, whereas as far as they're concerned I'm just some glorified face painter.'

'But make-up's a skill too. You'd think people in film and TV would appreciate that.'

'Mmm, you'd think. Funnily enough, the set make-up lady rarely gets invited to the wrap party.'

A painful silence settled on them. Cal fiddled self-consciously with the stem of his glass.

'Sorry you won't get to meet Hat after all,' he said finally. 'She's supervising a Duke of Edinburgh expedition with school.'

'That's a shame. Another time, maybe.' Joanna was quiet for a moment, staring into her glass, before suddenly bursting into laughter. 'Oh God, Cal.'

He blinked. 'What's funny?'

'We are. Sitting here all awkward, like we didn't share our lives for nearly a year. Honestly, this is so silly.'

He laughed too, relaxing slightly. 'I guess it is a bit.'

'There's loads I want to talk to you about. I was thinking about it all the way up here. I suppose it's just been so long, we've gone all shy.' She rested a hand briefly on his knee. 'Hey, you remember that summer we were flat broke and we hitch-hiked down to Southport with our last £50 for a weekend break?'

Cal smiled. 'Course I do. It rained the whole time we were there.'

'We had plenty of fun staying in though, didn't we? I'm surprised the B&B didn't fine us for disturbing the other guests.'

'I remember.' He sighed. 'It feels so long ago.'

'Hang on. I'll top us up.'

She stood up to fetch the bottle from the kitchen and refilled their glasses, then sat back down a little closer to him.

'You ever miss it?' she asked.

'What?'

'Being young. No responsibilities. I can't imagine trying to hitch-hike today, when so many people know my face.'

Cal took a sip of his refreshed champagne. He wasn't used to drinking fizzy stuff and it was going to his head a bit, making him feel woozy, but the alcohol was definitely helping his nerves. 'God, yes. All the time.'

'Who'd have thought we'd ever get this old, eh? Proper jobs, husbands, wives…'

'I know. I don't feel any older inside.' He smiled. 'Still, I can't wait to spend my life with Hat. Have kids with her. The next stage is pretty terrifying but it's exciting too.'

He looked up at Joanna when she didn't say anything. 'What about you and Conrad? Think you'll start a family?'

'We can't,' she said quietly, breaking eye contact. 'Conrad's… he's not able to.'

'Oh, Jo, I'm sorry. I should never have opened my big mouth.' Cal hesitated, then squeezed her hand. 'What about adoption? Is that an option for you?'

'Conrad isn't interested. If he can't have his own then he'd rather focus on his career, he says.'

'But you feel differently.'

'What does it matter if I do?' Joanna said. 'That's what Conrad wants, so… that's that. I knew the state of play when I agreed to marry him.'

Joanna had taken hold of his hand when he'd reached out to squeeze hers, and Cal didn't pull it away.

'You are happy though?' he said. 'You love the guy, right?'

Joanna shrugged. 'I do, but…' She trailed off into a sigh. 'I wonder, sometimes, how my life might've been different if it hadn't gone down this route. If I'd have been happier just being an ordinary schmuck, like you and Hattie.'

Cal laughed. 'Thanks.'

'Hey, that's a compliment,' she said, smiling. 'You don't know how lucky you are, babes. I'd kill to go out and not be recognised, or go to a party where I don't get sneered at by "proper" celebrities who think I'm a fraud. Some nights I dream of those days when we were together, eating chips out of the paper and sharing a can of Tizer. The ordinary things I never thought I'd miss.'

'I thought you loved that lifestyle. Mansions, swimming pools, all that stuff. You told me you dreamed of a life like that.'

'Course I did. When we met I was living in a back-to-back in Leeds, surviving on beans on toast.' She sighed. 'And now I spend all my time dreaming of that life I used to have. Ironic, isn't it? I never realised wealth and fame came at such a high price.' She pressed his hand and let it drop so she could pour them another drink from the bottle at her feet. 'Where do you think we'd be now, Cal? If we hadn't broken up, I mean.'

'Well not hitch-hiking to Southport,' Cal said, laughing.

'Why did we split up anyway?'

He shrugged. 'You got offered a job in Liverpool. I wanted to stay here. Just one of those things.'

'Do you think we'd have stayed together if I hadn't?'

'I don't know, Jo,' Cal said, gazing into his glass. 'It was fun while it lasted, but we grew up into pretty different people, don't you think?'

'It was fun, wasn't it?' Joanna said, her eyes clouding with nostalgia. 'We went well together. In the bedroom, at least.'

She was closer to him now. Cal could feel her body pressing against his side while they talked: feel the warmth of it, and smell the slightly sickly scent of her expensive perfume. Hattie wouldn't like that, would she? He tried to shuffle to put some space between them without it being too obvious, his brain foggy from the unfamiliar alcohol he was drinking.

'I guess we did,' he said. 'But let's not talk about that. It was a long time ago.'

'I know.' She sighed. 'Well, I'm glad you found someone you love, Cal. I wish Conrad and me could have what you and Hattie do.'

'I'm sorry. I never realised you guys were having problems. You look so happy in all your Facebook photos.'

'Of course. Putting a face on for the cameras is what we do,' she said with a sad smile. 'We rushed into things really, getting married so soon after we met. We got offered a lucrative deal by this big cosmetics company who wanted to sponsor our wedding and it felt too good to turn down.'

Cal blinked. 'Seriously, you guys got married for a sponsorship deal?'

'Partly,' she said, grimacing. 'Does that make me sound like an awful person?'

'Well, no. I mean, who am I to judge? It's just so far removed from the world I live in. I can't imagine committing my life to someone for the sake of a business opportunity.'

She regarded him for a moment. 'You take it very seriously, don't you? All this marriage stuff.'

'Course,' Cal said. 'I mean, it's for life, isn't it? I couldn't vow to love someone until death unless I was one hundred per cent sure I meant it.'

'Cal, you're like a Boy Scout or something. All those principles I used to love you for.' She sighed. 'You really must think I'm awful.'

'Don't be daft, I don't at all.'

She smiled. 'You know, I think this has been good for me. Talking to you. You're just so… ordinary.'

Cal finished his champagne. 'Gee, thanks.'

'Sorry, that didn't come out right. Real, that's what I ought to have said.'

He blinked. 'Right. What, like Pinocchio?'

'You know what I mean. My whole life now is full of fakes and flatterers. It'd never occur to them that there was anything odd about arranging a wedding for the sake of a sponsorship deal. You're the only person who'll still tell it to me like it is.'

'Oh. Well, er, happy to help, I guess.'

'Another drink?'

Cal glanced at the bottle. 'We finished it, didn't we?'

'We finished that one.' Joanna flicked her long blonde hair over one shoulder so she could reach into her capacious designer handbag, emerging with a second bottle of Veuve

Clicquot. 'What do you say we make a night of it, eh? It's so nice to have someone genuine to talk to for a change.'

'I really shouldn't, Jo. I've got work tomorrow, and a long drive to drop off a tent afterwards.'

'Go on.' She rested her long fingernails on his thigh. 'It's been years since we've seen each other, and I think we both know it'll probably be years till we see each other again – if we ever do. Let's drink to the old times.'

Cal hesitated.

'Well… all right,' he said. 'But just one more glass.'

SEVENTEEN

At 7am, Bridie's phone alarm went off. Sleepily she patted the area next to her in the tent, then forced her eyes open when she found it empty.

Ben was gone, and so was his sleeping bag. He must've cleared out before the kids and other teachers worked out where he spent the night, just like she'd asked him to.

That was good. Obviously sharing a tent had been through necessity only, to stop one of them freezing to death, but Duxbury would be bound to kick up a stink if he knew. The kids would take the piss something chronic too.

Still, Bridie couldn't help feeling a swell of disappointment that she hadn't woken up in Ben's arms. She'd eventually given in to the low temperature the night before and let him embrace her in a full cuddle, and his body around hers had just made her feel so... safe.

Of course, that would've been the same for anyone who'd happened to be here last night. She probably wouldn't even have objected if it had been Duxbury snuggling up to her, it had been that bloody cold. There was nothing special about it being Ben: he'd just been a convenient warm body with a decent pair of arms attached.

She sat up, groaning at the effort of changing her position. She felt stiff and sore all over after her day's walking, there were blisters on both feet, her shoulders ached from carrying the heavy rucksack and she had it all to do again today. At least tomorrow they'd be going home though. Bridie hugged herself at the thought of it. In twenty-four hours, she'd be back in the great indoors again. She was already fantasising about hot baths, Netflix binges and her warm, snuggly pyjamas.

Unfortunately, however, that was tomorrow. Right now the best she had to look forward to was a tepid shower and a singed bacon butty.

She threw on some warm clothes over her pyjamas, slid her poor sore feet into her crocs and unzipped the tent to go see about the possibility of a shower. Annoyingly the kids had beaten her to it, little sods, and there was already a queue for the two shower cubicles.

'All right, I'm cutting in,' she told the girl at the front of the line. 'Teachers get first dibs on showers.'

She grinned. 'Yeah, nice try, miss. Mr Duxbury said no queue-jumping allowed, not even for teachers. He told us we were to tell you that you had to queue just like the rest of us.'

'Huh. Should've known.' She glanced down the line, noting which students were missing. 'Where are Josh and pals? Are they still in bed?'

'Nah, they wandered off that way,' the girl said, pointing to a nearby bank of trees. 'Kelly said she'd found something interesting and came to fetch her mates to have a look at it.'

'Hmm, that sounds worrying. I hope it's not a hallucinogenic fungus they're gobbling down or something. We'll be overrun with wallabies.'

'You what?'

'Never mind.'

Bridie left them and headed into the trees to see if she could locate the missing kids. She discovered Kelly, Josh and Emma on their knees in the damp grass, snickering as they peeped through a bush at something.

'What're you lot gawping at?' she demanded.

'Miss, shhh,' Josh whispered. 'He'll hear you.'

'Who'll hear me?' She stood on tiptoes so she could see what they were looking at over the top of the bush.

There was a sort of waterfall a little way down in a valley – well, really more of a trickle than a fall, dribbling down a mossy rock face. Underneath it was Ben, shirtless, rinsing his long hair. He looked like a bloody Herbal Essences advert.

She frowned at the kids. 'You're spying on him having a shower? Not cool, you guys.'

Josh shrugged. 'He's got his trousers on, hasn't he? If he doesn't want people to look then he should use the proper showers.'

'All right, leave it now. Go get in the queue with the others. We have to be out of here in an hour and a half.'

'Aww, go on, just a bit longer,' Kelly pleaded. 'We've got a bet on which bit he washes next. I reckon definitely his bum.'

'You're not sitting around here waiting for him to get his bum out. Go on, sod off before I tell Mr Duxbury on you.'

'Ugh. We thought you were one of the cool teachers.'

'Well, you were wrong. I'm easily the uncoolest person I know. I still wear underwear with the days of the week printed on it.' She jerked a thumb over her shoulder. 'Now hop it.'

With a last lingering look at the topless Ben, the kids trudged off back to the shower block. When they were gone,

Bridie made her way precariously down the track that led into the valley.

'Oi. Prince of Thieves.'

Ben glanced around. 'Oh. Hi, Bride.'

'What the hell do you think you're doing?'

He shrugged. 'Just trying to wake myself up. The queue was a bit long for the shower block and I was craving cold water.'

'I just had to chase off three randy adolescents who were perving at you. Can you get your clothes on please, before there's a major scandal?'

He glanced up to the hilltop. 'Really, they can see me from up there?'

'Yes, they had a great view. They were taking bets on whether you might be about to get your arse out.'

'They'd have been disappointed.'

She glanced at the water tumbling down the rock face. 'Aren't you worried you'll get cholera or something?'

'Don't be daft, this is healthy running water. We survivalist types know what we're doing.'

She shook her head. 'You honestly think you're Bear Grylls now, don't you?'

'Yeah, he wishes.'

He pushed his sodden curls out of his eyes, and Bridie found her gaze dwelling on his broad, firm chest and well-defined stomach muscles. He really did have a great body, thanks to a combination of vanity and the sort of work he did. It was a shame it had to belong to someone who exploited it so shamelessly.

He grinned when he noticed her eyes lingering on his bare torso. 'Fancy joining me? Feel free to jump in.'

'No I don't. Just get your shirt on, can you? I can't talk to you when you're like that.'

She turned away from him, trying to banish the image of all that naked flesh. God, it really must be a long time since she'd last had sex if her thoughts were wandering in that direction…

'Overcome with lust, right?' Ben said, nodding soberly. 'Well, I don't blame you.'

'Ugh. You're unbearable.'

'And yet here you still are, unable to leave me alone.' He hopped out from under the flow, grabbed his towel from a rock and started rubbing his hair dry. 'So, did you sleep well?'

She snorted. 'I'm surprised I managed to sleep at all with you poking your boner into me all night.'

He shrugged. 'I didn't do it on purpose, did I?'

'Seriously, mate, are you permanently on heat?'

'No, that just tends to be what happens when attractive women wriggle their shapely backsides into my crotch. That's how men work, Bridie. I didn't design us.'

'Hmm. I hope Cal's there at the other campsite with an extra tent when we arrive, that's all.'

He smirked at her through the folds of towel. 'Why not just admit you enjoyed it? When I woke up this morning, you were snuggling up to me like a favourite teddy. Practically mounting me, you were.'

'I was cold and it's a tiny tent. You were the closest thing to a hot water bottle. Don't think it means anything.'

'Come on, don't go all prickly again,' he said, smiling warmly. 'You know, you can be surprisingly pleasant company when you deprickle.'

She could do without him smiling at her like that. The smile alone Bridie could cope with, but the smile combined with the wet curls dripping on his face, plus his bare, water-beaded torso and the year's worth of celibacy, was just too much.

'Ben, shirt, please,' she muttered, pressing her eyes closed.

'All right, if my body's so upsetting to you.' He pulled his T-shirt back on and approached her. 'There, all covered up. Happy?'

'Ecstatic. Come on, let's get out of here before people talk. I need breakfast, coffee and a shower before I can function today, in whatever order they happen to present themselves.'

'Hang on.' He rested a hand on her shoulder. 'Bridie, before we go back…'

'What is it?'

'Last night. What we talked about.'

She turned around to face him. 'Do we have to go through that again? I'm still trying to process it. There'll be other times… other places for this conversation.'

'There was something else I didn't tell you. Something I was too afraid to say, but… I think you deserve to know it.'

'What?'

'Back then, when we were kids, I actually think…' He drew in a deep breath and exhaled slowly before going on. 'I think… I was kind of falling for you. That's why I was so afraid of being with you that night. Those feelings were new and frightening, and I didn't know what to make of them. There's the whole truth of it.'

Bridie stared at him. 'You can't mean that.'

'I bloody do mean it. That's what I've been working out, these past few weeks since… since I started thinking some stuff through. There were a lot of things I had to dig in deep to find out about myself and that was the biggest one. I didn't understand it fully at eighteen but I do now.' He curled one arm around her waist to draw her to him. 'Bridie, I'm sorry,' he said softly. 'Sorry for not telling you then. Sorry for nearly wimping out of telling you now. You deserved to know all this a long time ago.'

She looked up into his eyes, keen and intense, fixed on her face. 'Ben, I… I really don't know what to say,' she whispered.

'You might tell me you felt the same.' He trailed his fingertips over her cheek. 'And that… maybe it's not too late for us?'

'Us?' Everything felt dreamlike suddenly, with the little waterfall chattering behind them, the scent of early-blooming heather and the wail of calling curlews in the air. Unreal, weightless, just as it had the night of Hattie's party, out on the veranda with Bruce…

'Us,' Ben repeated softly. He bent to connect his lips with hers, and Bridie's arms snaked around his neck as she allowed herself to kiss him back.

'God, I missed this,' he whispered when he drew away. 'You still taste like cherries, Bride.'

His eyes looked almost liquid this close up: a deep, mellow brown, with that expression in them – that old, familiar expression she remembered so well from schooldays, sort of laughing and sad both at the same time. And that jawline, covered now in Ben's customary designer stubble rather than clean-shaven as it had been the night… the night of…

'Oh my God!' She struggled out of his arms and pushed him away.

He frowned. 'Bridie? What's wrong?'

She shook her head, laughing. 'Christ, I've been blind! It was you, wasn't it? It was fucking *you*!'

'What was me?'

'Don't play dumb. That night at the party. Bruce.'

He looked taken aback. 'I... well, yes, all right. I'll admit it. It was me.'

'So *that's* why! That's why you suddenly decided to rehash all this stuff from the past.' She put a palm to her forehead. 'I can't believe I was that *naive*. This whole thing, it's just been one big seduction ploy, hasn't it? You knew how I felt about what happened at the ball, and so you... you exploited it to make me like you again! Why, Ben? Because I'm the only girl in town you haven't been to bed with yet? Had to have the full set, did you?'

'Bridie, no! That isn't it at all. Come here.'

He tried to embrace her again, but she pushed him away, tears in her eyes.

'For the second time in my life you've made me look and feel like a complete fool, Ben Kemp,' she whispered. 'You, a virgin, at eighteen! *Falling* for me!' She curled her lip in disgust. 'God, what an utter crock. And despite knowing exactly what you're like, what you've always been like, I went for it just like the stupid, inexperienced girl I was the first time you pulled this crap on me.'

'It wasn't a crock, Bridie. Honestly, that's what happened.'

He rested a hand on her shoulder, but she pushed it away.

'Don't touch me, Ben. Don't come near me,' she said in a choked voice. 'I might've made the mistake of believing you once, I might even have been mug enough to do it twice, but a third time? Not a chance.'

Shooting him a look that, if there was any justice in the universe, really ought to have the power to strike him stone dead, she marched off back to the camp.

EIGHTEEN

Hattie was frowning at her phone when Meg joined her at the fire circle.

'What's up, Hat?' she said.

'Just wondering why Cal hasn't rung me back. He said we could have a chat before bed last night but there was no answer when I called him.'

'Probably nodded off in front of the TV.'

'That's what I thought, but he ought to be up and on his way to work by now. I left him two voicemails and a text and he hasn't responded to any of them.'

'Because he knows he'll see you later. He's dropping off an extra tent for us at the next site.'

Hattie brightened. 'Oh yeah, I forgot about that. Hopefully we can sneak in a cuddle before he has to go home again. I know it's only been a day, but I'm missing him like mad.' She cast a glum look at the phone. 'A fair bit more than he's missing me, if he can't even manage to stay awake for my call.'

'Oh, give the lad a break. He's probably just tired.' Meg

nodded towards Bridie marching in the direction of the cluster of teacher tents in the distance, face like a wet weekend, with a sodden-haired Ben jogging behind her as if trying to get her attention. 'Looks like there's trouble in paradise.'

Hattie frowned. 'What's she got that face on her for? They seemed like they were on the verge of being all over each other last night when we left them alone, reminiscing about how much they fancied each other at school. I really thought we'd cracked it.'

'Well, something's obviously got her back up.'

Hattie watched as Bridie studiously ignored Ben calling her name.

'She knows,' she muttered.

Meg frowned. 'What, that Ben's her Batman guy? How would she have found that out? We've sworn everyone to secrecy.'

'I don't know but she does. I can tell.'

Bridie ducked into her tent, pointedly zipping it up in Ben's face when he tried to poke his head in after her. He hovered outside for a moment, then, obviously deciding it was best to give her time to cool off, wandered away somewhere else.

'Maybe we shouldn't have hidden it from her after all,' Meg said.

'No, this is good, I think.' Hattie turned to face her. 'We can use this to our advantage. It's time for stage two, Meggy, and I reckon I know just how to do it.'

'How?'

'Bridie's not had her shower yet. She's probably gone into her tent to grab her wash stuff. And I know for a fact that while she's got five full shampoo bottles in her rucksack, not a single one of them contains any actual shampoo. She forgot to pack any.'

Meg grinned. 'Ah. Gotcha.'

'Me, you and Ursula need to lurk somewhere she can't see us and watch. When she works out she hasn't got any shampoo, she'll nip into our tent and help herself to mine, like the thieving mare she is. That's when we all take our places outside to have The Chat.'

Meg nodded. 'Right. Let's find Ursula and get cracking.'

———

Bridie yanked the tent zip down in Ben's face, only narrowly missing the skin of his stupid freckled nose. Then, when he could no longer see her, she burst into tears.

She did her best to be quiet, whispering her sobs, while she waited to see if he'd try to follow her inside. He didn't though; she could hear him walking away. Once she was sure he'd gone, she gave in and let herself have the good cry she so badly needed. She seemed to be spending a lot of this trip in tears, for some reason.

Well, not for some reason. For one specific reason. Ben bloody Kemp, of course. What else?

This was what happened when you lowered defences. She'd been lulled by exhaustion and vodka and kindness into forgetting the one promise she'd ever made to herself: that she'd never, ever trust Ben Kemp with anything again as long as she lived, least of all her heart. Why had she let herself believe him? She knew he had a line for every woman he met; that when it came to sex he'd say anything to get what he wanted. The nostalgia evoked by finding herself on another expedition with him, reminding her of when they'd first begun a physical relationship – the heady thrill of those early fumbling, exploring touches – had overruled every jot of good sense she had.

So he'd been laughing at her, had he? This whole time, he'd been laughing in his sleeve at her – and sneering at her too, probably. He'd tricked her into a kiss at the party, when she hadn't known who he was, and again just now when she'd allowed herself to forget, briefly, that promise she'd made to herself.

God, the party. Her cheeks burned with humiliation whenever she thought of it. The way he'd let her open up to him, tell him her most painful secret, when at any time he could have revealed who he really was. What for? To score off her? To seduce her? He hadn't wanted her ten years ago, but that didn't mean to say he wouldn't sleep with her now if the chance arose. Bedding her would be the ultimate victory for him, wouldn't it? Then he could finally declare himself the winner in this little war they'd been trapped in now for nearly a decade.

'Ugh!' She glared at her washbag, then, on a sudden impulse, picked it up and threw it hard at the side of the tent. It bounced off the canvas and hit her in the face.

'*Fucking* thing!' she muttered, rubbing her cheek. 'He's even trained his bastard tent to injure me. Stupid tiny bastard fucking stupid *Ben* tent.'

She heard a voice shouting outside – Duxbury's voice.

'Last call for showers!' he yelled. 'I want everyone lined up here, washed and fed with their kit packed, in no more than an hour. Spit spot, you lazy sods.'

Bridie sniffed, wiping her eyes on her sleeve. There was no time for wallowing now. She had to get showered and dressed so she could go do her job. She started pulling out the various bottles of shampoo she'd packed.

Dry hair, greasy hair, coloured hair, conditioner, heat treatment serum...

'Bollocks,' she muttered. Every single one of them was filled with booze. How the hell had she managed to forget to bring actual shampoo? She had five bottles of what were ostensibly hair treatment products but not a single one she could actually put on her hair, unless she wanted to spend the day stinking of sauvignon.

Hat would have some though. She was always the organised one. Bridie unzipped the tent and looked around the campsite for her friend.

There was no sign of her, or Meg or Ursula either. Where were they? Helping the kids pack up?

'Come on, Ms Morgan, get a shift on,' Duxbury said sternly, noticing her head poking out. 'We need to be out of here soon.'

'Yes. I just, um... need to get something I left in Hattie's tent.'

'Mmm. Need to swap some of your shampoos, do you?'

'No. Er, toothpaste. She's got our toothpaste.'

'All right, off you go then. Don't drag your boots.' He wandered off in the direction of the children's tents to give any malingerers a poke with a sharpened stick.

Bridie unzipped Hattie's tent and crawled in, fastening the door behind her. Her friend wouldn't mind her going through her stuff, she was sure. They did it all the time at home. Housemates of three years' standing could have no secrets from each other, just like they couldn't have any property to call their own.

At least, for as long as they were housemates. Bridie was currently trying very hard not to think about the fact that in just three weeks' time, she'd be losing her Hattie when Cal came to take her away. Another Kemp determined to cause trouble for her, she reflected savagely, even though she knew that wasn't fair.

Which rucksack was Hat's? It was a bit dim inside the tent, with the sunlight filtering through the orange canvas to make everything look the same colour. Deciding it was almost certainly the middle one, Bridie started pulling out the shampoo bottles nestled among pairs of walking socks and thermal underwear.

She popped open the first bottle and gave it a sniff. Nope, that was definitely merlot, not the aloe vera extra moist it claimed to be. The second... pinot noir, she was sure. The third was vodka...

Hang on, no, that couldn't be right. Hattie hadn't packed any spirits. This must be Meg's bag.

She turned to the one next to it and started unpacking a liquor cabinet's worth of shampoo bottles from that instead. God, this was going to take a while...

Footsteps squelched in the mud outside, and Bridie froze. It wasn't Ben, was it, come to seek her out again? He was the last person she wanted to talk to now, just when she'd managed to get her emotions back under control before another long day's walking. She kept completely still, breathing as quietly as she could while she waited for him – if it was him – to go search for her somewhere else.

'Well, our lovesick little puppy looked very cheerful last night, don't you think, girls?' a voice said.

Bridie frowned. That was Ursula, wasn't it? What was she talking about, lovesick puppies? Not Adrian? Bridie knew things were going well with him and Meg, but it was a bit early for that kind of talk. They'd only had four dates so far.

'I know,' another voice said with a laugh – Hattie's voice. 'He had that dreams-do-come-true look in his eyes when Bridie was being all soft and smiley with him, didn't he?'

Bridie stiffened. Her? They were talking about her?

'Cal's definitely sure, is he?' Meg asked Hattie. 'I mean, do you really believe Ben's feelings for her are as strong as his brother makes out they are?'

What? Bridie gripped the tent's groundsheet, her head spinning.

'I don't need to believe it. Cal had it straight from the horse of a different colour, as Duxbury might say,' Hattie told her. 'Ben confided everything to him over a beer two weeks ago. It all just came spilling out: how he'd fallen for her when they were kids; how he went travelling to try and get over it, but as soon as he saw her again it was back as strong as ever. How afraid he was to let her see his feelings because of the way she always is with him.'

Bridie couldn't have moved now if she wanted to. She felt numb in every limb. Her breath seemed to be stuck in her throat.

Fallen for her… when they were kids… the very echoes of Ben's words at the waterfall, right before he'd kissed her. But that had been a lie, surely. Just a trick, because she'd made the mistake of telling him he'd broken her heart when she'd believed he was Bruce that night.

'She is very hard on him,' Ursula said. 'Poor lad, you can see in his eyes how it upsets him.'

'I know,' Hattie said soberly. 'Mind you, he did hurt her a lot once. She's got a right to be sore about it, hasn't she?'

'That was so long ago though.'

'Yes, but it's part of her now, that pain. I honestly don't think she'll ever be able to put it behind her and trust him again.' Hattie sighed. 'Poor Ben. Ten years trying to suppress how he feels; keep it all inside. Cal told me that when Ben confessed it all to him a fortnight ago, it was the first time he'd seen his brother cry since they were kids. I think that was the day Ben finally realised he couldn't lie to himself about it any more.'

Bridie felt a twinge in her chest. A fortnight ago – that was when she'd seen Ben at the flat. The day he'd claimed to be ill from some unspecified sickness, when he'd looked so rough and behaved so strangely towards her.

Now she thought about it, Bridie wasn't sure she'd ever seen Ben cry as an adult either. He wasn't the sort to show emotion easily: he never had been. Had she done that, made him cry? She hadn't meant to really hurt him when they'd been trading insults. She thought he was impervious to emotional pain: as undentable in that respect as he was shameless. Besides, he'd always seemed to enjoy their sparring, just as she did.

And yet... no, it couldn't be true. She didn't believe it – she wouldn't. Cal must've got the wrong end of the stick somehow. Ben Kemp, in love with her! Ben, who didn't do marriage or love or relationships or even second dates, sobbing into his pint because he didn't dare tell her how he felt. It simply wasn't possible.

'I think you're right,' Meg said to Hattie. 'She really sounds like she hates him when she talks about him. I don't think she ever will be able to put it behind her, what happened between them.' Meg fell into thoughtful silence for a moment. 'It's a shame, I've always liked Ben. He's got a good heart under that put-on cockiness. I hope he can get over it and meet someone else to make him happy.'

'He'll have plenty of women who can comfort him in his little black book, I suppose,' Ursula said.

'I don't think casual sex is a very healthy way to get over lovesickness, do you?' Hattie said. 'Cal reckons all those years sleeping around, never having a proper girlfriend, was just denial about his feelings for Bridie. I doubt yet another one-night stand is going to be anything more than a temporary sticking plaster for him.'

'Does Bridie know it was him who kissed her at your party?' Meg asked.

'Course she doesn't. We promised we wouldn't tell, and there's no one else who knows about it.'

'Why did Ben swear us all to secrecy like that? Adrian's not too happy at having to pretend it was another man I was with that night.'

'I guess he was embarrassed. Embarrassed that he'd let his feelings get the better of him and given in to that desire to be close to her. He told Cal it was just so wonderful to see her being sweet to him for a change, he couldn't help himself.'

'So what will he do? Do you think he'd ever tell her?'

'I don't know. I sort of thought last night, when she seemed to be softening to him, there was a chance. But she had a face like a slapped arse on her when I spotted her running away from him earlier so I think it's back to business as usual this morning.' Hattie sighed. 'Well, it's none of our beeswax, I suppose. I'm certainly not going to stick my beak in when there's a risk of my future brother-in-law getting hurt. They'll have to sort it out between them.'

'And if they don't?'

'Then that's that, isn't it? It's a pity though. I think they could really make each other happy, if they could just put their past behind them,' Hattie said. 'Come on, let's go see if the kids have got these bacon sarnies going. I'm starving.'

Bridie heard their footsteps retreat as they wandered off to the cooking area.

She slumped back, feeling dizzy. What had she just heard? Ben Kemp, the major crush of her teenage years, the first and last boy she'd ever loved, her worst enemy... and one of her best friends, when you got right down to it. He loved her. He loved her! The only words she'd wanted to hear him say at one point in her life. His failure to do so – his total and utter rejection of her, and his subsequent embrace of what felt like the entire female population of their hometown – had sown the seeds of discord and bitterness towards the whole idea of love. And yet all this time, all these years, he'd…

That meant it was true. He really had fallen for her at school, just like he'd said. When he'd told her that under the layers of swagger and ego there'd been just an insecure, sexually inexperienced teenage boy, falling in love for the first time, confused, terrified of getting it all wrong… that had been true too. He'd hidden his identity at the party, kissed her, not as a trick but quite simply because he hadn't been able to help it. Tricks and games, taunts and teases, the foundation of their relationship as adults – it was all just a shield to hide what he really felt.

What about her, how did she feel? Her heart was thumping in her ears; her stomach was flipping double somersaults; she felt dizzy, light-headed and sort of strangely elated, but that didn't mean she had any romantic feelings for him. It was far more likely to be an anxiety attack.

What should she do? Find him? Talk to him?

No, not now. She needed time: time to think. She needed to get through this trip and go back home where she could work things out.

There was the sound of the tent unzipping, and she jumped.

'Ben,' she said when his head poked through. Her lips flickered with the beginnings of a smile at the sight of his face. It was funny how different he looked to her, now she knew what he felt. How much softer.

'I wondered where you'd got to,' he said, in that deep

voice with the eternally laughing edge to it that she knew so well. 'Can we talk now you've calmed down a bit?'

'Not now. There isn't time, we have to leave soon. And besides… no, Ben, sorry.'

'I won't go until we're friends again. Look, I'm sorry about the party but I genuinely wasn't lying. Everything I've told you this weekend has been one hundred per cent the truth, I swear to you.'

'Yes. I know that now.' She managed a smile. 'I'm not angry, not any more. It's just all so… overwhelming. I have to get through this expedition then take time to think about it properly. Will you respect that?'

'Of course, if that's what you need. Just tell me you believe me and I'll give you as much space as you want until you're ready to talk.'

'Thanks, Ben. I do believe you.'

'What made you realise I was telling the truth?'

'Oh, just… thinking it over. Sorry, I shouldn't have been so quick to flounce off.'

He smiled. 'I thought you didn't flounce.'

'Maybe on very special occasions,' she said, returning the smile.

'All right. Well, you know where I am.'

He withdrew his head and left her alone. Bridie, feeling more confused than she had done since she was eighteen years old – waiting outside the school sports hall in a Monsoon ballgown and a lacy thong set for a date who was never to appear – exited the tent with her head whirling. The bottles of shampoo lay forgotten on the groundsheet.

NINETEEN

Bridie sat on her bed, smiling as she flicked through the photo album she'd dug out of storage.

So many memories. Photos of her as a child with her mum and dad in the garden of their old house on Messington seafront, before her parents had left the town two years ago for a seaside of rather warmer persuasion in Italy. Her as a gawky teen with her fringe in her eyes, sitting with the rest of the kids in her English set on the last day of school after GCSEs.

Where was Ben? Bridie scanned the group and soon located him in the back row with the popular kids, next to Louise Marsh, trying to look cool by casting a bored glance anywhere but at the camera.

That was around the time Louise had bragged to Bridie and a group of other girls about how she and Ben had celebrated finishing their exams, with a big bottle of Blue WKD and a quickie under the slide in the kiddies' playground. Louise had always relished telling stories about her sexual feats to an audience of awed virgins. Had it really been total fiction, all the time? There'd been a lot of detail. Bridie still remembered Louise's in-depth descriptions of the goodies Ben had been packing underneath his grey school trousers as a sea of unblinking schoolgirls had listened rapt. No wonder she'd always got such good marks for creative writing.

Bridie flipped the page to look at the next photo. Ben was in that one too. It was his birthday party – his fifth, she guessed – and he was sitting behind a huge cake, beaming broadly, with chocolate all round his mouth. Bridie soon found herself in a group of kids behind him, giggling as Ben's dad Jonny entertained them with a couple of hand puppets.

Ben and Cal never saw their dad now, or spoke to him as far as she knew: not since it had all come out eleven years ago. The string of affairs their mum had known nothing about; the mistresses Jonny seemed to have squirrelled away in every town he travelled to in his job as a sales rep. The scandal had rocked Messington. Jonny Kemp had been – or at least, had seemed to be – a kind man, well liked around town and devoted to his family. Bridie remembered him as being funny like Ben, but quieter in his disposition, more like his younger son. And all the time it had been nothing but a smokescreen for his womanising. One day, one of the mistresses decided she'd had enough of being someone's dirty little secret and contacted Alison Kemp to fill her in on her husband's extra-curricular activities.

Bridie looked at the little boy in the photo, grinning as if nothing bad could exist in the world as long as there was chocolate and cake, and felt a surge of pity for him. Back when it had all happened, she'd been smarting so much from being jilted at the ball that she'd never fully considered what a horrific shock it must have been for him. She could only imagine what it felt like to discover something like that about someone you loved.

She flicked through a few pages of photos spanning the decades, instantly homing in on Ben in each one he was in. They'd shared a lot of their lives, now she thought about it – the number of photos they both appeared in was testament to that. Here was Ben dressed as a robot for the town fete procession aged about eight, his skinny little legs painted silver and his head in a foil-covered box. Teenage Ben with his arms around two girls in some nightclub, looking mightily pleased with himself. A passport-sized photo of Ben and her in a photo booth, Bridie grinning at the camera while he kissed her on the cheek. It had been taken in the days when they'd been not-quite-dating, not long before it all went tits up.

She stopped on that one for a moment, smiling, before taking it out and slipping it into her pocket.

It was three weeks now since they'd arrived home from the Duke of Edinburgh trip and Ben had been as good as his word, leaving her alone apart from a few businesslike messages about the Sten arrangements. Bridie knew she needed to talk to him, but what the hell did she want to say?

Her feelings were… confused, to say the least. She'd spent a lot of time thinking about Ben these last three weeks – in fact, she'd struggled to think about anything else. One minute she'd feel white-hot anger towards him, remembering how he'd kept the truth from her all these years about one of the most painful experiences of her life. She'd reflect on all the bad dates she'd been on, all the failed relationships, every one of them stemming from that formative night of the leavers' ball when Ben Kemp had stood her up. The next minute, she'd remember the look in his eyes when he'd kissed her at the waterfall, recall everything she'd overheard her friends saying about the strength of his feelings, and experience a rush of fondness for her lifelong friend-slash-enemy that reminded her of those heady days when they'd first become more than just friends.

She'd loved him then, in her naive schoolgirl way. But now she was an adult, and love at seventeen was a long way from love at twenty-nine. Over and over Bridie asked herself the question: how did she feel? Was she in love? In love with… with Ben Kemp?

She stumbled over it every time she tried to think about it. Her brain seemed to be rebelling against coupling the word 'love' with the name 'Ben Kemp'. For ten years she'd been telling herself he was the last person she could ever love, and now she tried to think about whether that had only been a screen for other, deeper feelings – the sort of feelings that might end with her getting hurt again – there was some invisible barrier stopping her from admitting it to herself.

And yet it was *Ben, Ben, Ben,* over and over again in her head. Visions of him as a kid, and a teen, and a man. All her life he'd been there, driving her crazy. Making things interesting. Maybe she loved him, maybe she hated him, maybe it was a bit of both, but one thing, at least, Bridie was forced to admit to herself: she couldn't do without the bastard.

She jumped as a knock sounded at the bedroom door.

'Can I come in?' Hattie called. 'Brought you a drink.'

Hastily, Bridie closed the album.

'Yeah, come on,' she said.

Hattie came in and put the cup of tea down on Bridie's bedside table before perching on the bed beside her.

'The final cuppa, eh?' she said, smiling a little sadly. 'I can't believe I've spent my last night in this place. Feels weird, doesn't it?'

Bridie sighed. 'It feels awful, Hat. I mean, sorry, I know

you're excited for your new life with Cal and everything. I'm going to miss you something rotten, that's all.'

'I know, love. Me too.' Hattie glanced at the photo album. 'What's that?'

'Just some old pics I was looking through.'

'From sixth form?'

'Yeah, some of them.' Bridie frowned. 'Why?'

Hattie shrugged. 'Just a hunch. What've you hunted those out for? Feeling nostalgic?'

'Not especially. I just thought I might stick a few up on the school alumni page.'

'Any of Cal in there?'

Bridie smiled. 'How did I know you were going to ask that?' She flicked to the photo of Ben's fifth birthday party. 'There you go. Cute as buttons, wasn't he?'

'Aww.' Hattie simpered at the four-year-old surreptitiously trying to steal a Smartie from a bowl at his brother's elbow. 'I hope our kids get his cuteness gene.'

'That's their dad,' Bridie said, pointing out Jonny.

Hattie scowled at him. 'That prick. He looks so nice, doesn't he?'

'Yeah, he seemed it too. It was a massive shock when everyone found out what he'd been up to. Although not nearly as big a shock as it was for Alison and the boys, obviously.'

Hattie pulled the album to her and flicked through some pages.

'Oh,' she said when she got to the place the passport photo of Bridie and Ben had until recently inhabited. 'There's one missing.'

'Is there?' Bridie tried to look surprised.

'Yeah. Did you take it out?'

'No. Must've come loose. I'm sure I'll find it in a drawer

somewhere.' Bridie took the album back and closed it. 'You all right?'

Hattie shook her head. 'How do you always know when I'm not?'

'I've lived with you for three years, Hat. Some women get synchronised periods; I get synchronised mood swings. What is it then?'

She sighed. 'I was standing in the supermarket queue with Mrs Bradley this morning. You know, Cal's neighbour? Well, my neighbour as of later today, I guess.'

'All right. I know Penny Bradley can talk for England but she isn't all that traumatising, is she?'

'No, it's just… well, you know her eyesight's pretty poor.'

'Yes, and?'

'She asked me… she asked me what had happened to the new hairdo.' Hattie's tone was filled with suppressed anxiety.

Bridie frowned. 'What new hairdo?'

'That's what I said. So she said she was sure last time she saw me, I'd gone blonde. I told her I'd never dyed my hair; I had a bad reaction to bleach. So she just said "Oh", and tried to change the subject.'

'That's weird.'

'I thought so too.' Hattie looked down at her fingers twisting together. 'Anyway, I pressed her on it and she said she thought she'd seen me going into Cal's three weeks ago with this new look. She'd remarked on it to her husband; said it suited me.'

Bridie shrugged. 'It probably was you. Like you said, her eyes aren't what they used to be. She is eighty-four.'

'It couldn't have been me though, could it? We were away on the D of E trip.' Hattie closed her eyes. 'And she said… Bride, she said she was sure it must've been me, because her and her husband were sitting in their conservatory all night and… and this woman, whoever she was, never came back out. She must've stayed overnight.'

Bridie shook her head. 'Nah. Penny'll have nodded off and not seen whoever it was come out. Who would Cal be having sleepovers with?'

'All right, suppose she did come out. Who was she in the first place though?'

'A mate, probably. He has got mates who are girls, you know. I can think of half a dozen old schoolfriends it might be.'

'I know.' Hattie fell silent for a moment. 'I just keep thinking, that would've been the night he was supposed to wait for my call and I couldn't get hold of him. Then he turned up to camp with that tent, obviously hungover, saying he'd fallen asleep on the sofa. If it was a mate, why be coy about it? I'm not so possessive I mind him having women over; I just worry when he goes out of his way to hide it from me.'

'He didn't go out of his way. He just didn't mention it, that's all.' Bridie put an arm around her to give her a squeeze. 'Hat, you know I'm quite prepared to believe in any amount of twatty behaviour by men, but Cal Kemp is the perpetual exception to that. He wouldn't do anything to hurt you. If he didn't mention it, there'll be a perfectly innocent reason why.'

'Like what?'

'A surprise for the wedding, probably. I bet she's a baker or something and he's plotting with her about cakes.'

Hattie brightened a little. 'Yeah. I guess that might be it.'

Bridie smiled. 'You know, you never used to be this paranoid before you were getting married.'

'Bad, isn't it? I don't know if it's the nerves or that it feels like I've suddenly got more to lose.'

'Talk to Cal about it if you're worried. I'm sure he'll put your mind at rest.'

'You're right. Thanks, love.' Hattie looked up as the doorbell rang. 'Speak of the devil. That'll be him, come to help me finish packing.'

'Shall we ignore it and hope he goes away?'

Hattie smiled. 'Sorry, Bride, but we can't put it off forever. One way or another, I'm moving out today.'

Bridie sighed. 'I suppose I'd better help then, if you will insist on leaving me. You two finish upstairs; I'll pack up the living room.'

———

Ben glared at the notepaper he was writing on, covered in scribbles and crossings-out, before crushing it into a ball and throwing it over his shoulder to join the mountain of crumpled sheets currently filling the wastepaper bin in his bedroom.

Ugh! Why was this so *hard*? The words were all there in his head. It was just getting them onto the page in the right order that seemed to be giving him trouble.

He hadn't heard from Bridie since they'd come home from the Duke of Edinburgh expedition, aside from some brief, perfunctory replies to his messages about the arrangements for the Sten trip to Blackpool next month. He had no idea, right now, what she was feeling. All he knew was, he couldn't stop thinking about her.

Now he'd finally admitted his feelings to himself, he found that Bridie Morgan was in his thoughts night and day. He went to work and every little thing reminded him of her, whether he was taking a group of kids climbing at Little Monkeys' Junior Activity Centre (monkeys were Bridie's favourite animal and top of her ideal pets list), leading a canoeing trip (Bridie hated canoeing but had always wanted to go on a gondola ride in Venice) or eating his lunchtime sandwiches (never prawns, because he knew Bridie hated the smell of them on his breath). He thought about her when he was falling asleep, remembering how she'd snuggled into him that night on the expedition and imagining how it might feel to fall asleep like that with her every night. He thought about her when he was actually asleep, when both teenage and adult versions of her haunted his dreams. And when he woke up, she was the first thing on his mind.

He had to tell her. It was the only way to exorcise the Bridie-ghost currently living rent-free in his brain. And if she rejected him, well, then he'd... he'd... shit, she wouldn't do that, would she? She loved him – Cal had said so. That was all that was keeping hope alive right now.

The question was, how to approach the thing. She might love him, but she didn't trust him: that much was obvious. Well, why should she? He'd broken her heart, then spent the ensuing years sleeping with half the girls in town while teasing her mercilessly every time they ran into one another. Not that she hadn't always given as good as she'd got in that respect, but trading verbal blows all the time was hardly the foundation of a solid romantic relationship.

And Ben knew, now, that a relationship was what he wanted. For the first time in his life, the idea of settling down with just one woman didn't fill him with existential dread. Cal was right: he couldn't live the way he had been doing forever, and if he was going to take a punt on monogamy then there was no one else he wanted to do it with but Bridie Morgan. She was perfect.

Well, all right, not perfect. She had a quick temper, that was certain. A sharp tongue, too; he had the scars to prove it.

He'd noticed when she wore her hair up that her ears stuck out a bit. But when Ben thought of those things, they just made him smile to himself and long to see her all the more. God, he missed her: temper, sarcasm, ears and all.

Had she believed him when he'd confessed everything to her at camp? She'd said she had, but then why hadn't she been in touch? Was she still angry with him for kissing her under false pretences at the party?

He stared at the fresh sheet of paper, again trying to arrange the jumble of words in his head into some sort of order. This had seemed like such a good idea, getting them all down on paper where Bridie could read them instead of having to listen to the sort of gibbering nonsense he tended to come out with when he tried to speak to her in person. But every time he put pen to paper, it came out wrong.

He tried again.

Dear Bridie,

I wanted to write to explain about stuff, since it always sounds daft when I try to say it to your face. The truth is, I think you rock. You're really fit and I don't even mind your sticky-out ears or anything like that. I wouldn't change a thing about you, Bride, promise, because I—

This was the bit where he always lost the flow. The word he wanted to write, the word he knew he had to write, just sounded so... final. He had a horrible image of Bridie reading it to herself then cracking up laughing, right in his face.

But it needed to be in there, or what was the point? He closed his eyes, then forced himself to go on.

—because I love you. There, I finally said it. I actually don't think I love anything in the world as much as you. That's weird, right? I suppose I've been hiding from it for years, just like you have. I thought you hated me so I buried it deep inside me. Now I know that's not true, I know that it's OK to tell you I feel the same way you do. Or I hope you

do. Cal said you did. Anyway, I guess what I'm asking is: Bridie Morgan, will you go out with me? Sorry that question's ten years later than it should've been.

That's all,

Ben x

PS: I miss you when I don't see you for ages.

PPS: I think you're really funny even when you're being a dick to me. Also, your arse is fucking amazing.

PPPS: Sorry this letter's so shit.

RSVP (that's French for write back)

When he was done, he looked over what he'd written and grimaced.

Ugh, this was worse than his last attempt. *I think you rock? I don't even mind your sticky-out ears? Your arse is fucking amazing? Christ almighty, Ben.* Evidently he was not a natural composer of the classic love letter. And Bridie was an English teacher: she was used to reading poems and sonnets and all that sort of soppy crap. He crumpled it up and sent it to join its brothers in the bin.

Ben stared at the blank sheet of paper underneath for a moment, hesitated, then got to his feet.

Right. This was not working. If he couldn't confess how he felt in writing, he'd just have to man up and go do it face to face.

He looked at the box that had been delivered that morning, containing the T-shirts for the Sten do in a month's time. That gave him an excuse to go over to Bridie's place without looking too desperate or stalky, at least. But first, he needed to get changed: something a bit more fitting for a love declaration than his current outfit of baggy T-shirt and lounge pants. He opened the cupboard to select an outfit.

TWENTY

'What about Jeff the Giraffe?' Cal said, picking up the stuffed toy from the top of Hattie's chest of drawers. 'Am I throwing him in a box with the rest of your rubbish or do you want to transport him separately? I know you've been weird about putting toys in storage since I let you watch *Toy Story 3*.'

Hattie was sitting on the edge of her bed, gazing absently at a framed photo of the two of them she always kept on the bedside table.

'Hattie?' Cal said when she didn't answer.

'Hmm?' She looked up. 'Oh. Sorry, love, did you ask me something?'

'Come on, Hat, wakey wakey. I can't pack you up all on my own.' He pecked at the side of her face with Jeff the Giraffe, hoping to make her laugh, but she only smiled vacantly.

'What's up, sweetheart?' he said gently, putting the toy down and sitting by her on the bed. 'I thought you'd be bouncing with excitement today. I've been thinking about nothing for weeks but the day I could finally take you home with me to keep.'

'Sorry, Cal.' She leaned over to kiss his cheek. 'I am excited, promise. I suppose I can't help feeling sort of sad at the same time though. The end of my old life, beginning of a new one. I can't wait to wake up with you every day, but I'll still miss Bridie to bits.'

'Hey, Hat!' Bridie's voice called up the stairs. 'I found your Zara top in with my whites all shrunk, so I'm going to cut it up for dusters, all right?'

'She pinched it out of my ironing and hid it in her room, she means,' Hattie whispered to Cal. 'She always did think it looked better on her.' She raised her voice to shout back. 'Yeah, OK. If it's ruined you might as well have it.'

'Thanks! Hey, do you really want this *Tape Deck Heart* album? Because the sleeve would look great on the wall in my bedroom.'

'Oh, no. You're not having any of my vinyls. Put it in the record box with the others.'

'Ugh. All right.'

'You sure you'll miss her?' Cal asked Hattie, smiling.

'To pieces,' Hattie said. 'Although I'm beginning to regret accepting her offer to help me pack. I'll have nothing left by the time I make it to your place.'

'Our place, you mean. You'd better get used to calling it that.'

'I guess I had.'

Cal lowered his voice. 'How's the plan going, do we think?'

'Well, Bride seemed a bit dazed after we worked the old "overheard conversation" trick on her at camp but I think it definitely worked,' Hattie said. 'She's barely mentioned Ben to me these past few weeks.'

'Is that a good thing?'

'When she insults him to me at least four times a day usually? I think it is. Plus, get this: I caught her going through an album of old photos before. She had the gooiest look on her face when I walked in on her, and I know for a fact she snuck one of them out. I'd bet anything it's of Ben. How's your guy getting along?'

'A bit the same. Half in a dream, forever gazing off into the distance like he's modelling underpants or something, irritable for no reason. He hasn't even looked at a woman since he overheard me and Pete talking, let alone chatted anyone up, which is a miniature miracle in itself.'

Hattie smiled. 'We make quite a team, don't we? Dishing out happy endings like workaholic fairy godmothers.'

'I like to think so.' Cal held his palm up for Hattie to high-five.

'Shall we give them another nudge, do you think?' he asked her. 'They can't just sit around being lovesick forever.'

'No, we've played our part. They'll come together of their own accord in the end, I'm certain of it. Especially with a lovely romantic wedding on the horizon.'

'Except they hate romance. And weddings,' Cal said, laughing.

'They want us to think they do. That'll soon come crashing down when they give in to their feelings.' Hattie looked back at the photo of her and Cal together and smiled. 'That was a good day, wasn't it? When we went to the fair?'

'And there'll be many more good days to come. I can't wait to spend my life with you, Hat.'

'Yes,' she murmured, her gaze still fixed on the photo. 'Yes. I genuinely believe that.'

'All right. Not quite the response I was expecting.' Cal

took her hand and gave it a squeeze. 'Are you sure you're OK, love? You've been away with the fairies all afternoon.'

'I'm OK. I told you, it's just overwhelming. Everything changing.'

'Are you sure that's all?'

'Yes.' She sighed and put the picture down. 'No.'

He felt a stab of worry. 'What is it then?'

'Cal… that night I was away, when I rang and you didn't answer…'

'I said I was sorry about that. I fell asleep.'

'Is that all?'

'Well, yeah.' He frowned at the anxious expression on her face. 'Why?'

'I wondered if, um… if you might've had friends over or something. You looked rough as hell the next day at camp.'

He looked into her eyes, filled with worry and love, and sighed. 'All right, I'll come clean. I wasn't lying; I did fall asleep waiting for you to ring. But before that… Joanna came over.'

'Joanna! Your ex Joanna?'

'Yeah. She was up this way talking at a conference or something and she asked if we could meet to catch up.' Cal knelt in front of her to take her hands. 'Sorry I didn't tell you, Hat. It was supposed to be the four of us meeting up for a drink – me and you, and her and that actor bloke she married. Then you were away, and she wanted to come to the house, and when she turned up without the husband and a bag full of champers…' He sighed. 'I thought it might upset you, the idea of us alone together. I know you don't like thinking about me with her.'

Hattie shook her head, drawing her hands away. 'What upsets me is you hiding it from me, Cal. I mean, what am I supposed to think when I hear about attractive blonde women dropping round while I'm away and not leaving until the next morning?'

Cal frowned. 'Eh? She left around ten.'

'That's not what Mrs Bradley said.'

'Well, she got it wrong. I told Jo to go out of the back door so the neighbours wouldn't see.' He took one of her hands again and gave it a squeeze. 'You didn't honestly think I'd spent the night with her, did you? You can't believe I'd do that to you, Hat.'

'Well, no, of course not, but… I mean, obviously I trust you, Cal, but you did lie about her coming over.'

'I didn't lie about it. I just didn't mention it. I didn't want you to get upset over such a little thing, that's all.'

She raised her eyebrows. 'A little thing?'

'Well, it was a little thing. It just might've looked like a bigger thing and I didn't want it preying on your mind in the run-up to the wedding.' He bowed his head. 'Sorry. That was stupid, wasn't it?'

She nodded. 'Enormously. What did you get up to then?'

'We had a few drinks, talked about old times. It was pretty awkward, to be honest, but I didn't have the heart to cut it short early. She seemed so… dunno, sort of sad.'

Hattie snorted. 'Sad? Cal, she looks like a supermodel and she's got an Olympic-size swimming pool in her backyard.'

'Her marriage doesn't sound very happy. I felt a bit sorry for her,' Cal said. 'Anyway, I'm glad it's over and we can go back to being just Facebook friends.'

'Are you?'

'Yeah. I told you, the whole thing was a bit awkward. She seemed pleased to see me, but we didn't have anything to talk about except stuff we did together years ago. Honestly, I was squirming the whole time. It feels like we don't have much in common now she's living this new life. Our worlds are just too different.'

Hattie smiled. 'Thanks, Cal.'

He pressed her hand to his lips. 'So, am I forgiven?'

'You're forgiven. Just be honest with me next time, all right? However dodgy something might look, it looks ten times worse for hiding it. That's not what husbands and wives do, is it? We need to be able to trust each other completely if we're in this thing for life.'

'I know. I hated to think of you brooding on it, that's all. When we look back on this part of our lives, I want it to be filled with joy and wonderful memories. I don't want it spoiled by something so silly.' He sat by her on the bed and pulled her into his arms. 'I love you, OK, Hat?'

'I love you too,' she said, smiling more warmly than he'd seen her do all day.

He smiled too. 'So was that it then, our first big fight?'

'I guess it was.'

'What do you say we try to make it our last?'

Hattie laughed. 'I don't think marriage works like that, but it's a noble aim.'

'Let's get the rest of your stuff packed up, eh? I've got a bottle of prosecco chilling in the fridge to celebrate our first night as roomies.'

'No, love. No prosecco for me tonight.' Hattie put a hand on his arm to stop him standing up. 'Cal, there's something else I need to talk to you about.'

———

After the last box of her things had been packed, Hattie threw her arms around Bridie, who was waiting in the living room for her last goodbye.

'Bride, I'm going to miss you so much,' she whispered.

'Me too, sweetie.' Bridie swallowed a sob. 'God, you've got no idea how much. Best housemate in the world.'

'I'll visit all the time. Three times a week. No, four. And stay over on Fridays so we can still do marshmallow hot chocolate night. Promise.'

'Um, am I going to get to see anything of you at all?' Cal asked.

Bridie released Hattie to glare at him. 'No one's talking to you. Housemate thief.'

'Yeah. I'm sorry about that.'

'You don't deserve her, you know.'

'I know I don't, but I'm lucky enough to have her all the same,' Cal said, smiling fondly at Hattie. 'I hope you can forgive me one day, Bride. I never meant to make her fall in love with me; it just happened.'

'Yes you did. You and your evil male wiles, seducing inno- cent young women. You know, between you and that brother of yours—' She stopped.

'Between us what?'

'Nothing.'

He came over to clap her on the back. 'Well, you know you're welcome to come round to ours anytime. I hope your new housemate lets you steal their stuff just as much as this one always has.'

'No, I'm done with house-sharing. I don't think there's anyone else in the world who could put up with me apart from Hattie. I'm going back to living alone, like I was before.'

Hattie frowned. 'You're not going to advertise for someone else? You never told me that.'

'Well. I didn't want you to feel guilty.' Bridie embraced her again. 'All it means is that your room will still be your room, whenever you want to stay over. And of course when it doesn't work out with Cal and you inevitably come running back to me.'

Cal shook his head. 'You're wicked, Bridie Morgan. Putting a curse on us when we're about to get married.'

'Oh, you know I'm only kidding,' she said, smiling. 'You guys are perfect together. Come here.'

She let Hattie go and pulled him into a hug.

'All the happiness in the world, Cal,' she whispered. 'Just you look after my Hattie, that's all, or you'll have me to answer to.'

'I will.' He gave her a fond squeeze and released her. 'You're sure you won't be lonely rattling around this place on your own like Miss Havisham?'

'Are you kidding? I can't wait. I can put my feet up on the sofa without getting told off by Miss over there, I can pick all the telly, I can walk round in the buff and I can sing in the kitchen as loud as I like while I cook. I'll be living the dream.'

'You never know, it might not be for too long,' Hattie said with a smile. 'I'm still convinced you'll meet someone perfect for you one of these days. Before long I bet this place will be heaving with husbands and bouncing Bridie babies.'

'You know, Hat, it's traditional to just have the one husband at a time,' Cal said. 'At least, I'm hoping that's something me and you are on the same page about.' He nudged Bridie. 'What do you reckon, Bride? Is there life in the old girl yet?'

'Well… we'll see,' she said, flushing slightly.

Cal raised an eyebrow. 'We'll see, will we? That's certainly progress from "men suck and I'm taking holy orders". You're not thinking about getting out dating again, are you?'

Hattie clapped her hands. 'Ooh, yes please! I've missed Bridie dating stories.'

'No. Not dating,' Bridie said. 'But… I guess I'll take what comes. That's my new life motto.'

'I like it. Very carpe diem.' Cal looked at Hattie. 'What do you think, future wife?'

'I think there are good things on the horizon for all three of us,' Hattie said. 'This time next year, I predict happiness and love for everyone in this room. You wait and see.'

Bridie smiled. 'Well, thanks, Mystic Meg. Go on, you'd better go while you still can. I'm literally seconds away from throwing myself at your legs and begging you not to leave me.'

'Yes, I suppose it's time.' Hattie gave her a last peck on the cheek. 'Bye, my love. You take care of yourself, eh? We'll see you really soon, I promise.'

When she'd gone, Bridie took one look around the bare, cheerless living room, denuded of all Hattie's possessions, and burst into tears.

TWENTY-ONE

Bridie was still snuffling to herself half an hour later when the doorbell rang. She swore at it for interrupting her pity party, then wiped her eyes on her sleeve and went to answer it.

'Ben,' she said when she found him on the doorstep. 'What are you doing here?'

'Um...' He looked awkward, and kind of smartly dressed, as if he was going out somewhere. He also reeked of Hugo Boss again. 'I came to show you the T-shirts. For the Sten weekend.' He nodded to the box in his arms. 'Can I come in?'

'Well, OK. I guess so.'

He followed her into the living room, dumped the box on the coffee table and untucked the flaps to extract a T-shirt.

'Good, right?' he said, holding it up against him.

The T-shirts were classic stag and hen fare: blue for the boys, pink for the girls, with two special bride and groom shirts in white and black. Each bore the legend 'Cal and

Hattie's Stag and Hen' above the date and a cartoon of a stag and a hen gazing lovingly into each other's eyes.

'Stag and hen?' Bridie said. 'I thought we were going to have "Sten" and let the picture do the work.'

Ben grimaced. 'Yeah, but when I came to order them I couldn't stomach it. It sounds like a pharmaceutical company.'

'You could've asked me.'

'Sorry, Bride. It was just a spur-of-the-moment decision. You don't mind, do you?'

'I don't mind the change. I mind not being consulted. We're supposed to be equal partners in this thing.'

'Well, you're right, I should've asked.' He smiled warmly at her. 'Come on, don't be cross with me. I've missed you.'

She flushed. 'Ben, I…'

'That's all right. You don't have to say anything back. I just wanted you to know, that's all.'

'Um, what's the back like then?' she asked, hurriedly bringing the conversation back onto the subject of nice, safe T-shirts.

He turned it around so she could see. 'Just like we agreed. Everyone's got the nickname we picked for them, and then there's the list of dares.'

She scanned the dares, each with a checkbox next to it for ticking off. They were the usual sort of thing, although nothing too naughty for mixed company: make a prank phone call, get a selfie with a celebrity, photobomb a stranger, convince someone to buy you a drink. Bridie lifted an eyebrow at the final one.

'Serenade somebody? I don't remember that being on the list.'

'I wanted to add a surprise one just for you.'

'What for?'

He smiled. 'Well, maybe I fancy singing to you.'

'No thanks. I've heard your karaoke.' But she couldn't help smiling back.

'So, what do you think?' he asked.

'They look great. Thanks for sorting it, Ben.' She grimaced. 'I suppose I should order one of those stupid L-plate and veil sets for Hat. Why do these things always have to be so clichéd?'

'Where is Hattie?'

Bridie smiled sadly. 'Gone to pastures new. Your brother stole her away from me about half an hour ago.'

Ben pressed a palm to his forehead. 'Oh God. I'm sorry, Bride, I'd completely forgotten it was today she was moving out.'

'Well. It had to happen sometime, didn't it? Still, the sudden empty-nest feeling hit me pretty hard, I have to admit.'

'Here, sit down with me.'

He took her hand and guided her to the sofa.

'You've been upset,' he said quietly when they were both seated, examining her bloodshot eyes.

'Not upset really. I'm not such a selfish cow that I resent my best friend getting the happy ending she obviously deserves.' She sighed. 'But… wistful, I suppose. Everything's changing, Ben.'

'I know. Everything feels different since…'

'…since the party.'

'Yeah.' He looked at her for a moment, frowning.

'What's up?' she said, rubbing her eyes self-consciously.

'Nothing. I guess I just don't like seeing you sad.'

She laughed damply. 'Times really have changed.'

'No they haven't. I never liked seeing you sad.' He ran a

finger under her puffy, salt-swollen eye. 'You want a hug, Bride?'

'God, do I? Right now, I'll even take one off you.'

'Good, because you're getting one off me.' He gathered her up in a tight embrace. 'You know, you really ought to stop pretending so hard that you hate me. I'm being nice, aren't I?'

'Sorry, love. Force of habit.' She snuggled deep into the hug and let out a sigh, relishing the feel of those big, safe arms – the ones she'd been dreaming about ever since they'd held her at camp – wrapped around her once again.

'So can we talk?' Ben whispered in her ear. 'You said we could.'

'I know. I ought to have called, I'm sorry. I just… wasn't sure what to say to you.'

'I've been struggling to get the words right too. I actually came here today to…' He relaxed his embrace a little so he could look into her eyes. 'You know now, don't you, that what I told you at camp was true? I really did have those feelings back in school. You were very special to me, Bridie. That's why I chickened out of going to bed with you.'

'Yes. I believe you now.' She tried to bury her face in his chest again, to lose herself there in the warm oblivion of his embrace. That aftershave, the same stuff he'd wear on a big night out when they were teens – the scent she'd always associated only with him – was so familiar and comforting. But he held her back.

'Wait,' he said quietly. 'I want to see your face.'

'Why?'

'What are you feeling, Bridie? No snark today, just God's honest truth. I need to know.'

She took a deep breath. 'I guess I feel… confused, because everything I knew – or thought I knew – is different suddenly. And relieved that there was more to what happened at school than I thought, and… hurt, I suppose, that you only told me now.'

He drew a finger over her cheek. 'I'm so sorry. I'd have told you sooner if I'd known it was still causing you pain.'

She smiled at him. 'How long have you been like this?'

'Like what?'

'I don't know. Sweet. Gentle. Emotionally articulate. Where's that shagging, bragging, swaggering bastard we all know?'

He smiled back. 'That guy? I heard you hated him so I thought it was time he retired.'

'I didn't hate him; not really.' Half unconsciously, she reached up to run her fingers through his hair. 'I mean, he drove me insane, constantly. I always felt that what him and his ego needed more than anything was a really good boot in the balls from one of the many women he'd humped and dumped around here. And yes, I never could quite forgive him for rejecting me when we were kids. But he was fun, and he made me laugh more than anyone else I know, and secretly I missed him like crazy when he wasn't around. Deep down, I knew that if I was ever in any trouble then he'd drop everything to help me out. And… he was one of my best friends. That's the truth.'

'Aww, Bride…' He pulled her closer and buried his face in her hair. 'I always knew you loved me really.'

'Don't go all insufferable about it, will you? I was just starting to like this new you.'

'Don't worry, he's not going anywhere.' He inhaled deeply against her neck, getting her scent. 'You're right, I would've done anything to help you out. It pissed me off that every guy you went out with was too much of a prat to see how incredible you were.'

She smiled. 'Fibber. There's no way you thought that.'

'Hey. Just because I wouldn't have been caught dead admitting it doesn't mean I didn't think it. I even warned one of them off.'

She lifted her face from his shoulder to look at him. 'You never did.'

'Yep. Chris. You remember, he dumped you after your third date? It was right before I went away.'

'What, you were behind that? Gee, thanks. I quite liked him as well.'

'But you deserved better. That guy was bad news, Bride. He's got a worse reputation than I have, and with none of the cuddliness. He'd only have hurt you.'

'A worse reputation than you? Is that possible?'

'There are bigger twats than me in the world, hard as that might be for you to believe. All right, so I've slept with a few girls—'

She snorted. 'A few?'

'More than a few,' he conceded. 'But I'm not a Chris. I'm not one of these bastards who gets off on making women fall in love with them just so they can break their hearts. It's not a crime to have safe sex with people who want to have sex with you, is it?'

'What, so you've never broken a heart?'

'Just once,' he said quietly, his fingers stroking the nape of her neck in a way that made her shiver. 'And I regret it every day.'

She smiled. 'How many women have you slept with anyway?'

'Not nearly as many as you think I have, I reckon. I'm sure I'm not half as bad as this despoiler of maidens and wrecker of marriages you make me out to be.' His eyes darted over her face. 'God, you're hot, aren't you? When did that happen?'

'Why, was I really such a moose at school?' she said, laughing.

'You were gorgeous at school. Now you're something else as well though. Sort of... sensual.'

She raised an eyebrow. 'Sensual?'

'All right, so I was just trying to find a fancy way to say sexy. Could've been worse. I could've said voluptuous.'

'True. That would've been unforgivable.'

He smiled. 'Be patient with me, eh? I'm still finding my feet with this romance stuff.'

'Is that what this is?'

'That's what I was hoping.' He stroked her cheek. 'I've been a pillock, haven't I? We could've been doing this for years, if I'd only told you...'

'Told me what?'

'When I said you were special to me, back at school... Bridie, I want you to know that's still true now. That's why I came here this afternoon, to tell you. The T-shirts were just an excuse.'

She frowned. 'What are you saying, Ben?'

'Well, I...' He rubbed his neck. 'Fuck, this is hard. If you laugh when I say it I'll die on the spot. I mean, you know anyway.'

'I can't be sure until you say it though, can I?'

'All right, then I... Christ.' He closed his eyes for a moment, as if it was a struggle to get the words out. 'Fine. I love you then. Happy?'

She laughed. 'No need to sound so grumpy about it.'

'I'm fighting a battle with the other guy here, Bridie. The one who's convinced I must've gone off my head to even consider it.' He drew her to him. 'Well? What are you thinking?'

'I'm just wondering when you're going to pull your finger out and kiss me.'

He smiled. 'I thought you'd never ask.'

Ben covered her mouth with his, a soft kiss at first, but growing deeper, harder, as all the feelings they'd been bottling up for the past ten years were finally unleashed. Bridie pushed her fingers into his hair, loving the feel of his fingertips pressing into her back, and loving the kiss and his lips and his tongue, so familiar, and yet so strange and new now the two of them were all grown up. She could feel his arousal, his body quivering against her and the echoing tremors that rippled through her own.

'Wow,' she gasped when he broke away for air. 'We're not eighteen any more, are we?'

'Bloody hell.' Ben laughed breathlessly, pushing a few unruly curls out of eyes that had fogged with lust. 'I didn't see that coming. We've seriously been missing out, Bride.'

Already needing to feel him again, she claimed his mouth for another deep kiss, her fingers reaching for the buttons of his shirt.

'Will you stay?' she whispered as she planted kisses on the now exposed flesh of his chest.

'With you? Here?'

'No, with Bug-Eyed Billy in Timbuctoo. Where do you think, thickie?' She nuzzled against his shoulder. 'I don't want you to go away from me just yet.'

'Well…'

She glanced up at him through lowered lashes. 'You don't want to?'

'If you can't tell I do, then I'm seriously worried about how much you know about men.' He stroked her hair. 'I know you've been upset today, that's all, with Hattie moving out. I don't want to take advantage.'

She shook her head. 'You really have changed.'

He smiled. 'You can't possibly have thought that badly of me. Just because I've been a bit of a slut doesn't mean I wasn't always a gentleman. More or less.'

She trailed one finger over his moist, parted lips, still panting slightly from their last kiss. 'It's OK, Ben,' she said softly. 'I know what I want.'

He kissed along her neck, letting his lips linger tantalisingly in each sensitive spot before moving down. 'Dunno, Bride. I'm not sure I'm that sort of boy.'

She snorted. 'I'm sorry?'

'Well, if you're just going to treat me like a sex object. I told you how I felt. I think you owe it to a guy to make him feel valued before he drops his pants.'

She drew her breath in sharply as his lips fell on the exposed skin above her breasts.

'What do you want me to say?' she whispered.

'Come on.'

'All right. I… I suppose… you're very special to me, Ben.'

'Nope. Give it another go.'

'And… I've been thinking about it for weeks and I've realised… I care a lot about you.'

'You're not going to get in my boxers with that sort of talk. That's top-half-only material at best, Bride.'

'Ugh. Fine.' She pressed her eyes closed as his hand slid up her inner thigh. 'All right, I… I love you. There.'

He smiled. 'That's the one.'

She smiled too. 'Feels good to get it out, to be honest. Although it doesn't half sound bloody weird. I never thought I'd say that to anyone, least of all you.'

'Nor me. I didn't believe I was capable of it.' He lifted his head from her chest to kiss the tip of her nose. 'Or maybe I told myself I wasn't, because I never thought I'd meet anyone who'd think I was worth loving back. And then… there was you.'

'Let's go upstairs,' she whispered. 'After all these years, I don't want our first time to be squashed on the sofa.'

'Lead the way.'

TWENTY-TWO

Bridie took Ben's hand and led him up to her bedroom. He followed her in and closed the door.

'Oh,' he said, glancing at her George Clooney cut-out. 'I didn't realise we'd be having company.'

'Don't mind my friend. He's terribly discreet.'

'He's a bit off-putting though, Bride.' Ben swayed from side to side, keeping his gaze fixed on the cut-out. 'Look, his eyes follow you around the room. I don't think I can get naked while he's smirking at me.'

She pushed him down onto the bed. 'Just shut up and get your clothes off. I'll see to George.'

'Bloody hell, this is what you're like in the bedroom?'

'Sometimes.'

'You're terrifying.'

'You want me to stop?'

'Are you kidding me?' he said, laughing. 'Keep going, please.'

Bridie left him taking his shoes and socks off to go to her

cupboard. She took out a scarf and tied it around George's eyes.

'There, happy?' she said, turning back to Ben. 'Or do you want me to dig out some earmuffs for him too?'

'No, the blindfold'll do.' Ben shrugged off the shirt that was already hanging open and stood up to remove his jeans and boxers. 'I'd hate to intimidate him.'

He was completely naked now. Bridie looked his body over and gave an appreciative nod. 'I see what you mean.'

Ben walked towards her and pulled her into his arms. He heard her inhale sharply as his erection pressed against her leg.

'So? Are you going to get undressed as well?' he whispered.

'You do it for me,' she said, smiling. 'This is your area of expertise, isn't it? If we're finally doing this then I want the full Ben Kemp experience.'

'All right.'

He kissed her neck as he removed her top with trembling hands, then reached for the catch of her bra.

Christ, what was wrong with him suddenly? Why was he shaking like that? He'd done this so many times he could usually manage it with just a flick of his thumb and forefinger, yet now he was fumbling away with both hands like a schoolboy on his first go at it.

'Hurry up,' Bridie breathed in his ear. 'Don't tease me, Ben.'

'I'm not teasing.' He leaned over her neck to look at his fingers fiddling with the bra catch. 'Where did they manufacture this thing, Fort Knox?'

She laughed. 'Seriously? That's disappointing. I thought you were an expert in the art of seduction.'

'I was until it was you. Typically you've Bridied it right up. Here, turn around.'

'Oh, give it here. Honestly, you're rubbish.' She pushed his hands away so she could unfasten her own bra and tossed it to one side, then removed her jeans and knickers.

'Fuck,' he whispered, looking down her body.

'What?'

'Nothing, just… you're beautiful, you know that?'

She smiled and stepped forward to kiss him. 'Come to bed with me, Ben.'

'Right.'

Bridie slid under the duvet. Ben climbed into bed next to her, skin pressing against skin.

'So, um, now what?' he asked.

'Don't you know?'

'Well, yes, obviously I know.' He ran a hand over her hip and thigh, trying to smother this strange awkwardness that had arisen in him all of a sudden. It had only got worse when he'd finally seen her fully naked for the first time. 'Is that all right?'

'Yes,' she whispered, peppering kisses over his neck and shoulder. 'That feels good, Ben. Don't stop.'

He shuffled down to kiss her breasts, but as incredible as they were, he knew that things weren't right with him. Somehow, he seemed to have forgotten everything he'd ever known about the art of foreplay. If there was one thing he thought he knew how to do it was please a woman in bed, and yet with Bridie he seemed to be all thumbs. This time it really mattered – this time it was with someone he loved, and knowing he had to get it exactly right was making him a bag of nerves.

God, Ben, snap out of it! He'd fantasised about this since he was a clumsy teenage virgin, and now, finally, he was in bed with Bridie Morgan for real. She was right there under his fingers, his lips; no longer the sarcastic, prickly girl he knew but naked, beautiful and moaning as he caressed parts of her body he'd only ever dreamed about before. And… and he felt like he'd been reset right back to that trembling, inexperienced kid he'd been the last time she'd let him touch her.

He sucked on a taut nipple, then ran his tongue around it. Bridie let out a little gasp of pleasure.

Right. He could do this. He'd done it plenty of times, and he'd not had a complaint yet. She was enjoying it, see? Moaning, arching her back. He just needed to make sure this was the best sexual experience of her entire life, that was all. No pressure.

'Hey, can I go down on you?' he whispered.

'Sounds good to me,' she whispered back.

'OK, great.' He flexed his knuckles. 'I'm good at this.'

'That's for me to decide, isn't it?'

'Honestly, I've had loads of compliments. I've got a technique, I don't just do that alphabet stuff. Grab a pillow and strap yourself in.'

He was about to dive under the duvet when she put a hand on his shoulder.

'Ben, wait,' she said gently.

'What?'

'Love, what's up with you? You're shaking all over, and I don't know what that expression is in your eyes but it's not what I'd call slumberous with desire. You look like you're about to get stuck into some gardening. Why so determined?'

'I'm fine.'

'You're not though.' She ran a tender finger over his cheek. 'You're actually nervous about this, aren't you? Ben Kemp, afraid of having sex. That has to be a first.'

'Not quite. It has happened once before.' He sighed. 'I'm

sorry, Bride. It's just… I cocked this up once for us already, didn't I? I've got a feeling I'm only going to get one shot with you and I want to get it right.'

'Why do you think you'll only get one shot with me?'

'I don't know. Because I blew the last one, maybe.'

'Come here.' She wrapped her arms around him and kissed him softly. 'I love you, OK? I want to be with you. You've got absolutely nothing to prove to me and we can take a million attempts to get this right if we have to. I'm not going anywhere.'

He stroked her hair. 'Yeah, I guess so. I'm being daft, aren't I? Thanks, Bridie.'

'I, on the other hand, have got a hell of a lot to prove to Messington's most notorious ladies' man.' She rolled on top of him and grinned. 'Brace yourself, Ben. I'm about to be the best you've ever had.'

———

When Bridie woke up the next morning, she was still in Ben's embrace. He was fast asleep, both arms wrapped tightly around her and his legs twined with hers.

She lifted the duvet to peep at him. She'd never seen him fully naked before last night, not even back when they were teens. Bridie felt a zing of excitement and arousal when she remembered sitting astride those thick thighs, gripping his hair, calling out his name as orgasm took hold of her. Once she'd taken charge and helped him overcome his initial nerves, it had been just… wow. Ten years' worth of suppressed lust crammed into one evening's energetic love-making. She ached all over this morning, but every sore limb and muscle was so worth it.

'Morning, new girlfriend,' Ben whispered as he woke up, nuzzling her nose with his.

'Morning, new boyfriend.'

He blinked. 'Shit, that sounds weird.'

'I know. Still, we'd better get used to it, hadn't we?'

'Suppose we had.' He glanced at George Clooney. 'What do you think, can we take Georgie Boy's blindfold off now?'

'Not until you're dressed. He gets very jealous.' She planted a row of soft kisses along his shoulder. 'Besides, who says I'm done with you?'

'If I'd known you were this hot in the bedroom, Bride, I'd have snapped you up years ago.' Ben ran one hand over the curve of her breast. 'Do you know how much of a turn-on it is to hear you go all bossy in bed?'

'I could sense you were a fan last night.'

'I should've known there was a closet nymphomaniac hidden under that sensible, uptight teacher act. It's always the quiet ones.'

Bridie rolled on top of him. 'You're a bad man, Ben Kemp.'

'Which of course only makes me more irresistible.'

She shook her head, smiling. 'And to think I thought the prospect of commitment might make you a bit less cocky.'

'After my athletic feats last night? You must be kidding, love. I'm a god.'

'Oh, you're a god now, are you?'

'Yeah, one of the minor deities, I reckon,' Ben said, nodding. 'Is there a god of multiple orgasms? If there is I'm probably that guy, but if he's not available then I'll take the one with the flying shoes.'

'Comparing yourself to a god is definitely far too cocky, even if it is only the flying shoe one. That's going to require a punishment, I'm afraid.'

He trailed the back of one finger over her hip. 'Go on then, make me an offer.'

'How about you ravish me again? I bet you won't enjoy that at all.'

He pulled a horrified face. 'God, no. That sounds like torture.'

'I want to hear your screams though. Just so I know you're getting a good, solid punishing.'

'Ah, now you're talking.' He rolled her over and she giggled as he burrowed into her neck to nibble her ear.

'Ben?' she whispered.

'Mmm?'

'Are we going to tell people?'

'About our sex life? I'm not sure they'd want to know, Bride.'

'About us. That we're… you know, us.'

'I don't know. What do you think? It's a bit early for those sorts of announcements. Plus, well…'

'…they'd take the piss out of us something chronic after we both swore blind we hated each other and we were never going to settle down? Yeah, I know they would, the bastards.'

'Let's leave it till after the Sten thing, eh?' Ben looked up to grin at her. 'Right now, I'll just settle for making you scream.'

She shook her head. 'No, you've got it backwards. You're supposed to do the screaming. That was the arrangement.'

'Well, we'll see which one of us caves in first. Now then, where was I? Oh yes. Punishment…'

Bridie wriggled pleasurably as he found his way back to the sensitive spot just behind her ear and his hand slid down between her thighs.

TWENTY-THREE

Meg shook her head. 'I can't believe Cal had Jojo Fitzroy over and he never told you, Hat.'

'I know, serious error of judgement,' Hattie said, sipping her bellini. 'Everything's woop-te-doo in paradise again now we've talked it over though.'

'Not that. I mean, there was a celebrity in your house!'

Meg was wearing the starstruck look Hattie had become used to seeing on the faces of her best friends whenever Joanna was mentioned – or two of her best friends anyway. Bridie, who'd known Joanna before she was famous, was thankfully immune.

Hattie laughed. 'Seriously, Meggy, that's what you're taking from this?'

The prospective bride and bridesmaids had gathered at a cocktail bar near to a boutique owned by one of Sandra Leonard's business contacts, where she'd booked them an appointment to try on some dresses. Hattie was currently filling Bridie, Meg and Ursula in on what she and Cal now fondly referred to as 'our fight' – although really, when she thought back on it, Hattie supposed it was more of a disagreement than a full-scale row. Still, she felt it deserved its status as The Fight all the same. It felt like she and Cal were a proper nearly married couple now they'd had one, like it was a rite of passage or something.

'How come he didn't tell you?' Bridie asked, detaching herself from the straw through which she was slurping some pinkish concoction called a Woo Woo.

'Oh, he was just being a typical obtuse bloke, trying to paper over a little problem with a much bigger one,' Hattie said, flicking a hand. 'Sounds like he sort of got sucked into it. He thought Joanna was bringing her husband and they were going to catch up at a café or something. Then she turned up at his place, alone and bearing champagne, Cal panicked that I'd think there was something wrong and like an idiot decided not to tell me.'

'Huh. I've had stories like that from exes before,' Ursula muttered. 'That's why they're exes.'

'This is Cal though. Mr Nice,' Bridie said. 'I can totally see that happening to him. He'd be mortified at the idea of being rude and doubly mortified about potentially hurting Hattie. I bet he was in purgatory the whole time Joanna was there.'

Hattie smiled. 'Yeah, I think you're right. And I do trust him. Her I'm not so sure about.'

'Naaaah,' Ursula said tipsily. Hattie suspected her mojito might've come with double measures of spirits. 'She's married to wossit. Conrad Benson. I mean, no offence to Cal, but that guy's… well, he's…'

Hattie raised her eyebrows. 'Yes, Ursula? Something to say about my future husband?'

'I just mean Conrad's… well, buff. Has Cal got a six-pack?'

Hattie considered this. 'He's got a two-pack.'

'Plus Conrad's off telly,' Ursula went on. 'And if she's had enough of him, I bet she can take her pick of rich, famous hotties. Her boyfriend before Conrad was thingy, you know, that premiership footballer who does all the aftershave ads. Why would she be running up from Chester or wherever she lives to have a go at seducing Cal? For his two-pack and lovely personality?'

'All right, maybe you've got a tiny smidgeon of a point,' Hattie conceded. 'But still, who turns up alone at an ex's house with a handbag full of Veuve Clicquot?'

Meg shrugged. 'Famous people, probably. I bet they drink that stuff like pop. Jojo probably never leaves the house without a couple of bottles on her.'

'You're all loved up again now though, right, Hat?' Bridie asked. 'Enjoying being housemates?'

Hattie smiled. 'Yeah. The best part is, Cal feels so guilty about it that I've been getting some serious attention. Flowers, chocs, and, um, a few other treats, if you know what I mean, girls.'

Meg nodded to Bridie. 'One of us does, I reckon.'

Bridie frowned. 'What's that supposed to mean?'

Ursula laughed. 'Yeah, come on, Bridie, what's his name?'

'Eh? Whose name?'

'It's no good playing innocent. Whoever it is that's been putting the spring in your step and colour in your cheeks this past fortnight.'

Bridie flushed. 'What? No he hasn't. I mean, no there isn't.'

'Yeah, bollocks,' Hattie said, grinning. 'We've all noticed the signs since the new term started. Yawning constantly, swigging coffee by the gallon, humming to yourself, looking all moony over secret text messages we're not allowed to see. I'd bet some serious money you've spent every night of the past two weeks getting laid.'

'Don't talk daft. Who would I be getting laid with?'

Hattie shrugged. 'You tell us. It's pretty obvious you've been taking advantage of your new housemateless state to make a bit of noise with someone.'

'Maybe I treated myself to a new vibrator to cheer myself up.'

'All right, if that's how you want to describe him. What's he called then, this "new vibrator"?'

Bridie stood up. 'I'll go get us another round. We've got time for one more before the dress shop lady's expecting us.'

'Not for me,' Ursula said. 'I'll fall down if I have another one of these. I swear it's ninety per cent rum.'

'Me neither,' Hattie said, holding up her still half-full bellini. 'I've got plenty left. Besides, I don't want to bloat up on fizzy stuff before the fitting. You and Meg go ahead though.'

'What's in a bellini anyway?' Bridie asked. 'I've never had one.'

'Peach juice and prosecco, I think.'

'Hmm. Sounds a bit sweet for my taste. Think I'll stick with the Woo Woos.'

'Because your new man's sweet enough, right?' Meg said with a grin.

'Ha-terribly-hilarious-ha,' Bridie said, rolling her eyes. 'So that'll be a tap water for you then, Margaret.'

Hattie smirked as she watched Bridie leave.

'Now there goes a woman who's quite obviously spent the last fortnight being thoroughly made love to,' she said in a low voice. 'We did it, you two.'

'You think it's Ben?' Meg murmured back.

'I know it's Ben. Cal's been noticing exactly the same symptoms in him. Constantly tired yet grinning like a loon all the time, forever on his phone texting someone. Cal even found a love letter Ben had been trying to write to her.' She glanced over at Bridie, who was smiling goofily at something that had popped up on her mobile while she waited for the barman to pour their drinks. 'You see that look on her face? That, girls, is true love: I'd recognise it anywhere. I'm calling this a definite win for Team Cupid.'

———

'Welcome, ladies,' the proprietor said when they arrived at the dress shop. She glanced around. 'Oh. No Sandra? I thought we'd have the mother of the bride as well.'

'My mum booked the appointment, but she wanted to leave us to try the dresses on by ourselves,' Hattie said. 'I think she worries she might end up taking over things, with it being her job.'

'Ah, so you're the bride-to-be.'

'Um, yes,' Hattie said, flushing slightly. It still felt strange to think of herself as a bride-to-be – a wife-to-be – although she and Cal had been engaged for nearly four months now. It made it feel like it was really going to happen when she heard other people use the word.

'Well, dear, you've picked a good day to come for an appointment. We've got a new Suzanne Neville range just in that I know you're going to love.' The boutique owner turned to the other three. 'Ladies, feel free to look around and see what takes your fancy. Try a few things on if you like. I'm just going to steal your friend away to see what we can find for her, but I'll have her back to you in a blink.'

When Hattie had gone, Ursula fished out the price tag on one of the dresses and whistled.

'These things cost a bomb,' she said. 'It was nice of Hattie's parents to offer to buy them for us, wasn't it?'

'I wish I had rich parents,' Meg said. 'If Adrian ever pops the question, we'll be funding the whole thing on a couple of teacher salaries. Hope you like the potato sacks you'll be wearing on my big day, girls.'

Bridie turned to another rail and started skimming through the dresses in their plastic covers. 'I feel mega guilty having the Leonards pay silly money for something I know I'm never going to wear again.'

'You might do, you never know,' Ursula said. 'Maybe your new man will want you to escort him to an embassy ball or something.'

Bridie shook her head. 'How many times? There is no new man except the one you lot have dreamed up for me. The only bloke allowed in my bedroom these days is George Clooney, as you well know.'

'She's really a terrible liar,' Meg observed to Ursula.

Ursula nodded. 'I wonder why she bothers, don't you? She knows we'll find out who he is in the end.'

'Do you two really lead such quiet lives that my non-existent love life is so fascinating to you?' Bridie demanded.

Ursula shrugged. 'Yes.'

'Come on, let's pick out a few of these dresses to try on before Hat comes back.' She pulled out a silky red dress with a slit down the side and curled her lip. 'Ugh, I can't believe I have to wear one of these things. If God had meant us to wear dresses, he'd have invented ladderless tights.'

'Ooh, I love that!' Meg dived forward to grab it from her before she put it back on the rail. 'It's just like the sexy red dress Jessica Rabbit wears. You should get it,

Bride. You're the only one of us with the tits for it. I bet your new man won't be able to keep his eyes off you in that.'

'He will because his eyes, like the rest of him, are entirely imaginary.' Bridie shook her head. 'No, it's too loud to wear to a wedding. I think there's some sort of rule about not being in red, and I'd just look tarty following Hattie up the aisle with a slit right up to my knickers. Anyway, we all have to match, don't we?'

Ursula took out a more conservative peach number, full-length and in a Grecian sort of style. 'This look would be good on all of us, don't you think?'

Meg extracted a dusky pink off-the-shoulder gown. 'I prefer this one. It's classy but it doesn't cover everything. Obviously we don't want to outshine the bride but we still want a bit of sex appeal.'

'Well I couldn't care less, so I'm happy to go with either,' Bridie announced. 'Let's try them on then.'

They'd each visited the changing rooms and jointly decided Meg's choice of dusky pink was their preferred style when Hattie reappeared from the back room, blushing all over her face. She was in a stunning ivory backless gown with a lace bodice and full-length sleeves. The chiffon and satin skirt clung to her curves before dropping to pool elegantly at her feet.

'Well, what do you all think?' she asked shyly.

'Oh my God,' Meg whispered. 'Hat, you're beautiful.'

'Give over.'

'Honestly. You look like Audrey Hepburn.' She turned to the other two. 'Doesn't she?'

Ursula shook her head slowly. 'Tell you what, Hattie, Jojo Fitzroy's got nothing on you. Cal's going to be blown away when he sees you in that.'

'What does our foremost wedding cynic think?' Hattie asked, turning to Bridie.

'I think… this is the one,' Bridie said in a hushed voice. She came forward to run soft fingers over the chiffon skirt. 'Sweetie, you look incredible. Absolutely perfect.'

Hattie raised her eyebrows. 'Bride, are you crying?'

'No.' She dashed away the tear at the corner of her eye. 'That's just… hay fever.'

'In September?'

'Yes. Shut your face.'

'Aww, Bridie.' Hattie gave her a hug, being careful not to crush her dress between them. 'I can't wait to see you in a big white dress of your own one of these days.'

Bridie smiled as she hugged her back. 'You know I don't do dresses except under extreme duress. Or weddings either, for that matter.'

'I'm still positive there's someone out there wonderful enough to change your mind. Who knows, eh? Maybe this time next year, we'll be back here for another fitting.'

Bridie laughed. 'Yeah, and maybe I'll have made a fortune pursuing my new career as a professional unicyclist for the Moscow State Circus.'

'We'll see, that's all I'm saying, Ms Morgan. We'll see.'

TWENTY-FOUR

'All right, you lot! All aboard the Debauchery Express!' Bridie clapped her hands to attract the attention of the assorted stags and hens milling around the coach they'd hired to take them to Blackpool, most already in their pink and blue T-shirts and sipping a pre-Sten glass of bubbly each.

Hattie and Cal were there, of course, as well as Meg and Ursula. The parents of the bride and groom had all sent a pass on their invitations, presumably feeling that the presence of mums and dads might put a bit of a dampener on the young folks' fun. Some of Hattie's cousins were coming, however, and a handful of Cal and Ben's buddies from the climbing group they both belonged to, plus three of Hattie's friends from yoga and a couple of Cal's mates from the car repair shop he ran. Adrian Verges had been invited too, and of course Pete Prince from the Garter: always to be found where there was any chance of a good time being had. In a place like Messington, the local pub landlord was everyone's mutual friend and Pete had been on more stag dos than he'd poured cold pints – including three of his own. Altogether, there were twenty-one of them set to paint the town red that weekend.

Well, twenty at the moment, since Ben wasn't here yet. Bridie had to keep stopping herself from looking around to see if he'd arrived. They both knew they needed to act just the same as normal if they weren't going to arouse any suspicion in their friends this weekend – which, of course, meant not appearing to be too nice to each other.

'Ben.' She beamed when he appeared at her elbow in his stag T-shirt, then quickly rearranged her face into the more usual pre-shagging expression of curt irritation. 'You took your bloody time, didn't you? We're supposed to be coordinating this thing together. Typical of the best man to leave the maid of honour doing all the hard work.'

He glanced behind her at Cal and Hattie, who were pulling on their bride and groom T-shirts before getting on the coach, and assumed his old expression of cocky indifference.

'I had to make myself all sexy for the hen side of the party, didn't I?' he said, gesturing down his body.

Bridie nodded solemnly. 'I can see why that might take you a while.'

He patted her bum. 'Got your pulling pants on then, Sweet Pea?'

'Of course.'

Ben clasped a hand to his chest. 'What, not the beige M&S ones with the tummy-flattening panel and reinforced gusset? Be still my beating libido.'

She smiled drily. 'You'll be commando for ease of access, I suppose?'

'Naturally. You can't expect a man of my virility to be contained by mere underpants.'

Ben watched as Cal and Hattie boarded the coach. When

he and Bridie were alone and unobserved, he bent down to give her a quick kiss.

'Missed you,' he whispered.

'I missed you too, love,' Bridie said, returning the kiss. 'You're not really commando, are you?'

'Would it turn you on if I was?'

'Er, definitely not.'

'Oh. Then no.' He trailed his fingers over her hip. 'I hope you've really got your sexy knickers on though. Thinking about them is the only thing that'll make the long journey bearable.'

'Tell you what, I wish we'd known when we drew up the room-sharing list that we'd be sleeping together by the time the trip came around.'

'If Future Us had turned up to tell Past Us about it, I very much doubt we'd have believed them.'

She smiled. 'That's true. Gender-segregated twin rooms aren't the best idea for anyone hoping to smuggle someone in for hanky-panky though, are they?'

'I'm sure Hattie won't mind letting me have her bed. She can swap you for Cal.'

She prodded his arm. 'But then we'd have to 'fess up about our naughty bedroom shenanigans, wouldn't we?'

'And submit to the merciless mockery we so richly deserve. Yeah, I know.'

'Come on, let's get on the coach. Don't forget to be mean to me.'

———

Hey, babes, did you get my message? Up your way again in a couple of weeks if you want to meet. Still thinking about last time xxx

The message had come through about an hour ago. Cal's

finger hovered over the keypad on his phone. He knew he needed to reply, but what to say? He'd really hoped Joanna's sudden curiosity about his life now had been exorcised the last time they'd seen each other. He'd ignored the previous message about meeting she'd sent him, hoping she'd take a hint, but apparently she wasn't going to just let it drop.

He glanced at Hattie, at the front of the coach queueing for a couple of hot drinks from a tea urn someone had had the foresight to arrange, then back to his phone.

Cal hadn't told Hattie that Joanna had messaged him again. Perhaps he should have – she was right, it wasn't good for them to have secrets from one another. No doubt she'd be peeved if she found out he'd kept this from her. He just knew that if he told her, she'd start doing that thing she did: comparing herself unfavourably to his ex. He wished she wouldn't – she must know she was more beautiful in his eyes than Joanna had ever been – but he guessed it was human nature. Anyway, it'd be bound to take some of the shine off all the exciting things they had planned in the run-up to the wedding. Better to just fob Joanna off and hope that this time she'd take the hint.

He had no idea why she was so keen for another meeting. The way they'd ended things last time, Cal had been pretty certain he and Joanna were on the same page about it being a bad idea to ever see each other again.

Me and Hat are pretty booked up with wedding stuff, to be honest, he typed at last. *Maybe another time.*

Hopefully she'd realise that *maybe another time* actually meant the exact opposite. Cal was careful to emphasise *me and Hat* too. He didn't want to be rude, but Jo must know perfectly well why he didn't want to be alone with her again.

A reply pinged through almost immediately.

OK. Just thought we should probably talk now we've had chance to process what happened, that's all. We were pretty drunk at the time, weren't we? x

Cal winced.

I'd rather just forget it, he messaged. *You should too, Jo. I'm getting married in three weeks and I really want to focus on that. Sorry.*

He watched the screen for a moment, but no reply appeared. Was she upset? If she was he was sorry for it, but she needed to understand.

'What are you up to?' Hattie asked as she joined him with a styrofoam cup of tea each for them. Cal jerked guiltily, turning the phone over so the screen was facing down.

'Oh, nothing. Just amusing myself with Candy Crush while I wait for my gorgeous wife-to-be to join me.' He held down the power button to switch off his phone and shoved it into his jeans pocket, then turned to give her a kiss. 'You shouldn't stay away from me so long.'

She laughed, handing over his tea. 'Cal, it's been ten minutes.'

'I know, and that's still too long.'

'I wonder if you'll be talking this way when we've been married twenty years.'

'I'll be talking this way when we've been married a hundred. I know when I'm onto a good thing.' He nodded to Ben and Bridie, sitting together near the front of the coach. 'Speaking of true love, look at that, eh? Seat buddies.'

'Apparently as the organisers, they have to sit together to "discuss the arrangements",' Hattie said. 'They don't want to, naturally. It's entirely through necessity.'

'Well, obviously. They seemed to be extra sarcastic when they met today, didn't they? It's clear they can't stand each other's company.'

'Absolutely.' Hattie lowered her voice. 'They are so sleeping together.'

'Yep.'

'When do you think they'll tell us?'

'When they think we won't take the piss, I guess,' Cal said, shrugging.

'Right. So, never then.'

Cal smiled. 'We'll catch them in the act eventually. They'll never be able to keep their hands off each other for this whole trip – I guarantee it.'

———

The coach arrived in Blackpool around two hours later and everyone piled out.

'All right, you lot,' Bridie barked, clapping her hands. 'Get into groups. Hens on one side, stags on the other. It's time for some strictly regimented good-time-having.'

'Ooh, yay. Organised fun, my favourite,' Hattie muttered to Meg.

'I knew you'd made a mistake putting her in charge. She enjoys this stuff far too much.'

Bridie glared at them. 'Oi. No talking in the ranks.'

'Sorry, Sarge,' Hattie said, saluting.

'All right, best man, your go.' Bridie nudged Ben at her side.

'Right,' he said. 'After much discussion, Bridie and me thought it'd be good for the stags and hens to separate and enjoy a bit of male/female bonding time before we all meet up later for a night on the town. To please the traditionalists among us.'

'So, lads, you're free to do whatever you want, just so long as you don't get completely trollied and you stay out of the strip clubs,' Bridie said. 'This is a high-class Sten do.'

'Oh, what, no strip clubs?' Pete muttered.

'Sorry, mate,' Ben said. 'Tried my best for us. Bossy Knickers here overruled me.'

Adrian raised his hand.

'Yes?' Bridie said.

'Um, am I a stag or a hen?'

'Eh?'

'Well, I'm in the bride's party, aren't I? I'm Hattie's friend, not Cal's.'

Bridie turned to Ben. 'It's a point. We didn't think of that.'

Ben shrugged. 'I'd say he can take his pick. If he prefers cocktails and cake with the lasses to beer and boobies with the lads, he's welcome to go with your lot.'

'Suits me,' Adrian said, slipping an arm around Meg. 'This side comes with boobies supplied.'

'Well it doesn't suit me.' Meg patted his cheek. 'You go drink beer with the other boys. I want some girly time where I can talk about your bedroom performance behind your back. Sorry, Ade.'

Hattie nudged Cal, who had a vacant look on his face. 'What's up with you? Scared I'm going to be sharing notes on your bedroom performance with the other girls? Because you're right, I am.'

'Hmm? Oh, nothing.' He leaned down to kiss her. 'Bye, love. I'll see you this evening, eh? Behave yourself and don't tell that lot too much about my willy.'

'All right. Same goes for you though.'

'Hat, I swear I won't tell the boys a thing about your willy,' Cal said, crossing himself.

She smiled. 'I'm glad to hear it. And no strip clubs, remember?'

'Hey. Why go out for hamburgers when you can have steak at home?'

She patted his arm. 'Well said, future husband. See you later.'

'Yeah. See you, Hat.'

He headed off with the other males of the party.

'What's up with him today?' Bridie asked. 'He looked like he was on another planet all the way down here.'

'Not sure,' Hattie said, watching him walk away. 'I guess he's just stressed out with the wedding planning.'

'Well, where are we off to then, ladies?' asked Samantha, one of Hattie's yoga pals.

'Are we allowed to go to strip clubs?' Meg asked.

'Seems a bit unfair us going out for a letch when we just banned the lads,' Ursula said.

'Nah, that's all right. When they do it, it's misogynistic male-gaze exploitation of female sexuality. When we do it, it's redressing hundreds of years of sexual repression. Very liberating.'

'I've got a plan,' Bridie said. 'I made a list of fun stuff we could do today and I think I know just the place to take you randy mares first.'

'Will there be men with no clothes on?' Meg asked hopefully.

'Well, not quite the full monty, I'm afraid, but there'll certainly be plenty of sexy fellas with flesh on display.'

'What is it, like the male version of Hooters or something?'

'Better. Come on.'

TWENTY-FIVE

'All right, who else feels like they've been swizzed?' Meg muttered to Hattie as they watched an act called Dolores de Luxe gyrating around a pole.

Bridie shrugged. 'You wanted sexy men, you've got sexy men. What's the problem?'

'It's a drag club, Bride.'

'So?'

'I just sort of thought there might be more lunchboxes packed into tight Speedos and fewer sequinned feather boas,' Ursula said, watching Dolores strut her stuff across the stage while she belted out 'I Am What I Am' from *La Cage aux Folles*. 'God, girls, wouldn't you kill for those pins though? Lucky bastard.'

'I'd kill for those boobs,' Meg said, eyeing Dolores' impressively horizontal rack enviously. 'I mean, I know they're not real, but she knows how to work them.'

'I'd have been a great drag queen,' Bridie said, smothering a slight hiccup as she sipped her mojito.

'You're missing a few key ingredients, Bride,' Hattie said.

'Discrimination.'

'Plus you can't sing, you can't dance and you don't like crowds. Or people,' Hattie went on. 'I can't help feeling it's not the job for you.'

'Yeah, but I've got…' Bridie waved a hand vaguely. 'Presence, that's it.'

'Presents?'

'Pres*ence*. Like, sass or whatever. I'm well sassy.'

'You mean you're a sarky cow.'

'Pretty much. I do fancy the wig and make-up though. That'd be such a rocking look on me.' She slapped the table with her palm. 'Right. Games. Fun. Debauchery. Dares. As chief hen I demand there to be dares.'

'Here,' Ursula said, twisting around so Hattie could see the back of her T-shirt. 'Read us the dares, Hat.'

'Right.' Hattie skimmed down the list. 'Photobomb a stranger. Make a prank phone call. Get someone to buy you a drink. Get a selfie with a celebrity…' She glanced at Dolores. 'Is she a celebrity?'

Bridie shrugged. 'Kind of, I guess. It says on their website she's been on that RuPaul thing. She's a bit busy though, Hat.'

'Oh look,' Meg said, leaning around to look at the back of Ursula's T-shirt. 'Answer any question you're asked truthfully or you have to down your drink, it says here. What do you say, Bride, are you up for a bit of Truth or Dare?'

Bridie frowned. 'Eh? We never put that on there.'

'It's true, honestly. Says it right here.'

Bridie tried to twist so she could read the back of her own T-shirt, but all that achieved was to make her head, slightly woozy after two cocktails, spin a bit.

'Why do I have to go first?' she demanded.

'Because you insisted we all had to do dares. It's only fair you get the ball rolling.' Meg turned to the others. 'What do you think, hens? What shall we ask her?'

Hattie smiled. 'Oh, I think she can guess what we want to know.'

'Yep,' Ursula said, grinning. 'Come on, Bride, who is he? You're bound by the unwritten rules of hen-do sisterhood and therefore compelled to confess the name of your secret boyfriend to us.'

Bridie opened her mouth to deny any such person existed, but was interrupted by Meg.

'And if you fib when the rules of the game state you're obligated to tell the truth, you'll be cursed.' She licked her finger and made a squiggly occult-style symbol in the air. 'Seven years of bad sex if you lie. Better tell the truth, Bride.'

'What was the alternative? Down my drink?' Bridie picked it up and squinted at it. There was quite a bit left and she'd definitely get brain freeze from the crushed ice in the bottom, but if it was between that and telling them it was Ben who'd been putting the smile on her face this past month…

'Aw, come on, Bride, tell us,' Hattie said, fluttering her eyelashes. 'We're your best friends, you have to share. We promise we won't spread it around, don't we, girls?'

'At least tell us if there really is someone if you won't give us his name,' Ursula said.

Bridie flushed. 'Well… all right. Yes then.'

'Ha!' Hattie clapped her hands. 'I bloody knew it. You've been at it like a soon-to-be-disgraced MP, haven't you?'

'I may have been having a moderate amount of inter-course, yes,' Bridie informed her loftily. 'I'm entitled. It's been ages since I last had sex.'

'Is it just sex or is it more serious than that?' Meg asked.

Bridie felt her cheeks heat, and she sipped her icy drink in an effort to cool them down. 'I only have to answer one question, don't I?'

'Yes, but you refused the first one so now you have to answer a bonus question as a forfeit,' Hattie said. 'New rule.'

'You can't just invent rules.'

'Er, yes I can, I'm the bride,' she said, straightening her veil. 'I can do anything I want.'

'Well… then yes, I guess it's serious,' Bridie muttered. 'I mean it's pretty new still, but I like him. I really like him actually, if you're that desperate to know.'

'Oh my God!' Hattie reached over to give her hand a gleeful squeeze. 'This is major stuff, Bride!'

'It's not that major.'

'Yes it is! You hardly ever like anyone you go out with after the third date, if it even gets that far.'

'You're exaggerating. I've liked loads of people.'

'You know you haven't. You're insanely picky and all your dates seem to go tits up within minutes. It was only a few months ago that you were talking about giving up on blokes full stop. If you like someone, really like them finally, then that is massively major.'

'The sex is obviously pretty good if your grinning face at school recently has been anything to go by,' Ursula said.

Bridie smiled. 'I'm not going to deny that. Better than pretty good.'

It was kind of nice to talk about Ben with the girls, now they'd wheedled the information out of her. Bridie was trying to exercise caution in this new relationship, given her general romantic history – her history with Ben in particular – but she was really excited about how things were going. She couldn't help it. For maybe the first time in her life she was actually happy: really bloody happy.

She'd been wary, at first: still cautious after being hurt by him before, and worried that someone with Ben's background might get bored of his first dabble in monogamy and fall back into old habits. But that hadn't happened, thank God. He couldn't seem to get enough of her, and there was a core of sweetness under the laddish, swaggering boy she thought she knew that she'd never suspected existed. Slowly, she'd allowed herself to drop defences and let her feelings for him show fully.

But she still didn't want to reveal who her mystery boyfriend was to her friends; not just yet. Aside from the fact they'd tease her mercilessly after all the years she and Ben had apparently been mortal enemies, Bridie liked having her own special, secret Ben she could keep to herself. Everything was still so new and beautiful: the intoxicating excitement of being in love making her feel like she was a teenager again. They had plenty of time to share their relationship with other people, but right now she loved the fact it was just for them.

'So will we ever be allowed to know who he is, this perfect boyfriend and all-round sex god?' Hattie asked.

'Soon, if it keeps going well.' Bridie smiled to herself. 'But not just yet. Sorry, girls.'

'Well, drink up, ladies,' Meg said as she downed the last of her drink. 'What do you think? One more then we hit the Pleasure Beach?'

'Sounds good to me.' Bridie glanced at the dregs left in Hattie's glass. 'What's that, another one of those bellini things?'

'Yep.'

'Here, let's have a try then. I might have one next.'

Hattie looked alarmed as Bridie swiped her glass. 'Bridie, I'd really rather not—'

But it was too late, Bridie had already taken a sip. She frowned.

'Wait. This isn't…'

She trailed off as she noticed the pleading expression in Hattie's eyes.

'Um, this isn't… at all what I thought it'd be like.' She downed the rest, stood up and rested a hand on Hattie's shoulder. 'Hat, come help me get another round in.'

'Oh my God oh my God oh my *God*!' Bridie hissed as soon as they were out of earshot of the others. 'OK, there's only one reason I can think of why a bride would be swigging pure virgin fruit juice on her hen do and telling her mates it's a bellini. Is it? Tell me it is.'

Hattie flushed, smiling. 'It is.'

'Arghhh! Come here immediately, you.'

Bridie grabbed her friend for a tight hug, rocking her from side to side in her excitement.

Hattie laughed. 'All right, don't squeeze me to death.'

'Sorry.' Bridie loosened her grip slightly. 'I'm just so thrilled for you, Hat. I know how much you've always wanted this.'

'Bride, you have to cover for me with the girls, OK?' Hattie said in a low voice. 'Cal and me only found out a month ago ourselves. I really want to keep it quiet until we've had the three-month scan – even my mum and dad don't know yet.'

'I won't tell a soul, cross my heart.' Bridie released her friend from the hug and gave her a big kiss on the cheek. 'God, this is the best year. Now I get to be a maid of honour and an aunty-in-waiting all in one go.'

Hattie smiled. 'I thought you hated being a maid of honour.'

'Well, it's starting to grow on me.' Bridie gave her arm a

squeeze. 'Come on, Mummy, let's get these drinks in. Then I guess I'll just have to do my best to pretend I'm not buzzing with excitement for the rest of the trip.'

———

'We could just make a quick stop at Heavenly Bodies,' Pete said as the stag side of the party wandered around Blackpool Pleasure Beach. 'I know the bloke who owns it and he'd give us ten per cent off lap dances.'

Ben shook his head. 'Let it go, can you, you randy old bugger? You heard the girls. No strip clubs allowed.'

'Well what the girls don't know won't hurt them, will it?' He patted Cal on the arm. 'It's your brother I'm thinking of. This is Cal's last big boys' weekend as a single man.'

'Yeah, but I don't want a lap dance,' Cal said.

'But I bloody do.' Pete glanced at the rollercoaster track rising high above them. 'Sorry, but these aren't the sort of high-octane thrills I usually associate with stag parties.'

'They used to call my dad the Big Dipper,' Adrian observed to nobody in particular. 'Till my mum caught him at it.'

Pete nudged Ben. 'I thought at least you'd be on my side. I've never known you to say no to naked girls.'

Ben shrugged. 'Well, maybe I'm finally growing out of all that stuff.'

Pete scoffed. 'What, you? I don't believe it. How come?'

'There just comes a time in a man's life when he starts to reflect on what's really important, that's all. Makes you think, turning twenty-nine.'

'Have you been down the vet's to have your nadgers off or something?'

'Or something.' Ben nodded to a rollercoaster called the

Avalanche, with a bobsled-style track and cars. 'Anyone fancy that? Looks like a laugh.'

'My lap dance idea was better,' Pete muttered.

'Look, Pete, if it'll cheer you up then I'm happy to sit on your knee while we go round.'

'That's not really much of a substitute, thanks all the same.'

'I'm up for the bobsledding thing,' Adrian said. 'I've wanted to have a go ever since I saw *Cool Runnings*.'

'I won't bother,' Cal said. 'I can wait for you all here.'

Ben glanced at him. 'You sure, bruv? It's your stag and you haven't been on anything yet.'

'Yeah, I feel a bit sick. Long bus trips don't agree with me.'

'All right.' Ben was about to go join the queue with the others when an instinct held him back. 'You're sure that's all?'

'Course. What else would it be?'

Ben hesitated a moment before going back to his brother.

'You lot go ahead,' he said to the rest of the party, waving them on. 'I'll sit this one out with our Cal.'

When they'd gone, he took his brother's elbow and guided him to a nearby bench.

'All right, what's really wrong?' he asked. 'I might not be the most perceptive of brothers, but it's obvious you're lacking the joie de vivre that I'd expect to see in a man on his stag do.'

Cal shrugged. 'Just tired, that's all. Weddings are a bastard to organise. I feel like I haven't had a break in months.'

Ben examined his face for a moment.

'There's something else,' he said slowly.

Cal sighed. 'Yeah.'

'Go on then, fill me in.'

'All right. But first you have to promise not to bollock me.'

Ben frowned. 'Why, what've you done that I'd need to bollock you for?'

Cal grimaced. 'I kind of – totally accidentally – spent the night with Joanna.'

'You did *what*?'

Cal clocked the horrified expression on his brother's face and shook his head. 'God, no, not like that. I just mean she came over for a drink. When she was in the area last month.'

'You never told me you saw her.'

'Well no, because you'd go all glarey about it, wouldn't you? I know you can't stand her.' Cal groaned. 'And now... Jesus, Ben, I'm in a right mess. I've really cocked up. I mean, it wasn't my fault – I only ever agreed to have a coffee with her – but it seemed to sort of spiral and then Hat found out about it and we had a big row—'

Ben held up a hand to cut him off. 'All right, stop. Tell me from the beginning, Cal.'

'Right.' Cal took a deep breath. 'So. Joanna sent me a message a few months ago asking if me and Hat fancied meeting her and the new hubby for coffee when they came to town.'

Ben frowned. 'Hmm. I don't like the sound of that.'

'Why not? It seemed like an innocent enough proposal to me. OK, Jo was always pretty adventurous sex-wise, but I was sort of working on the assumption she hadn't got into swinging since me and her broke up.'

'I don't trust her, that's all. You can never take anything she says at face value.'

Cal shook his head. 'Why are you always like this about her?'

'I'm just wary of her. She's slippery as fuck, that woman,'

Ben muttered. 'Anyway, I must be right or you wouldn't have that look on your face.'

'She didn't do anything all that wrong really. Like I said, things just seemed to spiral. She texted me when Hattie was away at camp with you guys, asking to come round because she's too big a star to go out in public or whatever. Then she turned up without the husband and a bagful of posh booze and suddenly it all just felt a bit like a date.'

'But it wasn't a date. Was it?'

Cal grimaced.

'Cal,' Ben said in a low voice. 'Seriously. What did you do?'

'Nothing! I swear I didn't do anything. I mean she was pretty touchy-feely all night, but she was kind of down about some marital problems she'd been having so I just thought she was lonely. Then she…' He winced. 'She kissed me.'

'I fucking knew it!' Ben said. 'I told you she was no good. Please God, tell me you told her where to go.'

'Well, no. Not exactly.'

'You didn't kiss her back though? You put a stop to it?'

'Course I didn't kiss her back.' Cal closed his eyes. 'But… let's just say I could've put a stop to it a bit faster.'

Ben shook his head. 'Oh no, Cal.'

'I didn't do it on purpose! She'd got me sloshed on fizzy stuff so my reactions were all sluggish. I mean, the shock of it was enough to freeze me to the spot for a second.'

'But you didn't kiss her back. You're certain of that?'

'Course I didn't.'

'Right. Where were your arms then?'

'Just sort of dangling about, I think,' Cal said. 'Not on her, that's for sure.'

'Your tongue? Where was that?'

'In my mouth, obviously. Which was clamped firmly shut, by the way.'

'And your lips, what were they doing?'

'They were as inert as a pair of dead slugs, Ben, I promise you. I just sat there like a pissed, dopey lemon with Jo's mouth stuck to my face for a few seconds till my brain caught up with what was going on and I pushed her away.'

'Well, then what happened?' Ben asked.

'God, it was so awkward. I tried to make a joke of it, there was a bit of forced laughter on both sides, then she gave me a hug and left with what I thought was mutual unspoken agreement we'd never see each other again.'

'She's like a bloody albatross, Joanna Fitzroy,' Ben muttered. 'Wherever she goes, disaster follows.'

'You're too hard on her, Ben. It wasn't like that.'

'Yeah? She's coming on to you when she knows you're about to marry someone else, with a husband of her own at home. How does that make her any better than Dad?'

'She was drunk. Drunk and upset,' Cal said quietly. 'I think she lives a pretty lonely life now. I got the impression talking to me was the first time anyone had listened to her in a long time. Honestly, I felt sorry for her.'

Ben examined him keenly. 'Be honest, were you even a bit tempted? You thought she was the mutt's nuts once upon a time, didn't you? Couldn't get enough of her.'

'Maybe the smallest amount,' Cal admitted. 'But that was just instinct and hormones; it didn't mean anything. All I had to do was think of Hattie and everything I stood to lose, and that was that. I mean, after everything that happened with Dad, that's the last thing I'd ever do to someone I loved. I swear to you, I didn't do anything wrong except being too British to just tell Jo to bugger off when she asked to see me.'

'Hmm. And you said Hattie knows all this?'

'No,' Cal muttered. 'She only knows Joanna came over. I didn't tell her about the kiss. We had a big enough row just about me seeing her; I didn't want to rock the boat any more.'

'Is she still pissed off about it?'

'No, we kissed and made up. It's not Hat I'm worried about.' He sighed. 'It's Joanna.'

'Oh, screw Joanna,' Ben said, scowling. 'Let her sort out her own problems. She's not your responsibility.'

'I mean, I'm worried I might've led her on or something. You know, because I didn't push her away as quickly as I would've done if I'd had my wits about me. She keeps messaging me, asking if we can see each other again.'

Ben shrugged. 'Tell her to sod off then. Block her if you have to.'

'I don't want to be cruel for the sake of it, Ben. She's going through a rough time. I just wish she'd find someone else to be her shoulder to cry on, that's all.'

'Why doesn't she?'

'Who knows?' Cal said. 'Like I said, she seemed lonely. Said she wanted someone real to talk to. Her world's full of frauds and phonies now, it sounds like.'

'Then she ought to fit right in,' Ben muttered. 'You want my advice, little brother?'

Cal sighed. 'God, do I?'

'Come clean to Hattie. Tell her everything – the kiss, everything. You'll feel better for being completely honest.'

'Yeah, but it sounds bad, doesn't it? It could sound kind of like I kissed Jo back, and Hattie already feels threatened by her. I don't want Hat thinking I'm capable of doing something like that when we're about to get married.'

'It'll sound worse if she hears about it from someone else.'

'Like who, Joanna?' Cal shook his head. 'No, I really don't want Hat being worried or upset by anything. There's more at stake now than there was before.'

'How do you mean, more at stake?'

Cal looked bashful. 'I mean, now Hattie's got another little life depending on her.'

'Another little…' Ben's eyes widened. 'Shit! Really?'

'Yep.' Cal glanced towards a cloud of pink with one little white blob in the centre floating through the entrance. 'Those are our hens, I think. Don't say anything, will you, bruv? It's early days yet. We don't want to tell anyone until we get into safer territory.'

Ben laughed and grabbed his brother's hand to give it a hearty pump. 'Not a soul. Well done, eh? Mum's going to be made up.'

'You see now why I don't want to tell Hat? It'll sound worse than it was. It's not good for her to get upset in her condition, and this really isn't something worth getting upset over.'

'Course. Course I do. You made the right call, kid.' Ben left off shaking his brother's hand, but only so he could start slapping him on the back instead. 'Bloody hell. A baby! I can hardly… Look, if I can do anything you let me know, OK, Cal?'

Cal smiled. 'Thanks, Ben. I appreciate that.'

'Now put all this business with Joanna out of your mind and enjoy the rest of your stag weekend, eh? Me and Bride worked hard to organise this.'

Cal lifted an eyebrow. 'Been spending a lot of time with her, have you?'

Ben shrugged. 'Not had much choice really. We've had a lot to sort out.'

'That must've been tough. I know you two can't get on

for more than a maximum of thirty seconds without going for each other's jugular. Sorry for inflicting it on you, Benjy.'

'Yeah, well. Anything for my kid brother, eh?'

Cal glanced archly at him. 'Still, I don't think you need to be going over to hers every night. I'm sure it doesn't take that much organising.'

'Who said I'd been going over every night?'

'Just something I heard on the grapevine.' Cal nodded to the hen party, who'd spotted them and were heading their way. 'Here come the girls.'

TWENTY-SIX

'What're you doing here?' Bridie demanded when the group of women reached Ben and Cal.

'Getting our endorphin fix before tonight, since strip clubs have been declared off limits,' Ben said. 'What are you lot doing here?'

'Eating candy floss. Here, help yourself.' Bridie handed him her stick. 'Where are the other boys?'

Ben pointed to the Avalanche. 'On that thing. Me and Cal were just taking a timeout.'

Bridie glared at Cal, who'd made a beeline straight for Hattie and was currently hugging her around the middle while she held her candy floss up in the air, smiling fondly at him. 'Oi. Calvin and Hobbes. No fraternising between stags and hens until this evening.'

'Sorry,' Cal mumbled from Hattie's shoulder. 'Couldn't help myself.'

'Well, we might as well join together now since we're all here,' Ben said, noticing the rest of the menfolk staggering unsteadily towards them. He nudged Bridie. 'What do you reckon, Sweet Pea? Fancy a trip up the Tunnel of Love with me? All euphemisms entirely intended.'

She smirked before quickly turning it into a disapproving eye-roll for the benefit of the others. 'I think the Chamber of Horrors is more appropriate to us, don't you?'

'Fine by me. Feel free to hold my hand if any ghoulies jump out at you. Or any other parts of my anatomy that might comfort you.'

'All right, go on then,' Bridie said. 'I mean, not all right to grabbing your bits, all right we can join up now.' She turned to the rest of the group. 'If we get separated then don't forget we're meeting at the Sunset Bar and Grill at six, OK?'

Ben took her elbow to hold her back as the others wandered off to explore the rest of the park.

'What?' she whispered.

'Leave them to it and come play hooky with me. They can manage to organise their own fun for a while, I'm sure.'

'They'll get suspicious if we both go missing.'

'Nah, they'll just think we got lost in the crowds. Big groups get separated in theme parks all the time.' He watched until the others were out of sight, then tossed the remains of her candy floss into a nearby bin and pulled her behind one of the soft toy crane machines for a kiss.

'Well?' he whispered when he drew back.

She smiled. 'All right, that was a pretty persuasive kiss. But just for a bit, that's all.'

He took her hand and gave it a squeeze.

'You're a bad influence, Ben Kemp,' she told him as they snuck off hand in hand in the opposite direction to the rest of their group.

'What can I say? I missed you. I don't want to hang around that lot pretending to be mean to you and not being allowed to touch you for the next hour.'

She glanced up at him. 'Aren't you bored of this yet?'

'Bored of what?'

'This. Me. Being Mr Boyfriend Guy. I thought you might've started to find commitment tedious by now.'

He frowned. 'Is that a joke?'

'I guess… yes and no,' she said, shrugging. 'You've always been the country's leading advocate for single life: having the freedom to flit between women and ditch them when you've had enough. I can't help worrying the novelty of doing the relationship thing might wear off eventually.'

He stopped walking to pull her into his arms. 'This isn't some new hobby or challenge for me, Bridie. I meant it when I told you I loved you. Why would I want to be with any other women now I know I can have something like this with someone like you?'

'Something like what?'

'You know. Sex with someone who's a mate as well as someone I really fancy. Someone who turns me on and makes me laugh, not infrequently both at the same time.' He kissed the top of her head. 'Someone who's you.'

She smiled. 'That's sweet, Ben.'

'So, do you feel better?'

'Yes. Sorry. I can't help feeling a bit insecure, that's all, when I think about all the water that's passed under our particular bridge.'

'Well, we're done passing water now.' He frowned. 'That didn't come out how I meant it to.'

She laughed. 'I could tell.'

'I just mean, we've found each other now. The people we've been, the things we've said: that's finished. My days of casual sex are very much over, I promise you.' He kissed her again. 'And I'd really like it if you could try to move on too.

It's a long time since we were eighteen. I'm not going to hurt you again, I promise.'

'I know that. It just takes a bit of adjusting to after all this time, knowing you really love me.'

'And for me too.' He pressed her hand. 'But it's amazing. No one ever fell in love with me before.'

'They would if they'd really known you.'

He smiled. 'Like you do, you mean?'

She laughed. 'Yeah. Let's conveniently overlook the fact I was convinced I hated you for nearly a decade.'

'You've been making up for it the past four weeks though. Parts of me are feeling very well-loved.'

'Shameless as ever. Some things never change.' She nonchalantly examined her nails. 'Sooo... you and Cal seemed to be shaking hands pretty energetically when I spotted you on the bench. What was that all about?'

'Oh, nothing. Just a new... carburettor he's getting. He's pretty excited about it.'

'Mmhmm. Nothing else?'

'Such as what?'

She smiled. 'Come on, Uncle Ben. You know, don't you? Cal told you.'

'All right, yes,' he said, smiling too. 'Who told you?'

'Technically, no one. Hattie gave herself away when I took a sip of her virgin bellini.'

'Aunty Bridie and Uncle Ben.' He shook his head. 'The kid's doomed.'

'I know, poor sod.' Bridie glanced around the park. 'Well, where shall we go to play then?'

'Back to the hotel? If I'm banned from going to strip clubs then I think it's only fair you fill the window in my schedule with some nudity.'

'We haven't got time, sadly.' She pointed to a nearby rifle

range. 'There you go, there's something phallic and explosive you can play with if that's where your mood's taking you.'

'That looks like a suitably manly pastime for the chief stag,' he said, nodding. 'Maybe I can earn myself some boyfriend points by winning you a cuddly toy.'

They approached the range and Ben paid for a go.

'Right,' the man running the game said, handing him a rifle. 'Three shots per go, mate. You get ten points for hitting the outer circle, twenty for the inner circle and thirty points for a bullseye. Ninety points'll get you one of the big cuddly toys; the other prizes are all ticketed. Good luck.'

'OK. I've got this.' Ben lifted the rifle to his eye to take aim, and Bridie smiled.

'You look like you're in a Western or a gangster film or something.'

'Quiet, moll. You're putting me off.' He took a shot, hitting the target's dark blue outer circle. 'See? I'd have got a bullseye then if you'd kept schtum.'

'Mmm. I'm sure you would.'

Ben took aim again, this time managing to miss the target completely. His third and final shot hit the inner circle.

He sighed. 'Well that was crap. Sorry, Bride. I've failed as a man.'

Bridie patted his bum. 'Never mind. I still love you now you've been downgraded to mere beta male.'

'What do I win for thirty points then?' Ben asked the bloke running the game.

'Anything off this,' the man said, holding out a tray of small plastic toys and tacky jewellery for him to look at.

Ben selected a cheap-looking ring with a purple heart-shaped gem in the centre and eyed it critically. 'And that's four quid's worth, is it?'

'Sorry,' Bridie said to the man. 'He's a Yorkshireman: getting his money's worth is in his veins.'

Ben guided Bridie away, then took her hand to slide on the ring he'd won. 'Here you go. Sorry it's not a teddy.'

She smiled. 'Really, that finger?'

'Heh. I hadn't even noticed.' He smiled at her left hand in his. 'Suits you though.'

She held up her hand to waggle her new ring, watching how the gaudy plastic gemstone caught the dying sunlight.

'I love it, Ben.' She stood on tiptoes to kiss him. 'Thank you.'

He slipped an arm around her. 'Let's get out of here, eh? We can have a romantic walk on the seafront and I'll share a bag of chips with you.'

———

Half an hour later they were sitting on the beach by the big pier, watching the sun sink into the ocean as they ate a ketchup-slathered cone of chips between them. The air was alive with sound: the brightly lit trams carrying visitors up and down the promenade to view the town's world-famous illuminations; the beeps, bells and whistles of fairground games and rides, and rowdy merrymakers visiting the bustling nightspots that looked out over the sea.

'It's funny going on holiday to the seaside when you live at the seaside,' Bridie said. 'Feels sort of treacherous, enjoying someone else's beach.'

'The others'll be heading to the restaurant now,' Ben said, taking a look at his watch. 'We should go back really.'

'Yeah. In a bit. It's nice here.'

Ben held out a chip to her, and she opened her mouth for him to pop it in.

'What have you and the boys been up to today then?' she asked him, resting her head on his shoulder.

'We went for a pub lunch, played a few testosterone-fuelled rounds of massively competitive crazy golf then headed to the Pleasure Beach. What about your lot?'

'We went to see a drag act with great legs called Dolores, drank more cocktails than we really should have at lunchtime and the girls pumped me for information about the secret boyfriend they think I'm hiding from them.'

'What, another one?'

She smiled. 'I like to keep a few on rotation.'

'Did they get anything out of you?'

'I did confess there was someone. I didn't say it was you though, obviously,' she said, helping herself to another chip. 'It was sort of nice, to be honest, chatting about it. I love having you as my little secret, but I've been dying to talk to Hattie too. I can't help it when it's all new and exciting.' She glanced up at him. 'How would you feel about telling them? I don't mean now, but when the time's right.'

'I'd feel simultaneously massively embarrassed about all the times I've railed against romance and love and massively proud of my fit new girlfriend.' He leaned down to kiss her. 'But it'll be worth it. I've never been happier than I have this past month and I want everyone we care about to know it, no matter how humiliating it is for me personally.'

She smiled and snuggled into the arm he'd stretched around her. 'Ben Kemp, talking about feelings and all that girly stuff. I feel like you've been body-snatched.' She glanced up. 'Don't let them swap you back for the other guy, will you?'

'The other guy was just a front to hide the fact I'm a bit of a soppy bastard, apparently. That came as a surprise to me as much as anyone.' He pressed his lips to her head. 'All it took was you, Bridie.'

'You really don't miss the playboy lifestyle? Not even a bit?'

He drew her body tighter against his and inhaled the scent of her hair. 'Doesn't matter. Even if I did, it could never compare to this. If I have to choose between the joys of single life and being with you, you win every time.'

'I know what you mean,' she said, reaching up to squeeze his fingers on her shoulder. 'I owe Hattie and the girls a lot really. Not that I'd ever admit that to them.'

He frowned. 'The girls? Why, what have they got to do with it?'

'I just mean that if it wasn't for them, I'd never have known how you really felt about me. It was only overhearing them talking about how you'd confessed it all to Cal that made me realise you'd been telling the truth when you told me how you felt at camp.'

'Eh?' He looked down at her. 'How I confessed all what to Cal?'

She blinked. 'Well, you know: your feelings for me. How you'd been in love with me for years, but you were too afraid of me knocking you back to tell me. I guess Cal couldn't help himself telling Hattie. You know how those guys are. If you tell one then you might as well be telling them both, right?'

'What?' Ben shook his head. 'Hang on a minute. *What?*'

————

'What happened to your brother and the maid of honour lass?' Graham, a friend of Cal's from work, asked him as the stags and hens sat around a group of tables at the Sunset Bar and Grill with a drink each. 'I haven't seen them since we left the Pleasure Beach.'

'They'll have got lost in the crowds somewhere, probably,' Cal said. 'There are a few others we're still waiting on too. I'm sure they'll all turn up sooner or later.'

'Are they a couple then?' Graham sounded disappointed. 'Shame, I was going to take a crack at her later. Bit bossy, but she's a nice-looking girl.'

'Well, no, they're not exactly what you'd call a couple. At least, not officially. It's a bit complicated.'

'Those two have definitely snuck back to the hotel for a quickie,' Hattie whispered when Graham's attention had been claimed by someone else.

'Almost certainly.' Cal put an arm around her and squeezed her tight. 'Hat?'

'What?'

'I love you, all right? I mean, I really bloody love you. Don't ever forget that, will you?'

She laughed. 'OK. How much beer did you drink today?'

'This isn't beer talking, it's me. I want you to know, that's all.'

'I do know, don't I? You asked me to marry you, which was a pretty big clue. What's brought this on, love?'

'I've just been thinking about how lucky I am. And how I'd never do anything to jeopardise that.'

'Like what?'

'Just… anything.' He drew her closer to him. 'I'm going to miss my cuddle tonight. It feels weird now, falling asleep without you next to me. Sure you don't fancy sneaking in after Ben's asleep?'

Hattie smiled. 'You know that's not allowed. No hotel sex shenanigans or we'll get in trouble with the organisers.'

'Right. The organisers who are even now back at that very hotel sneaking in a shag before we go out.'

'I know, the massive hypocrites.' She patted his knee. 'Never mind, one night apart won't kill us.'

'No, I suppose not. We've got our whole married life ahead of us to catch up on that sort of fun.'

Hattie frowned as Bridie and Ben appeared in the restaurant, striding towards them with some seriously black expressions on their faces. 'Hello. Here comes trouble.'

'Oh knickers,' Cal muttered. 'Hat, I strongly suspect that we've been rumbled.'

TWENTY-SEVEN

'Right,' Bridie said when she reached the group at the table, folding her arms. 'You lot have got some serious explaining to do.'

'You. And you,' Ben said, pointing accusingly at first Cal, then Pete.

'Yeah, and you three as well.' Bridie glared at Hattie, Meg and Ursula, who did their best to assume innocent expressions.

'Who, us?' Hattie said sweetly.

'Did you or did you not tell Bridie I'd confessed, in my own words, that I was secretly in love with her?' Ben demanded.

'I don't remember telling her that.' Hattie glanced at Meg. 'Meg, did you tell Bridie that?'

'I cannot recall telling Bridie that. Urs, did you tell Bridie that?'

'All right, stop,' Bridie said, holding a hand up for silence. 'You had a conversation at camp about how Cal had told you

Ben confessed he'd been in love with me for years. Don't play innocent.'

'There may have been some such conversation,' Hattie admitted. 'We didn't know you were eavesdropping on us like a dirty little spy, did we?'

'Bollocks you didn't. You set me up, you bastards!'

'And you,' Ben said, scowling at Cal. 'My own brother. You and Pete deliberately lured me to the doors of that bloody beer cellar, didn't you?'

'Well…' Cal cast a guilty glance at Pete, who shrugged. 'All right, let's just say we didn't not do that.'

Bridie shook her head. 'Ben, can you believe these guys?'

'I know. Our best friends. Destroys your faith in human-ity, doesn't it?'

'Entirely.'

Ben turned to glare at Cal again. 'What did you lie for?'

'We didn't lie. Or not exactly.' Cal pointed at Pete. 'It was his idea.'

'Grass,' Pete muttered.

'Well? Was it your idea?' Ben demanded.

'Yeah, and a bloody good one it was too,' Pete told him stoutly. 'We were doing you a favour, mate. By rights, you should be offering to buy me a drink and name your firstborn after me in exchange for sorting you out with such a top bird.'

'Come on, you know you guys have got feelings for each other,' Hattie said soothingly to the two wronged parties. 'All right, so maybe we set up the conversations, and it was a fib about hearing you confess it – or a little white lie anyway. We didn't make up the part about you being secretly in love with each other though, did we? Everyone knew it but you; it seemed only right to give you the push you needed towards realising it for yourselves.'

'Who are you to tell us what we feel?' Bridie demanded. 'You're not the bosses of us.'

'Yeah,' Ben said. 'You lot can't just play God with people's emotions. Me and Bridie are the only ones who get to decide what we're feeling.'

'You've spent ten years dancing around each other, shagging every lass but her in your case and dating every lad but you in hers,' Pete said to him. 'I've watched you at it since you were barely out of school, and at nearly thirty you still haven't moved any further forward. How long were you going to wait to stop lying to yourselves? Till you were both on Zimmers?'

'That's not your call to make.'

'So you're saying you didn't have feelings for each other, are you?' Cal said.

Bridie flushed, waiting for Ben to speak. But he remained silent, standing at her side red-faced and seething while he scowled at his brother.

Right. He was just going to let that hang there, was he?

'Well yeah, obviously we always cared about each other,' she said after it felt like a few millennia had passed, trying not to catch Ben's eye. 'You know, as friends. You had no bloody business chucking the L-word about like that with no evidence. Totally out of order, right, Ben?'

Ben continued glowering at Cal, then blinked and turned to frown at her instead. 'Sorry, what do you mean, as friends?'

'I… well, I mean, they made the whole thing up, didn't they? That is how you felt about me before they started manipulating us, right? Just good friends?'

He stared at her for a moment, and if there was anything like hopeful appeal in her eyes he evidently couldn't see it.

'All right, fine,' he muttered. 'Yeah, if you like. Just good friends then.'

'So when you told me…'

'Listen, love, Cal and Pete swore blind you were eating your sweet little heart out for me. I had to do something about it, didn't I? Only gentlemanly.'

She snorted. 'Gentlemanly? You? Please.'

'Why, was it true what they said? Did you love me?'

She shrugged. 'Yeah, I mean, naturally I loved you a bit. As a mate, obviously. If that lot hadn't made me believe you were half dead with grief brought on by unrequited love…'

He scoffed. 'Unrequited love? Do us a lemon, darling.'

She narrowed her eyes at him. 'Hang on. You weren't in on this too, were you?'

'Eh?'

'Well, this isn't the first time you've tricked me into something like this, is it? It definitely isn't the first time you've lied to me. The kiss at the party? The leavers' ball?'

'Christ, are you ever going to let that bloody leavers' ball go?'

'No,' Bridie snapped. 'Ben, I swear, if this was all a scam to get in my knickers then I just hope you're proud of yourself, that's all.'

'All right, well how do I know you weren't in on it if it comes to that?' he demanded, crossing his arms to match her stance. 'I bet this whole thing was an attempt to teach me a lesson, wasn't it? Get your own back for what happened at school?'

'What?'

'You've always said the thing I needed most to puncture my ego was to have some woman I'd shagged make me look a tit in front of everyone. Well, congratulations, Bridie. You are that woman, and I feel totally and utterly humiliated right now. You win.' He gave her a sarcastic round of applause.

'I promise neither of you were in on it,' Hattie said, but they were deaf to anyone except each other and the paranoid voices in their heads.

Bridie turned away from Ben, scowling blackly. 'Fine. I wasn't in on it, for the record, but you can believe that if it makes you happy.'

'Fine. Neither was I, but if you really have such a low opinion of me that you think I get off on tricking girls into bed under false pretences, you just go right ahead and keep on thinking it.' Ben's gaze fell on a woman sitting by herself at the bar. 'Right. I'm off to do one of these fucking dares. What was the last one on the list: serenade somebody? That lass on her own there looks like she might have lost that lovin' feeling.'

'Oh, so that's how it's going to be, is it?' Bridie scanned the room until she clocked a man having a quiet pint by himself. 'Well if it comes to it, I reckon there's a bloke there who definitely wants to buy me a drink.'

'Enjoy yourself then. Hope he doesn't have genital warts.'

'You too. Hope she's not a serial killer with a fetish for twats.'

'You know, Bride, I'm glad you're not really in love with me,' Ben snapped. 'It was bound to end with me turning into one of those men who practically lives in his garden shed to avoid his constantly nagging missus.'

'I'm definitely glad you don't really love me. It'll save me a world of pain when you inevitably ditch me for some Botoxed airhead during the hugely pathetic mid-life crisis you plunge into after your hair starts to go.'

'Good. I'm glad we agree.'

'I'm glad we do too.'

They glared at each other for a moment before stomping off in opposite directions to their respective chat-up prospects.

'Oh well, isn't this just great?' Cal muttered to Hattie. 'Straight back into denial, the pair of them, just when they'd actually started to be happy. Now what the hell are we supposed to do?'

———

Bridie strode over to the man scrolling through his phone while he enjoyed his pint and pulled up a chair next to him.

'Hi,' she said, summoning a smile that was as sweet and beguiling as she could make it – so not very, probably. 'This is going to sound very forward, but I don't suppose you fancy buying me a drink?'

He blinked. 'Um, I was actually just waiting here for my friend.'

'Yeah, sorry, I know I'm being mega rude. It's just, I'm on a hen do and we're supposed to tick off this list of dares. I have to get a stranger to buy a drink for me.' She rolled her eyes to hopefully convey she found the whole business as tedious as he did. 'Huge cliché, I know, but my best friend's the bride so I have to go along with it. I mean, just a tap water or something is fine.'

'Um, well, I guess that's OK,' the man said doubtfully.

'Thank you.' She cast a glance over at Ben, who was watching her from the corner of his eye while he chatted to the woman at the bar, and smiled as seductively as she could for her new friend. 'That's ever so sweet of you. It's Bridie, by the way.'

'Ely.'

'Pleasure to meet you, Ely.' She shook his hand, letting

her fingers trail his as she dropped it, and he smiled uncertainly before going to the bar for her drink.

She took another sneaky look at Ben. He seemed to be doing well for himself. The woman was already simpering at him, resting her fingers on his hand while they talked. He had his on-the-pull smile screwed in place, dripping charm. He was giving the woman all his usual lines, no doubt: his chat-up technique didn't seem to have suffered at all during the four brief weeks he'd managed to remain in a committed relationship. Maybe he was pretending he was in love with her too, the poor cow. Maybe he did it to all of them.

Had he been in on it? Probably not – Hattie would surely have refused to be involved in anything she thought would really hurt her friend – but he hadn't leaped in to reassure Bridie how he felt about her just now either, despite her giving him plenty of prompts. When she'd suggested his feelings were no more than friendly, he'd just shrugged and gone along with it. As if he didn't care… as if she hadn't meant a thing to him.

To think she'd believed there was more to him than she'd previously thought; that he might actually have had deeper feelings for her behind all the quips and the teasing. Ugh, the whole thing was just so humiliating! How could Hattie have done this to her? And how could Ben… Bridie had really believed him when he'd told her he loved her. God, she'd been so happy these past weeks, and now…

Her eye was caught by the gemstone on the cheap ring he'd won for her earlier, sparkling on her wedding finger where he'd slid it on. It was blood-red now, although it had been purple when he gave it to her. Must be some sort of mood ring. What did red signify, she wondered? Disappointment? Anger? Hurt? Betrayal?

'Here you go,' Ely said, putting a glass of white wine

down in front of her. 'That man at the bar told me this was your favourite drink.'

She scowled at Ben. 'Pay no attention to him. He's got no idea what my favourite things are. He knows nothing about me at all actually.'

Ely blinked. 'All right. Ex-boyfriend, is he?'

'No. Just some knobhead I'm unfortunate enough to know.'

He glanced at her ring as she lifted her wine to take a sip. 'That's, um, stylish. Christmas cracker prize?'

'Fairground rifle range.' She slipped it off and chucked it into her handbag before summoning a smile. 'So, Ely, tell me about you. I want to know absolutely everything there is to know.'

———

Ben tried not to stare too obviously at Bridie and the man she was talking to. She was leaning forward flirtatiously while they chatted, giving the bloke a great view of her boobs in her skinny-fit pink hen T-shirt. Jesus, she had amazing boobs.

Huh! That Brylcreemed bastard was looking straight at them as well. Not even trying to hide it. What a prick. As if Bridie could ever be interested in someone like him. Ben had a good mind to march right over there and give him a piece of his—

'Ben?' Mia, the woman he'd come over to talk to, rested her fingers on his hand to claim his attention.

'Oh. Sorry.' He turned back to smile at her. 'So you're a swimming teacher, are you? I'm in a similar field myself.'

'Are you?'

'Yes, I'm an instructor for this outdoor pursuits company. Trekking, canoeing, climbing, that sort of thing.'

'I thought you were too classically rugged to be an accountant,' she said, flashing him a seductive smile that he returned with interest.

This was going great. It was good to know he hadn't forgotten how to do it while he and Bridie had been... whatever he and Bridie had been.

God, it was refreshing to be single again: no girlfriend to clip his wings, just the freedom to do what he liked when he liked, with whoever he wanted to do it with. Yeah, that was the only way to live: free, unfettered and up to his ears in beautiful, sexy, willing women all desperate to go to bed with him. He was living every man's dream here. What had he been thinking with all that settling-down bollocks? That wasn't for him; he'd been saying so for years. Thank Christ things were back to how they should be. Thank Christ all was right with the world again, and now he could go back to... back to...

He suppressed a sigh as his inner monologue finally gave up, failing to convince even the most blokeish, obtuse, randy parts of his psyche that he really meant it. Who the hell did he think he was he kidding?

From the corner of his eye, he saw Bridie remove the ring he'd won for her and slip it into her handbag. Ben felt a pang that was a lot more painful than he'd have expected at seeing her take it off.

She was obviously trying to make him jealous. That had to be it – she couldn't really be interested in that guy. Well, two could play at that game. He turned his flirtatious smile up a notch.

'So according to this list of dares I've got, I'm supposed to serenade you,' he told Mia.

She laughed. 'Suits me. I've always wanted to have a

handsome man singing to me in public. Do you take requests?'

'I do, but unfortunately they all come out sounding like Nirvana.'

'Why?'

'Because I can never remember the words or the tune to anything. Apparently what that gives you is Nirvana, every single time.'

She smiled. 'You're funny.'

'Thanks.' He glanced at Bridie again and grinned. 'Ha!'

Another man, evidently the boyfriend of the lad she'd been chatting up, had approached and was leaning across Bridie to give her date a big sloppy kiss. Ben shot her a thumbs-up, and she flicked him a V-sign in exchange.

'What?' Mia said.

'Nothing. Just watching a mate of mine getting shot down in flames over there.' He smiled at her. 'All right, let's see if I can get myself into your good books with a few bars of something that isn't but will inevitably sound like "Smells Like Teen Spirit". Hold on to your eardrums, Mia.'

TWENTY-EIGHT

'Oh,' Hattie said when she got back to the hotel room she was sharing with Bridie at around midnight. 'Here you are, Bride. Everyone was wondering where you'd got to.'

Bridie was in bed in her pyjamas. She turned away when her best friend – former best friend – came in, sticking her nose in the air to make it clear this was a solid blanking.

'You missed the meal,' Hattie said. 'Aren't you hungry?'

Bridie gave a small grunt. If Hattie thought she was going to get any more than that out of her, she could think again.

'Some of the gang went on to a nightclub, but I made an excuse. I don't think clubbing's the best idea for someone in my condition, is it?'

She paused for Bridie to reply, but there was no response except her head disappearing under the duvet.

'Come on, Aunty Bridie, don't be that way,' she said gently, sitting down on the end of her friend's bed. 'You were all happy and excited earlier. I hate seeing you like this.'

She patted Bridie's leg, and Bridie immediately drew her knees up to get them out of her way.

'We were only trying to help you, you know,' Hattie said. 'You're completely, one hundred per cent in love with Ben Kemp and you have been for at least the four years I've known you – probably a lot longer. And he feels just as strongly about you, trust me. I know it, Cal knows it, Pete knows it, the girls know it – the whole of Messington probably knows it, with the two sole exceptions of you and Ben. You think I wanted to watch you being miserably single the rest of your life when I could see the opportunity for love and happiness sitting right under your stupid stubborn nose?'

'Wasn't your choice to make,' Bridie muttered sulkily from under the duvet she'd pulled over her head.

'Perhaps not, but you weren't going to do anything about it, were you? Nor was Ben: you were both too firmly wrapped up in denial. Somebody had to bite the bullet.' She yanked the duvet down and leaned round to look into Bridie's tear-stained face. 'Admit it. You've been bloody happy this last month.'

'Haven't.'

'Yes you have. Happy and in love, two things I don't think you've been at the same time in your life before. So stop being a stubborn cow and go make it up with him, why don't you?'

Bridie yanked the duvet over her head again. 'Don't want to. He hates me anyway.'

'He loves you, probably about as much as you love him. Are you seriously going to chuck that away just because you're both too proud to be the first one to admit it?'

'Yep.'

Hattie shrugged and stood up. 'Fine then. Die miserable. Just never say I didn't do my best for you.'

There was a knock at the door.

'Come in!' Hattie called.

Bridie's stomach jumped. Ben! Had he come to apologise finally? Not before bloody time either. But when she peeped from under the duvet she saw that it was just Cal, his pyjamas under one arm and washbag dangling from his fist.

'Sorry, girls. I know it's against the rules, but can I kip on your floor tonight?' he asked. 'There ought to be some spare pillows and a duvet on top of the cupboard I can use, if your room's the same as ours.'

'Why, what's wrong with your room?' Bridie's muffled voice demanded from under her duvet. 'Did they put a sign on the door saying "No devious lying gits"? Because we're already over our quota in here.'

'No, our Ben's gone and pulled, typically. He just rolled in with that lass he was caterwauling to at the bar earlier. I'm not staying in there listening to my brother getting laid in a single bed; it'll put me off sex for life.'

Bridie threw off the duvet and jerked up straight. '*What?*'

'What's up, Bridie?' Hattie asked innocently. 'No skin off your nose who Ben shags, is it? I mean, since you've got absolutely no feelings for him of any kind.'

'That… *bastard*!' Bridie jumped out of bed and grabbed her handbag. 'Right.'

'Where are you going, Bride?' Cal asked as she marched to the door in her pyjamas and bare feet.

'To shove something up your brother's tight little arse!'

She flung open the door, strode down the corridor and banged on Cal and Ben's room. Ben answered in his boxers, a toothbrush sticking out of his mouth.

'Bruhdff,' he mumbled. 'Mmm-mmfmf?'

'What?'

He beckoned her in and went to spit out his mouthful of

toothpaste in the en suite. 'What do you want, Bride? Come to apologise?'

'No. I came to give you this back.' She took the ring he'd won her earlier from her handbag and threw it at his face with force. He shielded his eyes as it glanced off his left temple.

'I don't want it back,' he said. 'Especially not if it's going to give me bruises. I won it for you.'

'Yeah, well I don't want it any more. So, where is she then?'

He blinked. 'Who?'

'Whatever tonight's unlucky recipient of your yo-yo-boxered charm happens to be called.'

'Eh?'

Bridie's phone buzzed in her bag. On the desk, Ben's did the same.

'Hang on,' Bridie said.

She fished it out and glanced at the screen. It was a WhatsApp message from Cal.

Sorry, guys. We did it again :-D #TeamCupid

Attached was a photo of a very creased sheet of notepaper covered in Ben's handwriting.

'What's this?' she said, holding it up to him.

He looked at it, and his eyes widened. 'Shit! Bridie, don't read that.'

'"I don't even mind your sticky-out ears"?' she read, glaring at him.

'Well, I don't. They're cute.'

'"Your arse is fucking amazing"?'

'Hey, that's a beautiful, romantic compliment.' He shook his head. 'Bloody Cal, I'll murder him. Creeping about going through other people's wastepaper bins.' He glanced at the message that had just come through on his phone and grinned. 'Oho! What's this, Bride?'

He held it up so she could see. On the screen was a message from Hattie, showing the passport picture of Ben and Bridie as teens that Bridie had snuck out of her photo album. It was tucked into the clear plastic pocket of someone's purse.

'That's… nothing,' Bridie said, flushing. 'Just an old photo from sixth form I found under the bed when I was cleaning up. Hattie had no right to sneak a photo of it.'

'And where do you keep it?'

'I told you. Under the bed. It's just waiting there until Bonfire Night with the other scrap paper.'

'Right. Show us inside your purse then.'

'No.'

'Why not? If you've got nothing to hide then you've got nothing to fear.'

'I can't. It's… at the purse-mender's.' She looked at his letter again and smiled. '"I actually don't think I love anything in the world as much as you." Aww. Did you really write that?'

He coloured slightly, looking down at his toes. 'Yeah. I was trying to get how I felt all written down for you, only it kept coming out wrong. I wrote that the same day I came over to tell you I loved you.'

'And this bit, where you say you've been hiding from it for years?' She looked up at him. 'Is that real? Or is it just part of another trick?'

'Yes, a very old one. A trick I was playing on myself for the best part of a decade, until that bunch of bellends we call our mates opened my eyes.' He smiled at the photo of their teenage selves, then glanced over at his love letter on her phone screen. 'And the evidence against us has come straight from our own hands. We can deny how we feel till Dooms-day, but our hearts can't help telling tales on us.'

'Very poetic. So, friends again?'

'I guess so.' He drew her gently against his bare chest. 'Although I hope you realise I'm taking you back out of pity. I'd hate to see you die miserable and alone, which is obviously what's going to happen if I don't snap you up.'

'Same here. It's clear you're half dead through pining for me, just like the girls said. I couldn't have your stiff, broken-hearted corpse on my conscience.'

'Give us that mouth then, love, if it's the only way to stop you wittering.'

Ben claimed her lips for a kiss, his fingers burrowing into her hair. Bridie relaxed in his arms, feeling that she was once again back where she was supposed to be.

'Not worried about life in your shed?' she whispered when they broke apart, stroking his ear with the tip of her finger.

'No. I've actually always fancied my very own shed. I can get myself a workbench and a subscription to Pornhub.' He brushed his lips against her forehead. 'What about you? Scared I'll be off to Bermuda with my secretary as soon as my hairline starts to recede?'

'No. I know you could never bring yourself to leave your beloved shed behind.'

'Well, we don't need to worry about how to break the news of our relationship to the others now, do we? I think after that blazing row in the bar earlier, it's safe to say there isn't a friend or mutual acquaintance who isn't aware we've been shagging.'

'Or anyone else out in Blackpool tonight, for that matter.'

'Here.' He picked her ring up and slid it back on her

finger. 'Keep it on for me this time, OK? I seem to suffer from sudden shooting head pains whenever you take it off.'

'I will.' She lifted her face to kiss him again. 'I'm sorry, Ben. I acted like a kid, didn't I? I was just so humiliated when you didn't respond to Cal asking if you had feelings for me, then when you said…' She sighed. 'Let's talk it out next time, all right? We can't keep relying on our mates to sort it out for us every time we have a fight.'

'And I'm sure we'll be having plenty of those in the years to come. It's obvious we're destined to be one of those couples. Although that also means plenty of vigorous make-up sex, so swings and roundabouts really.'

Bridie's phone buzzed again and she smiled as she looked at it.

'Looks like Hat's had the same idea,' she said. 'She's offered a swap. I can have Cal's bed and he's taking mine.' She glanced at the twin beds. 'What do you reckon, shall we push them together for a bit of fun?'

'I'll even offer to sleep in the crack afterwards.' He buried his face in her hair. 'God, I love you, Bridie Morgan, you enormous pain in my arse. No tricks this time. I really do.'

'I love you too, Ben. You equally enormous pain in my arse.' She glanced up. 'What happened to that lass from before? I stormed over here with every expectation of finding you in flagrante with her.'

'Mia? She was pretty keen at first, despite the singing, but she'd soon had enough of me. Seemed to think I was just chatting her up to make some other girl jealous.'

'What? Madness.'

'Right?' He grinned. 'You picked out another entirely unsuitable match for yourself tonight, I noticed.'

'I know. Instinctively homing in on lads who wouldn't go for me in a million years is my only real talent in life.' She smiled up at him. 'I do think this one might have potential though.'

'I've certainly got high hopes for him.' He gave her a last kiss and let her go. 'Come on, let's push the beds together and get naked. This make-up sex isn't going to have itself.'

———

'Well, she hasn't come back,' Hattie said to Cal over in her and Bridie's room. 'I think it worked.'

'Yep. Team Cupid to the rescue again.' He gave her a high five. 'This time with the added bonus that I now get to spend the night cuddling you. Win-win.'

'You mind if it's just cuddling tonight, love? I don't know if it's all the partying, the pregnancy hormones or a bit of both, but I'm worn out.'

Cal kissed her cheek. 'Of course I don't mind. Like I said, we've got the rest of our lives to catch up on that sort of fun.'

They got into their pyjamas, then pushed the two beds together so they could snuggle up.

'Hat?' Cal whispered when they'd turned out the light.

'Mmm?'

'That night with Joanna… you do believe me, don't you? That it was all innocent?'

'Course I do. I just wish you hadn't kept it from me. If you'd told me about it up front, I wouldn't have been worried.' She pressed her face against his chest. 'But let's not go over that again. It's in the past.'

'Right.' He rested a hand on her stomach. 'And we're all about the future now.'

'Yep.' She glanced up at him. 'You've been acting a bit oddly today, Cal. Everything's all right, isn't it?'

'Everything's perfect. As long as I've got you, how could it not be?'

'There isn't anything you want to tell me?'

Cal hesitated, his hand still resting on her stomach.

'It's nothing,' he said after a moment. 'Wedding nerves, that's all. Somehow, this weekend's made it all feel more real.'

'I know what you mean.' She kissed him. 'Night, Cal.'

'Night, beautiful.' He ducked under the covers to plant a kiss on her tummy. 'Night, Peanut. Love you both.'

Hattie smiled. 'I know it's only a nickname, but Peanut Leonard-Kemp is really starting to grow on me.'

'I know, right? Very minor celeb.'

'Just imagine the future he could have on reality TV.' Hattie snuggled deep into Cal's arms. 'See you in the morning.'

Cal stroked Hattie's hair while he waited for her to drift off to sleep. When her breathing had become soft and slow, he turned on his phone.

He groaned silently. Another new message had come through from Joanna. Cal hesitated a moment, then muted the conversation and snuggled into Hattie.

From now on, he was all about the future: him, Hattie and the baby. Ben was right. Whatever he had to do to leave Joanna firmly in the past where she belonged, that was what he was going to do.

TWENTY-NINE

Cal was packing a bag to go over to Ben's when a knock sounded at the front door. Hattie had already left to stay the night at her mum and dad's, so there'd be no tempting bad luck by seeing each other before the wedding – well, the wedding rehearsal, but Hattie felt it was important to do everything exactly as they would for the real thing in a week's time.

Cal chucked a pair of socks in his bag and went to answer, wondering if Hattie had forgotten something she needed for tomorrow.

'Fuck!' he said when he opened the door. 'Joanna! What the hell are you doing here?'

His ex looked awful. Her hair was unbrushed, her face pale and streaked with mascara.

'I didn't know where else to go,' she gasped between sobs. 'Cal, I'm so sorry. There… there wasn't anyone else I trusted. I messaged you loads but you weren't answering so I… I just came.'

'Christ, Jo! What happened?'

'It's… Conrad. It's over, Cal. He left me.'

'Oh God.' He sighed. 'I'm so sorry.'

'Can I come inside?'

'Um…' He cast a nervous glance at Mrs Bradley's house next door. 'It's not really a good time, Jo. I'm getting married tomorrow – I mean, I'm practising getting married tomorrow. I was just about to go out.'

'Please, Cal. I need you.'

Her face was so pale it was almost white, and her eyes were red and puffy from crying. Cal felt a stab of pity for the woman. She really looked like she'd been through the mill.

'All right,' he said, standing aside so she could come in. 'But it can't be for long, I'm afraid.'

Joanna went into the living room and took a seat while Cal went to fetch her some tissues.

'Thanks,' she said, taking them from him gratefully. She took out a pocket mirror and started cleaning up the carnage on her face. 'Oh God, look at the state of me. What must you think of me?'

'Give over, you look fine.'

She summoned a watery smile. 'Cal, you've always been the worst liar I know.'

'All right, you look pretty rough,' Cal conceded. 'But that sounds like it's the least of your worries. Let me get you a tea and you can tell me about it.'

'Thank you.'

Cal went into the kitchen to make the tea. When he came back in, Joanna had cleaned up her face, applied some fresh make-up and was looking a bit more like her usual self.

'Here,' he said, handing her a mug before taking a seat beside her. 'Now come on, tell me what happened.'

'We had a blazing row,' she murmured. 'You know one of

those that starts over something really small and quickly escalates out of control?'

'No, not really.'

Joanna smiled thinly. 'No, I suppose not. I forgot other couples don't have those. It's become so much the norm for us now…' She sighed. 'But this one was different. Things were said that can't be unsaid.'

'What did he say?'

'Not him. Me.' She took a sip of her tea. 'I told him… told him I didn't love him. It just slipped out in the heat of the moment, but then when he pressed me on it… I couldn't take it back, Cal. I don't love him. I thought I did but I was wrong. The next thing I knew… he was driving away.'

Cal patted her shoulder. 'I'm sorry, Jo. But might it be for the best, in the long run? It sounds like you wanted very different things out of life, and if you don't love him, well… I'm convinced there must be someone better for you out there.'

'I hope so.' She looked up at him, her puffy eyes wide and appealing. 'Would a hug be out of the question?'

'Er… I'm not sure that's such a good idea after last time, are you?'

'Why not? We're not drunk now. I'm sure we can manage to behave.'

Cal hesitated, but Joanna's arms were already snaking around him. Not knowing how to extricate himself politely, he gingerly patted her back.

How was he going to get himself out of this? He didn't want to spend all night comforting his ex on the day before his wedding rehearsal. Obviously he felt for the woman, but what could he do? He'd only seen her twice in six years. She must have someone else she could go to for support. Cal couldn't help remembering the last time he'd seen her, and the kiss he wanted more than anything now to put behind him.

'Um, Jo… look, don't take this the wrong way, but what are you doing here?' he asked. 'I mean, why come to me?'

'I didn't know where else to go,' she whispered. 'There's no one genuine in my life now except you, Cal. No one who knows the real me.'

'Right. Right.' He hesitated. 'But, well, I'm not in your life, am I? This is only the second time I've seen you since we broke up.'

'I know, and I feel awful about that.' She let him go. 'Aren't you wondering why I got back in touch after all this time?'

'A bit, yes.'

'Because… because I realised I made a mistake. The problems with Conrad, and seeing you about to marry someone else, it finally made me realise…' She laughed wetly. 'God, do you know how many times I've wished I never took that bloody job in Liverpool?'

He frowned. 'What are you saying, Joanna?'

'It was you, Cal,' she said softly, resting a hand on his leg. 'It was always you. I lost the best thing that ever happened to me the day I accepted that job.'

'Joanna…' Gently he lifted her hand from his body. 'Look, you're upset. Let's forget this happened, eh? I know you're going to regret saying all this tomorrow.'

'No. You're wrong. I've been thinking about this ever since we kissed.'

'We didn't kiss. I just… failed to stop being kissed as quickly as I should have.'

'I know you did.' She summoned the seductive smile that had always had such an effect on him back in the days when they'd been dating. 'Because you were tempted, right? Look me in the eye and tell me there wasn't a big part of you that wanted me that night.'

Cal looked her in the eye. 'All right. There was a part of me. But there was a far, far bigger part of me yelling through the champagne fog that I love Hattie.'

'What does that matter? I'm talking about something far more visceral than love here, babes.' She slid her hand up his thigh, bringing her lips close to his ear. 'You remember all the fun we used to have, when I used to get you all hot and bothered out in public? All I had to do was whisper that I wasn't wearing any knickers underneath my skirt and you couldn't wait to drag me into the nearest—'

Cal flinched. 'Joanna, stop.'

'I know you don't really want me to.' She lowered her voice to a husky purr as her fingertips trailed over his leg. 'Do you know the sort of life you could have with me, Cal? All the things I could give you? More than that frumpy, uptight little schoolteacher ever could. Think about that.'

'Really? That's what you think I care about?' Cal got to his feet. 'I love Hattie, Joanna. I'm going to marry Hattie and I'm going to have kids with her. I get that you're not thinking straight right now, but this… this is wrong. I think you'd better leave.'

She shook her head, scowling. 'You're seriously turning me down for *her*? You know how many men send me messages online telling me all the things they want to do to me? How many have left wives and girlfriends just for a chance of being with me?'

'I don't know and I'm not particularly interested in finding out.' He flung open the living room door. 'Bye, Joanna.'

'Come on. You're throwing me out?'

'I'm asking you politely to leave. I've got somewhere else to be.'

'Fine, if that's what you want. I've never begged a man in my life.' She stood to go, then hesitated, her expression softening. 'Look, Cal, I'm sorry. You're right, I'm not thinking straight tonight. I was upset and I... I wanted to be with someone. Let's not leave it like this, eh? If this is the last time I'm going to see you, I want to go as a friend.'

Cal's frown lifted slightly. 'Look, there's no hard feelings. I am genuinely sorry your marriage didn't work out. I hope you meet someone else to make you happy.'

'How about a last hug to show you mean it?'

He hesitated, then nodded slightly, not resisting as she wrapped her arms around him.

'You know, we could just have tonight,' she whispered while she held him. 'For old times' sake. Hattie doesn't need to know.'

'I'd know though, wouldn't I?' He extricated himself from the hug. 'I'm sorry, Joanna. There's only one woman I want to be with, and I'm afraid you're not her.'

THIRTY

At 7.30am, Hattie's mum Sandra woke her daughter up with a cup of tea.

'Time to get up, my love,' she said, putting the steaming brew down on the bedside table. 'Today's the big day. We've got lots to do.'

Hattie smiled. 'Not quite, Mum. Today's only the big day rehearsal.'

'Well yes, but we have to pretend, don't we? That's the whole idea, to give it a trial run so we're all set for the real thing on Saturday.'

Hattie yawned as she sat up and reached for the tea. 'You didn't need to wake me quite so early, you know. It's not a dress rehearsal. At least three hours on the actual day are going to be dedicated to getting into my dress, getting my hair done, make-up, nails and all that. All I have to do today is chuck a pair of jeans on and run a brush through my hair.'

'Listen, Hats, you've given me an itinerary and I'm sticking to it,' her mum said firmly. 'I've got one child, and since I firmly believe that you and Cal are made for each other, this is my only chance to help organise a wedding for someone I love rather than a stranger. If this is my one go at being the mother of the bride, I'm bloody well going to do it properly.'

Hattie laughed. 'Well, I'm glad you're taking it seriously.'

'Someone has to, don't they?' Sandra said, flicking her daughter's ear fondly. 'Now drink your tea and up you get. Breakfast first, then at nine we need to start getting you into your dress.'

'I told you, Mum. I'm not wearing the dress today.'

'No, but you have to pretend to get into the dress all the same.' Sandra tapped her watch. 'Itinerary, remember? Drink up, sweetheart.'

She went out, leaving Hattie to sip her tea in quiet thoughtfulness.

It had felt strange, sleeping back in her childhood bedroom. It wasn't enormously different now to how it had been when Hattie had left home to go to university at eighteen, even down to the posters of My Chemical Romance that still adorned the walls. Her parents were constantly talking about turning it into a home gym, but somehow that never seemed to happen. Hattie got older but her old room stayed the same, other than the junk and boxes that seemed to accumulate in there now it was no longer inhabited.

She wondered how Cal was doing this morning after a night in the spare room at his brother's: if his heart was fluttering the same way hers was. It all felt a lot more real now the Sten do was over and they were counting down in days rather than weeks to the big event. Hattie could feel the butterflies dancing in her stomach, hyperactive on a diet of nervousness, stress, excitement and burgeoning pregnancy hormones.

Feeling suddenly queasy, she pushed her tea away. Was

that nerves or morning sickness? She'd been feeling a bit bloated and sluggish lately, but she'd avoided any of the really bad symptoms so far. It would be nice if Peanut could carry on behaving himself until at least after the wedding, if not the honeymoon.

In just six days' time she and Cal would be husband and wife, preparing to fly off to Venice. As filled with trepidation as Hattie was about the various things that had the potential to go wrong, she couldn't wait to marry Cal. There was no one else she could imagine raising a family with… growing old with. Cal Kemp, sweet and funny and warm and lovely; Cal who loved her unreservedly, demonstratively and without embarrassment, and who did a million little things for her every day to remind her how lucky she was to be with him.

Hattie hugged herself as she pictured his handsome, smiling face. Not everyone was fortunate enough to meet their soulmate in life; it almost felt unfair that she should be one of the lucky ones. Not that she was about to start complaining.

Her dad was cooking a fry-up when Hattie went down to the kitchen. After she'd eaten – her mum commenting on how little appetite she had, but without seeming to suspect any reason for that other than nerves – Hattie had a shower and got dressed in her best jeans and a nice silk top, which she'd selected as about the right amount of smart-casual for a wedding rehearsal.

Getting ready took around an hour, compared to the three hours reserved on the itinerary for dress, hair, make-up and other beautification rituals, so she had quite a bit of time to fill before the bride, groom and a few select guests were due to gather at the stately home where the wedding was to take place. She tried to occupy herself with a book, but she couldn't focus and the words swam before her eyes. Despite the lack of a big dress or fancy up-do, the prospect of this rehearsal was rendering Hattie nearly as restless as the real thing.

'Mum! Dad! I'm going to go out for a walk,' she called to her parents from the hall as she put on her coat. 'If I'm not back in an hour just head to Lindley House without me and I'll meet you there, OK?'

'All right, but don't be late!' her mum called back.

'I won't. See you in a bit.'

Outside, Hattie breathed in a deep lungful of sea air to help calm her nerves and started walking along the clifftop path towards the steps that led down into Messington town centre.

It was a quiet morning, with hardly anyone about, but she soon felt someone fall into step behind her. She glanced over her shoulder and blinked.

'Um, hi.'

Naturally, Hattie recognised the woman smiling awkwardly at her immediately. She must've seen her face on a dozen magazine covers and advertisements for make-up – and of course, on the ubiquitous 'Beauty with Jojo' channel.

'You know me, right?' Joanna said.

'Of course. You're Jojo.'

'And you're Hattie.' Joanna glanced at the Leonards' house. 'I've been waiting here hoping to catch you. There was something I wanted to… I felt like I owed you an apology. I couldn't go back home easy in my mind until I'd seen you.'

Hattie blinked. 'Um, OK.'

'You know me and Cal saw each other a few months back, when you were out of town?'

'Yes, he told me. He said you were around for a conference or something.'

Joanna sighed. 'I told him that, but… Hattie, please don't hate me for this. It was a lie. There never was any conference. I came to see him, not for any other reason. I tricked him into agreeing by implying it was going to be a double date, the four of us, when all the time I knew you'd be away from home that weekend.'

Hattie frowned. 'You came especially to see Cal? What for?'

She shrugged. 'Because I missed him. Because I realised I'd made a mistake all those years ago when I ended it with him. Because… because I was hoping I might be able to win him back.'

Hattie took a step back. 'What?'

'I know, it sounds awful. I knew he was with you, and yet… I couldn't help myself. I haven't been having an easy time of it lately, Hattie. Conrad and me were having problems, I wasn't in a great place, and I suppose… I suppose I fixated on Cal as the one person who could make me happy again. Then I saw you two had announced your engagement and… well, it felt like my last chance to convince him I was the one for him after all.'

'Why? I mean, why Cal, out of everyone? You two hadn't seen each other for years.'

'He was different from the others,' Joanna said quietly. 'I've been with a lot of men, Hattie, but I've never had another lover like Cal. So sweet, so passionate…'

'I don't think I want to hear this,' Hattie muttered.

'No. Sorry.' Joanna reached out to rest a hand on her shoulder. 'Anyway, I sought you out to say I'm sorry, and I'll be going now to let the two of you get on with your lives. It was wrong to try to tempt Cal away from you. When I saw him last night and he told me he had no intention of leaving you, it finally made me realise that I was being a real bitch and there was no excuse for it.'

Hattie felt like she was in a dream. Was this really happening? Jojo Fitzroy, beautiful, famous, larger than life, standing right in front of her, apologising for trying to steal her boyfriend. If Hattie ever told this story afterwards, she was certain no one would believe her.

'Oh,' she said. 'Well, that's… um, that's very big of you, Joanna.'

'And here. Just to show there are no hard feelings and it's genuinely all over now.' Joanna reached into her handbag and took out a little pink envelope, which she handed to Hattie. 'These are all the love notes Cal ever gave me, and all mine to him as well. You can burn them or do whatever you like with them.'

Hattie stared at the envelope. Cal had been in the habit of writing Joanna love notes, had he? He never wrote anything like that to her. She drew out one little square note and skimmed the writing on it.

Jo, last night was amazing. God, I can't believe you let me do that. You are bad! Can't wait for round two tonight. Love you now and forever. Cal xxx

Hattie winced and stuffed it back into the envelope again.

OK, that had been a mistake. She hadn't expected it to hurt that much, being reminded he'd enjoyed sleeping with someone else – that he'd been sweet to someone else, loved someone else, just as much as he now loved her.

But it was fine. That wasn't her Cal, that was twenty-one-year-old Cal: a boy still becoming a man, and someone very different from the person she knew now.

She frowned at another note that had been partially drawn out of the envelope when she'd removed the other.

Cal's had looked old, but this… this looked new, on crisp pink notepaper and written in fresh blue biro.

Miss you so much. Sneak away soon, please: I need to be with you desperately. Counting the seconds. Jo xxx

'This doesn't look six years old,' she muttered.

Joanna blinked. 'Well, no.'

Hattie looked up at her, feeling slightly dazed. She'd half forgotten Joanna was there.

'What do you mean, no?'

Joanna looked puzzled. 'I told you I wanted to apologise. I mean, I thought you understood.'

'Well I don't, clearly. What exactly are you apologising for, Joanna?'

'Well, me and Cal…' Joanna paused for a moment. 'You do know, don't you? He did tell you what's been going on between us, since we spent the night together that weekend?'

Hattie stared at her. 'What?' she whispered.

'Hattie, I'm so sorry. I genuinely thought you knew.' Joanna rested a hand on Hattie's arm, her face a picture of mortified guilt, but Hattie pushed it away.

'No.' Hattie shook her head. 'No. Bullshit. You wrote that note to set him up.'

'Honestly, I didn't, I swear. Why the hell would I want to do that? Look through and you'll see his notes to me too, new as well as old.'

'Well, then… then you wrote those as well,' Hattie snapped. 'I don't believe it and I won't.'

'I don't get it,' Joanna said, blinking in confusion. 'Cal told me last night you knew all about it. He said he'd confessed and you'd forgiven him so there was no point trying to get him to go back to me.'

'No. You didn't see him last night. He would've told me.'

Joanna rested a hand on her arm. 'I'm so sorry, Hattie. It

was supposed to be one last time before the wedding, that's all: goodbye sex. I'm sure if you check with your neighbours, they'll be able to confirm I was there.'

Hattie gripped the rail that ran along the clifftop to steady herself. She felt like she was going to be sick.

'No,' she whispered. 'This… I don't believe any of this. Cal would never, ever do that to me. He loves me.'

Joanna smiled sadly. 'He told me that too, once. Love doesn't always last forever, does it?'

'You've made all this up,' Hattie said, glaring at her. 'These notes have to be forged, the newer ones anyway. I'm going to ask Cal and he's going to explain it and we're going to get married on Saturday and that's that. So just sod off back to your mansion, Joanna. Nice try but it didn't work. Game over.'

Joanna sighed. 'I was hoping it wouldn't come to this. I don't want to cause you unnecessary pain, honestly I don't, Hattie. But… there is something else.'

———

'How're you doing, mate?' Ben muttered to Cal as they stood in front of the lectern in the orangery wedding chapel at Lindley House, resting a hand on his brother's shoulder.

'Fine.' Cal gulped down a breath and exhaled slowly. 'Fine. I'm fine. So, so, so fucking fine here. Have you got the rings?'

'Eh? I thought we weren't bothering with them for the rehearsal.'

Cal's eyes widened. 'What? Yes we are!'

Ben grinned. 'Yeah, I know. Just winding you up. They're in the back pocket of my jeans.'

'You *prick*, Ben!'

'Hey. House of God here. Watch the mouth, little brother.'

'It's a civil ceremony, I can eff and blind as much as I like.' Cal glared at him. 'And no more jokes like that, all right? I'm nervous enough as it is.'

'Bloody hell. If this is what you're like at the rehearsal, how bad will you be on Saturday?'

'Well, I can't guarantee you won't have to physically hold me in an upright position if my legs give way.'

Bridie came over and stood on tiptoes to kiss Ben's cheek. He smiled down at her.

'Hiya, trouble,' he said. 'Any sign of the bride yet?'

'Yeah, Meg just saw the Leonards' car pull in.' She glanced around as the organ struck up the wedding march. 'Just in time too, it sounds like we're getting ready to start. Trust Hat to make an entrance, eh?' She slapped Cal on the arm. 'You all right, Kemp the Younger?'

'I can't feel my teeth, Bride. Or my tongue. Is that normal?'

'Er, dunno. Probably.'

'Oh God,' he groaned. 'What if it flops out of my mouth while I'm trying to say my vows?'

She smiled. 'You'll be fine. Just remember, it's only a practice run. You don't have to get it right first time.'

'I wish Hattie was here. It wouldn't seem so scary if we were going through it together. I could strangle whoever invented that stupid superstition about not seeing each other before the wedding.'

Bridie glanced at the door as Hattie's mum came in and took her seat. 'Hat'll be in the back room with her dad and the girls, I guess, getting briefed by the celebrant on what to do when we all walk down the aisle. I'd better join them and find out what I'm supposed to do. See you in a bit, boys.'

Twenty minutes later, the friends and relatives drafted in to fill out the rows were starting to get antsy. Irritated whispers rippled through the seating area.

'What's the hold-up?' Cal muttered to Ben. 'Should it take this much time to brief the bridal party or are they just doing it to turn me into even more of a quivering wreck? I mean, all they have to do is bloody walk.'

'I'm no expert, but twenty minutes does seem excessive,' Ben said. 'Want me to go check it out?'

'Please. Thanks, bruv.'

Ben made his way to the back room, feeling a growing sense of trepidation. What was the problem? Surely Hattie wasn't experiencing cold feet or something? It wasn't even a real wedding, for God's sake. He hoped this wasn't a taste of what was to come on the actual big day.

When he opened the door to the back room, he discovered Dafydd Leonard, Hattie's dad, in earnest, hushed conversation with the celebrant while the three worried-looking bridesmaids tapped at their mobile phones.

'What's going on?' he asked. 'Where's Hattie?'

Bridie looked up from her phone, her face drawn and pale.

'We've got a bit of a problem here, Ben,' she said quietly. 'The bride seems to have vanished into thin air.'

THIRTY-ONE

Half an hour later, all hope of Hattie turning up to the rehearsal had disappeared. There was no answer from her mobile, which seemed to be switched off, nor any response from the landlines at either her parents' house or the place she shared with Cal.

'Right,' Ben said when they'd dismissed the few guests and only Hattie's parents and closest friends remained. 'Let's work out what we can do. Who saw her last?'

'Well, we did,' Sandra said in a trembling voice. 'I woke her up this morning with a cup of tea, then we all had breakfast together. She got dressed and there was a little while before we were due to arrive, so she went for a walk to clear her head. She said to go ahead without her if she wasn't home in an hour and she'd meet us up here.' She turned to her husband. 'Oh God, Dai, do you think she's safe? Anything could've happened to her!'

'Now, love, don't worry,' Dafydd said soothingly in his lilting Welsh accent, putting an arm around her. 'It'll be a case of last-minute nerves, I expect. She'll be OK.'

'Did she seem nervous when you last saw her?' Ben asked Sandra.

'A bit anxious, definitely – she barely touched her breakfast – but no more than you'd expect. I didn't think anything of it. Well, it's only a rehearsal, isn't it?'

'We'd better split up and look for her, I think.' Ben turned to Cal, who looked like he might be about to faint, he was so pale. 'Cal, me and you will go back to your place and see if she's there. Sandra and Dai, go home and check if she's at yours. And everyone else… well, if there's anywhere you can think of that she might be hiding, check it out. Message in the wedding WhatsApp group if you find her, OK?'

Everyone nodded and dispersed to start the search, leaving Cal, Ben and Bridie together.

Bridie patted Cal's arm. 'Don't worry, love. We'll find her.'

'Jesus, guys, what if it's the baby?' Cal whispered, pushing his fingers into his hair. 'Hattie might be sick or bleeding or passed out or… or…' He trailed off, his eyes filled with pain at the horrors he couldn't help picturing.

'It won't be anything like that,' Bridie said, as soothingly as she could. 'It's easy to imagine the worst, but Ben's right: it'll be last-minute cold feet, that's all.' She gave Cal's elbow a squeeze. 'Now go home and look for her. I'd say there's a ninety-nine per cent chance she's back at your place, hiding under the duvet and whimpering.'

'Yeah. OK.' He summoned a wobbly smile. 'Thanks, you two.'

Bridie gave Ben a quick kiss before they left.

'Thanks for taking charge, Ben,' she whispered. 'I'm glad someone's able to keep their head in a crisis. Proud of you.'

'Text if you find her at your place, won't you?' Ben said.

'I doubt she's there. She gave her key back to me when she moved out. But yes, if I find her I'll let you know.'

———

The little square notes spread out over Hattie's bed swam before her eyes. They were all different colours, some in Cal's writing, some in Joanna's: curling and creased scraps of paper mingling with the new and fresh.

Her head felt odd, like it was trying to float away from her body. Everything seemed unreal. If this was a slasher movie, this would be the moment when the heroine finally makes the missing connection and realises the killer is the person she trusted most. The camera would be zooming in on her horrified face right now to the sound of a scraping violin.

Hattie looked at her white face, reflected in the mirror opposite her bed. It didn't look horrified. Just numb. Dead.

She thought she'd known that man, inside out and back to front. Thought he'd loved her as much as it was possible for one person to love another, just as she had him. Could she really have been so deluded?

Hattie heard the front door unlock and tried to call out, but it just emerged as a sort of strangled yelp.

'Hat?' Bridie's voice called out. 'Is that you?'

Hattie managed another little yelp.

A second later she heard feet thundering up the stairs and Bridie burst in, the draught causing some of Cal and Joanna's love notes to flutter off the bed.

'Hattie, oh my God!' Bridie threw herself at her friend and hugged her tight. 'We've been so worried! I've been scouring the whole town for you. How did you get in?'

'Spare key,' Hattie managed to whisper. 'Still under the plant pot in the back porch. Sorry.'

'Never mind sorry.' Bridie held her back and examined her pale face and red eyes. 'Sweetie, what's wrong? You look like you've been crying.'

Hattie shook her head. 'No. I wish… wish I could. No tears.'

'What is it? Not the baby?'

'No. Something else.'

Bridie sat down on the bed beside her and Hattie rested her head on her friend's shoulder.

'Now, don't you worry,' Bridie said softly, stroking her hair. 'Whatever it is we'll get it sorted out, you'll see. I'll just message the others to say I've found you safe and sound, then you can tell me all about it.'

She took out her phone, but Hattie rested a hand on her arm.

'Please don't,' she said quietly.

'Hat, I have to. Everyone's worried sick about you. Your mum and dad, Ben, the girls… poor Cal looked like he was going to pass out.'

She snorted. 'I bet he did, once he realised why I wasn't there.' She looked up at Bridie with pleading in her eyes. 'Please, Bride. I don't want them to find out where I am. They'll only turn up wanting answers, and… I don't have the strength for it right now. Especially not for Cal.'

Bridie cast a concerned glance over her friend's white face. 'All right, not if you don't want me to. Still, they need to know you're safe, Hat. They're all so worried. Cal was terrified you might be having a miscarriage somewhere without being able to get to a phone.'

'Oh God, Peanut,' Hattie whispered. 'I'm going to be a single mum, Bride. How will I… where do I even begin to…'

Bridie gave her a squeeze. 'Let me tell everyone you're safe, then we can talk about what we're going to do with you and Peanut.'

'Yes. I don't want them to think I'm in any danger.' Hattie bowed her head for a moment. 'Let me do it though. I'll tell them I've gone to visit some of my dad's family in Wales. My cousin Jen will cover for me if I ask her. Just for a little while, so I can get my head together. I'm not expected back at work for three weeks.'

'You sure you don't want to be with your mum?'

'Not right now. She'll only fuss. I don't want anyone with me but you, Bridie.'

Bridie took her hand and pressed it tightly.

'All right,' she said. 'If that's what you need. But do it now so they can call off the search.'

Hattie took out her phone. She'd switched it off earlier, and when she turned it on there was a slew of messages and missed calls – many from her friends and parents, but the vast majority from Cal. She ignored them.

She texted Jen first of all, asking if she'd mind letting people think Hattie was staying with her for a few days. Her cousin owed her a favour, and Jen quickly replied with a puzzled affirmative. Then Hattie opened up the WhatsApp group they'd created for everyone involved in planning the wedding.

Don't worry about me, guys. I'm safe, she tapped out. *Staying with Jen down in Bala while I think things through. Cal knows why. I need to be on my own right now and I don't want to talk to anyone so please respect that. Mum, Dad, I'll call you.*

She hesitated a moment, then added, *The wedding's off, in case that's not clear. Ask Cal. Sorry, everyone.*

Then she turned her phone completely off and stuffed it under her pillow.

'There,' she said to Bridie. 'They know I'm not dead in a ditch somewhere. That'll have to do until I feel up to talking about it.'

Bridie was looking at one of Cal's notes, frowning.

'What are all these?'

Hattie snorted. 'Love notes. Or lust notes in some cases. A lot of them are pure filth.'

'From Cal?'

'That one is, yes. These are all notes from Joanna to Cal, or Cal to Joanna. She gave them to me.'

'Why?'

'As an apology, apparently.' Hattie picked one up and flinched as she read the words. 'Here. Look at this one.'

Bridie's eyes widened as she read it. 'Bloody hell. Cal wrote this?'

'Yeah.'

'Never knew he had such a potty mouth. It just goes to show, you never can tell.'

'Yes. I've learned that today,' Hattie murmured, half to herself. 'Never assume you know someone, even if it's someone you love with your whole heart. Even if that someone is the father of your unborn child.'

Bridie reached up to stroke the head resting on her shoulder.

'I'm sorry you had to see these, Hat,' she said softly. 'I know it must hurt, thinking of Cal with someone else. But these are from his past, when he wasn't much more than a kid. We've all got something like this in our closet, I'm sure.'

Hattie barely seemed to hear her.

'He never wrote me anything like this,' she said, looking again at the note. 'I had no idea he was even into some of the stuff they talk about in these. He's obviously a lot more keen on getting adventurous in bed than he ever confided in me –

there's a whole side to him I never knew existed, one Joanna was apparently all too aware of. I guess that's why…' She swallowed. 'Why it happened.'

'Honey, honestly, just talk to him,' Bridie said. 'There's nothing here to really get upset about. So he wrote some dirty notes to his ex, so what? He loves you. These are old news.'

Hattie shook her head. 'Not all of them.' She picked one up. 'This one's new. Look, the ink's still bright and fresh.'

Bridie took it from her. 'This is Cal's writing?'

'Definitely.'

'And you think he wrote this recently?'

'I know he did. Joanna told me.'

'Can you trust her though?'

'I thought that at first. I was in total denial when she first gave them to me. Then I thought, why would she lie? She's got nothing to gain by it.'

'Hmm.' Bridie glanced at the note. 'Except breaking up you and Cal.'

'Why should she want to do that?'

'Well, because she wants him for herself, I'm guessing.'

Hattie sighed. 'Bridie, Joanna Fitzroy's everything I'm not. She's beautiful, famous, wealthy, desired – do you really believe she could be so desperate to get Cal for herself that she'd stoop to lies and forgery? She could have anyone she wanted. I'm sorry, but however much I might want to, I'm not going to be that woman who contorts herself with mental gymnastics trying to get her cheating boyfriend off the hook.' Hattie looked over the notes and swallowed hard. 'You were right, Bride, what you used to tell me every time you came back from another crap date. There's only one kind of man.'

'I was wrong about that,' Bridie said. 'Honestly, I really can't believe Cal would cheat on you. Call him, please.'

'No, Bridie. He can't talk his way out of it this time.' Hattie lifted her head from Bridie's shoulder to look into her face. 'It's not just the notes.'

Bridie frowned. 'What?'

'Joanna said it had been going on ever since we were away at camp. Her and Cal. Every time he told me he had to go away to a trade show or made some other excuse not to see me, he was with her. The notes make it pretty clear she had a lot to offer him that he didn't feel he could get from me. And I've felt so tired and gross lately, with the hormones, it's no wonder he… that he…' Hattie's voice broke as she choked back tears.

'It's just so hard to accept,' Bridie murmured. 'If you talk to Cal about the notes then maybe he can—'

'I told you, it isn't just the notes. I wish it were.' Hattie turned on her phone again, ignoring all the notifications from WhatsApp of replies to her message, and scrolled to one of the screenshotted Messenger chats Joanna had sent her. 'Look at this.'

Bridie looked at the exchange between Cal and Joanna and frowned.

Hat's off trying on dresses with the girls all day today, Cal's message read. *Fancy some fun while she's out? ;-p*

You betcha! Still thinking about last time. See you soon, sexy xxx

'That's… all right, that does sound bad,' Bridie conceded. 'Still, there are apps you can use to fake stuff like this.'

'How would she know though? That's dated from when we were at the bridal boutique. Joanna can't have that sort of inside information.'

'Well…'

'And there's worse.' Hattie took the phone from her,

scrolled to the next screenshot and pushed it under Bridie's nose.

'Christ, Hat!' Bridie hurriedly turned her face away, grimacing. 'A bit of warning might've been nice.'

'You can't fake that, can you? That's Cal, Bridie, I'd know him anywhere. Go on, read the message with it.'

'I am not looking at that again. You read it to me.'

'"Something to keep you warm until you get here",' Hattie read. 'Then a winky emoji. And then…' She winced. 'Then the photo.'

'Yes, but… I mean, you can't be sure that's Cal in the photo, can you? Let's face it, one cock looks a lot like another at the end of the day. She could've got anyone to pose for that.'

Hattie shook her head. 'That's Cal, Bridie. You think I don't know my own boyfriend's penis when I see it? Besides, I can see his birthmark. A little raspberry-shaped thing on his hip.'

Bridie thought back to the sly glimpse she'd snuck of Cal in the nude the morning of Hattie's birthday. She hadn't seen much really, but… there had been a birthmark, hadn't there? And yes, it was exactly the same shape and colour as the one in the photo Hattie had shown her.

'There's no way it can be anyone other than Cal,' Hattie whispered. She blinked hard at the image, then turned off her phone again. 'She sent me four, all similar but with differently angled dick pics. All dated from the past few months – since the night he saw her again, in other words.'

'I just… I can't believe it,' Bridie whispered. 'I mean, Cal! I know I've been harsh on men in the past, but I genuinely thought he was one of the good guys. I've known him and his brother all my life.'

'Perhaps those two have got more in common than we

thought,' Hattie muttered. 'Their dad was a serial adulterer too, wasn't he? Maybe womanising runs in the family.'

'Jonny always seemed like a nice guy on the surface as well,' Bridie murmured. 'You really don't think there's any way Joanna can have fabricated this somehow though? Got the photos under false pretences or... or hired a birthmark double or something?'

'Does that sound likely to you?'

'Well, no,' Bridie admitted.

'Let's face it, Bridie. Sometimes the most obvious explanation is the only one that makes sense, however much we might want to deny it.' Hattie covered her face as she let the tears flow. 'Oh God, Bride, I can't believe I was so blind!' she gasped. 'I mean, the evidence was all there, wasn't it? The gifts and flowers whenever he came back from a trade show, as if he had a guilty conscience. The boozy date he hid from me. And I was really naive enough to believe him when he said there was nothing to it.'

'Yes,' Bridie whispered. 'It does seem pretty damning when you consider it all, doesn't it?'

'He's been playing me, Bride, all this time. And I let myself fall hook, line and sinker in love with him. Christ, we were supposed to be getting married in six days! Everything's booked – the wedding, the honeymoon. My parents have spent a fortune on it all.' Hattie gave a wet snort. 'And I... I'm carrying his baby. I mean, what happens now, Bridie? What the fucking hell happens to me now?' She broke off into sobs.

'Aww, Hat.' Bridie pulled her into a hug, making soothing sounds over her as she wept. 'I'm sorry. Just know I love you and I'm here for you, OK? Fighting your corner, the same as ever. You're not on your own for this – not you or any little yous who happen to come along. With all my heart, I promise I will get you through this. Sisters, eh?'

'Thanks, Bridie,' Hattie whispered through her tears. 'Thanks for being here for me. Right now, you're the only person in the world I trust.'

THIRTY-TWO

Ben watched his brother on the phone from the corner of his eye as he brewed a mug of tea for him in the kitchen at Cal and Hattie's place.

'Dai, I swear to you—' Cal broke off, looking half bewildered, half desperate. 'No! No, you know I wouldn't ever – yes, I know it's not something she'd ever just imagine, but – no! Don't cancel a thing, please. I'm not giving up on the wedding yet, not without talking to...' He trailed off, bowing his head. 'Yes. Yes, I understand. Look, just if she calls you, tell her... tell her I love her. I just want to talk to her, that's all. Please.' He hung up.

'Any news?' Ben asked, coming back through from the kitchen.

'Dai and Sandra think I cheated on her,' Cal said in a toneless voice.

'I guess that's the natural conclusion people are going to come to.'

'They want to cancel the band and things. See if there's any chance of getting part of the deposits back.'

'It's a lot of money for them to just write off.'

'It's a lot of… life for me to just write off! I mean, we're talking about the woman I love. She's carrying my kid, Ben! This is my future – my family.' Cal buried his face in his hands and let out a despairing groan. 'Do you think it'd help if I told Dai and Sandra about the baby?'

'I don't see how, if they really think you've cheated. It'll just worry them more.'

'I guess,' Cal muttered. 'Christ, Ben, I have to see Hattie. I can't give up on the wedding – I won't. Not without hearing from her what all this is about. We were so happy.' He choked on a sob. 'So happy,' he whispered. 'I love her so much.'

'I know you do.' Ben pressed a strong cup of tea into his brother's unresisting hands. 'Here. Drink this.'

'Dai wouldn't tell me where this Welsh cousin lives so I could go find Hat and talk it out with her.' Cal glanced absently at the tea in his hands, as if unsure how it had got there, then put it down untasted and hid his face in his hands again. 'Shit, Ben, what can I do? Why won't she see me?'

'You've really got no idea what can have happened to make her call it all off?' Ben asked. 'She seemed to think you'd know what she meant right away. Could she have found out about the kiss with Joanna somehow?'

'I told you, it wasn't a kiss. Not a proper one. But I guess she might've heard…' Cal sighed. 'Ben, there's something I need to tell you.'

Ben frowned. 'OK.'

'Last night, before I came over to yours… Joanna came round.'

'Again! What did she want this time?'

'She was upset. Her husband had walked out on her after

a row. And then she…' He winced. 'She kind of came on to me.'

'She tried to kiss you again?'

'She tried to do more than that. I spent the whole time batting her hand away from my groin. First she cried all over me, then she made this big seduction play.'

Ben felt a stab of worry. 'Cal…'

Cal shook his head impatiently. 'Can you stop looking at me like that? I didn't go for it, OK? I told you, I wouldn't do that.'

'Well, what happened then?'

'She threw a strop after I turned her down so I told her to sod off, just like you told me I should. She apologised and we parted semi-amicably, mainly because that seemed the best way to get rid of her. And that was that.' He picked up his tea, looked at it, then put it down. 'I'm wondering if the neighbours have been gossiping. I was going to tell Hat about it, but I wanted to wait until after the rehearsal. Maybe she thinks I've been hiding things from her again.'

'Hmm. Could be. It feels like it'd have to be something bigger than that for her to refuse to even speak to you though.'

'That's what I thought. For Hat to run off like that and call off the wedding… it must be something major.' He stopped gazing worriedly at his jeans to look up at Ben. 'What though? I can't think of anything serious enough for her to behave like this.'

Ben looked thoughtful. 'You don't think…'

'What?'

'You don't think Joanna could've done something, do you? As revenge for rejecting her?'

Cal blinked. 'Like what?'

'Could she have set you up? Said something to Hattie to make her think you'd strayed?'

'You really think Joanna would go to all that effort just to get her own back on me because I turned her down for sex?'

'Do I think she's a vindictive, selfish, two-faced bitch, you mean? You're damn right I do,' Ben muttered. 'Cal, look. I never told you this before. I knew you loved Joanna a lot once, and I was worried it might drive a wedge between us, but... I'm the reason she broke it off with you. The job in Liverpool was just an excuse.'

Cal stared at him. 'You what?'

'I kind of... I kind of blackmailed her into dumping you. I told her if she didn't end it, I'd tell you something she didn't want you to know. I thought that that way, she could bow out gracefully and I'd be saving you pain. It was probably a stupid thing to do, but I was only twenty-three. It seemed like a good idea at the time.'

'I don't get it. Tell me what that she didn't want me to know?'

Ben grimaced. 'That she... she tried it on with me. Sorry, Cal.'

Cal looked dazed. 'No. What? She wouldn't have done that.'

'She bloody would. I bet I wasn't the first either. It was the weekend we hired that holiday cottage in the Highlands. You'd gone to bed and she made a play for me. Propositioned me with a full-on affair, as if I was the same sort of moral garbage she was. She knew I had a reputation with girls so I don't suppose it occurred to her I'd turn someone with her looks down. I think she got off on the idea of boffing your own brother behind your back.'

'And what did you do?'

'Well, I told her where to go, obviously. I said she had

three weeks to let you down gently and sod off out of your life before I told you what she'd done.' He patted Cal's leg. 'Sorry, kid, I should've told you. I knew how hurt you'd be, that's all.'

'I don't believe this,' Cal muttered. 'So that's why you always hated her so much.'

'Yeah. And if you ask me, she's more than capable of staging something like this for no other reason than revenge. I don't think Joanna would recognise a moral if it bit her on the arse.'

Cal was silent for a moment, looking blank.

'OK. Let's say I'll buy the idea she's behind it,' he said at last. 'How's she done it? I don't think Hattie would believe I'd done the dirty on her just like that because Joanna told her we'd kissed, or even if she lied and claimed we'd slept together. Not without talking to me.'

'I guess Joanna showed her some sort of proof. Forged presumably, unless there's anything incriminating you can think of that she might have from when you were together.'

'The only thing she might still have is some of our old notes – we used to slip them into each other's packed lunches; it was a bit of a game between us. There might be stuff in there Hattie would find upsetting. Nothing bad enough to make her refuse to see me though, I wouldn't have thought.'

'What is in them?'

'Jesus, I don't remember. It's years since I wrote them. I mean, some of them were just soppy sort of "miss you already" notes, others were a bit... naughtier. I couldn't quote them to you.'

'How much naughtier?'

'Well, quite a bit, I guess.' Cal rubbed his face. 'When I was first with Joanna I'd only slept with two girls, and they'd both been one-offs. Then suddenly I was with this person who was properly uninhibited in the bedroom – I mean, she was seriously up for anything, Ben. It was exciting, at the time, going out with someone as adventurous as Jo was.'

'And you talked about these adventurous sexytimes in the notes, did you?'

'Yeah, sometimes. It used to turn her on, finding a dirty note in with her lunch. Then when she came over, she'd…' He trailed off. 'It was a long time ago.'

'What sort of kink level are we talking about here?' Ben asked. 'I mean, if Hattie's just discovered you're into getting live armadillos shoved up your bum during sex then I can see why she might want to call things off, even if it's been six years since the last one.'

'Nothing like that. Nothing really dodgy. But… there'll be references to stuff me and Hat have never done together, stuff that might surprise her – shock her even.' Cal looked up. 'That wouldn't be enough to make her call things off without talking to me though, would it?'

'I shouldn't think so. Joanna's spun it somehow. She must've done.'

'What can I do, Ben?' He let out another strangled sob. 'I have to talk to Hat and make it right again. Have to.'

'I think you just need to wait until she wants to talk to you. She's asked for space; you probably ought to respect that.'

'Yeah, but only because she thinks I've cheated on her or… or something. I need to prove I've been set up, if that's what's happened. I'm not calling off our wedding on Saturday – I won't.' He struggled with tears for a moment, trying to get his frantically bobbing Adam's apple under control. 'God, I wish I could get hold of Joanna. I'd get her to own up to it if I had to throttle it out of her. I mean, she's trying to ruin my fucking life here!'

'Part of me wonders if it even is revenge, or just a game she's decided to play because she's bored. I wouldn't put anything past her.' Ben clapped Cal on the back. 'You want to stay over at mine tonight, kid?'

'No, I need to be here. Hattie might come home.'

'You never know, I suppose,' Ben said doubtfully. He stood up. 'I'll go home and get my night stuff then. You shouldn't be on your own.'

Cal smiled weakly. 'Thanks, mate.'

'I'll drop in on Bridie on my way back. She'll probably be pretty upset right now, plus she might have news from Hattie. If she was going to talk to anyone about what was wrong, it'd be Bride.'

Cal sighed. 'I guess Bridie'll hate me too, now.'

'Well, hopefully only temporarily. Don't worry, Cal. We'll get your name cleared somehow.'

———

Bridie was still in Hattie's room, trying to comfort her, when the doorbell rang. Once the tears had started to flow, Hattie hadn't been able to check them and it was only now, two hours later, that she'd finally fallen quiet again.

'Ignore it, sweetie,' Bridie whispered.

'What if it's Cal?' Hattie said, casting a worried look in the direction of the stairs.

'It can't be. As far as he's concerned, you're in Wales. Why would he come here looking for you?'

The bell rang again, more urgently this time.

'Perhaps I should go get rid of them.' Bridie gave Hattie

a squeeze before standing up. 'You stay hidden in here. I'll be back just as soon as I can.'

She closed the door carefully behind her, smoothed her hair and went to answer the front door.

'Ben,' she said when she found him on the step. 'What do you want?'

'To see how you are. Can I come in?'

Bridie glanced up the stairs. 'Um, it's… not really a good time right now. Could you call me later?'

'Just let me in for five minutes, please. I could really use a hug, Bride.'

He did look worried, his usually smiling face pale and haggard, and his voice sounded trembly too. Bridie couldn't help relenting when she saw the mute appeal in his eyes.

'Well, all right,' she said, standing aside. 'But it'll have to be quick. I'm kind of in the middle of something.'

He followed her to the living room and immediately took her in his arms, holding her as tight as he could without hurting her. Bridie sighed as she pressed her body against him. She needed a hug pretty badly herself.

'How are you doing, love?' he whispered.

'Not so great. What about you?'

'Not great either, but a lot better than poor Cal,' Ben said. 'He's distraught she won't even talk to him. I left him staring into space, trying not to cry.'

'Huh. I bet.'

He held her back to look quizzically into her face. 'What does that mean?'

'Nothing. Sorry.'

'Do you know something? Has she called you?'

'You saw her message,' Bridie said, looking away. 'She doesn't want to talk to anyone. She wants to be on her own.'

'OK, well that answer was just deliberately evasive. What

do you know, Bride?'

She sighed. 'You'd better sit down.'

He took a seat on the sofa and Bridie sat beside him.

'Ben… you love me, right?' she asked, turning so she could take his hands in hers. 'I mean, you trust me?'

He blinked. 'Well yeah, you know I do.'

'And I can trust you too. Can't I?'

'With your life, Bridie. What's this all about?'

'Love, if Cal had done something wrong, really wrong… would you take his part? Or would you be on the side of the wronged party?'

'That depends what it was,' Ben said cautiously. 'I mean, I love him, don't I? He's my brother.'

'I know.' She fell silent for a moment, frowning thoughtfully at the carpet. 'I know.'

'Bridie, what is it? What does Hattie think Cal's done?'

'It's not what she thinks he's done, it's what he's actually done.' She looked up at him. 'He's been shagging around on her, Ben.'

He shook his head. 'No. He wouldn't do that. It's Joanna who's planted this in her head, right?'

'Well, yes.'

'Exactly. She's set him up, Bridie, and I know why. He turned her down for sex last night and she's smarting about it. Not to mention the fact she's just fucking evil.'

Bridie sighed. 'I wish I could believe that, Ben. The evidence against him is pretty conclusive, I'm sorry to say. Joanna's got a lovely little collection of dick pics sent to her from Cal's Facebook account over the last few months.'

'Eh?' Ben frowned. 'No. She must've faked them.'

'She could've faked the messages but not the photos. Hattie's positive it's Cal in them. He's got a purple birthmark shaped like a raspberry on his hip, hasn't he?'

Ben was starting to look worried now. 'Well yeah, he has, but… I mean, that still doesn't prove anything. It could've been painted on in Photoshop or something.'

'The exact colour and shape? And what about everything else? The late-night visit he hid, the flowers and chocs for Hattie whenever he came back from some tryst that he pretended was a trip away for work, the messages containing information only he could've known, the mucky notes—'

'Cal told me about the notes. They're from back when they were together.'

'Not all of them. Joanna gave Hat a selection of nice new ones too,' Bridie told him. 'And yeah, I guess she could've forged them, but that along with everything else doesn't look good, does it?'

'No, I… I won't believe it,' Ben muttered. 'Not Cal. Joanna's set it all up to frame him. I don't know how but she has.'

'You won't believe it because you don't want to believe it. I get it. Neither did I,' Bridie said gently. 'But from these notes he wrote, it's clear your brother's into some stuff Hat had no idea about. It's not beyond the realms of possibility to think he might go to Joanna for some of his more specialised tastes, especially while Hat's been feeling all tired and mank from the pregnancy.'

'He wouldn't cheat. Cal's not like that.'

'I wouldn't have thought he'd have a penchant for light bondage or sex in public places either, but apparently he does,' Bridie observed darkly. 'Explain the photos, if you're so convinced he's innocent. Explain how Joanna could've known when Hattie had her dress fitting in order to fake the messages he sent her.'

'I… can't.' Ben reached up to rub his eyes. 'God, this is like being trapped in a nightmare. It can't be happening.'

Bridie pressed his hand. 'So? Can I trust you?' she asked quietly. 'If Cal's really done this thing, where do you stand?'

'Well, with you and Hattie, if he was genuinely unfaithful to her. Not that it'd ever stop him being my brother, but I wouldn't try to defend him.'

She smiled and gave him a kiss. 'Thanks, Ben. I knew you'd want to do the right thing.'

'I just can't get my head around him doing something like that, after everything our dad put our mum through when it came out about all the affairs. I mean, while Hattie's pregnant too! That really doesn't sound like something Cal's capable of.'

'No.' She sighed. 'But he must have done it, mustn't he? There's no other explanation that makes sense.'

'Bride, how do you know all this?' Ben asked. 'You're talking like you've seen these notes and things. Did Hattie send you photos?'

She regarded him for a moment. 'You promise I can trust you?'

'I told you. With your life, if it ever came to that.'

'Then come upstairs with me a minute.'

He looked puzzled. 'All right.'

She guided him up to Hattie's room, opened the door and stood aside to let Ben see.

'Hattie!' he said when he saw her there on the bed. He let out a short laugh of relief and came forward to envelop her in a hug. 'Bloody hell, love, am I glad to see you. I thought you were in Wales.'

Hattie looked helplessly at Bridie. 'Bride? What's going on? What's he doing here?'

'It's OK,' Bridie said gently, going to sit by her friend so she could put an arm around her. 'We can trust him, Hat. I told him all about it and he wants to help us.'

'But…'

'Don't worry,' Ben said, giving Hattie's shoulder a pat. 'I'm on your side. That's my niece or nephew you're caddying about in there, isn't it? I just want to help get this to a happy ending.'

Hattie shook her head. 'Sorry, Ben, but happy endings are off the cards now. They have to be.'

'Well, we'll see.' He picked up one of the scraps of paper on the bed. 'So these are the infamous notes, are they?'

'Yes,' Bridie said. 'A mix of old and new.'

He squinted at it. 'You know, girls, I don't reckon this is really our Cal's writing.'

'You would say that though,' Hattie muttered. 'I can promise you, it's a perfect match. I've been staring at it for hours.'

'It's a lot like it, yes, but the As aren't quite right. Cal does his small As weird, sort of like a number four. Mum was always trying to correct him of it as a kid but he couldn't break the habit.'

Bridie watched as something like hope kindled in Hattie's eyes.

'You think Joanna forged them?' she said.

'Someone did.'

'Why would she do that?'

Ben shrugged. 'Because Cal rejected her, for one. Because she loves stirring up shit to make her vacuous, empty life more interesting, for another. Anyway, I'd bet money my brother didn't write these.' He picked up an older note in Cal's handwriting and handed them both to her. 'See for yourself.'

Hattie studied them and let out a damp laugh. 'Oh my God, Bridie, he's right. The As are different in the older ones.' She looked up at Ben. 'There's still the photos though.

They're definitely not forged. And the messages where he tells her to come over because I'm at my dress fitting, with the date an exact match.' She choked on a sob. 'Every time I think about it, it's like someone's kicked me in the stomach. How could Cal do this?'

'I admit, it does look bad.' Ben was silent for a moment. 'Look, Hattie, will you let me talk to Cal? I won't tell him you're here, but I need to get his side of the story. I can't believe the worst of him without giving him a chance to defend himself.'

She looked wary. 'I don't know, Ben. I really don't want to see him right now. I'm not strong enough for it yet.'

'Please. This isn't just about you: there's Peanut to think about too. Let me talk to your baby's dad, eh?'

'Well…'

'Hat, if Cal convinces me he's been set up then I personally am going to prove this has all been faked if I have to drag Joanna Fitzroy here by her hair to confess it to you. Just promise you won't cancel anything to do with the wedding for the next three days, that's all.'

Hattie looked at Bridie. 'What do you think? Can we trust him?'

'Definitely,' Bridie said with a firm nod. 'Ben has my complete confidence. He wouldn't give us away.'

Hattie managed a weak smile. 'What happened to you? I remember a time when you insisted you wouldn't trust any male of the species further than you could chuck him.'

'Well that was before I got to know this one a bit better, thanks to you and your meddling,' Bridie said, smiling at Ben.

'I won't let you down, Bride.' He stooped to kiss her. 'I have to go talk to Cal and find out if there's any way to put this right. I'll be in touch, OK?'

THIRTY-THREE

Cal was trying once again to get a message through to Hattie, the phone keypad swimming before his tear-filled eyes.

He'd never felt more lost; more afraid. Hattie was God knew where, refusing to either see him or talk to him. He didn't have a single ally except his brother – every one of his and Hattie's friends and relatives now believed he was some sort of cheating scumbag. Dai and Sandra, his biggest fans since the day Hattie had first introduced him to them, were threatening to cancel the wedding right away if he couldn't explain himself – and he had no idea what the fuck it was he was supposed to be explaining. What had Joanna said to Hattie – what had she shown her? How could he defend himself against something when he didn't even know what it was?

It had to be something big. It couldn't just be the notes. Hattie would've talked to him about the notes, even if she'd seen things in them that might disturb her. OK, there was some stuff that might not put him in the best light – a bit of mild kink and experimentation, not particularly shocking in general, but enough, perhaps, to worry someone who'd been his sexual partner for the last eighteen months and was about to sign up for the rest of her life. They belonged to his past, though, not his present. There must be something more – something truly damning in Hattie's eyes, even to the extent she wouldn't speak to him to talk it over.

He threw down the phone. What was the point sending more messages? He'd sent dozens already, and Hattie hadn't responded to a single one. She was miles away in Wales with her phone switched off, no doubt crying her eyes out and wondering what was going to become of her – her and the baby.

He couldn't get hold of Joanna either. He didn't have her number – she always contacted him via Facebook, and when he went to send her a message, he discovered her profile had been deleted. That just left her YouTube channel, but he couldn't imagine she was going to reply to the comment he'd left under one of her videos among the thousands there already.

It all felt so hopeless. He was accused of something but didn't know what it was, the person probably responsible for setting him up had disappeared, and the person he needed to talk to, to find out what this was all about, was refusing to have anything to do with him.

It must be cheating Hattie suspected him of. There was nothing else that held up. But what could Joanna have faked or forged to make his fiancée believe it of him? And whatever it was, how could he possibly prove he'd been framed with only six days to go before the wedding? Even if he could get hold of Hattie, if Joanna had been convincing enough to talk her into this, would he really be able to talk himself out of it? It broke his heart to think that even if Hattie could be persuaded to listen to him, she might never look at him again with that familiar expression of love and trust in her eyes. And then… then there was the baby.

Cal wiped his eyes and got to his feet when his brother walked back into the house.

'You were ages,' he said. 'Did Bridie have any news? Has she spoken to Hattie?'

Ben strode forward with a look of grim determination on his face and in seconds had his brother pinned against the wall by his shoulders.

'Did you do it?' he demanded.

Cal blinked. 'What?'

'Just answer me honestly, Cal. This is no time for playing games. Did you do it or not?'

'Ben, please, don't you start. You're the only person I've got who still believes I don't know what this is all about.' Cal looked down at the hands gripping his shoulders. 'Or do you?'

'Just tell me if you did it,' Ben said, regarding him with a steely expression. 'Did you cheat, little brother? The truth.'

Cal shook his head, completely bewildered. 'I already told you I didn't. I wouldn't. Why are you asking me?'

'Swear it.'

'Eh?'

'I want you to swear on Mum's life that you didn't sleep with Joanna while you were with Hattie. On Mum's life, Cal, so I know you mean it.'

'What the hell did Bridie say to you?'

'Just swear, if you're really telling me the truth. And if you can't… well, then I'll know, won't I?'

'All right, if it'll make you happier then I swear,' Cal said, feeling more confused by the second.

'On Mum's life.'

'On Mum's life, on yours, on Hattie's, on the baby's; on

the lives of everyone I hold dear,' Cal said, putting one hand on his heart. 'I haven't slept with Joanna, or with anyone else since I've been with Hat. Now are you going to tell me what the hell this is all about?'

Ben let out a sigh of relief. He pulled his brother into a hug.

'You don't know how happy I am to hear you say that, kid,' he murmured, patting him on the back. 'For a bit there, I really thought you and your cock might've been stupid enough to throw away the best thing that ever happened to you.'

'Why would you think that? I told you I hadn't done anything worse than being a bit slow to stop a kiss. Don't you trust me?'

Ben released him from the hug. 'In general, yes, but Bridie's seen some pretty compelling evidence against you. Hattie sent her screenshots of private Messenger chats with Joanna that look like they've come from your Facebook.'

'Well yeah, there were a few messages asking if we could meet up a second time – I told you about those in Blackpool. I mean, I can see why Hat would be pissed off I hid it from her after we promised to be honest with each other, but not to the extent of refusing to see me and calling off the wedding. I didn't want to put her under extra stress while she was pregnant, that's all. You said you thought I'd done the right thing.'

'Oh no, what Hattie's seen are some very different sorts of chats,' Ben said with a dry smile. 'You'd probably describe them as… intimate.'

Cal frowned. 'Intimate? Did you see them?'

'Thankfully not. I'm told they're pretty X-rated.'

'Eh? And they came from my account?'

'Or some sort of app that can fake it, I guess.' Ben

nodded to the sofa and they both sat down. 'So, come on then. Explain to me how Joanna might have got hold of a nice little collection of snapshots featuring Little Calvin.'

Cal raised his eyebrows. 'What, dick pics? That's what she showed Hattie?'

'So I'm told.'

He shook his head. 'Well, then… they must be fake. You said you thought she was capable of going to any lengths. She must've got someone else to model for them.'

'Well whoever it was, they've got your birthmark.'

'Shit, really?'

'Hattie was positive they were of you. I guess she knows that part of you pretty well by sight.' Ben squinted at him. 'They couldn't be you, could they? Maybe from when you and Joanna were together?'

'No, I can't see how they could be – oh. Hang on.' Cal stared into the distance for a moment, frowning.

'Well?' Ben said.

'There were some photos,' Cal said slowly. 'God, I'd forgotten about those. Right back in the early days, Jo sent me some nude pics while I was away at a trade show.'

Ben nodded. 'Right, now we're getting somewhere. And you responded in kind, did you?'

'Yeah,' Cal said quietly, looking embarrassed. 'It was just a bit of fun, same as the notes. Joanna liked stuff like that. She deleted them though, the day we broke up. I watched her do it on her phone, and I deleted the ones I had of her.'

'Could she have made a backup copy?'

'I guess she must've, if she's shown them to Hattie. It never occurred to me she'd want to hang on to them.' Cal looked a little brighter. 'Do you think Hat'll forgive me when I explain that's what must've happened?'

'Hmm. I don't know, Cal. There are other messages too. Messages with information only you could've known.'

'Like what?'

'Like the date Hattie went for her dress fitting. There's a message from you to Joanna that morning, inviting her over for sex while Hattie's out.'

Cal frowned. 'What? But... how?'

'I don't know, but it doesn't look great for you, does it? Then there's the very date-like evening with Joanna that you hid from Hattie—'

'I explained that to her already. We'd moved on.'

'And then you had Joanna over for a second time last night without saying anything.'

'I told you, I was going to tell Hat about that. I just wanted to get the rehearsal out of the way first.'

'What about the presents? The flowers and things whenever you spent a night away from Hattie for work stuff? That looks a lot like a guilty conscience.'

'It was a guilty conscience,' Cal said. 'But guilty because I felt bad about leaving her on her own, not because I'd been having it away with someone else. I've got a very low threshold for guilty consciences. That doesn't look suspicious, does it?'

'It does to women. They see too much of that kind of thing from cheating bastards. It was certainly one of Dad's favourite tricks.'

'I'm not like him though!' Cal protested. 'Honestly I'm not.'

'Plus there's the notes,' Ben went on, ignoring him. 'Hattie showed a few to Bridie – sent photos of them, I mean. Joanna's forged some pretty convincing new ones to go with the old, but even if you can persuade Hattie they're fakes, the mucky ones from when you were together don't look particularly good. Hattie's obviously worried you're into some stuff you felt comfortable sharing with Joanna and not her. It's bound to make her extra paranoid if she thinks you're not the man she thought she knew on top of the rest of it. When you consider everything together, it doesn't look good for you, does it?'

'But it's all circumstantial!' Cal said, his voice taking on a desperate edge. 'I didn't cheat. I didn't do anything wrong other than being a randy, impressionable prat when I was much younger. It's a big fuss over nothing.'

'Yeah. I know.' Ben patted his leg. 'I'm just trying to see it from Hattie's point of view, that's all. I mean, imagine if it was the other way round. How would you feel if some wealthy, handsome, successful ex of hers turned up with a load of dirty notes she'd written him plus photos of her fanny? It's not an easy thing to talk your way out of. That was a lot of "buts" you just gave me there that sounded a whole lot like the voice of guilt.'

'Except I'm not guilty, am I? If I can just get her to listen, convince her... I'm supposed to be getting married in six days, for Christ's sake.'

'The problem is, Cal, even if you can convince Hattie you're innocent, no one else is ever going to believe you, are they? Not with Joanna being who she is and looking the way she does,' Ben said. 'You claiming you didn't sleep with her, that she set you up to come between you and Hattie, is up there with "I must've got the chlamydia from the bike saddle at the gym, darling" or "honestly, Doctor, I tripped and fell on that cucumber". No one's going to believe in a million years that a nobody like you would say no to someone with the great Jojo Fitzroy's charms – no offence. Especially in the face of all the evidence to the contrary.'

'No,' Cal murmured. 'Everyone round here knows what

happened with Dad. They'll just think I'm a chip off the old block and Hattie's a gullible moron to take me back.'

'One person still has the power to clear you completely though,' Ben said, looking determined. 'Joanna bloody Fitzroy.'

THIRTY-FOUR

'I wish you'd let me get rid of these stupid notes,' Bridie said to Hattie. 'I understand that it's important for you to wallow in misery right now, but I really don't think staring at them is helping.'

She made a move to sweep them away, but Hattie stopped her hand.

'No. Leave them.' She picked a couple up and squinted at them. 'You know, I'm not sure the As in these old notes are that different from the new ones after all. See, the first A in "masturbate" from this newer one does look a bit like a four.'

'Hattie, please, just let me put them away or burn them or something. You're only torturing yourself.'

'And the handwriting from Joanna's notes doesn't look anything like the writing on the ones she's supposedly forged from Cal,' Hattie went on, as if she hadn't heard. 'I think I let Ben talk me into seeing what I wanted to see instead of what was actually there.'

'Right. I'm putting them away.' Ignoring Hattie's protestations, Bridie swept all the notes into the envelope they'd been delivered in and tucked it into her pocket.

Bridie felt her phone buzz and yanked it out of her jeans.

'It's Ben,' she said.

'You don't think he's told Cal where I am, do you?'

'He wouldn't. He promised me.' Bridie swiped to answer. 'What's up, love? Did you talk to your brother?'

'Yes, and I'm convinced Joanna set him up,' Ben said. 'He swore on our mum's life he hadn't cheated. That's good enough for me.'

Bridie mouthed an 'excuse me' to Hattie and left the room so she could talk to Ben in private.

'What about the dick pics?' she said in a low voice. 'Did he deny they were of him?'

'No, he admitted they probably were, but they're not recent. Apparently he sent some pics to Joanna years ago, but he believed she'd deleted them when they split. Obviously she had a backup somewhere.'

'What about that message about the dress fitting?'

'Yeah, he couldn't explain that,' Ben admitted. 'Still, I'm sure there are ways she could've got that information. If Cal says he was set up then I believe him.'

'I'm not sure Hattie will. She's already talked herself out of believing some of the notes were forged. She's completely paranoid after staring at them for the past three hours, and with everything that's happened, I can't say I blame her.'

'OK, it looks bad,' Ben said. 'If I was her, I'd feel just the same. But I know he didn't do it.'

'You're really positive he's telling the truth?'

'Well, yes. He's Cal. I mean, would you have thought he'd do something like that to her?'

'If you'd asked me this morning, then "no, absolutely not" would've been the answer,' Bridie said. 'But now I've seen his notes, I'm thinking there's another side to Cal Kemp that I never suspected.'

'Me too, but I'm certain that side is "randy, stupid kid", not "cheating, selfish bastard".'

'You would think that, wouldn't you? He's your brother.'

'And you're my girlfriend,' he said quietly. 'Bridie, I believe him – not just because he's my brother; because I know what the truth looks like when I see it. Will you trust me on this? For the sake of our future niece or nephew?'

'I…' She hesitated. 'Yes. All right. If you really think he's telling the truth, I trust you, Ben.'

'I knew you would,' he said, and she could hear him smiling down the phone. 'Look, are you able to leave Hattie by herself for a bit?'

'I don't like leaving her when she's upset.'

'She won't be upset for too long if this works.'

'If what works?'

'Bridie, Cal and Hattie managed to get us together when we were too blind to realise how we felt about each other and this is our chance to return that favour. Meet me at Scooper Dooper in fifteen minutes, OK? It's down to us to play Cupid this time.'

———

'All right, so what's your plan?' Bridie said when she was sitting opposite Ben inside the little ice cream parlour where they'd often hung out as teens.

'Well, getting you here was the first part of it,' he said. 'Then, er, after that I admit I'm kind of stumped.'

Bridie shook her head. 'Seriously, that's all you've got?'

'I did have an idea involving tracking Joanna down and

getting her to confess. I'm just not sure how that would actually work. I was hoping you might have some suggestions.'

'Ben, are you really positive she set Cal up?' Bridie said. 'I mean, I want to believe that, but to go to all this effort just to get her own back on the man who spurned her... it feels so out of proportion. Surely she can just go home to her big fancy house, wipe away her tears with a few £50 notes and move on.'

'Trust me, if you knew her the way I do you'd know she was more than capable of it,' Ben muttered.

'How do you mean?'

'Bride, you remember that night at the party when you thought I was Bruce? You called me the man who never said no.'

She flinched. 'Oh, don't remind me what I said then. I was jealous, that's all, because I thought you were getting off with Meg. I didn't mean it.'

'It's OK. I was just going to say, there was one significant occasion when I gave a woman who wanted me a very firm no,' Ben said. 'The night Joanna Fitzroy tried to get me to have an affair with her behind my brother's back.'

Bridie's eyes widened. 'No!'

'Yep. For Cal's sake I've always kept quiet about it, but I know first-hand that she's a nasty piece of work and always has been. I bet she wrecks homes for a hobby the way other people take up knitting.'

'Oh my God! I had no idea she was as bad as all that.'

'That was why her and Cal ended. I blackmailed her into splitting up with him.'

'Bloody hell. No wonder you always hated her.'

'Suppose we'd better order something,' Ben said as the waitress approached their table. 'Er, two scoops of strawberry for me and a double chocolate fudge for the lady. Cheers, love.'

Bridie smiled. 'How did you remember chocolate fudge was my favourite flavour?'

'Dunno. Must've stuck in my brain somewhere down the years.'

She reached out to squeeze his hand. 'Thanks for doing this, Ben. You're a good lad to want to help.'

'Well then? Any bright ideas, fellow sleuth? I spent half an hour on Google and discovered Joanna's going to be attending some awards bash in Manchester tomorrow, but I'm pretty sure we're not going to be able to gatecrash a swanky do like that.'

'Even if we did, if she's gone to this level of effort just to set Cal up, she's hardly going to just shrug and confess it all because me and you turn up demanding the truth.'

'I know.' Ben nodded to the waitress as she put two bowls of ice cream down in front of them. 'Thanks.'

They were silent for a while, chins propped glumly on fists while their ice cream steadily liquified.

'OK, how about this?' Ben said at last. 'We kidnap her going into the awards, lock her in a room, then I'll shine a lamp in her face while you question her. You know, like in the cop shows.'

'Right. So you pack the lamp, I'll fetch some duct tape, and hopefully Cal and Hattie will be allowed to send us some photos of the wedding while we're serving a ten-to-fifteen stretch each.'

'I wasn't suggesting we waterboard her or anything. We'd probably get eight years, tops.'

'What if we tell the actual cops?' Bridie suggested. 'Isn't it slander or something, lying about shagging someone to break up their relationship?'

'Hmm. I think that only counts if she sells her story to the papers. Plus we'd have to prove it, and all we've got at the moment is Cal's word against hers,' Ben said. 'What if we bribe her to come clean?'

'Ben, she's a multi-millionaire and we haven't got a pot to piss in.'

'See, you've hit on the one flaw in my whole plan.' He looked thoughtful. 'What we really need to do is trick her into confessing, ideally on tape. But how do we do that? She knows who we are. We're the last people she'll tell the truth to, if we can even get to her.'

'What about a disguise?'

He snorted. 'Yeah, OK. I'll dig my Batman suit back out, shall I?'

Silence descended again. Bridie sucked pensively on a spoonful of ice cream.

'Ben…'

'Mmm?'

'I might have an idea. A serious one.'

He looked up. 'Yeah?'

'We need to play to our strengths, that's what I think. Make use of our special skills. You know, like how in the detective shows the sleuth has always got some unusual characteristic or talent to help them solve the crime?'

'Right. So Jonathan Creek's a magician, Miss Marple's an innocent-looking old dear, Columbo's a scruffbag with an imaginary wife…'

'Exactly,' Bridie said, nodding. 'So, what are you best at?'

He blinked. 'Er… you think I ought to take Joanna canoeing?'

Bridie rolled her eyes. 'Not that special skill. The other one.'

'Bridie, I have no idea what the hell you're getting at.'

335

'What does every girl in this town know about Ben Kemp? Come on, you used to love bragging about this.'

He shook his head. 'Oh, no. You have got to be joking.'

———

'I'm really not sure about this, Bridie,' Ben muttered as she straightened his collar for him in their hotel room in Manchester the following evening. 'It feels wrong, thinking about being with someone else.'

Bridie smiled and kissed his nose. 'How far we've come, eh?'

He ran a finger under his shirt collar. 'You know what I mean. I don't do this shit any more.'

'You did it in Blackpool.'

'That was different. When I chatted Mia up, I was just trying to make you jealous so you'd admit you were crazy about me. This feels... real.'

'Just think of it as an acting job. Remind yourself what's at stake. Cal and Hattie's whole future happiness depends on you doing a good job tonight.'

'Jesus. No pressure, eh?'

'Here's your ticket for the bar. Don't lose it, I practically had to sell a limb to get it for you. Did you check with Cal he hadn't mentioned you to Joanna the last couple of times they saw each other?'

'Yeah. He was ninety-nine per cent certain my name had never come up.'

'And he's edited you out of all his Facebook posts for the past few years?'

'Yep, and blocked me temporarily. That still relies on the fact she hasn't been paying too close attention to his posts though.'

'I'm sure she's far too self-absorbed to have been hanging on to his every word. I doubt she'll remember everything he's put up, and there's nothing there now if she gets suspicious and goes to check. I know Cal said she'd deleted her account, but if she only temporarily deactivated it then she might still be able to access his posts.'

'You really think this can work, Bride?' Ben asked. 'I knocked Joanna back once before, don't forget. She's as likely to swing for me as snog me.'

'You knocking her back is exactly why it stands a decent chance,' Bridie said. 'Men don't say no to women like Joanna very often – or ever, probably, Cal aside. I bet she won't be able to resist finally bagging the one that got away. Plus no doubt she'll be keen on putting the boot into Cal a bit more by shagging his brother as punishment for turning her down. Just make sure you use all the seductive wiles in your arsenal, all right?'

He looked down at her. 'Bridie, are you sure this is OK?'

'It's the best plan we've got. I know it's a bit elaborate, but so was that frame job she did on Cal.'

'That's not what I meant.' He drew her into his arms. 'I mean, are you OK with it? I hate to think I might hurt you.'

'It was my idea, wasn't it? You're not exactly going to sleep with her.'

'No, but that doesn't mean there won't be stuff that'll upset you. I don't like the idea of you having to see that.'

'Ben, I trust you, OK? I know that whatever you do is in the line of duty.' She patted his cheek. 'Just try not to enjoy it too much, eh?'

He pulled a face. 'With Joanna? You must be kidding.'

'Well, she's a very sexy woman.'

'Bridie, she went out of her way to break up my brother's relationship. I can't think of a bigger turn-off.' He kissed her before he let her go. 'All right, if everything goes to plan I'll text you the code word when we leave the bar so you can get into position. If not, I'll ring you in about half an hour demanding reassurance that my sex appeal hasn't totally gone for a burton in my old age.'

'Right.' She squeezed his arm. 'Good luck, Ben.'

THIRTY-FIVE

When Ben arrived at Mystique, the posh bar where they'd discovered the unofficial after-party for the annual National Beauty Awards usually took place, it was just before 10pm. The ceremony would be drawing to a close around now, so he had a bit of time to find himself a seat at the bar where he wouldn't miss Joanna coming in. He flashed his ticket at the bouncer and headed inside.

It was a smart, modern-looking place, all mirrors and blue light. The mirrors were helpful anyway. Being surrounded by them meant he was unlikely to miss Joanna even if she was out of his eyeline.

There was a free barstool well placed between a mirror to the right and another behind the bar. Ben dragged it into the optimum position for door-watching and hoisted himself up.

'Grolsch please,' he said when the barman approached him. 'Er, no. Actually, make it a red wine. Something classy.'

The barman nodded and turned to pour him what was probably the priciest wine on the list.

Ben took a deep breath as he tried to slow his racing pulse. Was this going to work? Joanna would be instantly suspicious when she saw him there, so soon after her dirty dealings with Cal and Hattie. The plan also relied heavily on Cal not having mentioned his brother to her recently, and Joanna believing the story he was planning to tell her about the role he'd played in breaking her and Cal up six years ago. It also relied on her still fancying him, which there was no guarantee of. She had a lot more options now when it came to sexy men than she had when she'd been working on the make-up counter at John Lewis.

But Bridie was right, it was the best plan they had. Shit, it was the only plan they had. For his brother's sake, for Hattie's, and for his unborn niece or nephew, he needed to give it his best shot.

Ben stiffened as the door opened and a crowd of attractive, well-dressed people came in. He didn't need to look round to see that Joanna was among them, in a long, tight white dress with a slit down the side, laughing easily amidst a crowd of admirers. She certainly didn't look like a woman devastated because her marriage had recently come to an acrimonious end, he thought wryly.

Hang on. Wasn't that the actor husband with her? Ben recognised him from an episode of *Midsomer Murders* he'd watched last week – he'd played the corpse. Joanna had told Cal he'd walked out on her. Had that been a lie too? She probably knew that making Cal feel sorry for her, appealing to his incurable good nature, was her best shot at getting him to be unfaithful.

God, she was slippery. You couldn't trust a word that dropped from the woman's lips. He hoped Conrad being there didn't mean their plan was already dead in the water.

The attempted seduction of his brother was the one

part of all this that Ben didn't get. He was more than willing to believe Joanna would try to ruin someone's relationship simply for the hell of it, but why go gunning for Cal? He'd never done any wrong to her – in fact he'd always been far more charitable towards her than she deserved, even after they'd broken up. And it'd been six years since they last saw each other. There must be other people in her life she could fuck with if she enjoyed it so much. Had she seen Cal's announcement of his engagement and decided she just couldn't bear to see her ex happy with anyone else?

Joanna had detached from the group now and was approaching the bar; Ben could see her in the mirror to his right. He pretended to be scrolling his phone as he sipped his red wine, so she wouldn't notice him looking at her. She was measuring her steps carefully, which meant she was probably already pretty tipsy from the free booze at the awards do. That could only help.

Oh God. His heart was pounding here. Could he do this? He couldn't do this.

But he had to, didn't he? For Cal, and for Hattie. They'd helped him and Bridie find each other; now it was time to repay the favour.

Relax, Ben. It's just a chat-up – you've done it a thousand times…

That was before he'd fallen for Bridie though – or at least, before he'd admitted to himself that he'd fallen for Bridie. Even with his girlfriend's blessing, Ben felt a wave of guilt every time he thought about what he was here to do.

But he couldn't back out now, even if he wanted to. Joanna was standing at his side, literally right next to him, waiting for the barman to serve her. It was crunch time.

He looked up from his phone with an expression of surprise he hoped wasn't too hammy. 'Oh my God, I don't believe it! Joanna – Joanna Fitzroy? What the hell are you doing here?'

She turned to look at him, and her eyes widened. 'Ben, shit!'

He tried to instantly assuage her suspicions by standing up and kissing her on the cheek. 'Bloody hell, I never thought I'd see you again! How long's it been, six years?'

'Um, yes. About that long,' Joanna said, looking taken aback. 'What're you… did Cal—'

'Oh, don't talk to me about that bastard,' Ben said, scowling. 'We haven't spoken in three years. As far as I'm concerned, I have no brother.'

This was the test. If Cal had mentioned his brother to Joanna at any point or if she remembered any Facebook posts that included the two of them, she'd know he was lying. But while she looked bemused, there was no disbelief in her face.

'You two don't speak any more?' she said. 'But you were always so close.'

'We were. Or I thought we were. Not close enough to stop him stealing my girl though.' Ben laughed bitterly. 'Can you believe that, after I… well, never mind. Serves me right for thinking there was any such thing as fraternal loyalty.'

'Cal did that? I thought he was such a goody-goody. What girl was it?'

'Bridie Morgan. You remember her?'

Joanna laughed. 'That chubby thing you were always arguing with? Well, no loss to you.'

'What? She's not – I mean, no. I guess not.' Ben took a seat on his barstool again. 'So, can I buy you a drink? I feel like I owe you one, after the way we parted. Trust me, if I'd known then what I know now, things could have been very different.'

'Well, I'm here with some people.' She cast an appraising look over his body, and the outfit Bridie had carefully curated for him from all his sexiest clothes. 'But I think they can probably spare me for a little while.'

Ben smiled his most seductive smile as she pulled up a stool next to him. It was going well. He'd been with enough women to know exactly what Joanna's body language meant. Dress pushed to one side and legs crossed where he could see them, leaning towards his body so they were almost touching; pupils dilated and fixed on his. She was definitely interested, thank God. He just needed to keep up the pretence long enough to get her back to the hotel. It was too noisy in the bar for him to be able to record their conversation with any clarity, and she was unlikely to admit anything truly incriminating in public anyway.

The husband though – Ben could see him watching them from the corner of his eye. That could still be a problem. Joanna was definitely flirting with him, but that didn't mean she'd be willing to go further as long as Conrad was there observing.

'So, what will the lady have?' Ben said, just briefly resting his fingers on her arm as he angled his body towards hers. 'Anything you want, price no object.'

'In that case, I'll have a glass of bubbly.' She nodded to acknowledge the barman who'd approached them. 'And put five bottles on a separate tab, will you, and send them to the table over there? I'll be in trouble with the hubby if I don't get drinks in as promised.' She pointed out the table of her friends before turning back to Ben. 'So. When did you become the last of the big spenders, Mr Kemp?'

'I'm doing pretty well these days. Marketing manager for a big outdoors company.' Sod it, if he was going to spend the night lying through his teeth – sorry, *acting* – he might as well make himself rich while he was at it. 'That's why I'm here. I'm in town for a business meeting.'

'Oh, really?' She looked impressed. 'I'm glad someone in the family made it.'

'How do you mean?'

'Well. I never could convince your brother he ought to be aiming for more than rolling around covered in grease at that two-bit car shop.' She rested a hand on his knee. 'But let's not talk about him.'

'No. Let's not.' Ben trailed his fingers over the hand on his leg, suppressing the feeling that he was doing something really wrong as he reminded himself again that this had all been Bridie's idea. 'The thing I hate him for more than anything is remembering all the fun I missed out on for trying to do the right thing. Know what I mean? I wouldn't make that mistake again.'

'I really hope not.'

'I fancied you rotten when you and him were together, you know,' Ben said, feeling like he was getting more into the part now.

Joanna raised an eyebrow. 'Is that so? You said some very mean things to me that night in Scotland, darling. I still haven't fully got over them.'

'Perhaps I felt guilty about how much I wanted you. My brother's girlfriend. That's why I needed you to get out of his life, before I gave in to temptation and did something I'd regret.'

Discreetly he ran his hand up the leg revealed by the slit in her dress, and she smiled. 'How can I believe anything you say? A man with your reputation.'

'You used to like the idea of a man with my reputation.' Ben glanced at the group she'd come in with, and Conrad watching them with a blank expression on his face. 'But now you prefer a man with his reputation. Is that right, Joanna?'

She held up her hand to gaze complacently at her wedding ring. 'Oh, don't mind him. We've got an understanding.'

'Is that right?' His hand slid further up her leg. 'Care to elaborate?'

'Well, Conrad has his little flings, I have mine.'

'So it's an open marriage?'

She smiled. 'You seem awfully interested, Ben. I'm a free agent, that's all you need to know.'

'I'm just checking I'm not going to get a punch in the nose for what I'm about to suggest.'

'And what's that?'

He leaned forward to whisper in her ear. 'I've got a suite at the Peninsula Hotel. I'd love to take you there so we can pick up where I wish we'd left off up in Scotland. What do you say, shall we have a party of our own?'

———

Bridie was lying on the bed in the hotel room, trying to watch TV, but she couldn't focus. All she could think about was Ben, and what might be happening at the bar. Had Joanna shown up? Something must be happening; he'd been gone for over an hour. Surely he'd have phoned by now if it hadn't worked.

Her mobile was beside her on the bedside table, and she jumped as it buzzed with an incoming message.

It was from Ben. It just said *#TeamCupid*. That was the code they'd settled on if the plan was a success. It meant he was heading back here now… with Joanna in tow. She jumped up, pocketed her phone and went to hide in the wardrobe.

———

'Here we are,' Ben said as he showed Joanna into the suite, trying not to let his eyes wander to the wardrobe where he knew Bridie was hiding.

Joanna glanced around. 'Very nice. Homey.'

Ben smiled. 'I suppose it's not as grand as you're used to, but there's a fully stocked minibar.'

'Mmm. And a king-sized bed.'

'I was hoping you'd notice that.'

Joanna pulled her to him by his shirt front, and Ben tried not to wince as her lips connected with his. There was no avoiding this bit. He just had to get through it so they could get to the next bit. But it felt awful, kissing someone who wasn't Bridie. He hoped it wasn't too painful for her to watch.

He couldn't hold back though, or Joanna would get suspicious. Her tongue slipped into his mouth and he tried to fake a bit of passion, sliding his hands down to her buttocks and pressing her against him. She started moaning slightly, and Ben felt her hands rubbing against his chest... and down towards his groin.

He broke away.

'As amazing as this is, I'd feel cheap if we didn't at least have a drink together first,' he said, forcing a smile. 'Let's make a toast, eh? To new beginnings.'

Joanna laughed. 'You're not the man I remember.'

'You're right, I'm not. I don't think I had any concept of delayed gratification at twenty-three.' He nuzzled into her neck. 'But I'm a big boy now – a very big boy – and I know the best things come to those who wait.'

She smiled. 'All right. In that case, I'll have a champagne if there is one.'

Ben went to the minibar, took out a couple of small champagne bottles and poured them each a glass.

'Well,' Joanna said when they were seated on the bed. 'To new beginnings then.'

'And to a lot of fun to come.' Ben clinked her glass with his and they both took a drink.

He glanced at her wedding ring. 'I'm still a bit worried about your husband. You're sure he won't be jealous? I saw him watching us leave.'

Joanna trilled a laugh. 'Oh, sweetie. Don't you get it yet? I'm really not his type.'

'What is his type?'

'Well, your type.' She smiled at his puzzled expression. 'Conrad's strictly boys only. Be sure to keep that to yourself, won't you? It's an open secret in the business, but he isn't ready to go public just yet.'

Ben frowned. 'Right. So what's the marriage in aid of then? People don't still do that lavender thing these days, do they?'

'That depends on the price.'

'Eh?'

Joanna leaned over to nibble his ear.

'I knew one of my YouTube sponsors, Padua Cosmetics, would make marriage very worth our while,' she said in a low voice. 'They offered us big bucks if they could be the exclusive sponsor of the celebrity wedding of the year. Con and I are really just good friends – friends who know how to strike a good deal.'

She put down her drink and her hand slithered up towards his groin. Ben saw what Cal meant about her being a crotch-grabber: she certainly didn't seem to be a big fan of foreplay. He had to keep her talking now she was on a roll though, even if that meant letting her cop a quick feel. He tried to ignore the wandering hand as he carried on their conversation.

'Oh well, I don't need to worry then,' he said, trying to show willing by kissing along her shoulder. 'Isn't that rather hard on you though? What if you meet someone else?'

She laughed. 'Who? You?'

'Anyone. It's rotten luck to be tied to someone who's only a husband in name.'

She looked up from his neck. 'Can you keep a secret?'

'Sure.'

'That was actually part of the plan all along. A big white wedding, then a big white divorce soon after. Once I've bribed a couple of journalists to out me as this heartless cheating bitch, I'm going to be everywhere.'

Ben frowned. 'You want the press to make you into the bad guy?'

'Bloody right I do. You're in marketing: I'm sure you know there's no such thing as bad publicity. I'm huge among the under-thirties but the older generations don't know me – but they do know Con. I'm hoping the story of how I broke his heart will raise my profile enough to get me a part on TV. I'm sure I can make it as an actor, once I get a break.' Her fingers wandered to the buckle of his belt. 'But I don't think you invited me here to talk about Conrad, did you?'

'You'd be surprised.' He raised his voice. 'I think that ought to do it, don't you, Bride?'

Joanna recoiled as the cupboard door opened and Bridie appeared, holding her phone aloft.

'I think so,' she said. 'Well done, love. You were brilliant.'

'Thanks. And can I just say, I wasn't enjoying any of that?'

'Well, just this once I'll believe you.'

He went to stand by her, slipping an arm around her waist. 'You weren't worried, were you?'

She kissed his cheek. 'Not even for a second.'

'What the hell is this?' Joanna demanded. 'You... you two set me up? Why?'

'Why do you think?' Ben said, turning a look of pure disgust on her. 'You reckon you can ruin my brother's life for the sake of your fucking career and I'll just sit back and let you get away with it?'

'I take it that was the plan?' Bridie said. 'That Cal's the poor mug you were planning to use as a stooge when you denounced yourself to the press? You certainly went to a lot of effort to make his so-called affair look convincing.'

Joanna laughed, shaking her head. 'Honestly, do you really think I'm so naive that I'll just admit to something like that? That even for a minute I trusted you, Ben? Listen back to your recording. You'll find there's nothing at all on there about Cal. Nothing you can use to get that little frump wife of his to believe I was telling her anything but God's honest truth, which I'm assuming was *your* plan. I've been very careful not to say anything that could incriminate me.'

Ben sighed. 'Seems like she's outsmarted us, Bride. Oh well, we did our best.'

'I suppose we did,' Bridie said. 'Except – oh, wait. That wasn't our plan, was it?'

'No,' Ben said, shaking his head soberly. 'Our plan was blackmail.'

Joanna frowned. 'What?'

Bridie skimmed to a certain point in her recording and

349

Joanna listened to her own voice, husky with lust, talking back at her.

I knew one of my YouTube sponsors, Padua Cosmetics, would make marriage very worth our while. They offered us big bucks if they could be the exclusive sponsor of the celebrity wedding of the year. Con and I are really just good friends – friends who know how to strike a good deal.

'I expect Padua would be keen to know you conned them out of all that money for the sake of a fraudulent wedding,' Ben said, casually examining his nails. 'And your other sponsors, the ones who pay you megabucks to use their stuff on your YouTube channel. I doubt they'll want to be associated with a tainted brand once this gets out. Your career, this lifestyle you've got used to: you'll lose it all.'

'Well. Seems there is such a thing as bad publicity after all,' Bridie said brightly as Joanna's face became a mask of horror. 'Better hope your old job at John Lewis is still open, eh?'

'No!' Joanna dived towards Bridie and tried to snatch the phone from her, but Bridie put it behind her back.

'It's no good, Joanna,' she said. 'It's already been uploaded to the cloud. You're screwed.'

Joanna stood in the middle of the room, looking shrunken now as she glanced helplessly from one of them to the other.

'Fine,' she said in a defeated tone. 'What do you want then?'

'For a start, I want some answers,' Ben said. 'Why did you target my brother? There must be other poor chumps whose lives you could've ruined.'

Joanna shrugged. 'Because it makes a better story, doesn't it? Ex-boyfriend does the dirty on dowdy fiancée with glamorous star – the headline practically writes itself. Famous person shags other famous person isn't a story. Famous person shags Yorkshire car mechanic days before his wedding: that's a story.'

'But it didn't work, did it? Because Cal wouldn't play ball,' Bridie said. 'You should've known better than to think he'd ever hurt Hattie like that.'

'I admit it never occurred to me he'd turn me down,' Joanna conceded. 'I could get him to do anything for me once upon a time. I should've anticipated his inner Boy Scout would win out.'

'Or his love for Hattie would win out.'

'Anyway, it didn't matter,' Joanna said, sounding bored now. 'I didn't need him to actually cheat. I just needed people to believe he did. Really, I did Hattie a favour.'

Ben shook his head. 'You did her a favour? By wrecking her relationship?'

'Yeah. She'd have been flavour of the month once the press ran stories on us. She could've done wonders with that kind of exposure – built a career of her own in the public eye.'

'She doesn't want exposure, Joanna. She wants Cal.'

Joanna shrugged. 'Well, there's no accounting for taste.'

'Hang on,' Ben said. 'How did you know when Hattie would be having her dress fitting to fake that message?'

'You'd be surprised what you can find out when you're me, darling. It didn't take long to telephone all the likely candidates and find out where the appointment had been booked. I only needed to mention my name and some rubbish about Hattie having won a competition, then the owners were more than happy to help. Now are you going to blackmail me or what? I've got places I need to be.'

'OK. We want, um…' Bridie glanced at Ben. 'What do we want?'

'Proof,' Ben said to Joanna. 'That Cal didn't cheat. A

signed confession you set the whole thing up. You can write it now.' He stood up and took a pad and pen from one of the drawers. 'Make sure you mention the forged notes and messages, won't you? And how you got those photos of his knob.'

'And then you'll destroy the recording?'

'You can watch me do it,' Bridie said. 'But first, I want that written confession in my hand to give to Hattie.'

THIRTY-SIX

'All right, come on,' Bridie said the following day, holding the door of Ben's Audi open for Hattie to get in.

'But where are we going, guys?' Hattie asked. 'I don't want to see anyone. Not just yet.'

'This'll be worth the trip,' Ben said. 'You might not want to see anyone, but there's someone who badly wants to talk to you.'

She eyed him warily. 'You didn't tell Cal I was hiding out here, did you? I told you, Ben, I can't be near him. Not until… until it all starts to feel real.'

'Don't worry about that. Just trust me and Bridie. You know we're on your side.'

She looked at Bridie, who reached out to squeeze her hand, and flashed her a watery smile. 'OK. If you say it's all right.'

Ben soon pulled into the grounds of Lindley House, the venue where the cancelled wedding would have taken place. Hattie frowned.

'What the hell are we doing here?'

'You'll find out,' Bridie said. 'This way.'

Dazedly, Hattie followed Bridie to the orangery wedding chapel. She recoiled when she saw who was there, standing at the front by the lectern.

'Cal,' she murmured.

'Hi, Hat.'

'I said I didn't want to see you.'

'I know. I was hoping you might change your mind after you'd read this though.'

Cal approached and handed her a sheet of paper, covered in vaguely familiar handwriting.

Hattie cast a puzzled look at Bridie. 'What is it?'

'A letter. Well, more of a confession really. It felt right that Cal should be the one to give it to you.' Bridie kissed her cheek. 'We'll be waiting just outside, sweetie, OK?'

'But… what's happening, Bridie?'

'I'm hoping I'm about to get my role as maid of honour at the wedding of the year reinstated,' Bridie said, smiling. 'See you soon.'

Hattie watched them go, feeling dizzy.

'Well go on, read it,' Cal said with an anxious smile.

'"I, Joanna Fitzroy, being of sound mind, do hereby confess"…' She looked at Cal. 'What is this, Cal? It sounds like a will.'

'Yeah, she obviously got a bit carried away with the language. Never mind that. Just read to the end.'

'"…do hereby confess that Calvin Kemp has at no time committed an act of infidelity with me, not even a little one. Under duress, I'm being forced to admit I made it up for reasons you don't need to know about. Suffice to say, he didn't cheat. I faked the messages, I faked the newer notes, I blagged the date of the dress fitting from the boutique owner and the photos are seven years old. I'm not sorry, but I am confessing. Signed, Joanna Fitzroy."' Hattie blinked at it, then looked up. 'Cal? I don't understand.'

'I don't either, or at least not completely. Yesterday morning Ben had me take any mention of him out of all my Facebook posts, then late last night him and Bridie brought this to me. God knows how they persuaded Joanna to write it but I'm assuming there's some connection between the two things.' He took in the worried look on Hattie's face. 'It's genuine, don't worry. I recognise the writing and signature. I'm told she's agreed to back it up verbally if you're still not convinced.'

'No, that's… that's OK,' Hattie whispered. 'I can see it's her writing, I recognise it from those notes she wrote you. So you didn't…'

'Of course I didn't. Didn't and wouldn't.' He drew her into his arms. 'I love you, Hat. More than I ever loved Joanna, more than I'll ever love anyone. There's no one in the world for me but you. You have to believe that.'

Hattie looked up at him, that handsome, familiar face she hadn't been able to talk herself out of loving through all these past three days she'd been so desperately trying to, and her lips finally spread into a smile.

'I do believe you.'

Cal let out a low whistle of relief. 'Thank God for that.'

'So those photos she showed me…'

He flushed. 'Yeah, that was me in them. But like she said in the letter, they're old, Hat. I sent them to Jo back when we were first going out, sort of a game. I'm so sorry.'

She squinted one eye at him, her lips twitching as she finally started to adjust to this new reality. 'You never sent me naughty photos.'

'Did you want me to?'

'Maybe.'

'Oh, well. That's the sort of affordable wedding present I can manage.' He leaned down to kiss her. 'I'm sorry, Hat. Forgive me?'

'I'm the one who ought to be sorry,' she whispered. 'I should've trusted you, shouldn't I? A really top-notch future wife would have known right away the man she loved wasn't capable of doing that to her, no matter how bad things looked.'

'To be fair, the evidence against me was pretty overwhelming. Joanna set it all up to look as damning as possible, and I did myself no favours by hiding things from you when I should've talked to you.' He rested his forehead against her hair. 'I was worried about stressing you out, with the baby and everything, but in the end I only made things worse. It won't happen again, I promise.'

'What did happen between you and Joanna, Cal? Tell me everything.'

'Well, that first time she got me drunk and tried to snog me. Then the night before the rehearsal she turned up again and gave seducing me her best shot, because apparently I'm just that irresistible. She should've known it was a lost cause though. I threw her out on her arse.'

'Weren't you even a little bit tempted? She's very beautiful.'

'I know she is. Rich too, and famous.' He kissed her. 'But she's not my Hattie. That's the only thing that can tempt me.'

She rested her fingers against her cheek, choking back a happy sob. 'God, Cal, I've missed you. It's been torture these past few days. I'm so glad... so glad.'

'You're right though, Hat, I'm not capable of it – cheating, I mean,' Cal murmured as he hugged her tight. 'Remember that if you ever feel suspicious of me in future,

OK? I love you, and I would never, ever consciously do anything to hurt you.'

'I know. I won't forget that again.' She winced when she thought back to some of the things she'd read over the past few days. 'Jesus, Cal. I don't want to make you feel bad when you didn't really do anything wrong, but it's been so painful. Those notes…'

'Those are from the past. Past Cal isn't Now Cal.'

'I know that. It's not what was in them so much. It's more having to picture you with her, and know that she saw a side to you that you've never shared with me.'

'She didn't really,' he said gently, running a hand over her hair. 'I was young, with not much sexual experience. Yeah, it was a novelty at the time to try out new things, but I wouldn't say the stuff in the notes is representative of my tastes in general. I'm really a pretty vanilla sort of guy.'

'Right. So you don't want me to start handcuffing you to things or shagging you in lay-bys.'

'Not unless you particularly want to.'

She shrugged. 'I wouldn't mind the handcuffs. Could be fun.'

He smiled. 'Well, we'll save them for the honeymoon. All I want right now is to take you home and cuddle you until my arms go numb. Is that OK by you?'

'God, yes,' she whispered. 'Sorry for not trusting you, Cal. I always will from now on, I promise.'

'And I'll always be honest and talk to you about things. No more secrets.' He held her back to look into her eyes. 'And the wedding?'

She smiled. 'Definitely back on. Bridie's going to be so pleased she gets to wear her maid of honour dress after all.'

EPILOGUE

It was a gorgeous autumn day, the trees outside the little chapel on fire with russet and gold, when Dafydd Leonard proudly walked his only daughter down the aisle.

The rows were filled with friends and relatives. Sandra sat on the front seat nearest the aisle, beaming all over her face as she watched her husband and daughter walk slowly towards the groom. In the corresponding seat across from her, Alison Kemp – Cal and Ben's mum – observed the scene placidly. Adrian Verges was there, sitting next to Mr Duxbury and trying to catch Meg's eye as she walked behind the bride with Ursula and Bridie. Pete Prince actually seemed to have a tear in his eye, despite his three divorces to date.

Ben, flanking a terrified-looking Cal, smiled at Bridie as she joined him by the altar.

'You look stunning,' he mouthed, casting an awestruck gaze over her dusky pink bridesmaid dress, and she flushed with pleasure.

He looked pretty dashing himself. Bridie had never seen him this level of smart before. Who knew he'd be able to pull off a waistcoat? He looked like one of the models in a Moss Bros catalogue. She slipped her arm through his, feeling ever so slightly smug as a couple of envious female glances drifted in her direction.

'Well, the bride managed to turn up this time,' he murmured to her. 'That's a good start anyway.'

The vows for the civil ceremony were simple, but strangely moving. Hattie blushed slightly as she repeated her declaration after the celebrant.

'I call upon these persons here present to witness that I, Harriet Sheila Leonard, do take thee, Calvin William Kemp, to be my lawful wedded husband,' she said, her eyes shining with a love that was stronger than ever now it had been tested and forged anew.

Ben raised an eyebrow at Bridie. 'Sheila?'

She nudged him, smiling. 'Shh.'

Cal beamed at Hattie like she was the only thing in the room he could see. 'Yeah. I do too.' He glanced at the celebrant as she cleared her throat pointedly. 'I mean, I call upon these persons here present to witness that I, Calvin William Kemp, do take thee, Harriet Sheila Leonard, to be my lawful wedded husband. Wife! I meant wife.'

The celebrant laughed. 'All right, let's move on to the rings.'

'Oh! This is my bit, isn't it?' Ben fished out the rings and handed them to Cal and Hattie. 'Here you go.'

'I give you this ring as a symbol of our love,' Cal said softly as he slid on Hattie's ring. 'All that I am I give to you. All that I have I share with you. I promise to love you, to be faithful and loyal, in good times and bad. May this ring remind you always of the words we have spoken today.'

A chorus of *aww*s rippled through the guests. Bridie glanced over at Ben.

'Here.' She passed him a tissue from her clutch bag, then took out another for herself.

'Thanks.' He dabbed his eyes. 'Allergies.'

'Right. Same here.'

When the service was over and the groom had sealed the deal by giving the bride a big kiss, Ben offered Bridie his arm and they followed the wedding party out of the orangery. The meal was taking place in the banqueting hall of the stately home next door. When they reached the bank of the little lake in the grounds, Bridie made to go inside with the other guests but Ben held her back.

'Wait a sec,' he said. 'I just want to get some air before we go in. Slow my pulse a bit before I have to give my speech.'

'All right. I could do with a timeout before I do mine as well.'

He put an arm around her waist and they turned to look at the lake, rippling with autumn colours.

'Well that was pretty damn ridiculous, wouldn't you say?' Ben said.

'I know,' Bridie agreed. 'I mean, was that ring bit vom or what?'

'Yeah, and what's with all the olde-worlde English in the vows? Are we in the sixteenth century here with all that "thee" and "thou" crap?'

'Exactly, what's that all about? And that stupid business of getting given away pisses me off every time.'

'I know, sexist much? I always said you must be mad to want a wedding.'

'Well, you know my views on the subject.' Bridie glanced up at him. 'How are your allergies?'

'Not great.' He turned away a moment to wipe his eyes. 'Bloody spores. How are yours?'

She let out a damp laugh. 'Worse than I expected.'

'I know what you mean.' He lifted her left hand and smiled at the mood ring he'd won for her in Blackpool, which had turned canary yellow for today. 'Can't believe you're still wearing this. What's yellow supposed to be for then?'

'Dunno. Wedding irritation, maybe.'

'I'm surprised that cheap thing hasn't turned your finger green.' He reached into his waistcoat pocket. 'Here. Put this one on instead: it'll be safer. Sorry it doesn't change colour.'

She frowned as he slid off the tacky fairground ring and replaced it with something gold and sparkly. 'Bloody hell. Is that a diamond?'

'That's what the man at the jeweller's told me. I hope he was telling the truth, because he seriously ripped me off if not.' He pulled her into his arms. 'You know, Bride, weddings aren't all bad really. There are some nice bits.'

'Such as what?'

'Well, celebrating having met your soulmate with all your friends and family. I can see why that might appeal to some people. And getting to spend the rest of your life with the person you love isn't too horrendous, as a concept.'

'Yeah. I suppose those bits are all right.'

'And really, you can do it however you want nowadays, can't you? I mean, you can probably say your vows hanging naked by your ankles in a sex dungeon if that's your idea of a good time.'

'I suppose you can. I wouldn't though, just to be clear.'

He smiled, burying his face in her hair.

'So is that a yes then?' he whispered. 'It sounded like a yes.'

'It's a yes to the wedding, but I'm afraid it's a no to the sex dungeon. Sorry, love.'

'Well, there's always the honeymoon.' He kissed her

softly. 'Bridie Morgan, you little witch. Whatever did you do to me?'

'The impossible,' she said, laughing. 'I somehow managed to turn you respectable. I'm sorry, I didn't do it on purpose.'

'Respectable? The nerve. You know, of all the insults you've ever flung at me, I think that one might've wounded the most.' He squeezed her hand. 'Better go in and do our jobs, since we're going to be asking the bride and groom to return the favour for us pretty soon. I love you, OK?'

'Definitely OK. I love you too, Ben.'

Cal and Hattie stood inside by the large arched window, watching the scene. Cal's arm was curled lovingly around his new wife's waist, his hand resting on her discreetly pregnant stomach. They smiled as their best man and maid of honour absorbed each other in a tender embrace.

'I love it when a plan comes together, don't you?' Hattie whispered.

———

If you enjoyed LOVE AT FIRST FIGHT then you will love THE NEVER HAVE I EVER CLUB, another fantastic comedy from Mary Jayne Baker!

ACKNOWLEDGMENTS

Huge thanks have to go to my agent, Laura Longrigg at MBA Literary Agents, and to Hannah Todd, my fabulous editor at Aria, for all their hard work and skillfulness in helping my story become the best it can be.

Big thanks too to all of my talented, supportive writer pals: Rachel Burton, Victoria Cooke, Rachel Dove, Sophie Claire, Jacqui Cooper, Kiley Dunbar, Helena Fairfax, Kate Field, Melinda Hammond, Marie Laval, Katey Lovell, Helen Pollard, Debbie Rayner, Rachael Stewart, Victoria Walters, Angela Wren, and many others. Thanks as well to the Romantic Novelists' Association for being such a wonderful and supportive organisation and its members.

As ever, thanks to my supportive family and friends – my partner and long-term beta reader Mark Anslow; friends Robert Fletcher and Nigel and Lynette Emsley; Firths, Brahams and Anslows everywhere.

I chose to open this book with a quote from the play that inspired the story rather than a dedication, but I wanted to say a special thank you to all the fantastic English teachers (like my heroine Bridie) who foster a love of words in their pupils. It's thanks to the teachers who encouraged and nurtured my early interest in stories and words that I'm now able to call myself an author, so thank you, Mrs Whitehead, Mrs Hales, Mr Birbeck, Miss Walker, Ms Thompson and all the others who helped me along the way. I also owe a massive debt to the teacher who first introduced me to Shakespeare and created a lifelong love of his work, although I sadly can't remember now which teacher that was!

And while I'm on the subject, a big thanks to Will for the plot. I hope he'd approve of Bridie and Ben, Beatrice and Benedick's modern-day counterparts, and their banter-filled journey to a happily-ever-after.

ABOUT THE AUTHOR

MARY JAYNE BAKER is a romance author from Yorkshire, UK. She is represented by Laura Longrigg at MBA Literary Agents.

Mary Jayne Baker grew up in rural West Yorkshire, right in the heart of Brontë country... and she's still there. After graduating from Durham University with a degree in English Literature, she dallied with living in cities including London, Nottingham and Cambridge, but eventually came back with her own romantic hero in tow to her beloved Dales, where she first started telling stories about heroines with flaws and the men who love them.

Mary Jayne Baker is a pen name for an international woman of mystery...

Find her online at: www.maryjaynebaker.co.uk